THE EIGHTH EXCALIBUR

BOOK ONE OF THE EXCALIBUR KNIGHTS SAGA

LUKE MITCHELL

Thank you for reading.

CHAPTER I

MAN'S BEST FRIEND

"Come on, boy."

Panting, Nate Arturi reached past the rust-red rain gutter and took hold of the rooftop edge with his fingertips. Rough, dark shingles dug into his palm like sandpaper. He was officially sweating now. And also officially at the part of the climb that scared the living shit out of him.

"Come on, Copernicus," he pleaded. "What are you doing up here, boy?"

A few yards ahead, at the peak of the angled porch rooftop, Copernicus the corgi turned and barked a chipper greeting, wagging his stumpy little tail as if to say, *Ah, good, you made it! Thank you for coming.*

Despite everything, Nate couldn't help but smile. "Do you know why I gathered you here this morning, boy?"

By way of reply, Copernicus barked once more then resumed his winning doggy smile, tail-a-wagging.

"Is he talking up there?" someone asked down below. Then, much louder, Emily's unmistakably exasperated voice called, "Are you talking up there, IT Guy?"

With a sigh, Nate adjusted his already tenuous footing and leaned out just far enough to see that a small crowd was gathering in Emily's front yard to watch him flounder.

Fantastic.

Emily Atherton herself was scowling up at him in her skimpy pink bathrobe, looking like she'd been interrupted midway through an epic battle with her makeup and hairdryer—and admittedly still looking like a brunette goddess despite the fact.

"Will you be careful up there?" she called. "I don't wanna pay for you breaking something!"

Him be careful?

"Yeah, sure!" he called down, shooting her a thumbs up before turning back to the roof to mutter, "As soon as *you* be careful letting your dog run away every goddamn morning while you pretty up. Not that I blame *you*, boy," he added when Copernicus cocked his head curiously, his tail stopping in place at Nate's irritated tone. "You're just an adventurous little spud, aren't you?"

At that, Copernicus resumed his tail wagging with gusto. Down below, in the Land of the Careless Assholes, Nate was pretty sure he heard someone murmur something along the lines of, *Oh my god, why is he such a weirdo?*

He did his best to ignore it and turned his attention back to the coming rooftop mount—the coup de gras of the little climb he'd already made three times too many in one lifetime. It was the part where he took the plunge, thrust off of his last footing, and pulled himself up onto the rooftop like a professional rock climber. *If* professional rock climbers were scrawny, uncoordinated Penn State information and technology majors with hearts of gold, that was.

Whatever. He'd done this just enough times now to know he needed to move before he could psych himself out and really give the peanut gallery below something to laugh about.

With that in mind, he tightened his grip, tensed his legs, and—

"Nate?!"

And psyched himself right the hell out, a second too late.

It happened like one of those stupid cat videos where the little guy goes for a jump—a jump he clearly could've made if only he'd followed through—and instead falls adorably into the chasm between the bed and the dresser.

Hilarious.

Except that Nate wasn't a freaking cat.

He had a single instant to register that alarming fact, right along with the gut-wrenching understanding that he'd just made a fatal error, and that there was nothing his shocked brain could do about it.

Then the world lurched.

He caught one last glimpse of Copernicus, sprinting down the angled rooftop toward him. Cloudy gray sky replacing dark shingles in his vision. Voices crying. Something thumped into his chest. Then the Hand of God itself punched him in the back about eight thousand times harder.

The ground, some numb corner of his brain pointed out as the world began to resolve from the singular sensation of dark, overwhelming impact into sights, and sounds, and the deep, breathless ache of whatever had just broken inside him.

"Oh my god, Nate!" a familiar voice cried. The same voice that'd just made him slip.

So he hadn't imagined it. Gwen was here. And just in time to watch him break his own spine trying to save another girl's corgi.

It just got better and better.

Something shifted on top of him, digging into his chest on pointy claws. He blinked down past his nose, scared to move his neck at all, and found Copernicus hovering over his face, panting excitedly.

"Good boy," he rasped, wincing at the fire the effort woke in his lungs.

Copernicus barked and gave his face a friendly lick. Tail-a-goddamn-wagging.

Then someone plucked the dog carefully off his chest, and the next second a blonde angel appeared over him, her blue eyes wide with concern, and no less radiant for the throbbing pain at his core or the gloomy morning sky overhead.

Gwen.

"Fancy seeing you here," Nate forced out past his stunned diaphragm, hoping he could still somehow manage to sound cool. Even if he was paralyzed now.

"I think I'm dying," his traitorous mouth added of its own accord.

And that pretty much nailed it for the *sounding cool* part.

"Is he alive?" someone called.

Gwen rolled her eyes at the heckler, not bothering to answer and instead leaning in closer to inspect the damage.

"Are you okay?" she asked, laying a gentle hand on his chest. "Can you feel this? And what the hell were you thinking, by the way?"

"I think I broke something," Nate said, remembering the sickening crunch he'd felt on impact and not sure where else to start with her rolling questions.

Her eyes widened a little. She looked so worried. So worried that, for a second, it almost felt worth it all just to see her looking at him like that. At least until his mind drifted back to the way his hips and back seemed to be laying horribly misaligned, as if…

As if he'd landed straight on his backpack, he realized, finally lifting his head enough to look down. The same backpack he'd set down before beginning his heroic ascent, right where he'd been sure it'd be out of the way.

Score another win for Nate.

"Come on, babe," called a voice that instantly set Nate on edge. "He'll be fine. This algebra test isn't about to study itself."

Todd.

Freaking Todd. Of course he was here too.

"Just a minute," Gwen called without looking back. She leaned down and pinched Nate's ankle. "Can you feel that?"

"I'm fine," Nate huffed, trying to sit up and immediately regretting the decision as his nerve endings dutifully shouted a full-body damage report.

"You're not fine," she said. "You just fell off a roof. I should probably get you to the hospital."

"I don't know," Nate grunted, trying more carefully this time to get an arm under himself and work his way up. "Sounds like you've already got a pretty serious situation over there. I didn't realize they even taught algebra in college."

She narrowed her eyes at him, but he didn't miss her grin as she took his arm and helped him up into a sitting position. "Well, at least you're feeling well enough to mock the troglodytes."

He looked up at her, and his mind went blank. Her face was only inches from his. Close enough that he could smell the lavender. Close enough that he would've taken a roof dive a day to stay in this place another few seconds.

"Did you, uh…" he heard his voice mumbling somewhere in the distance, "… just call your boyfriend a troglodyte?"

Why?

Why for the love of the Sith would he say that?

And more importantly, why was Gwen's lip suddenly quirking in that clever little cockeyed grin that drove Nate crazy every time he saw it?

"Pretty sure I'm just repeating your words," she said, backing up a few inches to give him space.

Nate tried to let out his built up breath calmly.

"That doesn't sound like something I'd say," he mumbled quietly, glancing over her shoulder at the crowd, and at the troglodyte himself.

Todd Mackleroy was pretty much the spitting image of the stone-jawed

Prince Gallant from every fairy tale under the sun. Except with way better abs. And way more Greek-lettered tank tops, apparently. He and his surgically attached bundle of frat bros were mingling with the crowd, most of them looking bored.

Except for Todd, who was chatting up a suddenly quite friendly-looking Emily, practically undressing her with his mindless grin and his hungry eyes. Not that her bathrobe left much to undress.

"Are you going to be okay?"

Gwen's voice snapped Nate back to the moment. She was watching him with that concerned look, apparently oblivious to her shining knight's wandering eyes.

"Seriously," she said. "I'll call Kells and get us to the hospital right now."

Nate tried to run through a quick mental inventory but instead found himself searching Gwen's perfect face, wondering how anyone could ever be distracted by another face again when they had this one giving them smiles and kisses and…

"Nate?"

He swallowed against a dry throat and shook his head. "I'll be fine. Thanks, though."

He made to stand, and she scrambled to help him, stabilizing him on the way up and then holding on after the fact, not trusting he wouldn't fall straight back down.

"Okay," she said, glancing uncertainly back toward Todd and the rest of the crowd.

"Gwen?"

She turned back to him, eyebrows raised, her face attentive.

"It was… good seeing you."

"Yeah," she said, frowning at the rooftop. "We'll have to do it again sometime." She took his hand and gave it a squeeze. "I'll text you later, okay?"

Nate nodded and bent to scoop up his backpack as she left to rejoin her group.

Todd slung an arm over her shoulders like it was mechanical reflex, like she simply belonged there, nestled in. It turned Nate's stomach, watching the grinning mountain of man muscle pull Gwen in for a kiss even as Emily stood there, all but baring herself for him.

Gwen said something to Todd, and next thing he was looking over at Nate, throwing him a sleeveless salute like they were old pals. "Yo, party tonight, IT Guy. Come drink it off."

Todd didn't wait for a response. Just turned and sauntered up Allen Street with Gwen, his posse trailing faithfully behind.

Part of Nate wished he'd had the courage to at least flip the mindless barbarian the bird behind his back. The rest of him, though, was too preoccupied wishing he could be the one sliding his well-muscled arm around Gwen's slender waist, swaggering off to greet the day. And probably to fail an algebra test. But who gave a shit about that? Class was...

Class.

He needed to get to class.

Still moving tenderly, Nate slung his backpack over one shoulder and limped toward the dispersing crowd. Copernicus, whom no one had seen fit to keep track of, trotted in from the sidewalk and looked up at him with his winning doggy grin.

"Oh, Copernicus," Nate said, bending carefully down to pat the corgi's head. "That's twice this week," he added to Emily, who was watching Todd and the rest of the Alpha-Sig-Sigs saunter off.

"Yeah, thanks I guess," she said, like she'd barely heard him.

"Maybe you could get a collar he can't slip out of."

"Uh-huh."

"Or block off wherever he's climbing up," Nate added, frowning at the bars on Emily's window above and wondering, not for the first time, how the hell the little corgi kept managing to get up there at all.

"Yeah, uh-huh."

Nate turned back and realized Emily was on her phone.

"Or," he said, ninety-five percent sure she wasn't hearing a single word he said, "you could, you know, just keep an eye on him or something."

She let out an explosive huff and whirled on him. "Dude, I said thanks. What, you want me to blow you or something just because you stopped to help again?"

Nate actually recoiled a few inches. "I—What?"

"Whatever," she said, shaking her head and looking off after Todd's retreating bro-fest again. "Whatever."

And with that, she turned and headed for her door at a brusque march.

Beside Nate, Copernicus watched her go in silence, then looked up at Nate, his tail picking up in a tentative wag.

"Go on, boy," Nate said, waving after Emily. "Go tell her how good she looks or whatever the hell she does with you."

Nate wasn't sure if he imagined the corgi's ears drooping slightly, but the dog certainly didn't look happy as he slunk across the yard after his half-primmed owner. Emily slammed the apartment door closed as Copernicus reached the porch steps.

The corgi looked back at Nate, head cocked quizzically, tail picking up. Then the door opened, and Emily called, having finally remembered her dependent companion. Ears definitely drooping this time, the corgi marched into the apartment and disappeared as the door swung shut again.

"Goddammit," Nate muttered to no one in particular.

He turned to retrieve his bike from the tree he'd leaned it up against, positive that he was not up to riding it the rest of the way to campus right now. He was already going to be late to Structure and Design anyway. But that was okay. Professor Hillman probably wouldn't give him much grief, as long as he turned in his…

Shit.

How had he forgotten?

With a sickened feeling, Nate slid his bag off his shoulder and dropped to one knee. He reached for the middle zipper, already knowing what he'd find, and trying to hold on to hope anyway.

The zipper rumbled across shiny black teeth, parting the middle pocket open until Nate could see the intricate wood, wax, and wire model he'd been working on all week. The model he'd spent hours and hours shaping and carving and shaping some more. More hours still with the paint, until it was perfection. Until it looked like an honest-to-god little alien Promethean dude, ready to spring to life and conquer Earth, one ant hill at a time.

And now the ten-inch figurine was smashed to hammered shit at the bottom of his bag.

He looked up, not knowing what to do, which way to even turn. Looked up and found Copernicus watching him from Emily's window, the curtain draped over his smiling little corgi head, his upper body visibly shaking with the energy of his no-doubt-wagging tail.

"Goddammit, boy," Nate sighed, turning for campus with his bike in tow. "Someday, we're both gonna get away from this bullshit."

Across South Allen Street, in the rooftop nook of an old, creaking gray house that was currently the residence of no less than five of Emily Atherton's neighbors, an old man shifted beneath his threadbare blanket and reached into his robe for his cup, watching as the lanky child below mussed his dark hair, gathered up his pack and bicycle, and limped off up the hill, toward the university.

"Am I hallucinating again," the old man croaked in a voice that suggested long bouts of disuse even beyond the troubled sleep he'd just been yanked out of by the commotion across the way, "or are you referring to that jittery runt down there?"

He glanced up at the overcast sky, back down to the boy in question, then smirked, as if someone had said something amusingly naïve.

"You do remember what they are meant to do, don't you?"

He cocked his head, listening, but no one was there. Just an old, ragged-robed man, and his cup of ale, mysteriously full, though he'd only just pulled it from his pocket.

"Very well, very well," he grumbled, taking a long pull from the cup and shaking his mangy gray mane in reserved exasperation. "Insufferable spirit."

He stood, and very nearly pitched off of the rooftop when his head went spinning harder than expected. He sniffed, gathering his balance and taking another swig. Something told him there'd be significantly less commotion were *he* to go falling from a rooftop. No lovely blonde lasses pampering him. But then again, he also wasn't quite so fragile as to worry about a little fall.

"Are you certain about this?" the old man asked, watching the boy limp out of sight in the distance and knowing even as he spoke the words aloud that it was pointless to question the way of things—that this was exactly why her infernally unerring whispers had led him here, to this happiest of valleys.

He listened intently to the silence, and added his own sigh to the stirring wind once she'd made her reply. It was time, then.

"Very well..." He downed the remainder of his ale breakfast. "But I'm going to need a drink first, M'lady."

CHAPTER 2

JUST ANOTHER FRIDAY

"Catch, Broku Brodinson!" was the first thing Nate heard when he arrived home and cracked open the door. He caught the strong waft of fresh pizza next. And the shiny rim of a beer can lofting straight for his chest.

Nate tried to stow his phone, fumbled the catch, and ended up juggling phone, beer can, and backpack for what seemed like a logically impossible amount of time before finally tripping off of the shoe mat and straight onto the faux wood floor between the couch and their extensive gaming setup.

By sheer nerd reflex, they all gasped and whirled around, all having experienced one too many times the horror of a console yanked from the shelves or a controller yanked from the hand by the clumsy idiot who decided to go tripping over the cables. Only their nerd reflexes were outdated.

"Ahh," Zach purred when the inevitable crash didn't come, his eyes returning to his round of Battle Royale. "The joy of wireless controllers."

"Tomorrow," Kyle added, adopting an ambiguous fantasy accent from where he was perched on the back of the couch like a sage, albeit overweight, sword master, "you will catch the beer."

"I thought we all agreed *not* to join a frat," Nate groaned from the floor.

"Bro..." Kyle said.

"Bro!" Zach agreed, not looking away from his game.

"You guys are starting to freak me out now."

Marty, as he so often did, stepped in to restore balance to the Force. Emerging from the kitchen in typical Meek Marty manner, he scooped the jostled beer can up, went to restock it safely in the fridge, then leaned back out, hefting a fresh beer in one hand and a bottled water in the other, a silent question written on his brow.

Nate pointed at the beer.

"Bad day?" Kyle asked as Marty shelved the water and brought Nate his first round.

"Give him a break," Marty said, handing Nate the can. "It's Friday. And you're already four deep. At 5 PM."

By way of reply, Kyle burped and cracked open the new can he'd had ready and waiting. "Five, brochacho."

Marty just shook his head, then added to Nate, in a conspiratorially low voice, "Bad day?"

Kyle splayed his meaty hands in dramatic indignation. "We're sitting right here, Marty."

"And speaking of which…" Zach said in the flat tone that told Nate without even looking at the TV that his friend had just entered the thick of digital combat, and was now too occupied to finish his request.

Not needing any clarification, Nate rose and followed Marty out of the gamer's critical line of sight and into the adjoined kitchen and dining space of their happy little Penn State house.

"So what happened, brohan?" Kyle asked through the wooden framework that acted as both Lo-Fi shelf and honorary divider between the living room and their cramped dining area.

Nate set his bag down on the table and cracked open his beer, absentmindedly watching Zach shoot it out with some random online opponent while he thought about where to begin. He took a sip of his drink, tasted the welcome bite of hops, and finally looked at the can. Founder's All Day IPA. Collectively—with the exception of Marty, whose parents were loaded—they probably couldn't rightly afford to be drinking anything better than the finest discount pilsners. But they'd come to the agreement that they were a household of marginally higher taste, as evidenced by the extensive and varied collection of empty craft bottles lining the divider wall and the other shelves throughout the living room.

If they couldn't get the girls, they figured, they might as well get the good beer, at least.

Nate took another sip, a sip that turned into a long pull and maybe even a bit of a glug, as he reflected on the day's steady-fire stream of injustices.

"Goddamn Todd," he finally gasped at the end of his glug.

His roommates traded a dark look. Zach even looked away from the TV for a moment, only to be rewarded with a swift in-game death.

"Goddamn Todd!" he shouted, tossing the controller down on the couch beside him. "It was down to the final five!" Then, remembering himself, he grabbed his own beer off the coffee table and turned to Nate. "So, what happened?"

"Copernicus got on the roof this morning."

"Again?" Zach asked.

"Dude," Kyle said, extending beer hand and open palm like he was fixing to reveal the mind-blowing secrets of the universe. "Ladders. Just sayin."

"Isn't that like the fourth time this week?" Zach asked.

"Second," Nate corrected, "but he's definitely seemed kind of... I dunno, agitated lately."

"Yeah," Kyle said. "Because of the alien mind control rays."

"That's not a thing," Marty said.

Kyle rocked back on his couch perch, eyebrows reaching for the ceiling.

"Not again," Marty muttered, opening the fridge to grab a beer.

From his couch back perch, Kyle held up three thick fingers.

"He's doing it," Zach said before taking a long sip of his own drink.

"Here we go," Marty said, cracking open his can.

"Three weeks," Kyle said, wiggling his raised fingers for emphasis. "Three weeks since NASA, CNSA, and no less than eight major observatories around the world all started reporting"—he made dramatic air quotes—"'peculiar activity' in the 'background radiation.'"

"Yeah?" Zach asked. "What else, Dr. Evil?"

"At the same time," Kyle said, jabbing a finger at Zach. "Namor and the oceanographers pop up to tell us there's some strange seismic activity going down in the great blue yonder, and no one's sure why. Meanwhile, reports of odd and unusual animal behavior are on, and I quote, 'an unprecedented rise,' according to the National Wildlife Federation."

At that point in the speech, Kyle paused to take a hearty swig of his beer. "This isn't just another 'storm Area 51 now' poseur-fest, gentlemen. Three weeks." Another swig. "Three batshit weird signs." Another swig.

"Now I ask you, gentlemen..." Zach picked up in a decent imitation of Kyle's throaty voice.

"If that doesn't sound like aliens to you..." Marty added, his imitation passable if not quite as good.

Kyle unleashed a mighty burp and crushed his finished can. "Then what the fuck would?"

Nate took another sip of his beer, feeling oddly perturbed by his friend's bogus conspiracy theory. Chalk it up to too much doom and gloom in one day.

Kyle turned back to him. "So what happened with Copernicus?"

"I fell off the roof trying to get him."

Zach's eyes widened mid-sip.

"Dude..." Kyle said.

"Are you okay?" Marty asked.

"Is the dog?" Zach added.

"Oh, Copernicus is great," Nate said, smiling a little at the memory of the corgi, then quickly sobering. "But I landed on my backpack and crushed the Promethean..."

"Nooo," Marty groaned.

"... And Gwen and Todd just happened to be walking by in time to see the whole thing."

"No!" Zach said.

"So, yeah," Nate said. "I got to play helpless invalid to Gwen. Meanwhile, Todd's all but getting it on with Emily Atherton right behind her back." He shook his head, too frustrated to find adequate words.

"Sounds like good news to me," Marty said. "Todd is obviously a dick, and Gwen obviously cares about you. Win-win."

Nate sipped his beer, considering Marty's wisdom. "She did offer to drop everything and take me to the hospital."

"See?" Marty said, cracking a smile. "That's great, man. She cares."

"Yeah, because we're fucking BFFs," Nate muttered, but he found himself smiling too. Maybe it was partly thanks to the beer he'd downed rather hastily, but Marty's smile always seemed to have that effect on him.

"Sooo," Kyle said, leaning forward excitedly. "Was Atherton wearing the bathrobe again?"

"Dude," Zach said, elbowing Kyle's knee. "Not important right now."

"Emily was wearing the bathrobe, yes," Nate said, glad for the chance to turn the spotlight off of his own public embarrassment. "Pink and skimpy. Practically falling out of it."

"See?" Kyle said, splaying his hands at Zack. "How is that not important? Imagine..." He ran his hands through the air, tracing unseen curves, then cracked open a fresh beer and took a sip, shaking his head longingly. "Almost makes me wanna start waking up before noon."

"Yeah," Zach said. "Emphasis on the almost, right?"

Kyle shrugged and sipped his beer.

"Dude, have some pizza and forget about the whole thing," Marty said to Nate, flipping open the topmost box of the Bell's pizza stack on the table.

"We've got noobs to slay and beers aplenty!" Kyle agreed, raising his can in cheers.

Stomach rumbling at the sight of cheesy goodness, Nate took a slice and dug in without argument.

"What did Hillman have to say about the Promethean?" Marty asked.

Nate shook his head and tried to talk around a full bite. "I think I'm dropping his class."

That caused another round of startled looks.

"It's just too much to juggle," Nate said, immediately feeling defensive. "It's an elective anyway."

Zach cocked his head. "But it's like…"

"The only class he cares about?" Kyle asked.

"Yeah, that."

Nate shrugged. "No software firm is gonna care if I took some art classes."

Merciful Sith, he sounded like his dad.

"I don't need the credits anyway," he added to wash the thought away, but his roommates' skeptical stares persisted. He turned and found the same look mirrored on Marty's face.

"What?" He pushed past Marty to grab a plate from the kitchen cupboard and returned to the table to load on a few more slices. "I can just make useless shit on my own time, can't I?"

"That he can," Kyle said with a clap of his hands. "Now get your beers and start your rigs, ladies and gentlemen," he added, pointing first to Marty, then to Nate, then to the bottom two flat screens of their Cartesian quadrant style Mother of All Gaming Shrines.

"Tonight, we game!"

A FEW HOURS and a few beers later, Nate was finally starting to feel comfortable with the idea that normalcy had returned. Sure, it had been a shit day. And sure, he might've nixed what little bit of his prematurely failed art career he had left—not to mention further buried his chances with

Gwen. But he had his friends, and he always would. And they had their games. And he had his buzz.

Things could've been a whole hell of a lot worse.

In fact, he decided, after another beer and an unexpectedly spectacular Battle Royale victory, he wasn't really sure they could've been any better than they were just like this. Things were exactly as they were supposed to be. He was sure of it. So sure that he was preparing to make it known via a grand—and possibly slightly drunken—declaration when his phone vibrated on the floor ahead of him.

He traded an arched eyebrow with Marty, who was sitting cross legged on the floor beside him, as was their custom—Zach and Kyle both perched on the couch behind them where they could see over their heads.

"Hold up," Nate said, ducking his in-game character safely into a corner and reaching for his phone. His heart fluttered at the name on the screen.

Gwen: "How are you feeling?"

He unlocked the phone, game temporarily forgotten as he tried to compose an adequately cool response.

"Who dat?" Zach asked, craning curiously from the couch.

"It's Gwen," Marty said with a knowing smile. "That's the Gwen face."

"Ah, She of the Many Cliques," Kyle said. "How is ol' Gwenneth?"

"I don't know why you insist on calling her that," Marty said. "Having other friends isn't a crime, you know."

"*Other* friends?" Kyle asked. "I'm sorry, did I miss the part where she's still *our* friend?"

Nate swiped out his reply and hit send.

Nate: "Feeling great… but sorry, who is this again?"

He wasn't surprised at the bitterness in his friend's tone. Once upon a freshman dorm, Gwen had been their on-again, off-again fifth controller jockey, and Kyle in particular had never seemed to forgive her for having slowly vanished into the college ether.

"She still asks about you guys," Nate said, returning to the ongoing game. He didn't mention the part where his own chances to see her had grown decidedly less and less frequent with each passing semester. "And to answer your original question, Kyle, aside from having caught a bad case of steroid fever, I think she's pretty—"

The phone vibrated in Nate's lap.

That was fast.

"Yeah, we know you think she's pretty, buddy," Zach said. "Now if you could kindly hide the erection, we've got an enemy team at…"

But Nate was already glancing down at the phone with a single-mindedness that would've made Pavlov proud.

Gwen: "Har har, Mr. Concussion. I probably shouldn't encourage you to drink, considering, but come hang out tonight if you're up for it?"

Excitement rose in Nate's chest, tinged with a twist of apprehension and joined shortly by the churn of guilt in his gut. Did he really want to—

"Nate!" Kyle cried, snapping him back to the war room. "Get your rockets out here and—Well, shit. Never mind. Because now we're dead. Go team."

Nate looked up from his phone and vibrating controller just in time to watch the enemy team finish sweeping the floor with their digital bodies. "Sorry, guys," he said with a guilty grin, brandishing his phone. "But yeah. She's good, I think."

The look on his face must've said the rest, because Zach and Kyle both went from looks of suspicion to ones of accusation in a flash.

"Dude, it's Friday night squads," Kyle said. "You can't bail to go hang out with the original squad bailer. She of the..." He frowned, having apparently stumped his drunken self.

"You need to stop with the nicknames," Marty said.

"And *every* night is squads night for us," Nate added.

Kyle shook his head, holding up a single meaty finger. "Not true. Zach and I totally played duos the other night when you and Marty were"—he made air quotes—"watching Prometheus."

"So spooky," Zach said in a mock whisper. "Hold my hand!"

"Well..." Nate said, swiping out a reply to Gwen.

Nate: "Might have jumped the gun on the drinking thing. Where would I find you if I were up for it?"

"... Maybe you guys have a Battle Royale problem," he concluded, looking up at Kyle and Zach.

"And that was also three weeks ago," Marty pointed out. "Just for the record. Pretty sure we haven't missed a night since."

Kyle and Zach shared a look of genuine surprise.

"Out-nerded?" Zach murmured.

"Three weeks," Kyle echoed, looking moderately disturbed by that news. "Goddamn aliens." He shook his head clear, his usual vigor returning. "Well in that case, I should probably make sure I fed Hector."

Gwen: "Follow signs of troglodytes. Big, big footprints. Many keg tracks."

Nate smiled down at his phone then almost dropped it as the couch creaked and Kyle thudded down to the floor. Their plus-sized roommate stopped to catch his balance, clearly feeling the effects of the innumerable beers he'd pounded since he'd last left his seat, then he steadied and jabbed a finger at Nate.

"And once I'm sure Hector's not dead, *then* it's Friday night squads! You wouldn't wanna make your pals go dropping in with some rando fourth, would ya?"

When Nate wasn't quick with a response, Kyle marched off down the hallway, muttering something about *randos* and *kids these days* and *the humanity, gods the humanity!* They listened to him bang open the metal door and thump into his room down the hall.

"If you're gonna go," Marty said, "could you come have a look at my Arduino first? I hit a little snag."

Zach, who'd been watching the two of them expectantly, took that as a sign to fire up a solo round. "Yeah, go look at his *Arduino*, Nate," he said, smirking a little drunkenly and looking at a sincere loss between finishing his pizza or his beer while the game loaded.

Nate grabbed one last slice of pizza and followed Marty down the hallway to his friend's room. Without question, Marty's room was the tidiest in the house, and he was undoubtedly the MVP when it came to keeping the rest of the house in order as well. Between that fact and the concerned look Marty turned on Nate the second he closed the door behind them, Nate couldn't help but wonder for the thousandth time if maybe his own mother didn't secretly have Marty on payroll as her designated worry-wart by proxy.

"Why are you dropping Hillman's class?" he asked.

Nate looked around the room. "The old *can you take a look at my Arduino* trick, huh?"

"Gets 'em every time," Marty agreed, sitting down at his computer desk and waking the sleeping beast. "I *have* been getting an error all afternoon, though. Driving me crazy."

Nate stood there while Marty pulled open the code he'd been working on for his utterly unnecessary and wonderfully nerdy automated bedroom wakeup system. Adjustable lights, music, motorized window blinds control, and retro LED message board—all controlled by a handy little Arduino.

Marty loved these kinds of projects. It was the kind of stuff Nate highly appreciated as well but never tended to initiate himself, preferring instead to spend most of his leisure time either gaming or sketching up his concept art alongside that little voice in his head that said maybe, just *maybe* if he kept it going he could one day find work as a real living, breathing video game concept artist. One day.

His phone buzzed in his hand.

Gwen: "So what do you say, sailor? Just like old times?"

He tucked the phone in his pocket, suddenly feeling a little sick for reasons he couldn't identify. Probably just the onslaught of pizza and beer, he supposed, but...

"I couldn't show it to him, Marty. The Promethean, I mean. It's stupid, but after all the work I put into it... I just couldn't show Hillman what was left. Not even to prove my story."

Marty frowned, clearly trying to understand. "So what? He threatened to fail you or something?"

Nate shook his head. "No. He just said he understood and asked me if I wanted to try again."

"But... That's good, right? Why don't you just, you know... try again?"

Nate leaned in to inspect Marty's code more to change the subject than anything else, taking the mouse to scroll through the lines.

"You love that stuff, Nate," Marty said quietly. "You don't have to drop it all just because..."

He trailed off, either unsure of what to say, or just unwilling to point out the truths that Nate already knew: that he *wasn't* a concept artist, and that he probably never would be. That there just *weren't* that many reliable, obtainable jobs out there in the field, as his parents had been quick to point out back when the college talks had started. And sure, that didn't mean he *had* to drop the art. But it also didn't mean there was any point pretending he was something he wasn't.

"You transposed this matrix in the wrong spot," he said.

"What?" Marty said, turning back to the monitor.

"The way you're opening this spreadsheet and accessing the... Never mind. Just, this matrix needs to be transposed every iteration, see? So it needs to be nested one loop deeper."

"Oh." Marty squinted at the screen and bobbed his head as he saw it. "Ohhh. Yeah, that's... that makes sense." He looked up. "That was quick, dude. You *are* really good at this stuff, for what it's worth."

Really *lucky*, was more like it. He'd just happened to start reading at exactly the right spot. But he still appreciated Marty's compliment. For a second, he thought about asking his friend to come with him, even though he knew the answer would be a solid *thanks, but no thanks... unless you need me to.*

"I still think you should stay in Hillman's class," Marty added, still looking at the monitor. "For the record."

"Duly noted," Nate said, patting his friend on the back. "Maybe I'll try to take a page from your wall display's book."

Nate opened the door and slipped out of Marty's room to go investigate his clean shirt situation, sure that behind him, Marty was meanwhile turning to look at the retro LED display on his nice, tidy wall.

"ERROR," it read. "INPUT INVALID."

CHAPTER 3

GO FRAT YOURSELF

Finding and following signs of the troglodytes, it turned out, wasn't all that hard, what with the earth-shaking bass beats and the extensive collection of frisbees, wiffle bats, crumpled red cups, beer cans, and even one passed out pledge all scattered across the lawn. And somehow, staring at the decimation that'd already occurred, all Nate's buzzed mind could seem to think about—for the hundred-and-eighty-second time—was whether he should've changed his shirt after all.

Jeans and plain black t-shirt was a timeless classic, right? Maybe. But he *was* also the guy who thought people should maybe try listening to real music at these parties for a change, and whose own book of timeless classics consisted of such chestnuts as *Mario Kart* and *Ocarina of Time*. What the hell did he know about clothes, aside from that his gray zip-up hoodie was clearly at odds with the Greek cutoffs and Team America trunks of the Alpha-Sig-Sigs who were hanging on the front deck?

The sight almost made Nate shiver. But the Alpha-Sig-Sigs were either too cool to be affected by the early October chill, or too drunk. Probably both. Maybe Nate should've had another drink himself before he left. He was still buzzed, but it was in danger of fading, and gods forbid he had to brave the next hour on his wits alone.

"You will never find a more wretched hive of scum and villainy," he mumbled to himself in a bad excuse for an Obi-Wan impression.

See? Hopeless.

On the way past Emily's, he'd half-considered going to sneak a quick doggy paw bump with Copernicus through the window to drink up some of the little guy's incorrigible energy. But even on a Friday night, with a roughly hundred percent chance the corgi would be home alone while Emily and her roommate tore up the town, that plan had felt just a little too creepy, even for him.

Besides, if her texts were any indication, Gwen was waiting for him.

Waiting for him at her *boyfriend's* douchey Alpha-Sig-Sig party, Nate reminded himself, also for the hundred-and-eighty-second time.

He started down the entry path from the sidewalk, reflecting that he should probably stop it with the *Alpha-Sig-Sig* thing for the evening too, lest he slip up and land himself as target for an entire household's worth of roid rage. Alpha-Sig-Sigs were just what Nate and his oh-so-clever roommates called stereotypical frat bro types. Which was probably stupid to start with. Calling someone a Greek A.S.S. wasn't exactly subtle, and even if it had been, spiteful name-calling wasn't really his style. Alpha bros had just always had a way of hitting a nerve for Nate and his nerdy brethren.

The *actual* lettering on the side of the huge house read "Iota Nu Nu House," which was almost as funny anyway, even if they *had* missed their chance to call it "The INN Inn." In the daylight, minus the thumping music and drunken sundry, it was the kind of old house one might've described as rustic—from the outside, at least.

"What's up, bro?" someone called as Nate finished parting the drunken sea of the front yard and mounted the deck steps.

He looked up and found three of them watching him from their dominant, triceps-heavy leans on the banister above. Not blocking his way, but definitely giving off a whiff of the *who are you and what do you want* vibe.

Fair enough. Nate had been here before, multiple times, but he wasn't exactly memorable, and he didn't recognize these three Adonises-in-the-making either. He wondered if he should mention Todd's name, or Gwen's —reticent to even imply any kind of kinship with Todd, but also less than eager to let these guys think he'd come sniffing after their Alpha's mate.

Goddammit. They weren't werewolves.

That you know of, whispered his unhelpful brain.

He cleared his throat. "Hey guys."

Great start.

"Uh, Gwen told me I should stop by."

Okay, on second thought, maybe they were werewolves.

"Gwen Pearson," he clarified, probably unnecessarily judging by the metaphorical bared fangs. Desperate, Nate pointed down Allen Street toward Emily's and added, "Todd Mackleroy invited me this morning over at—"

"Oh hey! IT Guy!" someone called from the door.

They all turned, and Nate breathed a small sigh of relief at the beaming face of Brad, one of the few Iota Nu Nus he sort of knew—and actually, in this case, even sort of liked, from what limited interactions they'd had.

"Heard you had a wicked fall this morning?" Brad called, still beaming.

Had he heard? Great.

"Yeah," Nate called back, cautiously climbing the last steps to the deck and approaching a glassy-eyed Brad. The Greek werewolves stood back, watching suspiciously. "Yeah, that… that happened. At least the dog was okay, though."

The intensity of Brad's laugh caught Nate by surprise. "Long live Copernicus, dude! Come on in, let's get you a drink."

~

INSIDE, the party was, as they say, *thumping.* Loudly. And with all the writhing bodies and flashing lights of an epileptic's worst nightmares. Nate wasn't sure he would've made it more than a step through the sensory overload if Brad hadn't looped an arm over his shoulder and pulled him along like they were age-old bros.

"Ahh, IT Guy," Brad said, patting Nate's back. "Hell of a night to see you, Nate. Hell of a night." Brad squinted over at him with a look of intense focus. "It is Nate, right?"

Nate looked at his glassy-eyed guide in surprise. "Uh, yeah. Brad, right?"

"So they say, man." Brad shook his head. "So they say." He frowned, looking around the flashing light chaos, and barely seemed to notice when a rather *noticeable* girl materialized from the crowd and began moving against him in time with the booming music. "What were we doing, again, IT Guy?"

Figuring he was about to get ditched—and not really blaming Brad one bit for the fact—Nate was opening his mouth to ask his stalwart guide if he might know where Gwen was when Brad jerked upright and tugged Nate onward toward the kitchen with a cry of, "Drinks! We need to get you a drink! Fuck yeah!"

Nate caught a fleeting glimpse of the indignant surprise from Brad's would-be dance partner, then they were pushing on through the crowd, unmistakably on a mission.

"I'm not gonna lie, IT Guy," Brad said, patting his back again, "I'm trippin' ALL the balls right now. But we're gonna get this done. Like, a quest and shit."

"Uh thanks, man," Nate said, not really sure how else to respond. "And while we're at it, have you seen Gwen Pearson around here tonight?"

"Another quest!" Brad cried, pumping a fist as they stepped out of the strobe-lit dance room and into the enormous and only slightly tamer kitchen. "Yo, someone get IT Guy a drink!" Brad called. "Dude fell off a windmill or something today." He squinted over at Nate. "Right?"

"Uh…" Nate looked around at the dozen or so faces that were now turned their way and gave them a little wave that he hoped said, *Never mind us, we're all good.*

Everyone in the kitchen went back to their conversations—or their heavy petting—as Nate guided Brad over to the side of the room, out of the main traffic flow. Brad didn't seem to mind. In fact, he seemed pretty stoked about life in general at the moment. And he seemed to be blinking a lot, too. And had his pupils been that gigantic a minute ago?

Nate was about to ask if he was all right when one of the younger Iota Nu Nus appeared beside them, offering Nate a red cup, filled to the brim with a neon blue concoction.

"Here you go, IT Guy."

"Uh, thanks," Nate said, too flustered and surprised by the service to do anything but accept the cup. Quick as that, the pledge who'd brought it was gone, leaving Nate staring down at the blue mystery drink.

As a rule of thumb, he tended to avoid jungle juice. Especially from guys who called him IT Guy like it was his legal name. He wasn't even rightly sure how that one had started, especially since there were at least two IT majors in Iota Nu Nu, and most of these people had no idea who Nate even was. Maybe he just had one of those *IT Guy* faces.

Nate turned to Brad, thinking to thank him and ask where he should look for Gwen, but Brad cut him off, holding up both hands in a clear sign to wait. He closed his too-dilated eyes, still dancing to the beat, brow furrowing in paradoxical concentration. Furrowing, and furrowing, and…

"Ah, you found us!"

At the sound of Gwen's voice, Nate turned faster than what could ever be deemed cool or collected. Beside him, Brad just clapped his hands victoriously, gave Nate one last friendly pat on the chest, and danced off chanting something about satellite minds.

"Wasn't sure you'd make it," Gwen said, her smiling eyes flicking between him and Brad's dance-retreating form.

"Not sure what that was about," Nate said, nodding after Brad, suddenly unsure what else to say as the rest of his brain shut down to drink her in and spill a nice migration of butterflies into his stomach.

She was wearing faded jeans and a rose-red top with minimum frills and just enough of a cut that Nate might've pulled a muscle trying not to let his eyes wander if he hadn't already been so riveted to her smile-crinkled eyes, which looked more green tonight than blue. He could never quite tell.

Reflexively, he sipped at his drink to buy himself a second, all reservations about the neon blue mystery juice momentarily forgotten. "Brad was just, uh…"

"Tripping balls?" she asked, her smile widening.

"Something like that." Nate cocked his head thoughtfully. "I think he might be psychic."

"He didn't earn the name 'Balls Brad' by accident, I'll tell you that much."

Nate smiled. "Is he gonna be okay?"

"Oh, yeah. It's probably the drugs that should be scared of *him* at this point." She frowned across the room to where Brad was now strutting his dance moves for the refrigerator, clearly questioning her own confidence in the matter. Then Brad's prospective dance partner from earlier came into the kitchen and dragged him back out to the dance floor by the hand, and Gwen relaxed and turned back to Nate. "How's *your* brain doing, Mr. Concussion?"

"Well, you know, it's all a bit fuzzy," he said, brandishing his red cup. "So if I say anything stupid tonight…"

"Free pass," she said, holding up her own drink. "Guaranteed. Cheers."

This time, it wasn't that he was too flustered to remember his aversion to communal jungle juice. It was just that, touching cups with Gwen, caught in the shine of her infectious smile, he just didn't really care anymore. Especially not when he noticed she was also drinking the mystery concoction.

"Come on," Gwen said, taking him by the arm and pulling him toward the back deck.

At least if they died, they'd die together. And in that moment, arms interlocked, her favoring him with a happy grin, Nate couldn't help but think that maybe it wouldn't be such a bad way to go.

～

While not quite free of the October chill or the sleeveless werewolves, the enclosed wraparound deck out back was at least slightly less crowded, and the music volume slightly more amenable to speaking below a scream. There was even some moonlight striking through the glass panes—though that hardly put Nate's mind at ease, what with all the werewolf analogies.

Gwen led him to a couch that arguably had two open spots. Really, it was probably more like one-and-a-half, but they crammed in as best as they could. By the time they'd settled, Nate could only imagine his face had shifted to the rose-red of Gwen's top, but at least the deck was dark enough to cover it up. To his surprise, Gwen shared his embarrassed smile, looking a little abashed by the contact herself at first, but she quickly shifted, draping her legs over his and putting her back against the arm of the couch to free up a little more lateral space.

"Okay," she said with a playful pat to his thigh. "Not sure either of us is getting out of here without a crane now, so I guess you might as well tell me how you've been."

Nate was still busy just trying to remember how to breathe with Gwen this close to him, but once he'd gotten past his reflexive, "Oh, same old, same old," and Gwen sharpened her questions, they fell into an easy conversation about how both of their years had been going.

She told him about her senior bioengineering thesis work in the enigmatic Millennium Science Complex, and he did his best to follow along, asking questions whenever she lost him with her talk of induced pluripotent stem cells. Even if he hadn't found it all fascinating—which he *did*—he would've been tempted to pretend, just to see the way she lit up talking about it all. He knew how important this work was to her. Or had a strong idea, at least.

Gwen had always been pretty close-guarded when it came to her family situation, but over the years, he'd come to learn that her brother suffered from some form of muscular dystrophy, and that his condition had played a huge role in Gwen's path of study. She'd always dreamed that one day she'd be able to do something about it, and to listen to her talk, it was evident she had every intention of seeing that dream through.

Similarly, it filled him with a soft, bittersweet warmth when she was every bit as mortified as his roommates about what'd happened to his Promethean art project earlier that day, as well as his decision to drop Hillman's design course.

It never ceased to amaze him, how he and Gwen could go months without a real conversation and then, right when he'd start convincing himself it had all been in his head, and that she'd only been showing him merciful kindness in the past, they'd fall straight back into it like two peas in a pod, and she'd be there asking him questions and listening to his answers like what he said *truly* mattered to her. Like she knew him every bit as well as he thought he knew her. Like the two of them simply belonged.

It was so easy to forget this feeling when they were apart—to forget that someone so perfect could care so much about what he had to say. That underneath the beauty that even now made his palms sweat, she was just another person, just like him.

Which was ridiculous, of course. Because look at her, and look at him. But still, it was a divine little fantasy. So Nate drank it in while he could, smiling and laughing with Gwen for he didn't know how long, neither of them minding when their drinks ran dry, or when the deck began to get even more crowded with the thickening overflow from the booming party.

It was only when their couch neighbors made a particularly frisky, lip-smacking claim for even more couch space, and Nate found himself with Gwen all but sitting in his lap, that their conversation hit a lull. Or screeched to a grinding halt, rather.

In that moment, feeling her warm weight on him, smelling the electric blue jungle juice on her breath and the lavender in her moonlight-struck hair... In that moment, locked in the depths of her eyes, intoxicated with the closeness of her, and with gods knew what else, Nate thought in earnest about kissing Gwen—about reaching up, looping a stupid, sweaty palm behind her head and pulling her face to his, just like he'd seen at least one guy do at pretty much every shitty party he'd ever been to. Just like the neighbors who were practically dry humping on top of them now had no doubt done a minute ago.

She was right there. She was watching him. Not shying away. Watching him. Searching his face for... for what?

Just do it.

His hand twitched like a defective toy on the arm of the couch.

Gwen shifted ever-so-slightly on top of him, the slight movement sending ripples down to the core of his being. The oddest smile was tugging at her lips—sweet and yet somehow sad, vulnerable.

Kiss her.

He should do it. Was going to do it.

Then he thought of Todd, and of the loyal goon squad that would no-shit happily murder Nate's IT Guy ass for even sitting here with their

Alpha's girl like this—assuming they could even stop laughing at him long enough to bother…

"I'm sorry," Nate whispered, so quietly he wasn't sure he'd made the sound at all. He was staring down at her thighs now, not even remembering having dropped his gaze.

Jesus, why was he like this?

He felt hollow. Clammy, almost.

Then she laid a hand on his chest, and tremors ran through him at the touch.

"Same old, same old, huh?" she said, almost as quietly.

Before he could rally himself to do or say anything, she shifted again, and then she was climbing off of him, rising from the couch, and the moment was dead and gone.

"Come on." She offered him a hand. "Another drink?"

Nate took her hand, too ashamed or embarrassed or whatever the hell he was to even meet her eyes. He should leave, some part of him knew. Save face. Run away. And yet he was too afraid of letting the space between them explode into a permanent rift to do anything other than hold on to her hand and follow along.

They hadn't made it more than five feet through the sea of party-goers—at least a dozen of whom were heavily making out, as if to mock him—when Gwen stopped and turned to face him again, getting close enough to be heard over the din.

"Todd's… not really my boyfriend, you know," she said quietly in his ear before backing away a few inches and watching his face for his reaction, like she was in the lab studying some peculiar anomaly. What an odd little specimen he must be. And maybe it was the defensiveness that welled up at that thought, or maybe it was some combination of jungle juice and a higher propensity for Grade-A Asshole-ism than Nate had ever suspected resides within his nerdy frame, but he couldn't stop the next words that spilled out of his mouth.

"He's just a guy who calls you babe?"

He could've bit his own tongue off. Probably should've.

Gwen didn't snap back or slap him or anything dramatic like that. She just arched an eyebrow, her expression… what? Annoyed? Slighted? Or was it expectant? Or bemused?

He would've taken a thousand falls from Emily's rooftop to know what that eyebrow meant. And maybe a thousand more to sink through the floorboards and out of existence when a familiar voice cut through the din beside them.

"Ah, IT Guy made it," Todd Mackleroy said, sweeping in, hefting Gwen into his bulging arms, and pulling her into a deep kiss before either of them could say a word. It nearly turned Nate's stomach to watch.

"What's up, babe?" their interrupting Adonis said, when he finally disengaged from her lips long enough to acknowledge her with words.

"What's up with you?" she asked, licking her lips and looking a little taken aback. "And his name's Nate, Todd. You know that."

"Mmm," Todd purred, juggling Gwen closer, his hands shifting decidedly asswards. "You know it turns me on when you say my name like that, babe."

Gwen rolled her eyes, but Nate didn't miss the way her exasperation cracked to giggles when Todd nuzzled her neck and collarbone with kisses. Or the wink Todd shot him out of the corner of his eye.

The bastard.

"So you wanna play that game of pong or what?" Todd said, finally setting Gwen down. "Me and Bonzer just finished wiping the last of the challengers, and I figured you"—he booped her nose—"might want a shot before we turn the tykes loose on the table."

"Such a sweetie," she said, patting Todd's angular cheek.

"You know it, babe. So what do you say?"

For some reason, they both looked at Nate, as if the question was directed at him too.

"Oh, he's playing with Bonzer," Gwen explained. "Can't risk taking on a civilian and losing a game in his own house."

"I didn't ask for these skills, babe, but I sure as shit gotta represent 'em."

"Which means that I need myself a sorry civilian partner," Gwen concluded.

"Oh," Nate said. "I, uh…"

Need to go, said the unhelpful voyeur watching from the corner of his brain.

"Come on," she said, taking him by the elbow. "One game, partner. What's the worst that could happen?"

CHAPTER 4
HOUSE RULES

On a basic level, as a guy who loved games, Nate could understand at least some of the appeal of beer pong. You had a clear objective, and a mechanically satisfying task to repeat. Who didn't love trying to land a ball in a cup? Plus, drinks. Fun times for all.

So no, beer pong might not've been such an awful game.

Losing beer pong to the muscle-bound not-quite-boyfriend of your four-year-crush-and-possible-soulmate, on the other hand, kind of sucked.

"Just to clarify," Gwen whispered in Nate's ear, sliding a ping-pong ball into his waiting palm, "turns out the ball's supposed to go *in* the cup."

His wounded pride momentarily forgotten, Nate turned to her with his best shocked face and mouthed, with all appropriate horror, *"What?!"*

She laughed, snapping her fingers. "I knew we were forgetting something."

For a second, Nate felt his genuine smile flowing back across his lips, drawn to hers like a moth to the light. Maybe he shouldn't care so much that they were getting stomped. Even if they *had* started with a handicap of four extra cups. Gwen clearly didn't. In fact, with the exception of their momentary awkwardness out on the deck, her smile hadn't left her face since—

"Come on ladies," Todd called from the other end of the table, yanking Nate straight out of the moment and back to their imminent loss. "Let's wrap this up. Bonzer's gonna pass out if we don't get him a pizza soon."

Nate glanced at Todd's teammate and was not at all under the impression Todd might've misspoken when he said *a pizza* and not *a slice* of pizza. Nate was still half-convinced this "Bonzer" creature was in fact a cave troll in human disguise. But Christ, could that troll sink some balls.

"I believe, grasshopper," Gwen said quietly to Nate, patting him on the back as he stepped up to the table.

He took a breath. Lined up. Took his shot…

And made a cup.

"Yes!" Gwen shouted, bouncing excitedly and thrusting her hands out for a double high-five, which Nate returned with a stupid grin. It was only their first cup. Out of six. But a cup was a cup, he supposed, and Gwen's energy was contagious.

At least Todd wouldn't have any grounds to try some kind of *flawless victory* hazing bullshit when they lost. That was something.

Then Gwen took her shot, and Nate felt a disturbance in the Force.

He could see from the moment the ball left her hand that the shot was going to go long. What he couldn't remember was why that mattered in the context of Iota Nu Nu's extensive list of household rules. Not until Todd screamed like a freaking Spartan king charging into battle.

"SQUANTO!"

Then he plucked the little white ball out of midair and whipped it straight at Nate's face.

Had Nate had time to use his rational brain, he might've stood there and simply taken it like a man. Maybe even slapped the shot away with his hand. It was a freaking ping-pong ball, after all.

Instead, he ducked back out of panicked reflex, staggered by the stakes of the game and the sheer bro-tality of Todd's war cry. The pong ball grazed the side of his forehead, then his foot caught on something, and he was falling. For the second time that day, he felt the air smacked from his lungs, and then he was looking up at a ratty chandelier and about two dozen laughing faces all around him.

"Squanto for the win!" someone shouted.

"Victory by Squanto!"

"Dude, I think this bro's dead."

"Nate?"

This time, at least, he managed to sit up before Gwen could go full bioengineer nurse on him in front of the entire Iota Nu Nu house.

"I'm fine," he wheezed preemptively, scrambling to his feet.

She took his arm, like she was afraid he'd fall over but said nothing, maybe because she could already smell the shame radiating off of him. Everyone in the room seemed to be looking at him. Laughing at him. He looked to the door, wanting nothing more than to be gone from that place.

Before he could take a step, though, Todd swooped in on them and scooped Gwen up in both arms with a cry of, "Victooory!"

"Todd," Gwen said, in a tone that actually gave the Greek God pause.

"Yo, you all good, IT Guy?" he added.

"Fine," Nate said, almost surprised to find himself turning for the door. "I'm fine."

And then he was walking—nearly running—for the door.

"Nate!" Gwen called after him.

"Good game, dude!" Todd called. "Careful with that noggin!"

Gwen must've said something to him, because he kept going.

"What? He says he's fine. And you know what that means. Rules is rules, babe."

"Rules is rules," someone else—Nate could only assume Bonzer—agreed in a low, rumbling voice.

Nate kept walking. Out of the room. Through the raving dance mass. Toward the front door. He was done. Never should've walked out on Friday night squads in the first place. Never should've—

"Nate!"

His traitor legs stopped even as his head insisted he at least find the spine to storm out with dignity.

"Are you okay?" Gwen asked behind him.

With a breath, he forced himself to turn and meet her eyes. "I'm fine, Gwen. I'm just gonna go, okay?"

"You're upset," she said, searching his face with that concerned look. "It's okay. Everyone here is too shit-faced to care anyway, and it was just a game. You—"

"I said I'm good. You're right, it's just a game, and I… well, maybe I've just had enough of them."

She recoiled a little at that, her eyes widening. "Nate, come on…"

"I'm sorry. I didn't mean that. I just… I should just go home, okay?"

She nodded, biting her lip. "Okay. Well, can we talk again soon?"

He nodded, some of the tension leaving his shoulders. "Yeah. Yeah, of course we can."

She wrapped him in a tight hug. "I enjoyed being with you tonight. Get home safe, okay?"

"You too," he said, returning the hug and turning to leave a little more reluctantly this time.

"Heading out, bro?" someone asked as he reached the front door.

Nate looked around and saw Brad watching him from nearby, where he had his dance partner from earlier pinned rather provocatively to the wall. And judging by the indignant impatience with which she was now eyeing Nate, he assumed they'd just been getting somewhere interesting.

"Yeah, have a good one, Brad. Thanks for the drink."

"Rough night?"

Nate hesitated, glancing toward the door and the cool, quiet evening that lay just beyond.

"Dude…" Brad parted from his lady friend, and wobbled over to Nate, clearly less than sober. Even in the strobe-fest, it was evident his pupils were still enormous. He put one hand on Nate's shoulder, and patted Nate's cheek affectionately with the other. "You're a good boy, Copernicus. Just don't go chasing anymore windmills, eh? That's the trick."

Part of Nate wanted to be outraged that even Balls-tripping Brad had more of a handle on his night than Nate did. Another part, and maybe not a small one, felt a strange urge to simply let it all out—to break down in Balls Brad's arms and let the trippy bastard tell him how it was all going to be all right, even if he did apparently think Nate was a one-foot tall corgi.

Mostly, though, Nate just wanted to leave.

And he was ready to, until he caught the flash of bleached blond hair ascending the stairs across the room, followed too closely by a muscular back. Gwen. Being carried away by King Squanto himself, who had her secured by two generous handfuls of Gwen rump.

For a second, Nate thought she looked unhappy about it. But then Todd jostled her around and gave her ass a firm smack, and she was laughing, clearly trying and failing to be stern with him. Clearly not needing Nate's sorry ass to step in and embarrass himself again.

"Fuck this," Nate muttered.

"Yesss!" Brad hissed, patting his shoulders enthusiastically. "That's the spirit, Copernicus! Fuck those windmills, boy! I knew you had it in you! Go, boy…" He jerked his head towards the door. "Go make your mark on the world. I believe in you!"

Unclenching one trembling fist, Nate gave Brad a pat on the shoulder. "You have a good night, Brad. Thanks for not being a dick." He started to leave, then hesitated. "Also, you should probably drink some water."

Brad just beamed like it was the nicest thing anyone had ever said to him.

Nate turned and slipped out the door, hurrying down the front deck steps and out to the sidewalk, feeling liable to explode at any moment. He never should've left his friends. Never in seven hells should have imagined there was any world in which he, IT Guy McFalls-A-Lot, could walk into Iota Nu Nu and just make off with King Squanto's girl.

What the hell had he even been thinking on that deck?

Kiss her? Seriously?

Whatever.

He reached for his phone, thinking to check the time, and realized his pocket was wet. Completely soaked, in fact. Like someone had spilled a whole damn drink on him, and he somehow hadn't noticed until now. Maybe because he'd been too rattled on account of the fact that he'd just bit it in front of Gwen and a hundred A-holes.

Muttering a string of curses, he pulled his phone free and pressed the unlock button, expecting the worst.

Nothing.

Completely dead.

"Fuck it all," he growled, turning toward town and setting off at a brusque hate march.

"Amen, bro!" someone called after him from the deck.

CHAPTER 5
THE LEAKY POCKET

Nate stepped out of McLanahan's and slid his dead phone into the bag of rice he'd just spent ten minutes begging the last cashier, who'd already closed down the registers, to let him buy. The day had gone from straight shit to a honest-to-god shit-nado, and as Nate stood there, watching his breath fog in the chilling evening air, he could only imagine he'd be struck down any moment by a falling jet engine, or maybe even take the mantle as State College's first documented case of spontaneous combustion.

"Why'd he have an open bag of rice in his pocket?" one of the coroners would ask as they inspected the remains.

"Who cares?" would reply the other.

At this point, the only reasonable move was to cut his losses, head home, and get a couple more hours of Battle Royale in with his friends before he turned in for whatever sorry sleep the day's long list of embarrassments would see fit to allow him tonight.

But for some reason, he couldn't seem to bring his feet to turn right, back toward home. Back toward Iota Nu Nu, and Emily Atherton's, and the growing list of the day's failures. Back toward the booming party where Gwen might well currently be writhing beneath Todd, moaning that Greek God A-hole's name and wondering to herself how she could've thought, even for a second, that an IT Guy like Nate could ever compare. Not that she *had* wondered that, he reminded himself. Not anywhere but in Nate's own head.

He could always circumvent the INN house. Go a few blocks either way. But somehow, he was pretty sure that would only make it that much worse, knowing that even in the midst of his sweet, sweet victory, Todd was still all but lurking over Nate's shoulder, waiting to push him down the Fraser Street hill.

And screw that.

Almost by accident, he found himself turning left instead, drawn by the hoots and hollers of drunk Penn Staters having a good Friday night, inexorably wondering to himself what he might do—where he might go—if he weren't Nate Arturi, but someone else entirely. Anyone else. What would he do if he were one of these people? What would he do if he were the guy who kissed the girl on the deck—and to hell with the consequences?

For a second, he looked through the window of Pickles Taproom. Too crowded, he decided. Too visible. He walked a little further and descended the steps down to Zeno's Pub, not really sure what he was after, but half-entranced by whatever had gripped him. He showed his ID to the doorman and stepped into the cozy little underground pub, looking around at the healthy but not quite overwhelming Friday night crowd. Friends laughing, talking about their weeks. There was music too—the exact same standard pop fare that always seemed to be playing at every single bar and party in Happy Valley—but at least it wasn't aggressively loud.

This would do just fine. Except he still didn't know what it was he was doing. Never once since turning twenty-one had he just walked into a bar alone like this. But here he was, someone who could do exactly that, exactly as he pleased.

He turned and headed for the bar, refusing to stop now.

The bartender, a portly man with a silk vest and a matching flat cap, finished up with a pair of girls and turned to regard Nate with an indifferent air.

"Can I help you?"

Nate looked at the tap handles—Zeno's had a great roster of taps—then stopped himself. Because Nate Arturi *would* order another IPA, just like any other night. But someone else...

The image of Todd sprang to his mind's eye—Mighty King Todd in the middle of their pong match, downing a hearty swig straight from a bottle of... what had it been?

"Uh, can I get a whiskey?" Nate asked.

The bartender arched a brow at him. "Jack? Jim? Johnny?"

"Uh…"

"Top shelf or bottom, kid?"

Nate felt his face warming. "Is middle a thing?"

The bartender, either sensing Nate was overwhelmed at this point or simply growing tired of the conversation, turned around and grabbed a short, square glass and a bottle with a white label, a red mark, and black lettering he couldn't make out in the dim lighting.

"Can you make it a double?" Nate asked.

The bartender glanced dubiously up at Nate. "Can I see some ID?"

Damn. He was just knocking this cool person act right out of the park, wasn't he?

After the bartender had double-checked the ID, he shrugged and handed the card back to Nate.

"You know what?" Nate said, desperate to stop feeling like such an idiot. "Make it a triple."

So much for that effort.

The bartender finished his pour and turned, shaking his head at Nate as if to say he was sure Nate wouldn't recognize a double from a triple anyway. Which, in the bartender's defense, he totally wouldn't.

"I think a double's fine, kid," he said, sliding the glass to Nate. "That's ten dollars."

Nate reached for his wallet and fumbled the money out, wishing more than anything he'd just gone home. What was he honestly hoping to accomplish here?

"Thank you," he mumbled to the bartender, handing the money over.

The bartender looked him over one more time then gave up and shook his head again. "Have a good night, kid."

Nate turned and scanned the room for an empty seat, inwardly wringing his own neck. The guy tells him he can't even order himself a triple-whatever and what does Nate do? He says *thank you*. So much for transcending Mr. Nice Guy for the night.

He spotted a small open table and shuffled over, frowning down at his double-whatever and wondering if he even had the stomach to down the stuff at this point. If his phone hadn't been dead, he would've at least texted Marty—if for no other reason than to share a laugh about his sitting here in the dim corner of a pub he never would've come to alone, with a drink he never would've ordered.

But he *was* here, wasn't he?

That was something. Not much. Basically nothing, really. But something.

Trying not to wrinkle his nose, Nate took a sip of his rebellious drink, pretending he was someone who enjoyed whiskey—and was seized by a sputtering cough as dragon's fire trickled down his throat and seared into every square inch of his mouth and tongue.

Mother of Smaug, people did this for fun?

It wasn't like Nate had never taken a shot before. Basic proficiency at the skill was like an unspoken requirement for anyone courageous enough to brave a party in Happy Valley. He'd just never dared to let the dragon's fire actually sit in his mouth, and now he had confirmation that his gut instinct had been in place for good reason.

But some people *did* like whiskey, didn't they? It was probably just an acquired taste. Just like hoppy beer.

Still not really sure why he cared so much about making this happen, Nate glanced around, checking if the coast was clear for a second attempt. After the day he'd had, he half-expected to find half the bar pointing and laughing at his feeble attempt at whatever this was. In his mind's eye, he even imagined Todd across the pub, raising his own glass of amber liquid in mocking cheers, Gwen curled up in his lap.

But there was no Todd. And no one was watching Nate.

No one, that was, except for the ragged-looking man Nate hadn't noticed sitting at the next table over.

The first thought that popped into Nate's head was that the dude looked like homeless Gandalf. He had an enormous mane of long hair and a great bushy beard, both of which might've once been white or gray but had since grown too tangled and greasy to tell. His robe—and Nate was pretty sure *robe* was the right word here—seemed to have undergone similar abuse, having once maybe been a flowing garb of a subtle blue, but now looking more like a matted, dirt-caked assortment of hole-ridden grayish brown rags.

To say the guy was in rough shape would've been an understatement.

And he was staring straight at Nate. Staring without a shred of self-consciousness—not unlike one would stare at a painting in an art museum.

"Can I help you?" Nate asked.

Immediately, he regretted his choice of words. If this guy wanted money or something...

"I sincerely doubt it," the ragged wizard said. His voice was raspy, like it hadn't seen much use in a while. With bushy eyebrows and hard, dark eyes, he frowned down at the clay cup Nate hadn't noticed he was holding. "It's actually an ongoing point of debate with my companion, here."

He spoke with an odd accent Nate couldn't place. Maybe it was just because Nate was thinking about Gandalf now, but he couldn't help but think the guy kind of sounded like he'd walked straight out of Middle Earth and into Zeno's Pub.

More importantly, though, what did he mean, 'an ongoing point of debate with his companion here?' His companion *where?*

The guy was sitting alone, and quite frankly ragged enough that Nate was a little surprised Mr. Flat Cap behind the bar hadn't called over Mr. Doorman to check on their wizardly friend. True, the guy had a drink, which implied he was a paying customer, but on second glance, Nate didn't see another clay cup like his new friend's anywhere else in the pub.

Who the hell was this guy?

"Well, have a good night, then," Nate said, pointedly turning back to the privacy of his own drink and his own table.

He was probably being a dick. The guy was probably harmless. But he couldn't ignore the gut feeling that this was either a potentially unstable homeless man, or an eccentric local who liked to dress up on Friday night and put on a strange act for the drunk college kids, to who knew what ends.

Whatever this was, Nate was pretty sure he didn't want to be a part of it —was pretty sure, in fact, that he should probably just get up and walk out right then and there. Almost as soon as he thought it, though, he chided himself for being so paranoid and judgmental.

So what if the guy was a little dirty? He was still human, wasn't he? Nate was safe here in the pub. There was no reason he couldn't finish his drink in respectful silence and make his leave without offending anyone.

Except the guy was still staring at him.

Unwavering. Un-freaking-blinking.

It was creepy as hell, and Nate was fixing to throw all that moral high ground stuff out the window and to stand and beat a hasty retreat—feelings be damned—when the ragged wizard spoke again.

"It appears you've sprung a leak."

Nate tensed. "What?"

He wasn't sure what he was expecting, exactly—maybe for the man to break into manic cackles, or to come lunging at him with a shiv. Instead, the ragged wizard just pointed to Nate's hoodie, and Nate realized in a rush of embarrassment that the bag of rice had shifted in his pocket and that he'd already spilled a dozen or so grains on the floor.

"Oh," Nate said, carefully resealing the bag, doing his best not to spill any more. "Right. Thanks."

His ragged pal raised his clay cup in cheers. "The leaky pocket gets the rice."

"Yeah, I..." Nate looked up from his unfinished drink to the door and back to his leaky pocket. "I should go. Have a good night, uh, sir."

For some reason, he expected the strange man would try to keep him talking, but the ragged wizard only waved his clay cup in farewell. Nate headed for the door, feeling at once both disconcerted and also foolish for having allowed his jittery nerves at a harmless old man to affect him so deeply.

Whatever. He never should have come here at all. It was stupid, trying to pretend like he could ever be anything other than Nate "IT Guy" Arturi—like he could just walk into a bar and suddenly become something more. That just wasn't how things worked.

Nate glanced back, afraid he might find his new friend following him, but the ragged wizard was still huddled over his table, muttering something into his clay cup. Nate turned back for the door, eyeing the doorman beside it. Hesitating.

Had it all been in his head?

Probably. But better safe than sorry.

The doorman frowned a little as Nate approached him.

"Excuse me. I don't wanna sound like an alarmist or anything, but that guy with the beard back there was sort of giving me a weird vibe."

The doorman studied Nate for a second, then turned to survey the pub. "Which guy? Over there by the post, in the flannel?"

"No, the one in the robe. Right..."

Nate turned, trying to remind himself not to overtly point, and trailed off. Because there was nothing to point at.

The ragged wizard was gone.

CHAPTER 6

DOGGY STYLE

Nate might not have jumped at *every* flickering shadow on the walk home, but his racing heart sure as hell did. He did scan every nook and cranny of the buildings he passed, expecting any number of horrors to come leaping out at him.

Christ, he wished his phone wasn't dead. He'd considered asking to use one at Zeno's before remembering he didn't actually know anyone's number by memory. Wonders of the digital age. Had his phone not been resting in peace at the bottom of a rice-filled pocket, he might've even broken the bank and ordered a rideshare—never mind that he'd just foolishly spent ten dollars he barely had on a drink he'd barely wanted. Saving a few precious bucks probably wasn't worth more than his life.

But his phone was dead. And he was just being paranoid, besides. He had to be. There was no reason to believe otherwise. No reason to believe this was anything more than another half-drunk walk home down Allen Street.

And yet he couldn't stop wondering: where the shit had that blinkless-staring, Gandalf-looking creepy bastard vanished off to?

Probably to the bathroom, he thought for the hundredth time. Hell, for all he knew, the guy might've ducked under a table just to give Nate a nice strong case of the willies for the walk home. Nate had been too chicken to check for himself after the doorman had lost interest in the drunk college kid's made-up dangerous wizard man.

So Nate marched on, whispering to himself that he was being crazy, but also making a shameless point to stick to well-lit areas wherever possible. As much as he felt like he'd been through the wringer that night, it still wasn't all that late, and he was glad for the fleeting company of multiple packs of passing students as he went. One cute redhead even smiled at him as he passed her group outside the library.

On any other day, that smile might've made his night. That night, though, he just marched on, head on a swivel.

It probably said something about his state of mind that he barely even remembered he was coming up on the dreaded Iota Nu Nu house until he was practically beside it. Nothing like a little madman scare to set his priorities straight. For the briefest of seconds, though, he couldn't help but wonder what Gwen would have to say about the strange encounter.

He crunched that thought against the pavement, marching on, into the darker downhill stretch of Allen Street. There was no way he was going back in that house right now. Even if there *was* a strange old wizard man prowling after him in the shadows.

Which there wasn't, dammit.

He needed to stop watching so many creepy movies. But first, he just needed to get home and forget all about this night.

He crossed Prospect Ave and stomped onto the even darker sidewalk of Emily Atherton's block, wondering despite himself what Copernicus was up to right now—if he was peacefully asleep, dreaming doggy dreams, or if maybe he was alert and awake at his favorite front window lookout, awaiting the glitter and glam of his forgetful master's return.

Nate hoped it was the latter, if only so he could catch a glimpse of the little guy's infectious smile, and maybe share a bit of telepathic solidarity. He kind of wished, not for the first time, that he could simply snatch Copernicus up and abscond into the night. It wasn't like Emily was running a five star resort for the little guy.

Approaching Emily's plot on the dark sidewalk, Nate slowed. One of the upstairs lights was on. Emily's room, he was pretty sure. Maybe she actually was home, then. Nate looked down to the dark ground floor windows, hoping to spot Copernicus anyway, but no such luck.

Then a flicker of movement caught Nate's eye above, right at the peak of the angled porch rooftop. For a second, there was nothing, but Nate thought he saw a slightly denser shadow there in the darkness. A small one. Then the shadow moved, and the faintest little whine carried down to his ears, removing any doubt.

Copernicus was on the goddamn roof. Again.

"You've gotta be kidding me," Nate whispered, looking up and down the sidewalk.

It was dead this far down Allen Street, and far too dark for a casual passerby to spot Copernicus. Not that it mattered. Even in the daylight hours, it wasn't like anyone else ever stopped to get the corgi down. No one but Nate. But standing there in the considerable dark, still half-drunk and already having had two major falls that day, even he couldn't help but think this might finally be the time he should throw in the towel.

Still, he could at least go knock and let Emily know. Maybe they could call the volunteer fire department or something. Dammit, she really needed to get a ladder. Or learn to accept basic responsibility for another living thing. One or the other.

With a sigh and one last wary glance at the shadows, Nate stepped into the pitch black yard—and froze as movement from the single lit window above drew his eye.

Emily Atherton backed slowly into view, clearly topless, clearly wearing nothing but a little black thong. Nate stood frozen, instantly and embarrassingly aroused by the unexpected sight. Above, Emily padded on past the window, hips swaying seductively, her hand raised to someone else in the room, index finger curling with an unmistakable *come hither.*

Nate tore his gaze away, the guilt at accidentally witnessing Emily's private affair winning out over the torrent of other thoughts and feelings buzzing through his now fully wired body. For a second, he wasn't even sure he should ring the bell and spoil the moment for her and whatever lucky bastard was up there with her. At that thought, though, his eyes flicked back to the window of their own accord. Just in time to see a shirtless Todd Mackleroy stride past the window after Emily, his styled hair ruffled, and a hungry grin etched across his mouth.

"You've gotta be *fucking* kidding me."

Nate was walking into the pitch dark yard before he even knew it—definitely before he'd had a chance to come up with an actual plan. But it didn't matter.

He'd just had what might've been the worst day of his life. He'd fallen off of a roof, to the great amusement of his public audience. He'd literally crushed what little remained of his artistic aspirations. He'd abandoned his friends just to go embarrass himself again in front of the girl he was pretty sure he loved, only to watch her be hauled off by the ass cheeks and swept away on a one-woman flight to Todd's Pound Town.

And now that Greek God A-hole had the self-important nerve to come calling for round two with a different woman on the same goddamn night?

"Fuck this," Nate whispered, taking his first handhold in the increasingly familiar climb.

Right foot up. Hand over hand. Left foot joins. Right foot to the power meter. Stretch for the windowsill fingertips.

"Fuck your windmills," he growled, not really sure what he or Brad had meant by that, and not really giving a shit.

He just climbed on until he arrived at the sticking point—the oh-shit moment that had claimed his pride, his mini Promethean, and almost his spinal cord that morning.

He reached over the rain gutter, past the shingles to the edge of the roof. "And fuck you."

He lunged from his foothold, at the same time catching the lip of the roof and pulling. He strained, and scrambled... and pulled himself safely onto the rough shingle surface of the rooftop.

For a second, Nate felt a stir of victory in his chest.

Then a faint feminine moan broke the silence from inside, and Nate wasn't quite sure what he felt, other than angry—and maybe slightly confused in the nether regions as he turned and realized just how clearly he could see the scene through Emily's barred bedroom window up here.

The first thing he saw was Emily Atherton in all her naked glory, face down on a pillow, curvaceous hips raised high and ready. The second thing, to his horrid fascination, was the golden ass of Hercules himself, thrusting into her, his strong hands clamped down on her slender waist with an intensity that looked borderline violent.

For a few seconds, Nate couldn't look away. It was like staring into the goddamn sun. Then, with a light skitter of claws on shingles, Copernicus appeared beside his head and broke the spell. Tiny tongue a-lolling, the corgi stared through the barred window, then to Nate, then back to the window.

"I know, boy," Nate muttered. "That's... that's just not right."

Copernicus cocked his head, as if to ask why Nate was staring so hard then, or maybe what he was going to do about it. Both of which were damn good questions. Because much as he didn't want to be seeing this shit in the first place, he *had* seen it. And he was pretty damn sure there was no unseeing it. The only question was what he was going to do next.

Probably, he should start by getting off of the freaking rooftop. For a brief instant, wild ideas of breaking up their fun and setting Todd straight for this bullshit flashed through Nate's head, but they were just as quickly followed by vivid imaginings of Todd ripping those iron bars off the window and busting out here to hurl Nate headfirst down to his death to keep Gwen from ever finding out. Or just for fun, take your pick.

Yep. Step one, get the F out of here. Because as deeply pissed as Nate was at Todd's boundless audacity, the one thing he knew for sure was that he needed to live long enough to make sure Gwen knew about this. Plus, the sight and sound of Emily Atherton getting pounded halfway through the headboard somehow made it kind of hard to picture him tapping on the window and putting Todd in his place.

"Come on, boy. We're gonna get you down and then—"

Why Copernicus chose that moment to bark, Nate couldn't have said. But the corgi did. And he did it loudly.

"—fuck was that?" came Todd's unmistakable voice from inside.

"It's nothing," Emily groaned, turning her head enough to talk and pushing herself against him more insistently. "Don't stop, babe. He'll be fine. Just—god, don't stop."

Nate lay perfectly still, his hand clamped over Copernicus' muzzle, and watched as Todd took a few half-hearted thrusts, still peering suspiciously at the window, practically staring straight at them. If the lunk hadn't been in a lit room staring out into the darkness, he would've seen Nate and Copernicus in a heartbeat. But he didn't.

Did he?

Nate stayed frozen, feeling some of that anger trickling back in. Anger that he should be made to feel afraid in this moment, having caught King Squanto himself red-handed in the act. That any one man, even one so divinely gifted as Todd, could actually have the audacity to be so bored with the attention of not one, but two beautiful women in a single night that something so benign as a dog bark could actually pull him away from Emily Atherton's gyrating pleas.

Why couldn't the chiseled prick just be happy?

Why couldn't he just turn around and forget about it?

For a second, Todd visibly thought about doing just that. Then he pulled out of Emily and bent to pluck something from the floor, just out of sight.

"Todd, what the fuck?" came Emily's muffled voice. "I was almost there. What're you—"

But whatever else she said was lost to Nate's numb brain as Todd appeared right in the window, glaring straight at them like a vengeful bronze god. For a second, Nate was too startled to move. Then Todd snarled and jabbed a finger at the window in a clear sign for, *I'm gonna kill you, IT Guy,* and Nate damn near rolled off the rooftop in his haste to flee.

"Come on, boy!" he hissed, gathering up Copernicus, who was now growling and barking at Todd in earnest. He scooted them back to the edge and realized with a curse that Emily wasn't here to do the chair-on-the-deck handoff they'd antagonistically perfected over the last few rounds of their begrudging alliance.

He eyed the descent into darkness. The drop was close to fifteen feet, he knew, but at the crash of a slamming door and the sound of Emily's startled, "Where are you going?" from back in the house, Nate decided a second fall was the least of the two evils.

"We're gonna roll, boy," Nate whispered. "You understand?"

By way of reply, Copernicus squirmed in his arms, legs kicking like he was trying to run in place.

"Good enough, then," Nate said.

And with a silent prayer to the gods of parkour, he jumped.

Cool, rushing air, and darkness swallowing him whole. He had all of a split millisecond to remember to keep his feet together like he'd seen in a video somewhere, then that rushing darkness kicked back. Hard.

Nate let it take him, knees buckling, pitching forward, thinking rolling thoughts, and straining above all else not to land right on top of Copernicus. The world spun, utterly dark. Something slammed into his shoulder. He thudded to his back and coughed out the better half of his breath.

And that was that.

Nate lay in the darkness for a few shocked breaths, trying to wrap his head around the fact that he actually felt fine, albeit a little jostled, and that Copernicus was happily panting away in his arms. Then a door ripped open and slammed back shut somewhere behind, and someone came thudding across the porch.

Todd.

Cursing himself for having wasted precious seconds, Nate set a barking Copernicus down and rolled over, scrambling for his feet. He planted his hands in the grass, getting his legs under him, and—

Impact ripped through his head, and the world exploded in a shower of pain and bright lights. Nate lay there, vaguely aware that he'd somehow ended up on his back, his vision swimming with a kaleidoscope of effervescent stars and iridescent blurs that he could only assume were the dying cries of concussed brain cells. In the darkness, Copernicus was growling.

"Arturi!" someone hissed.

Todd?

"What the fuck are you doing here, you little freak?"

For a second, Nate was so surprised to realize that, one, Todd Mackleroy actually knew his last name and that, two, the Greek God A-hole had just kicked him straight in the freaking head, that he almost forgot to be afraid. Then the shadows moved, something yanked him up by the chest, and the world lit up in a second eruption of bright pain.

"I asked you a question, fuck-face. What're you, some kinda perv? Or you just think it's funny, fucking with another bro's game?"

Game? Nate's twice-thumped brain tried to process. What the hell was he...

"You..." Nate groaned. Why was it so hard to form words right now? "You call this... a game?"

For some reason Nate couldn't wrap his spinning head around, Todd chuckled at that.

"Fucking virgins," he muttered.

Something constricted on Nate's chest. Todd's fist, he registered, yanking him up by the shirt again. Nate flinched, expecting another blow, but none came. Instead, Todd just patted his cheek in the darkness, leaning down close enough that Nate could just make out the dark shape of his face.

"Let me put this in terms you can understand, choir boy. You never saw shit. And if you ever say otherwise—if I get even the faintest hint that my Gwenny Bear thinks I'm getting it on the side, I'll fucking kill you, Arturi. I'll bake you into a fucking pie, and I'll feed you to Bonzer like the hundred pounds of IT Pussy you are. You understand me?"

Nate glared at Todd's silhouette, wanting to tell him to go fuck himself. Wanting to spit in his perfect face. For a second, he pictured himself striking up with his right foot, catching Todd with a swift kick right to his damn cheating nuts.

Then a thud of impact and a blinding stab of pain in his ribs brought him crashing straight back down to reality violently fast. Nate curled up in a ball, all but sure the next kick was coming in the darkness. Then something furry and growling flew past him, and Todd staggered away with a string of inarticulate curses.

If Nate hadn't felt Copernicus' tiny bulk pressed up against his back, he might've thought a feral wolf had come to his defense by the ferocity of the little guy's growling.

"Hey look," Todd said, "the dick-sized dog has more balls than you."

Copernicus barked, and Nate shuddered in relief as he heard footsteps climbing back onto the porch. He didn't look, but he heard Todd pause at the top of the steps.

"Go home, Arturi. Go home and leave my girl the fuck alone."

Then he opened the door and went back into Emily's.

Nate lay there in the dirt, cold and trembling and in more pain that he could remember having ever been in. He'd never been in a fight before. Never even broken a bone. Never even... Never even—

He shuddered again, tears welling in his eyes, and wrapped his arms tighter around his knees. He shook with a rising sob, trying to hold it in, refusing to give Todd the satisfaction, even if the bastard wasn't here to see it. But he couldn't hold it back. Before he knew it, Nate was lying in Emily Atherton's pitch black yard, gasping with quiet sobs, every emotion he'd felt that day and half a dozen more all spilling out of him like so much water from a broken dam.

With each gasping breath, he told himself to get up and walk away, but he couldn't. Couldn't do anything but lay there, crying. He never wanted to move again. And Gwen. God, Gwen. Nate didn't know what to do, what to think. Only that he felt nauseous thinking about what that well-manicured ape was doing behind her back.

Something padded past him in the dark. Then he felt Copernicus' warm breath panting on his cheek. The corgi licked him once, then gently nudged Nate with the top of his head, as if to say, *Time to move.*

"Okay, boy," he whispered. "You're right."

And yet he still couldn't seem to move until the corgi nudged him again.

He rolled to his stomach, careful to avoid the side Todd had rib-kicked like a freaking movie gangster. Slowly, carefully, he rose to his feet, clutching at his ribs with one hand and his head with the other. He shuffled across the yard like a blind man and paused at the edge of the thick shadows, glancing back at the single lit window above, wondering if even The Untouchable Todd would be answering to his mistress now for his undeniably odd behavior in storming out of the apartment.

If the faint and rapid thumping he heard on the still night air was any indication, it seemed not.

Nate stared at the window, feeling like he should be angry, like he should be utterly sickened. But all he felt in that moment was numb. Totally and completely numb to everything but the pulsing fire in his ribs and in his head.

He opened his mouth, thinking to whisper one last curse on Todd's name, then stopped and instead started off down the sidewalk, deciding he might as well hold on to what little scrap of dignity he could, knowing he hadn't wasted his breath.

Realizing Copernicus was following him, he paused, staring down at the corgi. Copernicus stared right back, his stump of a tail moving back and forth not excitedly but in a steady, almost somber rhythm.

Nate didn't try to decode what it meant, or what he should do about Emily Atherton's complete and utter lack of responsibility as a pet owner. He just shrugged and walked on, not minding one bit when the corgi fell into companionable pace beside him, tiny claws clacking away on the pavement in the cold, still night.

Across Allen Street, in the deep shadows of the foliage between Emily Atherton's neighboring houses, the ragged old man gave a mirthless chuckle.

"This one?" he asked, looking at the empty darkness beside him. "Truly? You're certain you don't mean the one inside? At least we know *he's* not afraid to get his sword dirty, as it were."

He started to lift his clay cup to his lips and then paused, as if listening.

"Nine hells," he finally muttered. "You truly are insufferable."

He thought for another handful of seconds, then shrugged and drained the last contents of his clay cup. That done, he slipped the trusty receptacle into one of his dirty robe's endless pockets and began rifling around, searching this hidey hole and that until, with a satisfied sound, he finally produced a small, intricately gilded sphere, not much larger than a ping-pong ball.

"Very well, M'lady," he said, holding the sphere at arm's length and squinting so that the device blotted the retreating forms of Arturi and his furry friend from sight.

"There's just one more thing I'd like to see first."

CHAPTER 7

A WALK IN THE PARK

"That's a good boy," Nate said to Copernicus' dark outline as the little corgi concluded his post-pee dirt scuffing ritual.

If he hadn't known better, he almost could've sworn Copernicus actually cocked an eyebrow up at him in the dim light, as if questioning who Nate thought he was to be deciding who was and wasn't a good boy right now. Maybe the corgi had a point. Or maybe Nate was just being hard on himself. But that seemed fair enough, seeing as the rest of the goddamn universe had apparently sworn a solemn oath to do exactly the same.

How he'd thought the night couldn't get any worse, he wasn't quite sure. All he knew in his aching heart—and severely *more* aching face and ribs—was that he needed to get home before the Fates could reach down and strike him dead in this field, just for giggles.

"Come on, Copernicus," Nate said, turning back toward the distant trickle of Atherton Street traffic, feeling at once safe in the enveloping dark expanse of the community field, and also lonely as all hell.

It helped when the corgi fell in happy step beside him, no leash required. There was one small light from this endless turd sandwich of a day, at least: a spineless IT punching bag Nate might be, but at least he was already a better pet owner than Emily Atherton, who probably wouldn't even notice her furry little dependent was gone until the morning, when she realized...

Nate paused, his gut tightening with an odd swirl of dread and exhilaration.

… Until the morning, when she realized Copernicus had been dognapped. Because that's what this was, wasn't it? He looked down at the corgi, who was looking cheerfully up at him, awaiting his lead.

Had he just stolen a freaking dog?

Maybe he *was* concussed. Or maybe he'd just been too emotionally shocked after getting stomped into the dirt to remember it wasn't exactly lawful to walk off with someone's pet. Either way, could he really be blamed after he'd taken multiple falls and had his bell thoroughly rung by a roid raging frat god all in one day?

It wasn't like he'd snatched Copernicus and run for it. He'd simply walked to the park, and the corgi had followed. It wasn't his fault Emily had failed for the thousandth time to keep him inside, or at least get him a new collar to keep him reliably tethered out in the yard.

"Go home, boy," Nate said anyway. "You should go home."

Copernicus just stopped wagging his tail and sat down in the grass, as if staking his claim. Nate turned and stared in the general direction of Emily's, absentmindedly watching the cars flit by back on the road, realizing more and more with each one that maybe he wouldn't make such a great pet owner after all. Because he hadn't thought any of this through.

He didn't have dog food. Or a leash. Or poop bags. Or gods knew what else he'd need to keep his furry friend occupied. And he sure as shit didn't have spare cash to run out and grab all these things. And even if he did, this was crazy, wasn't it? He couldn't just pluck Copernicus off the street like a wartime refugee, could he?

Maybe not. But he also wasn't about to go back to Emily's right now. Screw that, to the power of infinity. For now, the corgi was free to do as he pleased.

"Up to you, little guy," he said, turning right toward the distant lights of the Hamilton shopping center and their house just another block beyond. "I'm not stealing you," he added, knowing it didn't absolve him of responsibility, explaining the situation to a dog—even one as clever as Copernicus— but well beyond caring. "But you're welcome to crash at my place tonight."

The rest, Nate decided, he could figure out tomorrow.

Except Copernicus wasn't following him when he glanced back. The corgi had barely seemed to hear him at all, in fact. He was too busy staring off into the darkness. Tensed, Nate realized. Hackles raised.

Nate's heart picked up. Between having had his head kicked in and accidental dog-theft, he'd all but forgotten about the ragged robed man, and his own tight-chested fear of the shadows on the walk home earlier. Now, though, as Copernicus broke into a soft growl, that fear came crashing back with sweaty-palmed interest.

"Copernicus," Nate hissed. "What is it, boy?"

The corgi half-turned to give him a short yip, then rounded back on the darkness, tensing up, head cocked like he'd heard something. Nate strained his senses. Heard nothing. Smelled the chill of the October night. Then…

Something humming. Something in the darkness beyond Copernicus, humming like the freaking Death Star preparing to fire. Nate stared, frozen, part of him wondering what the hell could be making that sound, the rest of him screaming to grab Copernicus and just run for it. He bent down, reaching for the dog, then froze again at a sound like a tiny crack of thunder.

Somewhere ahead—not far by the sound of it—something heavy thudded to the ground. Copernicus barked.

A low, rumbling growl replied from the darkness.

There was something wrong with that sound. Nate couldn't process what—too deep, too monstrous—but he had Copernicus scooped up and was backing away even before he heard the thing shift, and felt the first few thunderous footsteps impact the ground.

It was huge. That was all Nate's shocked brain could process as one massive shadow detached itself from the rest. Impossibly huge.

And it was moving straight toward them. Fast.

Nate found his legs turning and running for dear life before he'd even thought to give the order. He ran faster than he'd ever run, too afraid to think, too afraid to even cry for help, Copernicus bouncing in his arms, barking over his shoulder at whatever the hell was stomping after them, shaking the earth beneath his feet like a goddamn earthquake.

He ran, infinitely aware that each thundering step was closing on him. That he was about to die. That—

With a mighty kick, Copernicus sprang free from Nate's arms and flew off to the right.

"No!" Nate cried, veering after the dog, reaching desperately to catch him. Too late. Copernicus hit the ground running—just as something enormous smacked down right where Copernicus and Nate had been running. Nate whirled around and damn near fell over at the monstrosity towering over him.

It didn't compute. Couldn't be real.

The thing was at least eight feet tall, and it looked like a mad scientist's failed attempt to cross breed a rhinoceros and a tree. It looked like a freaking ogre. And it was stalking toward Nate, clearly looking down at him, even if it was too dark to see the thing's eyes.

"Gar'jougo," it rumbled in a voice that left Nate frozen, insides shriveling and outsides shuddering at the sheer size and power of the thing. Then the creature growled and reached one massive ogre hand for him, and the panic took over.

He leapt backward, half falling over, then scrambled into a turn and nearly ran straight into the waist-high wire fence that lined the side of the park's baseball field. He saw the shadowy lines in the dark just in time to clumsily vault over. He hit the ground off balance, scraped knees and palms on the dirt, and kept running, not giving one fractional shit about the burning pains in his hands, knees, and ribs.

Behind him, he heard the thing break into a lumbering run. It tore through the fence like a runner's finish line and thundered after him across the field. Nate ran for everything he was worth. But it wasn't enough. He could feel the thing closing on him. Nowhere to go. Something hit his back, and the next thing he knew he was smashing face first into the baseball field dirt. He gasped for breath and got half a lungful of the gritty stuff instead.

"Gar'jougo deh jrak ith net," the thing growled right above his head, as he reached forward to keep crawling. For a second, Nate couldn't move for the terror, couldn't think anything but that this was the end. Then the creature growled something else and prodded at Nate's back with one huge finger.

Choking on dust and fear, Nate rolled over and raised his hands in surrender. "I don't... I don't understand."

"Jougo," it replied, a massive mountain of head and shoulders hovering over him, clearly expecting something more. They were close enough to the lights now that he could just make out the glint of its beady eyes staring down at him. "Jougo!"

Nate flinched as the thing raised its huge fist, but then it straightened, looking around confusedly. That's when Nate noticed the growling, and realized Copernicus had reappeared to sink his little corgi teeth into the thing's gargantuan ankle.

The beast let loose with a burst of guttural language, shaking its leg to kick the laughably small dog away. But Copernicus was faster. The corgi danced back, darting left and right, barking all the way. The bipedal tree of a rhino turned to stomp after Nate's furry little rescuer, and Nate scrambled to hands and knees, looking desperately around for something—anything—to stop the beast and save Copernicus.

He looked to home base, hoping against hope for a baseball bat or something, but there was nothing. Christ, even if he'd had a freaking machine gun, he wasn't sure it would've done more than irritate the hulking monster. But for some reason, when his hand slipped into his pocket and closed around the bag of rice therein, he didn't dwell on the fact. Not with the lumbering giant stomping after Copernicus, doing his hulking damnedest to stomp the corgi dead.

He just plucked the bag from his pocket and threw.

Nate was no athlete. He was no Todd. But damn if that bag of rice didn't hit the monstrous rhino tree dead in the back of its fat head. Nate had a fraction of a second to feel victorious. Another to remember his phone had been in that bag. One last instant to register he'd just made a huge mistake. Then the creature rounded on him with a chest-shaking growl, and he realized his plan hadn't included a Step Two.

The giant lunged forward, raising one mighty fist on high, clearly done with talking, clearly ready to make with the smashing. Nate fell straight on his ass, petrified by the raw ferocity.

This was it. Nothing to be done. He was already dead.

And somehow, the only thing that flicked through his head as his brutish end came stomping home was what a shitty injustice it was that there'd be no one left to tell Gwen what an asshole her boyfriend was after Nate was gone and pasted into the dirt as a fine meat jelly.

What a crock of shit this whole damn universe was, he thought.

Then there was a flash of azure light, and the ogre jerked in mid-step, teetering like its strings had been cut. Teetering, and tipping. Straight toward him.

In a blind panic, Nate clawed his way backward, distantly aware that someone was screaming, even more distantly aware that it was him. The giant crashed to the dirt at his feet, its raised fist smacking down just shy of his left leg. Nate coughed through a lungful of dust, choking on the sharp burn of ozone in the air and feebly scrambling further back, not trusting for one second that it was actually over. Copernicus came padding around the giant's body, pausing to sniff delicately at the thing's lumpy, noseless face before turning to Nate, visibly trembling.

Then there was a sharp crack out in the darkness of the park, and Nate was running with Copernicus in his arms almost before he knew it, clutching the trembling dog tight, running for the lights as fast as he could. Not looking back. Running for his goddamn life.

Straight into traffic.

Lights flashed. A horn blared its indignant call, tires screeching. Nate felt his center of balance going and kept pumping his legs anyway. No time. No time to do anything else.

He hit the sidewalk alive, straight on his bad rib side, and heard himself cry out as if it were another person. He scrambled back to his feet, the world a confusing blur around him, and kept moving. He didn't look back. Couldn't look back. He kept running, ignoring his body's screaming protests—ignoring the whirlwind of impossible thoughts, and the tiny voice that said he should go back, warn that driver, make sure no one wandered into that park.

He kept running until the house came into view.

Then he kept running some more.

CHAPTER 8

ONLY IN DREAMS

Nate stumbled into the house, heaving for breath, body burning with a thousand different hurts, screaming mind not giving one single damn about any of them. He was too busy pushing the door shut behind him, collapsing against its feeble wooden promise of safety, and trying to piece together any part of what in all of the unholy hells had just happened. Copernicus, still trembling in his arms, seemed to be in a similar state after his diversionary heroics back in the park.

It was only after several seconds of hyperventilating and questioning reality in general that Nate realized that one of the TVs was on, and that he wasn't alone.

Kyle and Zach had fallen asleep on the couch watching Firefly on the top left quadrant of the Mother Gaming Shrine, Zach's sleeping head having drifted down onto Kyle's sleeping shoulder. On any other night, Nate might've snapped a picture, or at least cracked a heartfelt smile. But tonight he couldn't. Because he'd just thrown his phone at a motherfucking giant ogre in the park.

Somehow, Kyle and Zach's napping arrangement didn't seem all that important in light of that little fact.

"Someone ever tries to kill you," Mal Reynolds was saying on the TV, "you try to kill 'em right back!"

Easy for him *to say.*

Copernicus was squirming in Nate's arms now, like he wanted to go check the coast over at the wide paneled windows. Which, Nate decided, wasn't such a bad idea. Until Kyle stirred, muttering something in his sleep, and Nate felt a surge of defensive panic at the thought of having to explain himself right then.

Because what the hell could he say that wouldn't sound twelve different kinds of bat shit crazy? Not much. Not even to Conspiracy Theory Kyle, who'd been ranting for three weeks now about how the aliens were…

Nate's eyes widened.

No way. It was ridiculous. That thing couldn't have been an alien. Of course, it *also* clearly couldn't have even been real to begin with, so maybe the *couldn'ts* and *shouldn'ts* were out the window. Or maybe Balls Brad had tagged him with a patch of LSD back at Iota Nu Nu. Or maybe he'd just hit his head—or had it kicked—far harder than he'd realized and was tripping balls the old fashioned way.

Nate gathered Copernicus tighter and crept across the faux wood floor, sure of nothing but the fact that he couldn't explain himself right now. Or maybe ever. Jesus.

Somehow, the sneaking only made his abused heart pound that much harder. What if that thing had friends?

It couldn't have been real.

What if they followed him here?

Stop it.

By the time Nate had padded down the short hallway to his bedroom door, he was hyperventilating again. He grabbed the doorknob with a shaking hand, desperate for the safety—or, at least the *privacy*—of his room, then flinched when Marty's door creaked open, flooding the dim hallway with the soft blue glow of LEDs.

"Nate?" his roommate's silhouette quietly asked, reaching for his main light switch. "Dude, where have you—"

"Not now," Nate hissed. It came out sounding harsh, but he slipped into his room and closed the door before Marty could say anything. Time enough for apologies later, assuming he was still alive.

With that cheerful thought in mind, Nate skipped the light switch and went straight to the windows to look out front.

Not a soul in sight. Nothing but dead, dark street. And certainly no rampaging rhino trees.

Closing his eyes and depositing Copernicus on his bed, Nate let out a long breath… Then tensed as the door opened behind him, and the room lights flicked on.

Marty was watching him from the doorway, his hand still on the switch.

"Nate, oh my god, your face. What happened? What—Is that Copernicus? What the—"

His friend sputtered on like that for a few seconds, then fell silent as Nate crossed the room. Nate yanked his roommate into the room with an authority that neither of them expected, then closed the door behind them and stepped over to have a look in the slender wall mirror beside his closet.

Marty had a point. Nate's face was a dirty, bloody mess, and the rest of him wasn't in much better shape. His unruly black hair was soaked with sweat and caked with dirt from the baseball field, his clothes were sullied with much of the same, and he barely recognized his own eyes. They were too wild, practically screaming out loud with the violent fight or flight reflex still racing through his every nerve to the tune of *oh-shit-oh-shit-oh-shit-oh-shit.*

"Nate..." Marty was frightened. "Nate, what the hell happened? Where were you? Why are you *bleeding?*"

For some reason, Nate looked to Copernicus for guidance, but the corgi was too busy on guard duty, stretching up to his full length on his hind legs to peer out the window. Marty watched them both, his expression growing more confused and concerned by the second.

Nate waved him to sit, trying to gather his thoughts—or at least stop breathing so damn hard. He went and looked out the window again instead.

"Nate," Marty said, not sitting, only nervously gripping the back of Nate's computer chair. "Please, tell me what's..."

He trailed off as Nate held up a hand for silence. "I will. I'm just... not exactly sure where to start."

"How about with why you're bleeding, and why Emily Atherton's dog is in your room?"

"Goddamn Todd," Nate muttered, crossing over and flicking the lights back off.

"Todd?" Marty asked as Nate went to rejoin Copernicus at the window. "What does Todd have to do with this? And why are you two are acting like you have the Yakuza after you? What's with the lights? Should we be calling the cops?"

Cops.

For a second, cops sounded like a damn good idea. Then Nate remembered just how big and brutally strong that beast had been, and he couldn't help but give a nervous huff of laughter at the thought of what it could've done to a police cruiser. But it was dead, wasn't it?

Sure. Maybe. Dead because of whatever had caused that flash of light. Whatever had been crackling after them as they'd fled the park.

"Nate…"

He let out his pent up breath in an explosive huff. "Okay, okay. Jesus. I—we got chased. Chased by… by something."

"Something?"

"A big something. Over in the park, past the square. I don't really know how to describe this without sounding like a crazy person."

He felt Marty work through several starts and stops, obviously struggling to find the best tact here, probably still thinking rational thoughts.

"Okay," he finally said. "Okay. So what happened? The thing chased you out of the park?"

"Sort of. I mean, it *was* chasing us, but… I think something killed it."

"*Another* something?"

"Yeah."

"Okay." Marty bobbed his head in the dim light, clearly trying to be calm and collected. "Okay. That's a lot of somethings."

"Dude"—Nate turned from the window long enough to shoot him a look —"if you knew the night I just had…"

"Yeah, I uh, kinda gathered as much after…"

Nate frowned at something in his friend's voice—something outside of the obvious *my best friend just stumbled home bloodied and carrying a dog that isn't his.*

"After *what?*"

"Oh, well…" Marty shook his head, starting to look like he had a hint of the secondhand shock creeping in now. "I mean, it seems kind of unimportant now, with all this… whatever this is. But Gwen stopped by looking for you."

"What?"

"Yeah, we were all pretty surprised too. And worried." He glanced out the window. "You just missed her by like ten minutes." There was just enough ambient light to make out his frown as he turned back to Nate. "Why weren't you answering your phone, by the way?"

"I, uh…" *Threw it at a goddamn alien ogre's head along with a bag of rice.* "…lost it. Long story."

"Right. Okay."

"What did Gwen want?"

"She didn't really say, but…" Marty's frown deepened. "I dunno, dude, is this really important right now? I don't understand what happened out there, and you're kinda freaking me—"

"Please, Marty, I just…" He squeezed his eyes shut, searching for a handhold in his own mind. "I just need a single normal thought in my head right now, okay?"

"Okay. Okay, man. She just… said something had happened at the party and that she wanted to talk to you about it, make sure you were okay, that kind of thing. When we asked, she just said it was no big deal. She did stay and have a beer with us, though. I tried to call you a few times, but yeah. She just watched us play a round and then we all watched a little Firefly, shooting the breeze like old times. It was actually kinda nice. Even Kyle admitted it. Then she said she should get going, and that she'd text you."

Nate thought about his almost certainly dead phone, lying in a heap of rice in the cold dirt. Next to a freaking dead ogre, no less.

"Great. That's just… great."

Some squirrelly part of him couldn't help but wonder what it was she'd wanted to say to him—not to mention if Todd had in fact buggered over to Emily Atherton's tonight *because* Gwen had walked out on him. The rest of his mind was busy wondering how the hell he could even be *thinking* about his college drama mere minutes after having nearly been stomped to meat paste by a giant… whatever the hell that thing had been. And that part probably had a damned fine point.

"I don't know what to do, Marty."

Marty considered that for a stretch. "About Gwen? Or about the rest of it."

"All of the above," Nate said, scratching Copernicus behind the ears. The corgi started to wag his tail, leaning into the affection, then shook himself off and shot Nate a look that said, *Come on, man, we've got serious stuff to worry about here!*

"Why don't you just tell me what happened from the beginning," Marty said. "Unless you'd rather get cleaned up first?"

Nate opened his mouth to point out that his personal cleanliness was the last thing on his mind right now. As soon as the thought entered his mind, though, he couldn't ignore how battered and grimy he felt—dried blood on his face, caked dirt there and pretty much everywhere else. Maybe a hot shower wouldn't be the worst idea in the world. Just to settle his nerves.

He glanced out at the silent street once more for confirmation that they were indeed not about to be besieged by another monster, then he nodded.

"Yeah, good call. I'll just be a minute."

Once Nate was actually under the glorious jets of hot water, though, feeling the grime and muck sluicing from his body, he decided to take two, just to enjoy the simple pleasure. It took a few more minutes to actually get himself clean—partly out of the necessity of cleaning tenderly around his scrapes and bruises, and partly because the orangish brown dirt from the baseball field seemed to have found its way into every nook and cranny he possessed.

It was kind of amazing how much more normal everything felt once he'd finished toweling off and slid into a fresh pair of sweats. Almost like all that wild shit in the park had just been a product of three or four too many head traumas, and some suspect Iota Nu Nu jungle juice.

Hearing Kyle and Zach moving around out in the kitchen, Nate padded quickly back into his room, dreading the thought of bringing anyone else into this already loopy conversation. Marty was waiting there in the light of Nate's desk lamp with a glass of water and a few ibuprofen tablets. On the floor beside Nate's bed, Copernicus was happily lapping up his own water from a bowl, having already apparently licked clean a small plate of something.

"I had a few boneless wings left over," Marty explained, following Nate's gaze. "Just took a wild guess you didn't have time to snatch dog food out on your adventures. You hungry?"

Nate glanced uncertainly in the direction of the kitchen, where Kyle and Zach were laughing about something or another. "Think I'm fine."

"I told them you had too much to drink and didn't feel like talking," Marty said, apparently reading his mind. "Here."

Nate took the water and the pills and sat down on the edge of his bed, feeling overwhelmed.

"Marty… Thank you."

Marty shrugged. "Just trying to be a good friend."

Nate arched an eyebrow. "*Good?* Dude, you didn't bat an eye when I showed up with a stolen dog spouting off about how we'd just been chased by, and I quote, 'something big,' in the park. I'd call that better than good."

He shrugged again, smiling. "Guess I'm just dumb enough to trust that poor mug of yours. Though I wouldn't mind hearing the whole story now, if you're up for it."

"Yeah…" Nate said, nodding slowly.

Marty sat down at his desk chair, waiting patiently until Nate gathered his thoughts, leaned forward, and started to tell his friend everything he dared of the Level 5 Shit Storm that had gone down that night.

~

SLEEP DIDN'T COME EASILY that night, and when it finally did, it was fraught with cold sweat nightmares of roaring monsters, and alternating snippets of Todd Mackleroy beating him senseless and taking Gwen and Emily both to Todd's Pound Town, just for Nate's stomach-churning delight.

The creepiest by far, though, were the feverish deliriums of cackling wizards watching Nate from the shadows. Once, he thought he'd actually awoken and pulled the blinds to find the ragged wizard from Zeno's staring straight at him through his bedroom window, bushy brows furrowed with sinister intent. It was only when he'd remembered that his window was at least fifteen feet straight up from the driveway below, and that the strange old man would've had to have been hovering there in midair, watching him sleep, that Nate actually woke up from that one.

Bad as the ogre nightmares had been, Nate was pretty sure that last part was the mental image that was going to haunt him for good.

When he finally woke properly, bright sunshine was flitting through the blinds and radiating off the old cream colored walls, and the events of the previous night felt as if they must've simply been a few more in the long line of odd nightmares—nothing more than the confused byproducts of some magically bad combo of beer, pizza, spiked jungle juice, and maybe a few concussions.

The fluffy corgi that yawned, stretched, and padded up from the corner of his bed to come say good morning, though, reminded Nate that at least some of it had really happened. Which in turn reminded him that he needed to go find his phone. Or get a new one. And maybe find Gwen, too. And probably swear Marty to some kind of secrecy after everything he'd told him last night—which, while admittedly lacking in any details about strange vanishing wizards or ogre space invaders, had still been more than a little packed with the crazy sauce.

Lastly, he realized with a heavy heart, scratching Copernicus behind the ears, he needed to decide what to do with his stolen goods.

"Did that really happen, boy?" he asked quietly, dreading every part of the thought of taking the corgi back to Emily's.

Copernicus yipped what might have been an affirmative. Nate was too distracted by Zach's voice out in the kitchen to tell.

"Was that a dog?"

Nate made a shushing gesture at Copernicus, as if the corgi might actually understand, then rolled his eyes at the futility of it when Kyle's foot-steps came thudding down the hallway.

"Who has a dog?!"

"I swear I just heard a dog bark in his room," Zach said.

"Naaate?" Kyle called.

"Don't—" Nate started, just before the door flew open.

And there was Kyle, hands spread wide. "Nate, m'boy! How goes it? Strange tidings of…" He trailed off, frowning at Copernicus. "Huh. That *is* a dog."

Zach poked his head around the corner. "That's Emily Atherton's dog."

Kyle's ears perked at that, and he glanced around the room as if half-expecting he might spot Emily herself hiding behind the dresser or under the desk.

"What the hell'd you get into last night, man?" he asked when his search proved inconclusive. His eyes widened as they settled back on Nate, like he was just properly seeing him for the first time. "What in seven hells happened to your face?"

Nate could only stare, his head whirling at once with everything and nothing, attempting to sift out some kind of workable answer. "Uhhh…"

"Hey, good, you're awake," came Marty's voice from the hallway, a second before he poked his head in beside Zach's and gave Nate a knowing look that shifted to surprise at something on Nate's face, then quickly back to controlled composure. "Can I show you something outside real quick?"

That settled it. Marty really was the best.

"Uh, yeah," Nate said, sitting up and crawling out of bed. "Yeah, can you guys just let me get changed real quick?"

Marty gave a thumbs up and vanished like a good guardian angel. Zach and Kyle stood there looking uncertainly between him and Copernicus for another few seconds.

"Did you get in a fight?" Zach asked.

"Uh…" Nate touched the dully aching side of his face and winced. It must've been a hell of a bruise. "No, I just kinda bit it at the party. Again. Long story."

"Guys," Marty chided from down the hall when neither of them looked particularly satisfied by the answer. They traded a look, then Kyle waved his hands in an *excuse us* fashion, and they shuffled off down the hallway.

Nate padded over—a surprisingly painful endeavor after last's escapades —and closed the door on their muttered questions to Marty. He let out a deep breath and turned back to Copernicus. "We're gonna have to work on your timing with the barks, boy."

The corgi made a small whining noise, and tipped his snout upward in what Nate could've sworn was a defiant gesture. Nate just shook his head and went to grab some fresh jeans and socks. He paused when he saw the black-and-blue hammered-meat-slab reflection that was his face in the mirror.

"Great," he murmured, reflecting that, at the very least, he could be sure someone had indeed pounded his face in last night. Not that that bit really mattered right then.

"Come on, boy," he said, pulling on the pair of sneakers he'd been too rattled to remember to leave at the front door last night. "Get your shoes. Time to go for a walk."

Copernicus, who Nate was sincerely beginning to suspect might in fact be fluent in human speak, gave an excited whine and did a happy little tap dance on the faux wood floor. It was only then Nate remembered he didn't even have a collar for the dog. Or anything else.

Add that to the long list of things to take care of today. Move over, computations homework.

Finishing with his shoe laces, he reflexively turned to grab his phone, remembering even as he did that the device was gone, and probably lost forever.

He stopped halfway, chiding himself, then froze.

His phone—the same phone he'd last seen sailing through the dark night to smack into the back of a giant *something's* head in an explosion of white rice—was sitting right there on the corner of his desk. With it was a small note, written in a script that somehow looked both elegant and shaky, like it'd been written by a drunken Shakespeare. Nate hardly cared about the odd handwriting. He was too busy gaping at the six words on that yellowed scrap of parchment.

The leaky pocket gets the rice.

CHAPTER 9

TO GET TO THE
OTHER SIDE

Aching head still spinning, Nate pulled the front door closed behind him and turned to find Marty and Copernicus watching him from the chipped-paint concrete steps.

"You okay, buddy?" Marty asked. "You don't look so good. In addition to the Mike Tyson Punch-Out look, I mean."

Wincing a bit with the effort, Nate sat down beside his friend on the steps, decidedly not okay, and not sure what to say about it. Not sure what to make of any of it, other than to feebly hope he'd simply been far drunker than he'd realized the night before, or that someone was playing the mother of all pranks on him.

Because otherwise, all signs pointed to the fact that the strange old man from Zeno's actually *had* visited Nate as he slept last night.

The leaky pocket gets the rice. Who else could have possibly left that note? It wasn't something that could've been intuited by anyone who hadn't been there. And if he'd recovered Nate's phone post-ogre, then... This was insane. So insane that Nate couldn't help wonder if maybe he hadn't simply fabricated all of it in a drugged stupor, and written the note himself.

Maybe there'd never even been a ragged wizard to begin with. That would certainly explain how the guy had mysteriously vanished when Nate had tried to tell the doorman. That part alone was mentally suspect as shit—not to mention the walking bullshit alarm that *was* his recollection of the beast in the park. It was all inconceivable.

What was much easier to believe was that some douchebag had spiked the Iota Nu Nu juice, and that Nate had tripped balls, imagined a strange encounter in a bar, and then gone and thrown his phone at a spooky noise in the dark. And sure, there was Copernicus here to corroborate some of last night's events, but just because he'd stolen a dog didn't mean he'd actually seen any of what he thought he'd seen.

People had done crazier things on drugs, hadn't they?

"Nate?"

He looked at Marty, a sick feeling in his gut.

"Dude, you look like you're about to unravel."

Unraveling. That was one way to put it. Nate couldn't imagine he looked much *less* insane when Marty's words reminded him of an old favorite song lyric, and a manic grin pulled at his lips.

"If you want to destroy my sweater…" Nate said, pulling the phone from his pocket and holding it up for Marty's inspection.

"Oh!" Marty's expression went from pleasantly surprised to confused. "You found it?"

"I guess I did."

Marty frowned between Nate and the phone, clearly not missing the lack of relief in Nate's voice. "Is it working?"

Nate thumbed the screen awake and showed Marty the list of texts and calls and the other various notifications he'd missed throughout last night.

"Good as new," he said quietly.

"Well that's… good," Marty said, still frowning.

Nate turned the phone display back to himself, wondering if maybe he shouldn't just agree with his friend and leave it at that. He stared at Gwen's name on the list of missed messages, wanting to open her text but all too aware of his brain doggedly pointing out that it didn't have the bandwidth to deal with his emotional bullshit while it was worrying about the ragged man who'd apparently invaded their home last night—the ragged man he might well have fabricated, though the presence of the note in his pocket did seem to beg to differ.

Unless Balls Nate had happened to have eclectic calligraphy skills and a hidden ream of parchment stocked away somewhere, that was.

It was all too much. Too many questions. Too few hopes for answers.

Luckily, Copernicus' bark yanked him free from his reveries before they could swallow him whole. The corgi was staring up at the pair of them from the base of the steps, tail wagging expectantly, having apparently grown bored with sniffing the bushes and reached his threshold for patiently waiting.

It was a perfect sunny October Saturday, that wagging tail said. A perfect day for a walk. Obviously. The leaves were even changing. How perfect could perfect get? And maybe the little guy had a point.

"I think I'm gonna go for a walk," Nate said, tucking his phone away and standing up to a rousing crescendo from the Orchestra of Odd Aches and Pains.

"Yeah, I figured we both could, if you're feeling up to it," Marty said, looking off in the direction of the park. "Look around, see if we can find any signs of what happened last night, that sort of thing. Animal control was already packing up when I went and scoped it out this morning."

That gave him a healthy jolt. Beaten and utterly bamboozled as he'd been last night, Nate had completely forgotten that Marty had mentioned calling the service after he'd finished with his less-than-complete retelling of the park stroll from hell.

"Did they, uh, find anything?"

Dead ogre, perhaps? Or maybe the droppings of one terrified college senior, right around home base?

Marty shook his head. "He said there was nothing unusual in the area. I didn't see much either. Just some Gandalf-looking dude drinking on the bleachers at the crack of dawn."

Marty might as well have pushed him down the steps.

"Uh…" Nate licked his lips, fumbling for words. "Actually, Marty, I… Would you mind if I went alone? I just, uh… I think I need a little time to get my head on straight."

It might not be the best idea, charging off to find the ragged man at all, much less to do it alone, and as battered as he was, but Nate wasn't really sure how else to play it if any single part of this madness was actually true.

Marty was eyeing him suspiciously. "You're not, like, trying to keep me out of danger or something, are you? Because, if so…" He pointed to Nate's professionally bruised face.

Nate shook his head, trying not to wince. "No, man. You said the coast is clear anyways, right? I just… Honestly, I just need some fresh air, and I need to think about what happened last night."

Marty looked less than convinced. Nate doubted his friend had missed the way he'd reacted to the mention of the Gandalf-looking drunkard. But finally, Marty gave a reluctant nod.

"Okay, man. Just call if you need anything?"

Nate patted the pocket where his inexplicably restored phone was tucked away. "Will do. Thanks, buddy."

Copernicus fell into happy step beside Nate as he descended the steps and set off across the street toward Hamilton, doing his best to keep his pace casual for Marty's watching eyes, wondering with each step if he shouldn't turn around and call his best friend in for backup. He didn't know. None of this made any sense at all.

He stuck his hands in his hoodie pockets and marched on anyway, sure that, no matter what, he wasn't going to be able to think about anything else until he'd at least seen that baseball field and confirmed for himself there wasn't a giant dead ogre thing lying there.

～

NO ENORMOUS ALIEN carcass in sight.

Just a group of guys playing ultimate frisbee, and a handful of park-goers out for leisurely strolls—or, in one case, a heated game of fetch—with their loyal pooches. From the far corner of Atherton Street, beyond the lanes of zipping traffic, all appeared right with the world. A normal day in the park. Textbook, even.

Except for the old man on the bleachers.

He sat by the baseball field in his ragged gray robe, tipping back the last contents from a cup that Nate knew, even at that distance, was the same odd clay cup he'd seen in the man's hand last night at Zeno's.

It hadn't all been in his head.

The ragged wizard was here. And as the wild-haired man set his cup down on the bleacher, Nate couldn't push aside the feeling that the man was expecting him—that he could in fact feel Nate watching right that very moment.

"I've got a bad feeling about this, boy," Nate muttered.

By way of reply, Copernicus touched a forepaw to Nate's leg in what was either a sign for *I've got your back, bro,* or *Please don't make me cross this street on my own four paws.*

Nate glanced back in the direction of the house, thinking again that he'd been a fool not to bring Marty along, and that he should probably just turn around right then and do his damnedest to forget any of this had ever happened.

But he couldn't forget. Would *never* forget the terror of being run down by that hulking monstrosity. Or the uneasy feeling that, somehow, this strange old man was connected, and that he knew where to find Nate—knew how to break into his bedroom in the dead of night, for Christ's sake.

No. He couldn't turn away from this. He needed answers. And the last thing he wanted was to drag his friends into this. So, he scooped up Copernicus, checked both ways on Atherton, and set off across the street at a jog. Once they were safely to the park grass, he reluctantly set the corgi back down and continued on, Copernicus trotting faithfully by his side.

The ragged man didn't turn as they approached, nor did he stir or even glance over as Nate rounded the bleachers. Nate paused, unsure how to proceed, wanting in part to start right in with the questions—to ask him who the hell he was, and what he wanted, and to embrace his inner Todd and not take "no" for an answer. But something about the man's aura stayed Nate's tongue.

Instead of demanding his answers, he cautiously mounted the bleachers, ascended a few rows, and stood facing the ragged wizard, instinctively waiting for the man to speak.

After an uncomfortably long stretch, the man stirred, his dark eyes returning from somewhere far away to fix on Nate from beneath his bushy, dirty gray mane.

"Are you ready then, lad?"

Nate frowned. "Ready for what?"

As soon as the words left his mouth, it was like a stopper had been pulled.

"Were you in my house last night?" he pressed on, unable to stop. "Were you here in the park? Were you—was that thing… What was that thing? And what do you want with me?"

The ragged man, looking either grim or bored, only gestured for Nate to sit. Reluctantly, Nate did. Copernicus posted up beside him, a silent totem of support. Their robed companion blew out a long sigh. Even from several feet away, Nate could smell the stale alcohol on his breath, yet the man's eyes were sharp and clear enough as they studied the distant tree line.

"There was once a time when I might have bothered answering such questions." He fixed Nate with a melancholy smile. "Perhaps I might even have deigned to ask a few of my own. But the truth of the matter…" He shook his head, scooped up the clay cup Nate swore had been empty a moment ago, and took a heavy swig of whatever was inside. "The truth of the matter is that it matters very little at this juncture what either of us have to say where tongue and mind are concerned."

"What are you talking about?"

He leaned forward with a predatory grin and a reek of strong booze and whispered conspiratorially, "I am so glad you asked."

The guy was mad. He had to be. He was speaking complete nonsense. But for some reason, Nate couldn't bring himself to do the sensible thing and walk away as the ragged man set his clearly not empty cup down on the bleachers and continued.

"Allow me to offer you a deal, Nathaniel Arturi. I will give you the answers you seek." He huffed to himself, as if amused by the simplicity of his own words, then continued on. "I will tell you exactly what that creature was and what it was doing here last night. I will tell you who I am. I will even tell you who you are."

"You already said who I am," Nate pointed out, more than a little creeped that this guy knew his name. Then again, if the inexplicably working phone in his pocket was any indication, the old man might know even more than that. His eyes sure seemed to say so.

Nate couldn't imagine many people had ever received such a look of pitying condescension from a guy who looked like his last shower might have actually taken place right before he'd dressed up in costume to go see the cinematic debut of *Fellowship of the Ring* almost twenty years ago.

"What's this deal you're offering, then?" Nate asked, looking around the park just for an excuse to escape that stare. "What am I supposed to do for these magical answers?"

"You must pass but one simple test."

Nate scanned the ragged man and their immediate surroundings more closely, trying to deduce what trick was at work here. Some part of his brain was sure that this was the part where he realized it'd all been parlor tricks up till now, and that this was merely another homeless dude looking for money. The rest was busy quietly digging up every bit of lore he'd ever heard about crossroad demons and fae tricksters.

This was ridiculous.

"What kind of test?" Nate asked anyway.

The ragged man tilted his head back and forth, swirling the contents of his clay cup in deliberation. "A measure of character, really. Conducted remotely, by my associate. You need only acquiesce for us to begin."

And that was Nate's cue. He wasn't sure where this was going, but he had a strong feeling the next step was a call-center associate named "Steve" asking for his social security number or some such on the other end of the line.

"Okay," Nate said, standing in preparation to descend the bleachers, and snapping for Copernicus to follow. "Well, this has been weird. Good luck scamming the next guy."

"And good luck to you, Nathaniel Arturi, in surviving the troglodan invasion, and all that follows."

Nate paused, hating that he couldn't *not* pause at that. Hating that some part of him—the part that *knew* he'd nearly been crushed not twenty yards from here last night by a beast whose existence he couldn't explain—actually wanted to bite at this madness.

He stared at that spot on the baseball field.

"Troglodan?" He finally asked, glancing back at the ragged man. "Seriously? You expect me to believe that thing was, what? The vanguard of some alien ogre invasion or something?"

"Expect?" The ragged man frowned and stroked his beard, looking genuinely stymied. "In the future, I believe it would behoove you to improve your skill at asking sensible questions, Nathaniel. What I *expect* has as little effect on the truth as what you *believe*. And the truth is that the troglodan armada is coming for Earth. Likely mere weeks away at this point. They won't be the last ones, either. Not by a long shot."

For several seconds, all Nate could do was stare, wondering who the hell this guy was and, if by some galactically screwed chance even a single word of this was true, why the crazy old bastard had thought to tell *him*, of all people.

Because the guy is bat shit insane, came his brain's exasperated answer. *Obviously.*

And also because Nate was probably the only kid in town who'd been stupid enough to even listen to the guy's mad rambling this long. Obviously.

"Look," he said, backing down the bleachers, "I don't know what you want from me, but—"

"Did I not make that bit clear?" The ragged man frowned down at his drink in confusion, then back at Nate. "My mistake. We have a vacancy of sorts, you see, and my associate believes you might be worthy of filling it."

"You have…"

Nate stared in disbelief.

A job?

Homeless Gandalf was offering him a job… to help stop the alien invasion?

He'd lost his mind. Maybe it had been drugs, or a psychotic break from sheer public embarrassment. Maybe it had been a goddamn brain bleed from the head trauma, or just a freak accident stroke. But clearly, somewhere along the way, Nate had lost his freaking mind.

"Nathaniel," the ragged man called as Nate turned to retreat.

"No!" Nate rounded on the crazy bastard, surprised by his own animosity, but hardly caring in that moment. "I don't know who you are or how you found out my name, but you stay the hell away from me. If I see you again, I'm calling the police."

"Nathaniel, there's really no point in…"

But Nate was already hopping from the bleachers and turning to jog off, only slowing enough to confirm that Copernicus was with him.

"Oh nine hells, don't you start too," the man growled from the bleachers.

Nate didn't engage. Just ran a little faster.

"I asked him your bloody questions. If you care so much why don't you…"

Only when the growling voice had faded from clear hearing did Nate slow to a hasty walk and glance back over his shoulder. The ragged man was evidently arguing with someone who clearly wasn't there, waving his hands animatedly. Nate felt a pang of pity for the crazy bastard. But he had his own problems to—

"Hey!"

Nate whipped around at the familiar voice, stomach sinking, and found its owner glaring at him from the sidewalk across the street.

"Hey!" Emily Atherton shouted again, jabbing a finger his way. "Is that my dog, you creep?!"

Shit.

Nate raised a hand and gave Emily a stiff wave, his mind racing with bad excuses. Did she know he'd been there last night? He doubted she would've seen them in the dark yard if she'd looked out during the pummeling, but would Todd have told her afterward?

He had no idea. All he knew was that she looked properly righteous and pissed over there, cocking her hips and spreading her hands in a clear demand for immediate and gratuitous clarification.

Nate gestured toward the corner of Atherton and Hamilton and pointedly headed that way to meet her, avoiding direct eye contact and desperately rifling his brain for some explanation. With a look of incredulous indignity that burned so bright it probably would've been visible from orbit, Emily slid out of her power stance and broke into a murder march, headed for the corner—and, by the looks of it, for Nate's life blood too.

Think. Think.

Nate glanced back and forth along the street, barely registering the cars speeding by in both directions, head and heart both racing so frantically that he might've forgotten all about the insanity of the ragged man—had the crazy robed bastard not chosen that moment to materialize from the bushes behind Emily and flick his wrist at the murder-marching brunette.

What happened next, Nate couldn't rightly say. Maybe the heel of Emily's svelte gray boots just so happened to break by random chance, but there was something unnatural about that snapping heel. Something unnatural, too, about the way she lurched haphazardly off the sidewalk, as if nudged from a distance.

Straight into the busy street.

Nate's mind went blank, but for the blaring of the horns and the look of pure shock gripping Emily's perfectly made-up face.

He sprang forward before he had time to think.

Horns droning in on either side. Emily's broken boot twisting under her weight as she tried to catch her balance, knee buckling in kind. Sheer terror in her eyes.

Nate ran faster, lunging for her, screeching brakes tearing at the edges of his awareness. Her wide eyes too far away. The air shimmering between them. He flew toward her, some corner of his mind screaming that something was terribly wrong—even beyond the cars coming to crush them both to paste. He reached out—

And watched in disbelief as the space between them ruptured, imploding in on itself in a way that laughingly defied his brain's feeble attempt at understanding. For the briefest instant, Nate flew on toward the rift between him and Emily, powerless to stop at this point, distantly aware of the headlights rushing in from the right, a mere moment from hitting them both.

Then the rift engulfed him, space itself seeming to dilate even as it swallowed him into its internally curling infinity. The world melted around him, running off like so much hot wax until he found himself alone, drifting and bodiless in an endless sea of darkness.

CHAPTER 10

ACROSS THE UNIVERSE

Wherever he was—and whatever had happened to his body—the first notable thought that passed through Nate's mind was that he was even still capable of thought at all. That seemed promising, even if he was stuck on the one rather useless thought, echoing through his mind and the bodiless darkness, ad infinitum.

What the actual fuck.

It was a stupid phrase—the sort that he and his roommates would've normally scoffed at as lazy and self-satisfied. Just a bad use of language in general, really. But if ever in the history of human existence there *had* been a justified use, Nate was pretty sure he'd just found it.

Of course, maybe that was just what everyone thought when they died.

Because that was the most likely explanation for what this was, right? One moment, he's lunging to save Emily Atherton from an oncoming car, the next he's drifting in endless darkness? It wasn't hard to put two and two together.

Except he was missing another *two*, wasn't he? There'd been the ragged wizard who'd pushed Emily—or had he pushed her?—and the bizarre distortion that had ruptured the space between them just as Nate lunged in to save her.

Had he imagined that part too?

His current predicament said no, and that *no* promptly graduated to a hearty *hell no* when the darkness around him began to flicker to life with first a few dozen, then a few thousand tiny winks of light.

Stars?

Hello, Nathaniel.

What the hell?

Do not be afraid. I do not intend you any harm.

The voice was tranquil, yet something about it made Nate feel small and afraid. It seemed to come from everywhere at once, and yet also from nowhere at all—like he'd simply thought the words out of thin air.

"Who's there?" Nate whispered, too startled to give much thought to the fact that he *could* whisper at all without any apparent body or mouth.

Who I am matters little to you here and now. What matters is what I bring you, Nathaniel. But, if it should ease your mind for the duration of this conversation, I am the one called the Lady.

The voice seemed to take direction at the end, shedding that odd everywhere-and-nowhere ambiance and forming up behind Nate—if there could be a "behind" for someone without a body. When he thought about turning to face the voice, though, he suddenly found some ghostly form to his presence. Not quite his body, but a wispy imitation.

Odd as it was, he accepted it for the moment, far more concerned about who and what was behind him. He turned, and there she was.

Whatever *she* was.

At first glance, she passed for an ethereally beautiful woman in a flowing white gown. But there was something off about her. Something uncanny. Like what he was seeing was only a thin veneer laid over a vast and impossibly complex power. Her beauty was preternatural. Her hair shining with the barely contained radiance of a thousand stars. Her dress fluttering with a subtle yet magnetic sweep that whispered of passing eons and the birth and death of galaxies.

Earlier, speaking to the ragged man, Nate's thoughts had turned to crossroad demons and other impossible things. Now, though, he found them dragging up a fabled entity of an entirely different caliber.

A celestial being.

Was this… Could it be…?

"Am I dead?" Nate asked.

The Lady favored him with a benevolent smile that made him want to fall to his incorporeal knees and weep for its beauty. "Not yet, Nathaniel."

"But Emily… Those cars…"

"In a manner of speaking, your physical body does remain in peril back on Earth. Rest assured, though, that I will not allow anything to happen to you while we speak. Should you pass the test, you will be returned home safe and sound, better than ever."

"The test?" Nate gaped, some of his awe receding as the pieces fell into place, brick-by-incredulous-brick. "This is… You're that crazy bastard's…"

What? *Associate?* Could any man so casually call such an illustrious being an associate?

"Yes," the Lady said, with a knowing smile. "But please, do not allow my *associate's* demeanor to spoil your appetite for our enterprise here."

Demeanor?! Nate wanted to ask. But that was hardly the most pressing concern here. He opened his mouth, thinking to ask what they wanted from him, and instead ended up wordlessly gaping as the starry expanse brightened around them, clarifying into breathtaking color and depth as if the Lady had magically removed the shades he hadn't realized he'd been wearing.

It wasn't just stars he saw, but the entire cosmos. The swirling, radiant spires of entire galaxies, painted milky hues of yellows and oranges, greens and blues. The kiss of starlight on untold lightyears of space dust, breathing life into an interstellar canvas of violets and pinks that would've defied any attempt to contain its magnificence with words, or even with thoughts.

It was incomprehensible.

"All will become clear in good time, Nathaniel," said the Lady, reaching out one slender, perfect hand to him. "But for now, we should not tarry. Come. Allow me to show you why you are here."

Nate wasn't sure why he glanced back, or even *how* he did—or how he and this Lady could hear one another in space at all, for that matter. Such details kind of felt insignificant. Especially when he finished turning, and saw the rift that'd swallowed him whole hovering right there behind him— an impossible, wriggling portal, juxtaposed against the grand expanse of space. A clear path straight back to Atherton Street, where two screeching cars and the shocked eyes of Emily Atherton were all frozen in time.

The Lady didn't speak as Nate looked, nor did she have to. Words couldn't have made it any clearer. He understood on a deep, intuitive level that he was being offered one last chance to turn back—the so-called "choice" the Lady's mad *associate* had apparently forgotten to offer.

But it hardly mattered now anyway.

Not when the Lady's fingertips brushed against Nate's cheek like a kiss of sunshine and spring breeze. Not when he turned back to her and found her reaching for his hands, watching his eyes for permission.

He couldn't speak.

Then her hands closed around his, and they *moved*.

The word seemed inadequate, but Nate wasn't sure how else to describe it. One moment they were floating above the sprawling cosmos, drinking in the never-ending beauty, and the next, the Lady took a single step forward, and they were simply elsewhere, and Nate's head was spinning with the feeling that they'd somehow just jumped light years in a single step.

He couldn't have said where they were. Only that they were in a cavernous room unlike anything he'd ever seen, and that it appeared to be housed underwater. The architecture was like a strange and beautiful collision between an old, vaunted cathedral and the Emperor's throne room from the second Death Star.

That was all Nate had time to process before the Lady took another step, and they *moved* again.

With a flash, he was standing on a mesh metal deck, staring at a pair of... he didn't know what. They were aliens. Of that, he had no doubt. One was tall and slender and decidedly feminine in her copper armor, with smooth green skin and waving tendrils that looked something like hair. The other, he realized with a surge of panic, looked like a bigger, stronger version of the ogre that'd attacked him in the park last night, encased in fearsome blood red armor.

Nate stumbled backward, trying to run, but the Lady held firmly to his hand, and Nate went nowhere. He watched in terror as the smaller one's hair tendrils came to life like a hundred emerald serpents, cocking Nate's way as if they could hear his ragged gasps. Then the tall green alien turned to look their way, cruel, dark eyes narrowed.

"I'm sorry!" Nate cried reflexively, throwing his free hand up in surrender.

But the Lady was already stepping forward, pulling him effortlessly along, and with another flash, they were drifting back in space, and Nate was staring at the fiery radiance of a nebula, trying to wrap his head around what was happening.

"You need not fear for your safety here," the Lady said in her tranquil tone, apparently unperturbed by the violent intent of aliens or the effort of phasing them across the universe, step by step.

They flashed on, untold stars and planets rushing by faster than Nate could register starts and stops. Impossibly fast. And yet on they flew, like Nate had tripped on all of the acid in the world, and now he was on his way to meet the Maker himself.

"You are not alone in this universe, Nathaniel," the Lady said as the universe flowed by. "In fact, contrary to what so many of your kind choose to believe, the humans of Earth are actually some of the most primitive of the known sentient species of your galaxy."

"How..." Nate started, but then there was a stutter in their flight, and Nate was too busy gaping at the shimmering spires and whizzing space traffic of a cluster of floating island cities, each one too enormous for Nate to wrap his head around. Some kind of space station, he thought, set to the backdrop of the most expansive, breathtaking nebula yet.

They flashed on before his brain could finish exploding, and then they were on a rocky, barren wasteland of a planet, standing at the base of what Nate first took for a mountain.

"Why..." It took Nate a second try to find his voice. "Why are you showing me this? I don't understand. I don't understand what's happening."

The Lady smiled at him. "And thus I believe you have answered your own question."

She looked toward the mountain, and Nate followed her gaze to the crumbling ruins of an entrance he hadn't noticed in the great stone structure ahead. At a closer look, though, it wasn't the entrance that held his attention, but the lone figure that stood there—a black-furred humanoid with a head that resembled that of a lion, or a panther.

"Earth's days of peace grow short in number," the Lady said beside him.

Ahead, the lion-thing bared its teeth and tipped its head back. A fearsome roar rumbled through the air. Then they flashed back to dark space.

"What the hell was that?" Nate gasped.

"But another outcome of a sentient's proclivity for meddling with forces they did not understand," the Lady said, slowly turning to point over his shoulder. "Truthfully, I would be more worried about *that*."

Nate turned, realizing only then that they were standing on a wide asteroid at the outer edge of a thick belt of thousands, maybe hundreds of thousands, like it. A planetary ring, he thought.

Then he saw what the Lady was pointing at.

He wasn't even sure what *it* was. Only that it blocked out the stars beyond, and that it put a fear like he'd never known deep in his heart as its dark, shimmering edge spilled across the asteroid belt, swarming in like an entire ocean of aggravated hornets.

Giant, bus-sized hornets, he realized, as the swarm closed in and ripped straight through the belt like it wasn't there at all. Straight through gods knew how many millions of tons of stone and ice and space dust. Decimating it all. Consuming it. Headed straight for them.

Nate would've fallen over backward if the Lady hadn't been holding him in her unshakeable grip. He did, however, scream his freaking lungs out as the swarm closed on them, evaporating everything in its path like a terrifyingly silent force of nature.

Then the Lady pulled him through another flash step, and the swarm was gone.

Everything was gone.

They floated in an empty space, not unlike the one Nate had surfaced into at the beginning of this interstellar nightmare. Not that he took much note in the moment. He was too busy falling to his ghostly knees, gasping for breath that wouldn't come.

"I understand that was what you might call 'a lot to take in,'" the Lady said, gently releasing his hand for the first time since they'd set off.

Nate gaped up at her, still sucking fruitlessly for air, tightness closing around his chest right along with the horrible thought that maybe the Lady had simply forgotten to give him air here, and that he was about to die for nothing after all of that. Then she laid her ethereal hand across his back, and he felt the first tendrils of relief spreading through him. He closed his eyes, welcoming it, focusing on that single point of contact until the panic receded and he felt calm enough to look back up at the Lady.

He still wasn't breathing, he realized. But that didn't seem to be a problem. Maybe he hadn't needed to all along. It hardly seemed to matter anymore.

"What do you want with me?" he whispered. "What did you mean when you said Earth's days of peace are numbered? What does any of this have to do with me?"

"I am afraid that is not my place to tell you. My role here is merely to determine whether you are the one to take up the mantle."

"What mantle?" Nate asked, tension creeping back in around his phantom chest. "You're not making any sense. None of this is making any goddamn sense."

The Lady showed him a wan smile. "All in good time, Nathaniel. For now, my associate must have his answer."

"What answer? Why are you even helping him? Why…"

Nate trailed off, not really sure what he was trying to ask, or why he should think to expect anything else. He wasn't even sure why he instinctively felt he could trust this Lady any more than he could trust the ragged wizard—aside from that one was a transcendent goddess of the stars and the other was a crazy old man in a dirty robe.

"We have something of a compact between us," the Lady said, when Nate failed to finish his thought. "It is, as your people might say, rather complicated. As for the question in need of answering..." She gestured to something behind Nate. "I believe you will be familiar with this part of the tale."

Nate turned, not really sure what new development he expected to find waiting in their quiet little null space. Not really sure he even wanted to know. What he definitely *didn't* expect, was the smooth gray boulder that'd appeared in the darkness. Or the medieval longsword sticking out of it, gleaming blade buried halfway to the plain hilt.

"I don't understand."

He felt the Lady draw up beside him. "I believe that you do."

He shook his head, eyes fixed on the sword in the stone, five fabled words drifting through his head. *The* sword in *the* stone? It couldn't be. Even after all the wild shit he'd just seen—strange new planets, terrifying aliens, freaking giant space stations—this still felt like the biggest hoax of all. Because they'd just jumped from unknown space straight into the magical fantasy land legends of yore.

"This is some kind of metaphor?" Nate's words sounded more like a plea for sanity more than an actual question. "Some kind of symbolic test?"

"This is the bridge to the Excalibur," the Lady said, favoring the weapon with an affectionate smile. "The very same Excalibur you have no doubt heard about since you were old enough to understand such legends."

"But that's... That's just a story. That's..." He couldn't help himself. "What good's a sword gonna do against an alien armada, anyway?"

"Take it, and find out."

Nate blinked. "You want *me* to...? No, I'm not... You have the wrong guy."

The wrong guy? There was the understatement of the century. Twelve hours ago, Nate had been getting his face pounded in by a freaking frat boy named Todd, and now they were talking about alien invasions and giant space ogres and Earth's numbered days?

She had the wrong freaking *species* if she thought Nate was the one to do anything about any of this. And yet the Lady continued watching him in all her calm, otherworldly wisdom, waiting for him to do what he already knew deep in his bones was impossible.

"I'm a goddamn IT major!" he blurted. "This is insane! What help could I possibly be to anyone?"

She didn't bat an eye. "That is exactly what this trial was designed to determine."

"But why me?" His voice sounded frail and weak in his ears. Like he was about to cry. And maybe he was. He wanted to go home. Wanted to crawl into bed and hide under the covers and forget that any of this had ever happened.

He couldn't do this.

"I'm no one," he whispered. "I can't."

The Lady waved a hand, and suddenly they were standing at the stone, and the sword was close enough to touch.

"Then test yourself, Nathaniel Arturi, and let us see your true worth."

Somehow, he didn't need to look to know the portal back home had opened up behind them. He did anyway, and there was a rippling ovoid window to Atherton Street, and to Emily and the two speeding cars that were stuck in freeze frame... waiting to come smash him to pieces the instant he stepped through?

"You will survive the accident, should you choose to return that way."

It was like she could see inside his head, he thought, as he turned back to the sword in the stone. Which only made him wonder that much more how she could possibly think he was the one for this... this *mantle*.

But fine. All he had to do was reach out and show her, right? It wasn't like he was actually going to be able to pull the thing free. Because even if this *wasn't* all just the mad ramblings of his balls-tripping, thrice-concussed brain as he lay dying in Atherton Street... and even if this radiant Lady *was* truly inviting him to follow in the steps of King Arthur himself...

Well, if there was any single person on Earth who was worthy of that mantle, Nate was positive it wasn't him.

So why couldn't he just grab the damned sword and show her?

"This is ridiculous," he growled to himself, finally shaking his ghostly arm loose from its paralysis.

Phantom heart hammering, he laid his fingers on the hilt. It was warm to the touch. Smooth. Not at all as he'd expected. It felt not so much like a sharp, dangerous weapon as it did a living thing, tingling with a subtle power he could only wonder at.

Was this really happening?

He looked back to the Lady. What next? Was he supposed to just give the thing a yank, simple as that? She didn't make any sign at all. But it hardly mattered anyway, he reminded himself, because he wasn't King freaking Arthur. And because this was all a load of shit anyway.

Right?

He gripped the hilt tighter, and it all but sighed in his hand, swirling with an energy he felt but couldn't consciously quantify.

All a load of shit. Right.

"When all seems lost," the Lady said, "remember this moment, Nathaniel."

He wasn't sure what to make of that, but the thought quickly dissipated anyway, blown to the wayside by the growing storm of the sword's agitation, dancing like a leaf in a hurricane. Nate gripped the hilt tighter, willing it to be still. Then he braced himself, and pulled.

Pulled, and nearly fell over backward as the sword slid free with a sound of grating steel, and Nate joined it in that building hurricane. The dark air thrummed with rushing power, rippling around them, buffeting Nate's ghostly form like gusts of a hard wind, growing in intensity until he was sure he'd be carried away. But there he stood at the eye of the storm, the darkness of their null space brightening around him with the surge of the sword's power.

Nate turned to the Lady, too shocked for words. She hovered in the maelstrom beside him like a pale goddess, her ethereal dress fluttering only gently in the gale force winds. She smiled at him—a smile so warm that it literally shone, bleaching everything around them until he could barely make her out at all in the blinding light. Until he could barely see his own ghostly hands holding the Excalibur.

I will see you again, Nathaniel Arturi, came the Lady's disembodied voice, like a loving mother's kiss on the forehead.

Then the world flooded to pure white light, and she was gone.

CHAPTER II

TRAFFIC DELAYS

It was like coming to after having been knocked unconscious.

One moment, Nate could've sworn he was on a psychic voyage across the stars with the one called the Lady, pulling the goddamn Excalibur from the stone like some kind of tripped out Flash-Gordon-King-Arthur wannabe. And the next, he was crashing into Emily Atherton, car horns blaring in from both sides.

They hit the asphalt, and Nate rolled, distantly aware of the screeching rubber tearing toward them and more than a little surprised to find Emily's weight trapped safely in the cage of his arms. He hadn't even had time to think about it and yet...

Something was different.

He wasn't sure how or why. Only that, as he poked his head up from their rolling tangle, nothing seemed to be moving even half as fast as it had been a moment ago. The cars slid across the asphalt in slow motion—a blue Honda on their side, and a gunmetal Audi in the other lane—brakes locked and squealing in a pitch that sounded too low. Down the sidewalk, Copernicus was running toward them, also in slow motion, having somehow already made it safely across the street.

For one moment, Nate observed all of this and more with a kind of detached calmness, slowly rotating through the air with Emily, whose mouth was peeling slowly open in a silent scream.

Then he came around and saw the blue Honda's front right tire closing on his left leg, watched in horror as the squealing hunk of rubber hit his ankle, driving it under, and—

Time sped back up. They tumbled roughly onto the sidewalk, Nate's heart thundering with the sudden and terrible certainty that his ankle had just been shattered into a thousand pieces, Emily still tucked tightly in his arms. Too tightly, he realized, from her too-wide eyes looking up at him. Or maybe that was just because he'd landed on top of her, one hand firmly latched to her buttocks, Todd style.

He started to release her, ankle all but forgotten, trying to sputter an apology, too wired on near-death adrenaline to manage words.

"Look out!" someone shouted at the top of their lungs.

Screeching brakes and rushing motion caught his brain stem and yanked.

He didn't think about darting forward to grab the incoming bike. He'd barely even registered it *was* a bike, by the time the leading edge of the frame was rocketing into his open palm. He just tried to stop it from hitting Emily, and the rest happened on its own.

Impact jarred through his arm, cascading down the line from the hard smack of metal bike frame on open palm. Hard pavement kicked up against his braced hand and foot and knees—unforgiving reactionary forces coming to flatten him out for his audacity in trying to stop a speeding bike with his bare hand.

Only he didn't get flattened.

Nate watched in shocked disbelief as the dark-hoodied rider careened over his handlebars and past Nate in slow motion, face frozen in a wordless cry, looking every bit as startled as Nate was. Time sped back up. The rider thudded to the sidewalk and bounced past Emily like an unwieldy human cannonball, coming to a rest in a groaning heap after three hard revolutions.

Emily watched him go with wide eyes, then turned her gaping stare back to Nate. "Oh my god." She gave it another moment's shaken thought, then reconfirmed. "Oh my *god!*"

In the street, horns were honking. People were shouting. The squeal of peeling tires yanked all eyes to the blue Honda, and to the thirty-some-thing driver who Nate swore had just run over his ankle. The guy was gunning the engine, eyes wide, both hands clamped to the steering wheel in a death grip. Nate watched in dumb silence as the blue car screeched off over the hill, still trying to piece together what the hell had just happened, and kind of wanting to laugh at the thought that anyone on the planet could be so worried about something so trivial as a reckless driving charge right now.

The car. His ankle. The slow motion bike crash. The freaking intergalactic psychedelic walkabout.

The Excalibur.

He turned unseeing eyes back to the bike he was still holding, half-expecting to find a magic sword there instead. It was impossible. Im-freaking-possible. Anti-possible. A fluke. That's what it was. Adrenaline, and close calls, and… and what?

"What the fuck is happening?" Nate whispered to himself, oblivious to the world around him. At least until his eyes properly focused, and he got a good look at what he'd done.

The bike frame was bent in his hand. Bent *by* his hand, some part of his stupefied brain registered. Bent like the thing had crashed straight into a freaking steel girder rather than his fleshy little palm. Bent like…

Like you managed to eke out an ounce of power, said a gruff voice. *Good.*

Nate dropped the bike with a crash, and nearly fell over backwards in his reflexive rush to distance himself from the speaker. Only there was no one there. Left, right, up, down. No one. He shuffled a few steps back, panic spiking… and then fizzling straight out—not gone, necessarily, but filtered down, like someone had slipped him a few benzos just to take the edge off.

What was happening?

No one there. No one but Emily Atherton and the recovering biker, both staring at him like he might be an alien. Nothing but the oddly distant pounding of his heart, and the pedestrians jogging over to come check on them, and the street full of cars, and spectators, and—

"Hey, dude!" someone called across the street. "Hey, dude! How'd you do that?"

Nate followed the voice and realized the speaker had his phone out, and pointed right at him. Recording, from the look of it. So were his friends. Looking around, Nate saw more phones, all pointed at him, and Emily, and the bike that he'd just… just *what*, exactly?

"—uys fucking *see* that?"

The panic rustled behind the curtains.

"—his bare hand."

He was numbly aware his heart was beating faster.

"—some kinda freakin' super—"

He couldn't seem to breathe. Couldn't—

"Hey, are you all right, man?" asked a too-close voice beside him.

Nate jerked away, surprise piercing through his divine benzo filter, yielding another few inches to the blunt panic closing around his chest like a giant steel mitten. His good Samaritan didn't seem to mind. The kid was too riveted to his phone display, more interested in filming Nate's reaction than in actually helping.

Nate's eyes flicked down to the twisted bar of the bike frame—twisted to the shape of *his* hand—and he fought down the sudden urge to take off running. That would only look worse, he thought. Worse than whatever the hell this already looked like. He didn't know. Couldn't think straight.

He should leave.

He turned for Emily and the poor biker, thinking to at least check on them first, but the biker was already sitting up, looking rattled but okay, and Emily... Emily was watching him like she wasn't sure who or what he was.

He started to step past her, mind too blank to come up with any better plan than to leave before people started asking questions he couldn't answer. Emily reached up and caught his hand before he'd made it three steps, her eyes flicking to his from the wrecked bike, understanding setting in, right along with a silent plea for him to explain to her what had just happened. He tried to move on. She didn't let go. Almost without thinking about it, he pulled her up to her feet. She was surprisingly light. Too light. But he still wasn't ready for it when her shaky legs gave out to lingering shock and a broken boot heel, and she fell straight into him.

Nate staggered back a step and caught her, both arms around her waist. She looked up into his eyes, clear surprise written across her face, lips trembling. Then, before he knew it, Emily Atherton was burying her face into his chest, shaking with sobs and holding onto him for dear life.

"That was—That was..." she sobbed between wet, ragged breaths. "Oh my god. I could've—You could've... We almost..." She pulled back and looked up at him, gasping through the tears, silently begging him to make sense of it all for her. It was only then that he even registered how instantaneously the entire double tap near death experience had just unfolded for her, unbroken by any mid-game galaxy hopping timeout. Unadulterated by the crushing knowledge of the Lady, and of the existence of giant-ass space stations and all the sentient life in the known galaxy.

"I'm sorry," was all he could think to whisper back past his spinning head, holding but not quite hugging her, painfully aware of the Nosy Phone Brigade closing in, and of the thousand questions they'd have. Had they seen? Had they noticed his body or mind or soul or what-the-hell-ever blipping off across the galaxy for a split second?

"I'm sorry, I have to—"

He faltered at the hiss of excited whispers back by the bike, and glanced around with a sinking feeling. A few of his charitable cinematographers were bent over the mangled bike, getting close-ups of the inexplicable damage.

"Hey, how'd you do this?" one of them demanded, pointing his phone from the bike back up to Nate. "Show us your hands!"

Nate was already turning, already setting off across the grass, skirting past the rest of the oncoming "helpers," cutting the corner to Hamilton Ave, not really sure where he was going, only that he needed to get away. Away from all these watching eyes and damned recording phones.

"Hey!" someone called after him. "Hey, dude, what about this guy's bike?!"

Nate wanted to laugh at that. Or maybe cry, or scream. It was all too much, too fast. Too many impossibilities, churning up and roaring for tangible release. Too many prying eyes.

It started with a slow jog, like his legs were trying to simply sneak him out of there of their own accord. He almost felt as if he were watching himself from the third person, just as surprised as everyone else to find himself running for it. He didn't look back. Not when someone called something about the police. Not when Emily called his name.

His legs moved faster, and faster, until he was all but sprinting down Hamilton. Barely registering the passing houses, or the jostle of his pounding steps, or even the burning aches in his palm and ankle. He ran. Copernicus appeared at his side, zipping along on stubby legs, eyes wide with doggy excitement, like out of everyone involved, the corgi was the only one who'd managed to glean how badly the entire goddamn world had just been turned upside down.

Nate kept running. Toward home. Then past it. Running for he didn't know what. Running right up until he saw the ragged wizard himself emerge from thin air farther down the block, shooting him a drunken grin and a sardonic thumbs-up.

CHAPTER 12
ALL HAIL

"You!" Nate growled, stomping down the sidewalk toward the grinning wizard who'd just tricked him into doing the freaking intergalactic time warp. On his heels, Copernicus added an angry bark of his own.

"I'll be a witch's teat," the ragged wizard said, looking Nate up and down. "You went and did it, after all."

Whatever divine benzo aura had been holding Nate's emotions in check began to crumble then. Before the old man could raise that damned clay cup to his lips, Nate had grabbed him by the ratty robes and yanked him close, too pissed to flinch at the reek of booze on his breath.

"What did you do to me, you son of a bitch?"

"Me?" He frowned back at the park. "I merely opened the door. She's the one you should blame."

"The Lady?"

"The *Insufferable* Lady," the ragged man amended. Then, as if to the sky, he added, "Yes, I am aware that you can still hear me. Thank you, M'lady."

"You're not..." Realizing he was still clenching the man's dirty robes in his balled fists, and that the ragged man didn't seem the least bit perturbed by it, Nate released him and took a step back, trying to catch his suddenly tight breath. "You're not crazy, are you?"

The ragged man thought about that. "Well, I'm not sure I'd say *that*. Not insane, though. Probably. Most days." He grinned drunkenly. "Or so the voices tell me."

Nate just stared at the strange old man with his dirty robe and his wizard's beard, thinking about the Lady, thinking about the sword, Excalibur.

"Are you…"

He felt too ridiculous to even say the name.

The ragged man seemed to pick up on his discomfort. "Emrys?" he asked, looking down at his own wrinkled hands as if inspecting them for the first time. "No, maybe it's Ambrosius? Aristotle, perhaps?"

"What?"

"Oh, don't mind an old man's ramblings," he said, waving a hand dismissively. "I am precisely who you think I am. I am also not he. Not in the least. Do you understand?"

Nate frowned. "Not really."

The ragged wizard's bushy eyebrows returned Nate's frown a hundredfold. "Hmm."

"Are you telling me you're…"

Those bushy eyebrows cocked in the stretching silence, waiting, but Nate had lost his focus at the sight of a pack of five students headed their way on the sidewalk. He glanced around, not really sure where or how to blend out of notice, but pretty sure he didn't want to be standing here out in the open, talking about aliens with a mad wizard.

"They can't see us, lad," the ragged man said, following his gaze. He stepped off the sidewalk into the adjacent yard, gesturing for Nate to do the same. "None of them can."

Nate stepped into the grass, eyes flitting between his ragged companion and the oncoming students, wondering if they'd truly pass on by without a clue. Apparently sensing his claim was being put to the test, the wizard leaned out in front of the student flock as they neared and started waggling his fingers, shuffling from foot to foot in an ostentatious little dance.

The five of them passed right by without so much as a sideways glance. Not ignoring. Simply not seeing.

Turning back, the wizard took in Nate's wide eyes and shrugged. "I had a feeling you might make a scene about all this. Precautions seemed prudent."

For a few seconds, Nate could only stare at the ragged man. The ragged *wizard.*

"Merlin?" he finally managed to ask.

"Ah!" The wizard pointed an emphatic finger at Nate. "There it is. *The Merlin*, if we're to be exact."

"But that's not... That's impossible."

Nate felt the earth wavering beneath his feet, his head spinning as whatever psychic dam had been holding back the inevitable meltdown suddenly sprung a gaping leak. Because if this man in front of him truly was what he claimed to be...

It had been real. All of it.

His legs felt weak. Too weak. Chest tight. Vision blurring. He tried to lean against a tree for support, and felt his legs give out completely. He thudded to the grass with a rush of expelled air, some corner of his mind wondering if he'd been drugged, the rest too busy overloading with visions of space ogres, and gleaming alien cities, and the gods-blessed Lady. And then Merlin—*the* fucking Merlin—was standing there, frowning down at him from his tangled mane.

"That's more like it," he said, thoughtfully stroking his filthy beard.

Copernicus stepped between them, growling, but the Merlin only waved a hand, and the corgi wobbled and promptly tumbled to the ground, fully asleep. Nate tried to tell the wizard to leave his dog alone, but he couldn't seem to form the words. Then, with a strength that defied all logic for a spindly alcoholic in an ancient bathrobe, the Merlin plucked Nate from the grass and sat him up against the tree.

"*Impossible* feels a bit funny in the head, doesn't it?" the wizard asked, settling down to the grass with a huff and then rifling in a robe pocket until he produced his trusty clay cup. "Not so easy for a rational mind to reconcile once it's set in its oh-so-wise ways."

Nate watched in mute disbelief as the empty clay cup began to fill itself in the wizard's hand. The sight only added to the clammy nausea spreading through him. The Merlin, seeming to remember himself, looked down at the cup and then offered it out to Nate, arching a bushy eyebrow in question.

Nate nearly retched at the thought of imbibing anything right then. His head was still spinning too hard for him to risk shaking it, but the Merlin accepted his silence for answer and contentedly raised the drink to his own lips.

"You said I had to agree to... whatever the hell that was," Nate said weakly.

He wasn't sure why that was the first protestation out of his trembling lips, but somehow it felt important.

"Yes," the Merlin agreed at the end of a long glug, wiping his mouth with the back of a hand. "And so you did when you willingly stepped into service."

"You gave me no choice," Nate growled. "You almost killed Emily. You… You knew I couldn't just stand there. You played me."

"Yes," the Merlin said, bobbing his head. For a second, his face drew as if he'd had an important thought, but then he let out a deep burp and continued on with a drunken thrust of his pointer finger. "And yet therein lies what I believe your professors would call a 'teachable moment.' You say I gave you no choice. I counter that you always have a choice, Nathaniel Arturi. Always. Lowering yourself to believe otherwise simply because you find yourself thrust into a situation you did not ask for…" He shook his head. "That way lies something far worse than madness. That way lies complacency and powerlessness." He grimaced and tipped back the remainder of his cup. "And what a shame that would be."

He speaks wisdom.

It said a thing or two about Nate's current mental state that it actually took him a second to recognize the voice in his head had not been his own. Nor had it been the Merlin's. Or the Lady's. Which meant—

Calm yourself, or I will be forced to intervene once more.

Nate felt the panic returning—the ground wavering beneath him, his chest tightening. It was the same voice he'd heard just after he'd stopped the bike. He was sure of it. And once *more?* What did it mean, once more?

He thought about the pharmaceutical-level calmness he'd experienced upon returning from the stars, straight into a near-death scrape. "The sword…"

Nate felt the ring of truth even as he mumbled the words.

The Merlin looked up from his cup. "What of the sword?"

"It's…"

Go on now.

"It's…"

Dare you say it?

"It's in my freaking head. It's talking."

Bravo, Nathaniel Arturi. Bravo.

"Interesting," the Merlin said, stroking thoughtfully at his long beard. "Very interesting."

"What's interesting?" Nate sat up from the tree, panic beginning to burn through the lightheaded nausea. "Is this supposed to happen?"

But the Merlin only continued stroking his beard, staring thoughtfully off.

"Hey," Nate said, waving a hand for his attention. "Hey, Merlin."

Jesus, it felt weird saying that out loud. But at least the spacey old wizard roused at the sound of his name.

"Hmm? Oh, the Excalibur." He waved a dismissive hand. "Yes, yes. All very standard. Your new companion will need some time to learn your ins and outs, as they were."

As they *were*?

It is, as you might say, like a jungle in here, the gruff inner voice agreed. *Except far more full of whining. And pointless cat videos.*

Nate felt the thing's growing disdain, right beneath his own growing panic.

Please. Spare me the indignant 'what has happened to my life' doom spiral. You have been bestowed the highest honor available to your species. Though Smithy's blackened hands if I can see why.

"How do I—"

Make me stop? That IS a good question, coming from such a spineless specimen. Nine hells, she really has gone too far this time. I am an Excalibur, gods damn it, not a fountain of miracles.

"Shut up!" Nate cried, clamping his hands to his ears.

"Well, that won't work, will it?" the Merlin said, frowning at Nate like he was a simpleton. "He's in your head, lad."

And no small wonder I despair.

"I need to speak with the Lady."

That makes two of us.

Nate did his best to ignore the Excalibur's grating voice. The Lady, at least, had seemed reasonable. Benevolent, even. If he could just speak with her, if he could just explain…

"She doesn't exactly do house calls, lad," the Merlin said, looking less than benevolent himself. Looking drunk and amused and completely unhelpful as he filled his clay cup from thin air once more. "I'm afraid you're stuck with me for the time being."

Stuck with him? Stuck with a drunk wizard and a sassy magic sword in his head and—

Sassy? You wish to speak about sass?

It was too much.

Nate was lurching to his feet and scooping up Copernicus before he even knew what he was doing.

Come now.

"Talk later, then?" the Merlin asked, squinting up at him.

Do not be unreasonable.

But Nate was already tucking the sleeping corgi in his arms and running for it, no idea at hand but to somehow escape the madness.

"All hail Nathaniel Arturi!" the Merlin called after them from the yard, not bothering to rise or follow. "All hail the Knight of the Leaky Pockets!"

Nate kept running, not looking back.

"All hail the Eighth Excalibur!"

CHAPTER 13
WE ARE NOT ALONE

Humans, the Excalibur reflected, tasting the word as if preparing for its latest diatribe.

"Shut up," Nate wheezed, running on.

Nowhere else in the galaxy could one hope to find a mind so steeped in self-denial as to actually attempt physical flight from the voice inside its own skull.

"Shut up," Nate repeated.

Make me.

Great. And now the voice in his head turned out to be that of a five year old.

You have no idea how amusing that condescension is coming from you. I might take it more seriously if your furry friend there were to tell me to mind my personal hygiene whilst he consumed his own excrement.

"Screw you," Nate growled, clutching Copernicus tighter to his chest. "I didn't ask for any of this."

Nor do any who live to see such times. But that is not for them to decide. All we have to decide is—

"Are you..." Nate huffed out between heaving breaths, burning legs beginning to slow despite his best efforts, "... quoting Gandalf... at me... right now?"

Paraphrasing, the Excalibur corrected. *Forgive me, I am still parsing the records of all that I have missed during my hibernation. I merely hoped you might relate to a story about tiny weaklings bumbling their way through a conflict that lay entirely beyond the scope of their meager powers.*

"I think you… might've missed… Gandalf's point, there," Nate said, shuffling on at a pace that was quickly becoming more *limp* than *run*, but refusing to stop out of principle. Even just slowing a little, though, his breath began returning unusually quickly. "But then again," he added, "you are a goddamn sword, so I'm not sure why that would surprise me."

I am not a sword, you imbecile.

"I saw you. I pulled you from that stone."

Did you? And have you not stopped to wonder, in your infinite wisdom, where in nine hells that blade went when you jaunted back to Earth? Have you not stopped to wonder where I reside even now?

Nate stopped running. He hadn't had a chance to piece that one out amidst the rest of the thunderous shit-storm falling on his head.

Yes, I hadn't noticed.

And to make things better, this Excalibur thing could apparently read his thoughts.

"Maybe I just assumed the Lady sent you back by means beyond my petty little human comprehension, and that you were floating around in the ether or something."

Your wisest assumption all day, to be sure. But only marginally accurate.

Nate scowled at empty State College air and only then noticed he was drawing strange looks from some fellow students across the street on their way toward campus. In his arms, Copernicus arched around and looked at him, tail cautiously wagging against Nate's chest. He hadn't even noticed the dog was awake, as mentally disheveled as he'd been.

"Fine," he muttered quietly, setting Copernicus down. His ankle was seriously starting to hurt, and he already looked bad enough talking to himself in public without clutching a terrified corgi to his chest.

"What did I pull from that stone then, Mr. Excalibur?" he added, much more quietly, as he continued slowly on.

In simpleton speak, you acquired the blessing of the Lady.

"And what does that make you?"

One unsatisfied Excalibur, amongst other things.

Nate opened his mouth to fire back that the Excalibur and all the rest of them could be his guest and bugger off, but the sword that was apparently *not* a sword pressed on.

You needn't take my derision personally, Nathaniel. I would be equally inflamed had I been gifted to a snargladorf.

"What the hell's a snargladorf?"

Think of a creature that, while widely admired for its alleged cuteness, is about as small, weak, and ultimately useless as little Copernicus here.

"Ah. Yeah, nothing says *don't take it personally* like comparing a man's physical prowess to a freaking ten pound corgi. Thanks for that."

You are welcome, Nathaniel.

Nate rolled his eyes and looked around. In his admittedly futile dash to escape the Merlin and the rest of the madness, Nate had ended up several blocks past home base on Irvin Ave, farther south than he normally had reason to venture. Not that it mattered. Going home right that moment didn't really seem like a valid strategy. Nothing felt like a valid strategy. Not with a persistent voice rattling in his head.

You might be persistent too, in my position. Imagine you had awoken only to realize your oh-so impressive human power and intellect was to be harnessed by that corgi creature there. Can you not imagine the frustration?

"Well then maybe your pal Merlin should've left me the hell alone if I'm such a disappointment."

Fool. The Merlin is wise beyond your comprehension.

"Wise beyond… You're talking about the same maniac who almost killed an innocent girl back there, right? The one who was too busy drinking to even stop me from running away just now?"

I said that he is wise, you sniveling ingrate, not that he is without vice. If he had wanted to stop you, you would not have made it three steps.

"Whatever." Nate glanced warily in the direction of home, not sure what his next move was, but pretty sure he should stop standing there talking to himself on the sidewalk like a… Well, like a Merlin.

Son of a bitch, how had this happened?

Lady's Grace if I know.

"Yeah, I get it, you're upset," Nate grumbled, starting around the block on an indirect path home. He checked to see that Copernicus was following, trying at once to figure out what the hell he was going to do next while also refraining from thinking any one thought too loudly for the Excalibur's waiting derision.

The end result was mostly a mental log jam, whereby Nate conjured a head full of would-be thoughts that was simply too packed for a single one to make its way anywhere useful. But at least the Excalibur didn't say anything. After a minute or so of blessed silence, Nate decided to try again.

"So… snargladorfs and…" He frowned at the next word, somehow feeling both ridiculous for playing along with this madness, and equally silly for even questioning it at all after everything he'd seen in the past twelve hours. "Snargladorfs and troglodans," he muttered, shaking his head. "It's all real?"

Obviously.

"Aliens and everything?"

It astounds me how desperately your kind clings to the belief that, among the hundreds of billions of planets in this galaxy alone, you are somehow the sole organic sentience in the universe.

"Right," Nate muttered, kind of wanting to scream just to be sure he was even still real, yet also kind of feeling like it all made perfect sense, in a weird way. It was kind of disturbing, how little it took to completely turn one's entire grip on reality upside down. Nothing more than a space ogre in the park, a celestial goddess, and a little jaunt across the galaxy.

"Fine. It's all real. And what you said a minute ago about 'harnessing' your power… What did you mean? What do you do? I mean, aside from tampering with my mental states, and—"

You left me little choice in the matter, there. I would like to see YOU try assimilating a few petabytes of relevant background data with a sniveling college senior having a panic attack in your face.

Nate clenched his jaw. "I'd kinda been through a lot at that point."

Never before had Nate perceived the silence in his own thoughts to feel so condescendingly judgmental.

"Whatever," he muttered. "That still doesn't give you the right to mess with my head. Do you hear me?"

Would that I could STOP hearing you.

"Yeah, well you and me both. Just… Just don't do that again, okay?"

Silence.

How encouraging.

With a sigh, Nate pressed on. "Can you at least answer my question? If you're not a sword, what are you? What do you do? Where did you come from?"

They truly did not tell you?

Hell no, they didn't tell me, Nate opened his mouth to say. No one had told him a single goddamn thing. Just threw a freaking ogre at him and then yanked him off on the Magical Galaxy Express. But before he could say a single word, the Excalibur cut back in.

Of course they did not tell you. I can see now that their words would surely have been wasted.

Nate scowled at the sidewalk. "What's that supposed to mean? That I wouldn't understand because I'm such a stupid little human?"

Silence.

"I'm not a simpleton, asshole."

More silence. And this time, Nate could've sworn he felt a kind of subtle amusement radiating from somewhere within his own head—amusement that was definitely not his own.

"I'm a goddamn IT major, okay? I might not be an Einstein, but I know four computer languages, and I can solve differential equations."

I know over ten-thousand languages and might well possess more total computational power than this entire backwater planet. Shall we compare phalluses next?

Wonderful.

Clearly, it hadn't been enough to have Todd and the rest of the world dishing out daily reminders of Nate's many inadequacies. Now he had an even bigger alpha asshole living in his head. And the Merlin hiding in the bushes. And freaking aliens. And Earth's allegedly numbered days. And—

His phone buzzed in his pocket, and he latched onto that familiar feeling with a focus that was half weary relief, and half drowning man reaching for a life raft.

Splendid, the Excalibur said as Nate fished the phone out. *More complications.*

"So sorry I had the audacity to have a life before I was sucked into this freak show unawares," he muttered, glancing at the lit screen and the new text from Gwen at the top of the long list of notifications he'd missed since last night. He wasn't sure what was worse: the fact that he was actually buying this giant crock of crazy, or that, despite all the world-shattering revelations, he still felt that little nervous flutter at the sight of Gwen's name on his phone.

He hesitated on the unlock button, sure that now wasn't the time, and more than a little put off by the thought of the Excalibur listening to his thoughts while he read whatever Gwen had sent him last night, before she'd apparently decided to just say screw it and come looking for him at the house.

Rest assured, I read that message within minutes of our merger, right along with every other digital transaction you've had with Miss Pearson. And with pretty much anyone else. Ever.

"You can… read what's on my phone?"

Did I mention that my phallus is bigger than yours?

Nate looked down at the phone, absentmindedly studying his own stupefied expression in the black mirror, trying to process the entirety of what the Excalibur was telling him.

Oh blackened hands, would you just get on with it? Or should I simply narrate the correspondence to you? The Excalibur's voice shifted to something seductively feminine, and disturbingly similar to Gwen's. *Do you want me to tell you it's all gonna be okay, Nate?*

Nate clutched at his temples, feeling like his head might actually explode this time. "Please never do that again."

On the sidewalk beside him, Copernicus gave a little whimper, wagging his tail and clearly concerned about whatever Nate was going through.

"It's okay, boy," Nate said, bending down to pat the corgi's head before unlocking his phone. "I'm just gonna read this highly-sensitive text message while the asshole voice in my head tells me what a hopeless waste I am."

Copernicus made another less-than-happy sound, his ears flattening.

You are both being melodramatic.

Nate ignored the Excalibur as best he could, and tapped the notification with Gwen's name on it. He read the most recent message first.

Gwen: "Hey, you make it home okay last night? We were worried about you."

He moved to the message from the night before.

Gwen: "Just tried to call but seems like your phone is off. I'm sorry about what happened tonight. I know you said you're fine, but can I buy you a peace-offering drink anyway? Just left INN."

He looked at the time stamp. It couldn't have been sent more than ten minutes after he'd stormed out on his own quest for a bag of rice and a life in someone else's shoes. She'd left. And while he'd been sitting in Zeno's, choking on a whiskey and inviting this madhouse intergalactic bullshit straight into his life, Gwen had been out there looking for him. Which he would've found out, had he simply gone straight home as he'd known he should've.

He could've kicked himself right in the groin.

I find that anatomically improbable.

"Goddammit, can you just stay out of my head for five minutes?!"

There was a stretch of pregnant silence.

Would you prefer I lie?

"My life is over," Nate muttered, more to himself than to the Excalibur. Not that the distinction seemed to matter all that much.

Yes. You were only chosen out of the blue to represent your entire species on the intergalactic stage—a privilege many would die for, by the way. But do go on about how hard and unjust your life is.

"You do understand not everyone wants to be a..."

A *what*, exactly? A Knight of the Leaky Pockets? Nate still didn't even understand exactly what the hell he'd been conscripted for.

You are an Excalibur Knight. Or you may become one, at least, with the proper training, and perhaps a minor miracle or two.

"Okay," Nate murmured, staring unseeingly at Gwen's texts. "And what does an Excalibur Knight *do*, exactly?"

A true Excalibur Knight stands as a beacon of hope for all sentient life in the galaxy.

Nate tucked his phone away, blinking at the empty air, waiting for more. "Suppose I'm not entirely sure what that means..." he finally said.

He swore he felt the equivalent of a mental sigh from the voice in his head. *A true Knight stands as representative, envoy, and warrior in service to the Lady and her loyal Merlin, and to all of the assembled civilizations of the known galaxy. A true Knight wields the power of an Excalibur as both sword and shield against the darkness that, left unchecked, would swallow this galaxy whole. A true Excalibur Knight knows his duty, and embraces it gladly, without fear of death or torment. A true Knight does not sit and snivel like a soft-willed fool, pitying himself for the honor of his planet's fate resting on his shoulders.*

Nate was too busy trying to wrap his head around the scale of the thing —and particularly around the whole *all the assembled civilizations of the known galaxy* bit—to even process the last string of insults.

"That all sounds... big," he croaked.

The biggest.

Nate hadn't really noticed he'd sat down on the Allen Street curb until a forest green hatchback zoomed by a little too close for comfort, and the startled driver over-corrected with a swerve and an indignant honk. Nate just sat there on the curb, feeling like he was floating ten thousand feet above his body—ten thousand light years across the galaxy. Just floating there, amid the clouds of *all the assembled civilizations of the known galaxy*, with the planet's fate apparently crushing down on top of him.

Kind of explained why he couldn't seem to breathe.

"What's coming for Earth?" he heard himself ask ten thousand feet below.

At present? I cannot yet say, in full. But I feel the Beacon's call even now, and I will not be the only one. When the troglodans come... Well, I have been too long in hibernation to speculate as to the current disposition of the Greater Troglodan

Empire, but the Merlin does not appear optimistic. It is safe to assume they will come with a planetary strike armada.

Nate stared through the pavement, buzzing with the magnitude of the words. It was too much. Too much to even comprehend. "This is… too big."

Not for a true Knight.

"Take it back then," he said immediately, looking around as if he might actually spot a handhold in the mess, or at least the specter of the Excalibur. "Un-choose me. Go back and tell them they got it wrong."

Would that I could. Alas, there is only one way this compact is to be broken, and it does not involve you walking away with your life.

"Then what am I supposed to do?"

That is for you to choose, Nathaniel Arturi, and for you alone.

Nate stared numbly into space until Copernicus nudged into his side with a soft whine. He absentmindedly scratched the corgi behind the ears, realizing as he did that Emily Atherton now knew exactly who had her dog. He was entirely too tired to care. Too acutely aware of every scrape and bruise on his aching body. His ankle was positively pulsing now. He still wasn't sure how it wasn't broken, or how he'd conjured the strength to stop that bike. Wasn't sure he even wanted to know, or that it especially mattered. He didn't feel strong now. Just weak, and afraid.

"I just wanna go home and forget any of this ever happened."

Then fly home, little hobbit, and let us see how long that works for you.

CHAPTER 14

ROOMIES

Marty was halfway to crisis mode.

That much was clear as soon as Nate's foot touched the front stoop and his friend darted out from their happy yellow-paneled house with the kind of jittery air that seemed to declare he'd been waiting right there ever since Nate had left for the park... what, an hour ago? Had it only been an *hour*? It felt like he'd been gone multiple lifetimes.

Fair enough, probably, seeing as he'd been across the galaxy and back.

"Dude," Marty hissed, splaying his hands in a clear, *What the hell happened?!* as Nate ascended the old paint-chipped steps. Before Nate could even begin with the excuses, Marty glanced back over his shoulder, as if expecting Kyle and Zach might be watching from the paneled living room windows. Which they actually *were*, Nate realized with an uneasy feeling, trying to mask his slight limp.

Lady's Mercy, don't tell me you are afraid of these little piglets.

Nate's mouth was open, the first words on his tongue, before he remembered that he couldn't just tell the Excalibur out loud to shut up, and that he didn't know how much he could safely tell his friends at all before they decided to call psych services on him.

Bah, the Excalibur growled, apparently getting the gist anyway. *You worry like a frightened hare.*

Nate took a deep breath, suppressing the urge to fire back. Marty was already giving him a strange look. Nate put on his best *business as usual* face, and waved at Zach and Kyle in the window. The two traded a look, then Kyle made his own *business as usual* masturbatory hand gesture, and they went back to whatever they were doing inside. Saturday morning Battle Royale, if Nate had to guess.

"Dude, what happened?" Marty asked, shuffling down from the stoop to pet Copernicus and give Nate a closer looking over. "Why do you look like you just ran a half-marathon in jeans? And are those fresh scrapes?"

This one worries like a mother hen.

Nate barely contained the burst of manic laughter that tried to escape, in part at the doe-eyed naïvety of Marty's questions, and in part at the fact that, for once, Nate actually agreed with the critical voice in his head. But what was he supposed to say? The truth?

"I had a run-in with Emily Atherton," he said, indicating the scrapes on his hands and elbows. They were nothing compared to the hot, deepening ache in his ankle, but his friend didn't need to know that part quite yet.

"Oh." Marty looked down at Copernicus, then confusedly back to Nate's scrapes. "Was there light wrestling involved?"

Nate failed to smile and instead settled for recounting the accident to his friend as best as he safely could, leaving out the bits where Emily had in fact been pushed by a drunk wizard who'd consequently thrown Nate through a portal to the other side of the galaxy where he'd ostensibly become the second coming of King Arthur—sans backbone, skill, or talent, and apparently tasked with preventing Earth's first extraterrestrial invasion, which might just be touching down any week now, by the by.

Marty's eyes were already wide enough without the extra bits. Which seemed kind of funny, given that Nate was barely even aware of the words leaving his mouth.

"So you, like, full-on saved Emily Atherton's life?" Marty asked, when Nate had finished. "And you're acting like this is no big deal because...?"

"Because no one got hurt, I guess," Nate said with a forced shrug, unexpected irritation prickling up. Was that the Excalibur's irritation, he was feeling? "And I guess because I've had some time to cool down."

He needed to get to his room. Needed to think.

"And that's where you've been?" Marty asked, clearly dubious, but politely trying to hide the fact. "Cooling down?"

Part of Nate was a little taken aback by how readily his bobbing head nodded its way into the lie. The rest—the part that was a thrice-jabbed bundle of raw nerves—just wanted his best friend to shut the hell up and get out of the way.

"Yeah," he said, still nodding. "I just needed to take Copernicus for a walk."

Just a nice cool-down stroll with the stolen doggo. That's all. No drunken wizards or magical talking swords or anything.

"And Emily was cool with that?" Marty asked, pointedly looking down at Copernicus.

"Yeah," Nate said automatically. Then he remembered all the amateur cinematographers on scene, and realized with an unsettling jolt that he didn't have any damned clue what he was going to do if and when his friends caught wind of what had actually happened. "I mean, I don't know."

What if they saw the way he'd stopped that bike?

Jesus, what if they saw him flicker off of the goddamn planet?

"Everyone was pretty shaken up, I guess," he added weakly.

Marty huffed out an incredulous laugh and swatted Nate's shoulder, apparently too excited about the entire ordeal to notice the non-explanation. "Probably because you saved her life, dude!" He wagged his eyebrows. "You know what happens next in the movies, right?"

Nate shook his head. "It wasn't like that. I promise."

It wasn't like that, because I left her crying on the sidewalk and ran away from an active crime scene with about two dozen recording witnesses, he didn't add. *You'll probably be seeing it on five different social media apps before the sun goes down. Assuming the alien invasion hasn't started by then.*

Shit.

You are being melodramatic again, came the Excalibur's gruff voice, nearly making him jump out of his skin.

Marty, spreading his hands in a knowing little *no judgments here* shrug, was apparently too jazzed up on the second-hand savior buzz to notice that one, too.

"Dude," Nate said, "after what she did with Todd behind Gwen's back…" He shook his head, feeling suddenly and quite inordinately angry about the whole thing—so much so that Marty actually shrank away, dropping his gaze and adding a pang of guilt to Nate's abrupt anger.

"Sorry, man," Marty said quietly, eyes on the bushes. "Did you find out what Gwen wanted last night, by the way?"

"Not really," Nate said, not wanting to delve into yet another personal failure right that moment. "I still need to text her back. There's just a lot on my mind after everything."

"Understandable," Marty said, bobbing his head. And bless his heart,

Nate could see his friend meant it, even knowing as little as he did about the true *everything* Nate had just been through.

Your tribe coddles you. Do not mistake such fallacy for kindness.

Nate tried to keep the scowl off his face as Marty looked back up to meet his eyes.

"So all that stuff last night, then… No giant park monsters, or anything?"

"Not in the light of day," Nate said, trying again to force a smile past everything. "Nothing out of the ordinary over there, just like you said."

The Merlin must have disposed of the thing—the *troglodan*—sometime in the night. Nate hadn't stopped to think about it earlier, but it seemed the only explanation. It only then dawned on him that the Merlin must've been the one who'd killed the thing too, with whatever had made that flash of blue light.

"I don't know, man," Nate added. "I'm starting to wonder if I didn't just hallucinate the whole thing last night. All that stuff I told you…" He just shook his head, letting the silence do the talking.

Trusting Marty with the story of the attack last night had been one thing. Nate had been terrified for one, and completely in the dark about what the hell was happening. But after everything he'd seen today…

Somewhere between the mystical jaunt across the universe and the talking sword in his head, it felt like a line had been drawn.

I told you, I am not a sword.

And that pretty much decided that. He couldn't tell Marty or anyone else about the Excalibur. Not until he could wrap his head around what was happening to him. Maybe not even then.

Luckily, Marty didn't press the issue. He just shook his head along with Nate, as if chalking the whole series of events up as standard mishaps of college life. "We can't let you out of our sight for five minutes, can we?"

Nate's smile fell away as soon as his friend turned for the door.

Inside, Kyle and Zach looked up from the couch as Nate and Marty walked in, their eyes moving as one from the Battle Royale menu, to Marty, to Nate, to the smiling corgi who trotted in on his heels, clicking and clacking and tail-a-wagging.

"About time you two finished your secret snuggle-fest out there."

"Also, we like, have a dog now?" Zach added. "That's a thing?"

"For the moment," Nate said, "assuming you guys are cool with that."

Zach just patted the couch beside him and quickly lost himself in playing with Copernicus as the corgi hopped up to join him. Kyle, meanwhile, was giving Nate's battered appearance a closer inspection.

"Nate's a part-time superhero now," Marty explained following Kyle's curious stare. "Yanking corgis off rooftops and tackling busty brunettes out of the paths of speeding cars."

"Huh?" Kyle said, perking up at the mention of busty brunettes and looking more closely at Copernicus. "Methinks a story there is, here. Pull up some wood, gents, and join us in battle whilst we confer."

"That's what she said," Zach murmured, scratching Copernicus' flank. "Isn't it, boy?" Copernicus only craned his head up in delight, hind leg furiously kicking in time with Zach's scratching.

"I'm in," Marty said, plucking his controller from the Mother Gaming Shrine drawers and firing up his system. "Nate?"

He wasn't ready for the cold gut punch of his friend's expectant look. It was the happiness that did it—Marty's contented certainty that the day's tribulations were already behind them, and that there was nothing left to do but to settle in with a few bowls of cereal and a few hours of quality time with friends. Because what could be more important than that?

Nate stared at the dark screen of his own quadrant of the shrine, wishing more than anything that he could simply forget that he'd just been savagely assaulted with an overwhelming answer to that question, and that even now, a strange entity was almost certainly sitting in his head, watching to see what he would do. All he wanted to do was go into the kitchen, pour himself some cereal, and join his friends like everything was well and right in the world. Just another Saturday. Not an alien or a psychotic break in sight.

But how could he?

"Oops," Kyle was saying somewhere back in the direction of reality. "We have lift-off, ladies and gents."

"Yo, Nate!" Zach called, cupping his hands around his mouth as if he were shouting a great distance, "you still alive up there?"

If only they could've realized how badly their friendly jabs burned at his insides in that moment…

"Oh no," Zach said, recognizing at least some part of the souring look on Nate's face.

"Dude, it's Saturday Squads!" Kyle added. "Come on, just one round."

Woeful longing took on a bite of bitter anger.

"Sorry guys. I really need to get started on a project."

"Bullshit," Kyle said, though he sounded less than certain. "That's what Sunday night is for." He looked at the others. "Right?"

"Out-nerded," Zach agreed, wholeheartedly bobbing his head. "Plus, what was all that about brunettes and speeding cars and stuff? And why are you bleeding?"

"Marty can fill you in on that one," Nate said, turning for the hallway. "Just give me an hour or two to clean up and get this thing, uh, started."

Half-hearted boos and affectionately mild insults followed him out of the living room, along with the click-clack of doggy claws on faux wood as Copernicus hopped off the couch to fall in behind him. Nate ignored it all, focusing on the impending safe haven of his bedroom. At least until Kyle said something about alien mind control rays, and his feet paused of their own accord, halted by a thought that was still only half-formed when he turned back to his large roommate, who was watching him with a cautious look, like he was afraid he'd just crossed a line.

"I was just wondering..." Nate explained, not really sure how else to start, "where do you normally read all that alien conspiracy stuff?"

Kyle's concerned look quickly shifted to one of mock affront. "Well, if by 'conspiracy stuff,' you in fact mean 'factual reporting,' my go-to is normally this blog called *They Walk Among Us*. There's another one called *The Truth Is Out There* which is pretty good too, but we *Walkers* don't really like to talk about that so much."

"Why the sudden interest?" Marty asked, watching him with a pensive frown.

Kyle looked at Marty as if he'd just asked Nate why he thought Emily Atherton was attractive, or why he found Bell's Pizza to be so delicious. Then, apparently registering that Marty's question had some validity, he turned and fixed Nate with his own suspicious look. "Yeah, why *are* you suddenly interested?"

Nate shrugged. "Just came up last night in conversation."

That earned him three skeptical stares.

"With Gwen," Nate added, "Not with the Alpha-Sig-Sigs."

He wasn't sure that detail actually added any authenticity to the lie, nor was he particularly happy to be lying about something so trivial to begin with. So he shot them a salute, said a quick, "GLHF, boys," and turned to limp down the hallway before they could press on with the questions.

"Oh, we will," Zach called after him.

"With a rando fourth!" Kyle yelled.

But Nate was already stepping into his room and closing the door behind him. He lingered there, leaning his forehead against the flimsy white door, allowing himself a few moments just to breathe, releasing the compressed air of all the lies and madness where no one could see.

He'd never been so simultaneously relieved and achingly hollowed to be alone in a room.

I am sad to say you will never be alone for the rest of your life, Nathaniel.

He closed his eyes, pretending for a moment as if he hadn't heard a thing. Then he turned for his laptop with grim resolve, ready for answers.

~

WHATEVER THE PENN STATE IT DEPARTMENT might have to say about Nate's academic prowess, he had to admit he might've been leaving some performance on the table all these years. Celestial abductions and Excalibur-themed auditory hallucinations, it turned out, were great tricks for improving task-oriented focus—even better, he wagered, than those little blue pills he'd seen more than a few of his classmates popping during long coding sessions.

Somehow, staying on topic felt a lot easier when said *topic* had beamed down from Lady knew where and taken up temporary residence in his own head. Aside from a few sweaty palmed breaks spent scouring social media feeds for damning footage of his Atherton Street heroics—not to mention a few brief hiatuses to check he hadn't actually developed some kind of super strength, which, according to his uncrushed metal water bottle, he totally *hadn't*—he barely even came up for air. The problem, it quickly became clear, wasn't one of focus, but rather that he was sorely lacking in reliable source materials.

In hindsight, he wasn't sure what he'd been expecting.

Much as he would've given for the comforting weight of an *Excaliburs, Extraterrestrials, and Other Enigmas* textbook in his hands, Nate hadn't found anything that seemed even remotely applicable in what felt like the few *thousand* alien conspiracy articles he'd read. Nor had there been anything in the extensive bodies of King Arthur mythology, aside from a few low-budget movies set in modern day and one King Arthur comic series that, while apparently based in space, seemed sadly lacking in quick-fix answers for *what to do when you've been attacked by a giant space ogre and wind up with an Excalibur trapped in your head.*

Nate was starting to get the impression it wasn't exactly a common problem. And the Excalibur in question wasn't being much help either. The sword-that-wasn't-a-sword had been almost completely silent since the research had begun. If Nate hadn't known better—which, on second thought, he really *didn't*—it almost seemed as if the thing was pouting.

A rich accusation, coming from the boy who has spent the entire afternoon hiding in his room, avoiding everything from his pathetic roommates to the girl he claims to love.

"I never claimed to…" Nate blew out a huff of hot air and looked out the window, to… darkness? Shit, was it already nighttime?

He pinched his temples, looking down at the sketch of the Merlin he'd been doodling as he read, and trying in futility to rub out the dull headache of hours spent monitor-gazing. "Did you want me on task, here, or not? One minute you're telling me I've got the weight of the world on my shoulders, and the next you're gonna criticize me for trying to do something about it?"

Apologies. Clearly, I missed the part where you were doing anything of value here. Do carry on.

"You know what?" Nate picked up his phone and plopped down on the bed beside Copernicus, navigating to his messages. "If you're gonna be a dick about it, I might as well take care of my own life first."

He pulled up Gwen's text, and started typing out a reply before the Excalibur could say otherwise.

Nate: "Sorry I took so long to respond. Turns out my phone had too much to drink at INN last night, but it's all better now. Can I buy YOU a peace-offering drink to make it up to you?"

"There," Nate muttered, even as his fingers tuttered with the phone, deleting and retyping the last sentence through a few different variations.

As I was saying…

"Screw you," Nate muttered, tapping out the sentence one last time and hitting the send button.

All hail the Knight of the Leaky Pocket, Tamer of Corgis and Conqueror of Nervous Butterflies.

Nate dropped his phone on his chest and plopped his head back onto the pillows with a sigh. Beside him, Copernicus rolled over and did much the same. He hadn't meant to—had meant instead to finally go have that shower and join his friends for some games—but Nate was on the verge of dozing off when his phone buzzed on his chest. He roused back to life with a familiar thrill of excitement. Then he looked at the display, and the excitement bled away, replaced by surprise and curiosity, and a healthy ripple of dread.

It was a DM request from Emily Atherton, short enough that he could read its entirety in the preview line.

Emily: "Can we talk?"

He stared at those three words, mind churning uneasily with the thoughts of what Emily Atherton would want to talk to *him* about. It was an impressively short list, beginning with a stolen corgi, and ending with what in the holy hell had happened out there today. Nate stared at the phone, unsure how to respond, hesitant to even unlock the device and allow her to see that he'd seen her message. The phone buzzed again.

Emily: "Wanted to say thx for what u did today"

The knot in Nate's stomach eased a little.

Emily: "And to ask if u kno where my dog is lol"

The knot tightened right back up.

Nate looked over at the corgi on his bed, reflecting that he should probably get food and water for the both of them. Copernicus, as if sensing a change in the air, went paws-up and cocked his head around at an interesting angle to meet Nate's gaze. The phone buzzed.

Emily: "I'm not mad, btw"

Emily: "Just wanna talk. Hope ur ok."

Nate let out a relieved breath. No wild demands or accusations. And still no viral catastrophe from all those not-so-helpful helpers earlier today. Maybe everything was actually going to be okay.

Lady be praised, we are safe from the fifty kilogram beauty queen and the army of tweeting college youths.

Nate frowned at an indiscriminate point on the ceiling, wondering if it was worth it to point out that no one his age really tweeted these days.

I implore you to explain to me how that particular detail matters when NONE of these so-called social networks appear to be anything more than an amalgamated planetary feedback loop of self-aggrandizing mental masturbation.

Nate chuckled despite himself. "Well, I guess we don't disagree on everything after all." He looked to Copernicus, wondering what he should do about Emily. "Are you doing okay here, little guy?"

Copernicus broke into a panting doggy grin.

"Well LOL, then," Nate muttered, scratching the corgi behind the ears before unlocking his phone to type out a reply to Emily.

Nate: "No worries about today. Really."

He paused on the keyboard, teetering on an outright lie, then decided that, with everything else happening, adding *two-time willing dognapper* to the résumé probably wasn't necessary.

Nate: "Copernicus actually followed me home earlier. Sorry, I was gonna bring him up this afternoon, but I guess the day sorta got away from me after everything."

Her response was quick.

Emily: "OMG say no more, I've been a total wreck all day. Just glad he's OK."

A few seconds later, the phone buzzed again.

Emily: "Do u want me to come over?"

He couldn't help it. Those seven innocent little words, coming from Emily Atherton, stirred an abashed little part of Nate's imagination that wasn't ready to be stirred. Stirred it with unexpected vigor, right up until the phone buzzed again.

Emily: "To get him I mean lol ;)"

Nate blinked at the new message, not really sure whether it was in fact cancellation or confirmation of any perceived flirting, and more than a little irritated with himself for caring at all. How many times had she treated him like nerdy pond scum? Was he really going to let himself start salivating the first time he thought she might be fluttering her pretty little eyelids at him? It was pathetic.

Well, I guess we DON'T disagree on everything after all.

"Cute," Nate muttered, tapping out a reply. "Real nice."

Nate: "Would you mind if I just bring him by tomorrow? I think we're both pretty spent."

A slightly longer delay.

Emily: "Yeah, totally. I kno you 2 are besties anyways. Could u let me kno ur address just in case?"

Nate shared their Irvin Street address, oddly reassured that the tone had returned to normalcy. He arched an eyebrow at the unexpected *sweet dreams* and additional winky face he got back in return, and was just setting the phone down again when he felt a strange flicker of… *something*. Something he didn't understand—kind of like a nervous flutter, but different. At first, he almost thought he'd received another text and that his fried brain had simply crossed wires and misinterpreted the sensation. Then the Excalibur spoke up.

We have a visitor.

Nate tensed, reflexively looking around the room as if maybe he'd somehow missed a troglodan hiding in the closet. Beside him, Copernicus had gone alert, ears at attention, but that might've been more because of Nate's own tension than because the dog had heard anything.

"Where?" he asked quietly, sweeping the room again, this time for anything that might be used as a weapon.

YOU are supposed to be the weapon.

"Yeah, this coming from the freaking Excalibur," Nate muttered, scooting over on the bed to look out the dark windows. "Remind me again why—"

He jerked and nearly dropped his phone when the thing buzzed in his hand.

"Jesus," he hissed at the device, as if it were all the phone's fault.

Hopeless.

Nate ignored the Excalibur and woke the phone. It was a text from an unknown number, and a rather odd one at that.

Unknown: "May I speak with you in the backyard?"

Three guesses who that could be.

Fool. You needn't wager even a single guess.

"Yeah, I know, it's an—"

An idiom. Ah, yes, I see that now.

The impatience radiating from the Excalibur was clear enough, but if Nate hadn't known better, he might've thought there was actually a hint of embarrassment there, too.

If there is any embarrassment present, Nathaniel Arturi—

"It's me," Nate sighed, climbing off the bed and reaching for his hoodie. "I know, man. I know. One day together and you're already getting predictab—Agh!"

His left leg buckled beneath him as he planted his foot and his ankle caught fire with a deep, throbbing pain. He caught onto his computer chair, hoping for balance, then hit the faux wood floor with a thud and curse when the traitorous furniture tipped on him.

Would you rather I be UNpredictable, then?

"What did you do?" Nate growled, reaching to pull up the leg of his jeans, as if seeing the pained region could somehow make it better, or at least help him make sense of what was happening. All he saw, though, were the same dark bruises that'd been there before, when he'd first made it to the safe isolation of his room to check. Ugly bruises, to be sure, but nothing compared to what he would've expected after getting run over. It was only the pain that had suddenly quadrupled, which didn't seem to make a lick of sense, unless—

Unless SOMEONE was managing the pain for you, and repairing the underlying tissue damage faster than your sad little body could shake a stick at.

Nate stared down at the mottled mess, trying to process what the Excalibur was telling him.

That was an idiom, by the way, his gruff companion added, right on the crest of a particularly vivid wave of pain.

Nate grimaced, his mind's eye replaying the scene of the blue Honda's rear right tire crushing its thousand-pound way over his helpless ankle. He hadn't been imagining it.

Your leg would be shattered right now, had we allowed it, the Excalibur confirmed. *Your hand, too.*

No wonder the driver had been so freaked out. He *had* hit something. And holy damn, was Nate noticing now.

So would you like me to kiss it and make it all better? Or would you prefer to continue being confrontational?

"Bite me, asshole," Nate groaned, climbing back to his feet. The pain wasn't *that* bad, if he just kept all the weight off of it. "You want a Knight..." he growled, pulling open the door...

And stopping dead when he found Zach standing at the bathroom sink right across the hallway, frowning straight at him, as if he'd been listening through the door while he patted his hands dry.

"Just talking to Copernicus," Nate lied quickly.

Copernicus trotted out of the room, corroborating with a little yip, and the two of them scooted off—or at least *hobbled* off—before Zach could so much as blink, heading down the hallway to go meet their not-so-mysterious visitor.

CHAPTER 15

HOW TO SAVE THE WORLD

Nate ducked left through the kitchen, masking his limp and hoping to reach the back door without drawing the attention of Marty and Kyle, who were hooting and hollering at their respective TVs in the living room ahead. They saw him the moment he poked his head into the dining area anyway.

"Yo, Nate!" Kyle called from his favorite back-of-the-couch perch. "Come play with us, man. Marty's getting too drunk to pull his weight."

"This is still my first beer," Marty said.

"Ooo…" Kyle scrunched his face up apologetically. "Bad news then, buddy."

"You're an A-hole," Marty said. "I had more kills than either of you last round, *and* I rezzed both of your sorry—"

Nate didn't bother interrupting to promise *just a minute* or make some excuse about taking Copernicus out to use the little doggy's room. He just quietly opened the back door and slipped out onto the porch while the two of them continued bickering about kills and revives and who had shot whom, and who had done it better and with more pizazz.

Outside, the night air was pleasantly chilly after an unintentionally long afternoon spent cooped up, stagnating in his own despair. It was darker than dark, this far away from the heart of town—the yard lit by only what light trickled out from the kitchen window. All was calm and quiet, relatively speaking, the thumping heart of a State College Saturday night only a faint hum in the distance.

"It never ceases to amaze me," came the Merlin's quiet voice from the shadows. "The further mankind removes itself from actually *living* the warrior's life, the more infatuated it grows with chasing the thing through video games and glorified pop culture media. What a farce it all is."

"Video games?" Nate asked quietly, stepping off the porch and treading carefully toward the wizard's voice in the darkness.

"Humanity. Sentience. All of it."

So it was going to be one of *those* talks, huh? Wonderful.

The Merlin possesses countless lifetimes of wisdom, Nathaniel. You would be wise to listen.

"Of course *you'd* say that," Nate muttered, though he also *did* have to admit he had about nine-thousand questions for the wizard.

"Am I to take it you are becoming properly acquainted with your new companion?" came the Merlin's voice from the thicket of trees ahead. There was barely enough light coming from the kitchen window to make out the wizard's outline.

"Yeah, he's a real hoot," Nate said. "So much so that I can't help thinking you might've warned me what the hell I was getting into before you threw me into that portal. You had my number, apparently. Would it have killed you to send a text?"

You embarrass us both with your sniveling, Nathaniel.

But Nate couldn't have cared less who he was embarrassing. It was his neck—or ankle, as it were—that'd been thrown under the treads today. His future that'd been blown sky high. His life that'd apparently been hijacked to a cause he still didn't even understand.

"Would you have responded to a casual message from the drunk hobo asking you to come have a chat in the park?" the Merlin asked.

"Hell no, I wouldn't have," Nate growled, "which is exactly my point. You forced me into this."

"Forced you? Did I not adequately illustrate my point on the freedom of choice earlier?"

"Giving me the option between keeping my life and watching an innocent girl die doesn't really count, in my book."

"Then perhaps this book of yours could use some refreshment on the meaning of the words."

Nate felt his fists clenching in the darkness. He wanted to hit something. Or someone. Which wasn't something Nate found himself often thinking, but hey, that was what these two wanted, wasn't it? Some kind of alpha warrior badass? A guy who punched first and asked questions later? For a second, he was tempted to test the theory.

You would be a fool to try.

"Fine," Nate said, trying to calm himself. "You wanna talk about choices? I *choose* to not be a part of this. And if that's not good enough for you, you should talk to Mr. Excalibur. He says it's a no-go, too, so you might as well just take him back and try again. Find one of those big strong warriors you mentioned earlier. I recommend you try the Navy SEALS instead of a goddamn college town next time."

For a few silent seconds, Nate thought the Merlin was actually considering his words. But then the wizard shambled a few steps forward from the trees, tipping the remainder of his clay cup's contents into his mouth, then shaking his dirty mane as if to sober up.

"You were chosen, Nathaniel Arturi," he said, drawing close enough that Nate could just make out the glint of his dark eyes in the reflected kitchen light. "And so you will remain chosen until such a time as you are not."

"Then un-choose me!"

"That is not how it works. Not if you wish to continue drawing breath, at least."

As you would know if you had been listening earlier.

Nate tensed and untensed his jaw, wanting to argue but not really seeing the point. "For the record," he finally said, "you suck at giving fair choices."

"There is no such thing as an unfair choice, Nathaniel. Only the unfair circumstances surrounding it. It was time for a Knight to be chosen, and you willingly charged through that portal. Here we are."

"This isn't right."

The Merlin gave an amused huff at that. "Hmm. Rightness. Well, luckily rightness is not why I am here."

"And why are you here?" Nate asked, glancing back at the kitchen window, all too aware that his roommates were only a stone's throw away. "You come to explain to me what the hell it is you dragged me into here?"

"Sadly, no," the Merlin said, and as abrupt as the denial was, he actually *did* sound a touch disappointed about it. "It seems your Excalibur will have to do the honors, there. I only came here to let you know that I must leave for a short while."

"Leave?" Nate was surprised by the depth of the panic the news woke in him. "You can't just *leave* me here with this thing!"

Funny, I might have said the same thing, were I an insolent little sniveler.

"Oh bite me," Nate growled at the darkness. Then, to Merlin, he added, "Aren't you supposed to… I don't know, train me, or something?"

"Stop complaining."

Nate rocked back on his heels, and was rewarded with a flash of pain from his bruised ankle. "What?!" he hissed through a wince.

"That's lesson number one," the Merlin said, almost cheerfully. "Stop complaining, and accept who and what you are."

"Well thanks for that, Shitty Yoda."

Insolent cur!

"Any chance I can get lessons two and three before you skip town?" Nate pressed on, too aggravated to care if he was being an insolent cur, or a sniveling one, or any other variation thereof. "You know, if you're not too busy, that is."

"Oh, lessons two and three are quite simple," the Merlin said, apparently indifferent to Nate's temper. "Prepare your body. And prepare your mind. The Excalibur can enhance both beyond your wildest dreams, but the effects will always be proportional to whatever raw materials you bring to the table, so to speak."

Nate paused, mouth half-open. He hadn't really been expecting a real answer, and now that he'd gotten one, it only opened the door to about three-thousand more questions—how the Excalibur had managed to protect him from a ton of rolling destruction, for starters, right along with how it had given him the strength to steel-arm a speeding bike, and then blunted his panic attack like a mad pharmacologist.

"Perhaps you should ask your new life partner," the Merlin said, holding up his hands to prevent the outpouring of questions. "And most of all," he added, before Nate could point out that his *new life partner* was an argumentative brick wall, "do *try* to remember that this is not about you, Nathaniel Arturi, no matter how much you might feel that your life has been unfairly affected."

"*Affected?*" Nate hissed. "That's real easy for you guys to say when—"

The Merlin swept forward so suddenly and fluidly that Nate barely had time to tense before the wizard's hand clamped to the side of his head.

"What the hell are you—"

Dark night flashed inexplicably to gloomy day around them. Thunder cracked in the distance, and suddenly Nate was staring down at a broken, burning cityscape, hollow dread ringing in his chest. Distantly, he was still aware of the Merlin's hand on the side of his head, but that hand somehow didn't obstruct his view, almost as if he were seeing through eyes that weren't his own.

And what he was seeing was chaos.

Gunfire and explosions in the streets. Broken glass raining from the skyscrapers, raining on fleeing pedestrians, refracting the flaring scarlet pulses of some kind of energy weapons. Dozens of stout, jagged ships that almost looked like hovering rock crags filled the sky, raining death from above.

For a second, Nate thought they'd flash-stepped to another world, like the Lady had done with him, but then he registered how familiar the crumbling buildings looked, and the cars and trucks burning in the streets, and on the highway overpasses, and—

"Jesus Christ," Nate whispered, finally registering the distant hulking forms among the chaos for what they were.

Troglodans.

They were flooding the streets of what looked like New York, tearing through everything they met—buildings and vehicles and humans alike. Nate watched in horror as military jets screamed in on an attack run and promptly blossomed into neat little fireballs, plummeting to the streets below, where what remained of the human ground forces were meeting similarly violent ends.

"This is but one version of what may come to pass should you fail to find the Beacon before they do," came the Merlin's bodiless voice.

As I tried to tell you earlier.

"What are you talking about?" Nate asked numbly at both of them, his mind already at max capacity with the sheer volume of destruction below. "What Beacon?"

The scene faded from view, and Nate found himself suddenly standing in the dark backyard at State College again, wobbling on unsteady legs as the Merlin released him and stepped back.

"The Beacon is what draws this conflict to Earth. It is the reason the Lady decreed a new Knight need be awakened in the first place. Every Beacon needs a Knight, you see..."

Nate *didn't* see—not even a little bit. He was still too busy trying to *unsee* the hellish nightmare the Merlin had just beamed into his brain. But the wizard wasn't done yet.

"The Beacon is... how do I put this? It is one of the most powerful objects in the known galaxy. And unless you wish to see that vision come to pass, you're going to need to help me find it and get it safely off planet as quickly as possible."

"I don't..." Nate shook his head, trying and failing to wrap his head around any of this. "I don't understand. If this Beacon thing is so... so important, and if it's already here, why can't you just go grab it right now?"

"It is... lost to me, for reasons I cannot explain."

"Can't, or won't?"

The Merlin was silent for a long stretch. "It is lost to me," he finally repeated, as if that was simply that.

"But... Well, what about the Lady? She can step across the galaxy like she's stepping out to get the mail, right? Why can't she come find this thing?"

"The answer to that question is... even more complicated. Suffice it to say, the Lady is equally bound from taking an active role in this matter, for reasons—"

"You can't explain?"

"For reasons that are not yet my place to explain," the Merlin corrected.

"Maybe you should try anyway."

"It is far more critical that *you* do, Nathaniel. You and your Excalibur are innately attuned to the call of the Beacon. Far more attuned than I could ever be. Or you will be, at least, once you have adequately completed your bonding and learned to work together."

We can find this Beacon, Nathaniel.

That caught him off balance. "We can?"

Yes. If you'd stop your sniveling long enough to listen to what the Merlin is telling you.

"And what exactly is he telling me?" Nate cried, throwing his hands up in frustration before remembering his roommates might hear, and dropping it back down to a hiss. "The call of the Beacon? Completing our *bonding*? It's all just riddles and insults with both of you assholes!"

Says the one who spent seven hours attempting to understand the alien technology in his head without once thinking to simply ask.

"I..." Nate faltered. "I *did* ask. Back on Allen Street."

And so I answered, did I not?

"Barely," Nate grumbled. It wasn't like the Excalibur had exactly been forthcoming. Not with anything but insults, at least. Could the thing really blame him for being skeptical when it had done nothing but berate him for his petulant worthlessness since they'd "met" that morning?

"Right," the Melin spoke up, tucking his clay cup into the inner folds of his shoddy robe. "I think I'll leave the two of you to it, then."

"Seriously? What, because you're so busy running off for... for what? A Saturday night bender? Where the hell are you off to that's suddenly so important anyway?"

"I'm off to do something I should have had the courage to do a long time ago," the Merlin said. He sounded desperately tired. "Something I hope will spare a good many people a great deal of pointless loss."

The gravity in the old wizard's tone stilled some of the frustration churning Nate's gut. "Something more important than finding this Beacon?"

"Something I am better equipped for, at least. If all goes well, the two will not be mutually exclusive." The Merlin shook himself free of whatever thought he was having. "For now, you must focus on learning your Excalibur and finding the Beacon in time. Get it off of this planet, Nathaniel, and quickly, or the troglodan invasion will soon be the least of Earth's troubles."

Nate was opening his mouth to ask what the hell that was supposed to mean when the Merlin cocked his head as if he'd heard something. The wizard leaned in close before Nate could speak, clutching his hand and whispering in a quick, hushed tone.

"Prepare yourself for battle, Nathaniel Arturi, and do not give in to despair. All of humanity may well be counting on you. I will return as soon as I can."

The jiggle and wooden squeak of the back door opening cut through the night before Nate could answer. He whirled to find Kyle's rotund silhouette in the doorway, with Marty craning over his shoulder.

"Yo, Batman, you want a light out here?" Kyle called.

The yard lights flashed on before he could say *no*, incandescent illumination spilling across the damp grass in time with the panic spiking through his chest.

"Nate?" Marty called somewhere far away, as Nate whipped around to hiss at the Merlin to take cover. "You get lost, man?"

Nate was too busy gaping at the empty space before him, the words stuck in his throat.

The Merlin was gone. Again.

"Were you talking to someone out here?" came Marty's confused voice.

"*Talking?*" Kyle said. "He looks like he just got caught consorting with demons."

Confused, mildly relieved, and more than a little frazzled, Nate turned back to his friends. "You guys just caught me by surprise, okay? It's just me and Copernicus out here."

Just a man, his corgi, and his Excalibur, apparently arrayed against the entire Troglodan armada—and worse—in The Quest for the Holy Beacon.

Ahh, and what a glorious quest it could be.

"*Could* being the operative word?" Nate muttered quietly enough not to be heard by the others.

That depends...

On whether he could get his shit together and stop sniveling?

Precisely.

This was starting to get weird.

Do try to refrain from sniveling about it.

"Let's wrap it up, little guy," Kyle called from the porch, where he'd sank to haunches and was reaching out toward Copernicus, his breathing marginally elevated from the effort. "Daddy's gotta come play Battle Royale with his squad like a responsible roommate."

Battle Royale.

The thought almost made Nate laugh out loud. Only ten minutes earlier, he'd been fully intending to call it a night on the crazy and join his friends in the living room, reasoning that he'd tried his best for the day, and that none of this was going to be for anything anyway if he let himself slide off the deep end and lose his mind. But now...

How could he even think about taking a video game break after what the Merlin had just shown him? How could he do anything but dive head-first into... into *what*, exactly? Bonding with the Excalibur? Finding the Beacon?

Saving the entire goddamn planet from death by aliens?

Nate stared numbly at the house, wanting nothing more than to run inside, chug a beer, and sweep all this crazy shit under the rug until he could re-examine it in the light of day.

I believe that is what you humans call cowardice at work.

"You coming, buddy?" Marty called.

Nate realized Copernicus had joined his roommates on the porch, and they were all waiting for him now. Three concerned stares and one wagging tail.

"Go on in," Nate said. "I'll be there in a sec. Can you just get the light?"

Kyle frowned. Marty looked like he might protest. Then Zach called something from the living room, and the three filed back inside, leaving Nate alone in the cool night air. The yard lights flicked off. From the darkness, he watched through the back door window as his friends collected their drinks from the dining table, shared a happy cheers, and shuffled back into the living room to resume their happy lives. Nate stood completely still, feeling adrift in the darkness. Completely alone.

Not completely.

That, at least, caught him by surprise enough to halt the negative spiral. Then Copernicus appeared in the kitchen window, happily panting out into the darkness after having apparently found a way up onto the kitchen counter. He put one little corgi paw against the window, and that did it.

In that moment, Nate very nearly could've cried—for *what*, exactly, he couldn't have said. No more than he could've said what the hell he was going to do about the galaxy-sized mess staring him right back in the face.

What the hell was there to do about any of it?

Prepare yourself for battle, Nathaniel, came the Merlin's voice in Nate's thoughts. *Prepare your body. Prepare your mind.*

Nate stood there in the dark, thinking it over for a long time.

He'd prepare himself, he decided. Starting tomorrow, he'd do whatever it took. He'd start training. He'd learn from the Excalibur—ask it every question he could think to ask. Maybe even play friendly, if he could. But first...

He slid his phone out of his pocket and woke the device, the loose threads of a plan beginning to form in his mind.

First, he needed to make the only sensible call one could make after everything he'd just learned.

CHAPTER 16

THE IRON MAN

With the occasional exception of the odd last-minute group project meeting—and one briefly lived attempt at "getting his shit together" junior year—Nate had rarely had cause to venture to the barren wasteland that was campus on a Sunday morning. To say the place was dead might've been a slight overstatement. Students *were* in evidence here and there. It was just that most of them looked like they'd left their better, thinking halves at home in bed, right where they sincerely wished they still were with them.

Last minute group project meetings, Nate guessed. And probably a few soon-to-be failed attempts at getting respective shits together. College life at its finest.

He trudged past the curved overpass bridge of the IT building, glancing across to the bioengineering building—wondering, as he so often did, where Gwen was and what she was doing—and reflecting that he probably wasn't in any position to be judging anyone alive at this hour as he continued on toward Rec Hall, bound for his first official workout in… well, pretty much *ever*, as his dear mom had been quick to point out when he'd called her on the issue of funding his broke ass for this apparently highly questionable extracurricular.

Of the two monumentally awkward calls he'd made last night, he still couldn't decide which had been the more embarrassing.

"Did you say a *gym* membership, sweetie?" his mom had asked on the phone in clear bafflement, reaffirming Nate's every doubt and hesitation about his audacious new plan.

The Excalibur had practically cackled with derisive delight.

But at least she'd eventually agreed to foot the bill—*after*, of course, running Nate through the entire treacherous track of the Mom Gauntlet.

Is this about a girl, honey? Because you don't need to change a thing to impress anyone. You're perfect just the way you are.

Oh, well is it bullies, then? It's okay to turn to a teacher for help, Nathan. I don't care if the cool kids call you a narc rat, or whatever it is.

Oh, well... are you sure *it's not about a girl, then?*

He was half-surprised the Excalibur hadn't blown a fuse or pulled a sword muscle or something as Nate had calmly reminded her that he wasn't in high school anymore, thank you very much, and that he really just wanted to start taking better care of himself.

And sure, he wasn't positive that *preparing for battle* actually rightly belonged in the *taking care of himself* column, no matter how much exercise was involved, but at least it had sounded good. A hell of a lot better than anything he'd managed to crap out in the call that had preceded it.

In hindsight, he still wasn't sure what he'd been thinking, calling the National Security hotline to report a goddamn alien invasion.

Not that he'd been so careless as to come right out with it. He'd tried to play it carefully, tried to get patched through to someone up the chain of military intelligence—someone who might actually be a position to *do* something about the imminent invasion.

Instead, he'd gotten Roger, loyal DHA call center operator. Roger who, bless his heart, had at least pretended to take everything Nate was saying seriously, right up until he'd realized that the *aliens* Nate had started talking about a few sentences back were not in fact of the *undocumented immigrant* variety. It had all gone downhill from there. For the first time in his life, Nate had actually resorted to the old *I need to speak to your supervisor* chestnut—which, it turned out, didn't actually work for matters of national security.

Nate had been written off as "one of those Area 51 nuts," briefly scolded for clogging up their precious call lines, and promptly hung up on. He'd sat there fuming for a good fifteen minutes after that, trying and failing to come up with a more useful plan than writing them a strongly-worded letter suggesting that they amend their hotline slogan accordingly: Your calls *can* make a difference. (Unless it's about aliens. Yes, the outer space kind.)

Shame on him for trying to do the responsible thing.

Stymied by the powers that be, Nate had done the next best thing he could think of, and called his mom. And so it was that he found himself standing at the Rec Hall gym sign-in desk at 8:58 AM sharp, shifting uneasily beneath the moody judgment of the Excalibur, and the equally flat and unamused stare of the curly-haired desk attendant. Because if Uncle Sam wasn't going to step in, at least he could pump some iron in the delusional hope that he might turn into some kind of magical King Arthur superhero, right?

Stop it. He was almost surprised to realize the voice in his head was his own, and not the Excalibur's. *You're here. You're doing this.*

Worst case scenario, he wasted a few hours and ended up a slightly less pathetic version of himself. Maybe. Even that much was kind of hard to imagine under the stare of Judgy McJudgerson behind the desk, there.

"Sorry, are you guys, uh, open already, or...?" He glanced off in the direction of the sounds of whirring machines and clanking plates within, wondering if he'd read the schedule incorrectly online.

"They're regulars," she said, as if that fact were self-evident. "Sometimes they slip in a few minutes early."

"Right..."

Nate had been surprised to see the facility didn't officially open till 9 AM on Sundays, having always figured gym-goers were the sorts to get started early, even on the weekends. Apparently even fit-fam college kids needed their hangover sleep.

It wasn't like anyone was training to save the world or anything.

"Well, uhh..." Nate said, holding his freshly charged ID card up. "Any chance I can slip in now?"

She rolled her eyes and gestured toward the card reader with a demeanor that suggested Nate's audacity was causing her significant personal detriment. He swiped the card, aware that a few burly early birds had just piled through the door behind him, and eager to be on his way.

The card reader gave an indignant squawk that was quickly taken up as an indignant stare from the desk girl. So maybe the gym charge hadn't gone through to his ID, after all.

Wonderful.

This is degrading.

"How do you think I feel?" Nate whispered under his breath.

Behind the desk, the girl turned from whatever she was doing on her computer to shoot him a shameless *crazy guy* look.

I meant for you. I do not care what these petty meat sacks think.

The desk girl gestured to the card reader again. All too aware of the growing line behind him, Nate swiped with a small prayer. The light flicked green, and he hurried past the desk with a muttered thanks.

"Well, that's good for you, buddy," Nate said quietly, glancing back to eye the stream of the Penn State Beautiful-Jacked-People Club sweeping in through the open doors now. "Because I have a feeling we're about to be rolling in the degradation."

Maybe coming first thing in the morning had been a mistake.

He'd hoped he might beat the crowd and get a chance to start figuring out what the hell he was doing in here without a few hundred eyeballs waiting to see him fail. But now here he was crashing the party with the A-Team, and he was pretty sure the odd looks he was drawing couldn't have *all* just been in his head.

Maybe it was just the shiny black eye he was sporting. But he was still half tempted to come back later anyway, as he watched the new arrivals disperse amongst the free weights and the rows of pristine machines with an air of familiar routine, pausing only to say hi here, or shoot Nate a disapproving look there. Even if it *was* busy later, at least Nate could blend in with all the other sorry-ass weekend warriors fumbling their way through their workouts in their half-hearted attempts to work off the beer and pizza.

If you are intimidated by these children, Nathaniel, you might as well go home now, and not come back.

Nate started to open his mouth, then decided that, seeing as the Excalibur seemed to have no trouble reading his thoughts, he should probably nip the whole talking to himself in public thing in the bud. *Well, THAT guy looks like he could bench press a car,* he thought carefully, *so forgive me if I'm feeling a little shy.*

A single unarmed troglodan could easily slay ten such men.

What little victory he felt at the success of the silent communication was quickly buried by the unbidden memories of the troglodan's ferocity in the park. *Is that supposed to be encouraging?*

I simply preferred the time when your ancestors grew stronger by crushing the skulls of their enemies rather than playing with shiny hunks of steel.

"Yeah..." Nate muttered, eyeing one of the empty squat racks at the far end of the row, and mentally running through the basics of what he'd read online. *Well, I'm fresh out of enemy skulls to crush, so I guess this'll have to do for now.*

The Excalibur didn't see fit to reply as Nate crossed the escalating battlefield of the gym, trying not to make eye contact with any of the aggregating bro clans staking claim to their machines and weight stations along the way. From the far corner ahead, where another rack and lifting platform were half-tucked away behind a divider wall, there came a low, clattering thud Nate felt through his leg bones. Then another. And another.

It sounded like the freaking hammer of Thor at work, and as Nate reached his target squat rack and caught a glimpse of the guy doing the lifting, the analogy only felt more appropriate. The guy was wearing a worn PSU sweatshirt, and he looked older from behind. He wasn't a walking mountain of muscle like some of the others in here, but he looked plenty damn strong as he hefted a heavily-loaded barbell up from the floor and stood to his full height, the bar dangling from his hands with so much weight on either side that it was actually bending.

A deadlift, some corner of Nate's mind remembered. That was what the articles had called a deadlift.

A freaking *huge* deadlift.

It must've been over four-hundred pounds on the bar. Nate didn't have time to count the plates and try to figure it out before the sweatshirted thunder god lowered the weight back to the platform with a low thud.

"Holy shit," Nate whispered, focusing back to the rack ahead before the guy could turn around and catch him staring.

That one may be admirable for a human, but such a feat would be nothing for a true Excalibur Knight.

"Well something tells me I'd still better start with just the bar anyway."

The Excalibur said nothing as Nate stepped into the rack and up to the empty barbell, checking its height against his chest, like the articles had said. It said nothing at all, but Nate could feel its silent judgment stewing all around him.

The articles all said to start with just the bar, he thought.

I am well aware, the Excalibur replied. *I read and indexed every one of the articles you are citing in the time it took you to think that.*

Nate wiggled his fingers and scrunched his face in what he hoped was an understandably sarcastic sign for, *Ooo, look at me and how smart I am.* Then he remembered he was in a public space, and he crossed his arms, glancing furtively around to see if anyone had noticed.

Do you know what I noticed? the Excalibur asked.

No, but I'm sure you're about to tell—

THESE ARTICLES WERE NOT WRITTEN FOR AN EXCALIBUR KNIGHT.

"—Me," Nate finished aloud, dipping down to check his shoelaces in a wasted effort to hide his flinch.

They are written BY sad meat sacks, FOR sad meat sacks. Are YOU a sad meat sack, Nathaniel?

"I think we both know your answer to that question," Nate muttered, standing back up. He gripped the bar and stepped underneath, resting it across his back like he'd seen in the videos. *Now can you keep it down in there? I'm trying to focus.*

Yes, we wouldn't want you to hurt yourself.

One of the Beautiful Jacked People walked past Nate's rack, frowning at Nate like he was a crazy person. Which, given what he'd just been saying out loud, was fair enough. As if to add insult to the Excalibur's injury, the Bro eyed Nate's empty bar and relaxed, moving on like Nate was simply too scrawny to reach the threshold where *crazy* actually became *concerning.*

Nate ignored them both and unracked the bar, standing straight and taking a few steps back with it nestled across the less-than-substantial meat of his shoulders. It felt uncomfortable. Not heavy, necessarily. Just foreign. And as he gathered his thoughts and tried to descend into his first ever squat, the discomfort only multiplied.

Things wobbled. Others stretched. Others found themselves in positions they couldn't remember having ever been in before, and didn't seem to believe they had any business being in now. Nate tried to keep straight all the mental cues he'd read about.

Hips back.

Chest up.

Knees out. *Out where?*

Grip the ground with your toes.

He nearly fell over at that one. But then he caught his balance and rose, feeling at least marginally in control. He tried another squat. And another. Each one feeling weird and wrong—but slightly less weird and wrong than its predecessor.

How fortunate that I took the time to heal your ankle for this.

I'm trying here, Nate thought, completing his fifth squat and carefully stepping the bar back onto the rack hooks. He looked down at his ankle, wondering at the Excalibur's words. His ankle *was* surprisingly pain free at the moment. Underneath the sweats, he knew he was still rocking some pretty gnarly bruises, but—

Are you? Check again, little hobbit.

Frowning, Nate bent down and slid his right pant leg up a few inches.

The bruises were gone. And come to think of it…

He pulled up the front camera on his phone, and watched his own dark eyes widen as he realized his Todd-induced black eye had magically cleared up sometime in the past hour, since he'd sat there downing his cereal and wondering at the wisdom of trying to come work out on an injured leg. But now there was nothing there but pale white skin above, and thin, wispy leg hair below. It was…

Impossible? You have no idea what we could accomplish together were you to relinquish your hold on such thoughts and rise to the challenge.

"Fine," Nate said, studying the array of plates suspended on either side of the rack. "You want me to rise to the challenge?"

He moved to the outside of the rack, his gaze drifting to the 25 pound plates. But he knew what the Excalibur would have to say about that: *Are YOU a sad meat sack, Nathaniel Arturi?*

Are you? the Excalibur asked.

Nate wasn't sure what he was, aside from maybe a scrawny little hobbit with delusions of grandeur and a magic sword in his head. But he reached for the big 45 pound plates anyway. He loaded one on each side of the bar, the weight feeling a little too much like that of ego and bad decisions in his hands.

Better.

Nate tried it again and was surprised to find that he didn't die. Not that it felt great. The bar dug into his back with an outrageously uncomfortable vengeance, and he almost lost his balance on the first three repetitions. But he didn't. And by the time he settled the bar back into the rack, he actually felt kind of good.

You can do more.

Seriously? Nate glanced at the plates on his bar. *This is already triple what the plan was.*

And the troglodans will be here a thousand times sooner than your sniveling carcass will be ready for them. Perhaps you should consider these words of eternal human wisdom, which I just located on the internet: If the bar ain't bending, you're just pretending.

Don't tell me, Nate thought, rolling his eyes. *That was Jesus, right?*

Just load the barbell, Nathaniel.

Nate sighed. *I thought the plan was to find the Beacon before all hell broke loose on Earth, anyway.*

Which will only happen if you actually manage to bond with me quickly enough to do so.

Kindly refer to the aforementioned 'I'm trying,' Nate thought, with all the mental acid he could muster. *Unless you wanna actually tell me something useful about how this bonding process works, outside of me needing to be less pathetic.*

Was it his imagination, or could he feel the Excalibur searching for the right words?

Curious.

What's curious? Nate wondered.

Never mind that. You have observed this movie titled, 'Thor,' correct?

Nate arched an eyebrow at the air, not really sure where this was going. *Yeah... why?*

I believe this bit of pop culture provides a relevant analogy. Whosoever holds this hammer, if he be worthy, shall possess the power of Thor, and so forth... Do you understand?

I don't know... Nate frowned. *But what do you mean, you BELIEVE it's relevant? You don't know?*

Was that frustration radiating from the Excalibur?

You are holding the hammer, Nathaniel. Try not to snivel about it.

Nate realized he'd been absentmindedly staring toward the girl squatting two racks down from him, and she was starting to notice. He turned his frown safely back to the weights, thinking about the Excalibur's metaphors. First the Gandalf quote, and now this comparison to Thor and his Mjölnir, yet for both analogies, he couldn't help but think there was some critical disconnect, and that the sword-that-wasn't-a-sword seemed to have missed the entire point of both legends.

Perhaps it is you who missed the point, Nathaniel, the Excalibur shot back, and this time there was no mistaking the frustration. *I am merely attempting to establish a common ground upon which we might build this shoddy farce of an alliance.*

I understand, Nate thought back quickly, meaning it even if he was a little unclear as to exactly which part of this was frustrating his companion. Maybe that didn't matter so much though.

I... Even thinking the words was difficult. *Thank you, Excalibur. I appreciate the effort. But... what about the Lady's test? The sword in the stone? Why wasn't that part enough?*

The Excalibur rippled with something like amusement, or maybe reverence. *Why, indeed. Though I am fairly certain the fact that you even think to ask that question is, in itself, part of the answer. Now, are you going to prove your worth, or aren't you?*

Nate pursed his lips, kind of wishing he could take that *thank you* back. As if to highlight his daily shortcomings thus far, the real thunder god in the corner chose that moment to start up with another set of floor-shaking deadlifts.

This is bullshit, for the record, Nate thought, as he stepped over to slide more weights free from the rack. Total Todd-level, Alpha-dog bullshit. But there was nothing for it. It might be stupid, and unsafe, and a thousand other things. But as vague as the Merlin's directions had been, the Excalibur probably had a point. If there *was* any version of reality where he was actually ready when this alleged armada arrived, it probably didn't involve moderation and holding back.

Not that that softened his embarrassment as he clumsily added a pair of 35 pound plates to the bar and felt the dubious stares multiplying around him.

There. That's... He counted. *That's 205 pounds. That's more than I weigh. Are you happy with that?*

That is a semantically confusing question. But I am satisfied, yes. For the moment.

Nate took his place under the bar, noticing a few more guys frowning his way while they pretended to be busy with their phones. Like freaking sharks sensing blood in the water, just waiting for him to bite it.

Perhaps we should move this endeavor to the ship next time, if you are going to be this sensitive.

Nate paused under the bar. *The ship? There's a... a ship? Like a...?*

A spacefaring vessel, yes, Nathaniel. Of course there is a ship. Did you expect a Knight would traverse the cosmos via intragalactic pedicab?

Nate wasn't sure what he'd expected. Hadn't really thought that far ahead, if he was being honest, mostly for the simple fact that he still had no idea what the hell an Excalibur Knight actually *did*. His head was already on the verge of exploding from his single earthbound objective as it was.

Continue your exercise. We will discuss the ship once I've... found it.

Nate might've insisted on a few hundred more questions then—what the hell the Excalibur meant, once he *found* it, for instance—but the sight of the Shark People still watching him brought him back to the gym, where he was still awkwardly standing in position beneath the barbell.

It said something about his mental state that his brain seemed content to simply file this bombshell away for the moment. Nothing but a few voyeurs and a rogue spaceship to worry about? Not like he hadn't seen weirder. Might as well squat two-hundred pounds. Screw it.

That's the spirit.

This time, taking the weight on his back felt less like a localized discomfort and more like a full body trampled-by-troglodans experience. By the time he managed to walk the bar out from the rack hooks, his body was shaking with the effort of even stabilizing the weight. There was no way, his indignant brain informed him. No freaking way. No—

Squat, little hobbit.

Nate tried to take a breath—it was like sucking against vacuum through a straw—and unlocked his knees. *Hips back.* Body trembling. *Chest up.* Full on shaking now. Body whipping like the freaking Tacoma Narrows Bridge, moments before collapse.

In a panic, Nate tried to reverse direction, only to find that he couldn't. His hips were locked in place. He strained with everything he had. Stuck. Hips beginning to sink. Strength bleeding away.

Are you a sad meat sack, Nathaniel Arturi? Or are you a Knight?

A flicker of fire in his heart. Nate clenched his teeth, head on the verge of exploding, and *heaved*. He wasn't sure where the strength came from, only that he needed to live long enough to tell the Excalibur to kiss his ass. But the bar was moving. Inch by trembling inch, it was moving.

He was freaking doing it.

Then something smacked into the side of the squat rack, and Todd Mackleroy's sneering face appeared out of nowhere a mere foot in front of him. "Yo, Arturi! What the shit is up with—Oh damn, bro! Looks like you're about to blow a—"

Nate didn't hear whatever else Todd said. His magical drive had stalled. His balance was off kilter. Something gave way, and before he could even say what, everything was collapsing in a rapid fire explosion of jarring impacts and loud crashes.

When it was over, Nate's tail bone was aching, his legs and back burning, and he was looking up at Todd's gleeful face from a crumpled heap at the bottom of the squat rack.

"Oh my god," Todd said loudly, touching his hands to the sides of his head in dramatized concern. "Are you okay, bro?"

Nate looked blearily around and realized half the gym seemed to be watching—alerted, no doubt, by the crashing weights. Half of them had their damned phones out.

Not again.

"Maybe the IT Guy got confused," said one of Todd's pack members. "Maybe he hit his head too hard in that fall yesterday." He stepped away from the other three followers to point through the windows of the gym's front wall, over toward the IT Bridge. "Your building's over there, little guy."

Head still spinning, Nate tried to get an arm under himself to sit up, and felt hard resistance behind his shoulder blades. The bar. He'd fallen on the bar. Better than *under* the bar, some dazed part of his brain pointed out. The rest was busy just trying to focus on those three words: that fall yesterday.

The accident. How did they know about the accident? Unless—

Nathaniel, I have located five skulls ripe for the crushing.

"You've gotta be kidding me," Nate murmured.

"What'd he say?" growled Henchman Number One, puffing his chest in the universal sign for *come at me, bro.* Todd, like a good bro pack leader, held his man back with a hand to the chest, watching Nate with a suspicious look all the while.

Kick their rectums!

The Excalibur was so giddy with excitement that, for a split second, some crazy part of Nate even wanted to listen to the damn thing—delusions of badass grandeur dancing in his head. Then Todd stepped forward and shoved his phone in Nate's face, and Nate could only stare in astonishment as a tiny version of himself leapt across the screen, plowed into Emily Atherton, hit the pavement rolling, and came up to stiff arm a speeding black bike to a dead halt, moving entirely quicker than Nate had ever moved in his life.

He winced as the rear tire kicked up, and the hoodied biker went flying.

"What the hell gives, Arturi?" Todd asked, watching him closely as Video Nate pulled Emily Atherton to her feet and held her for a few breathless moments, only to turn and run off when the videographers started closing in.

Nate could only gape at Todd as he paused the video and leaned closer.

"What are you hiding?" he asked in a quiet voice, looking more serious than Nate had ever seen. His expression only darkened as he glanced at Nate's left eye socket, probably noting the lack of the bruising that'd been evident even in the shaky video.

"Look at him, bro," one of the I.N.N. henchmen broke in, waving at the mess of Nate's spilled weights as if to point out how pathetic he was. "I *told* you it was just a bout of retard strength."

"Dude!" another chided, shaking his head and smacking his fellow bro's shoulder as if to tell him off. "It's the pills, bro. Those computer jockeys eat 'em like candy."

Nate couldn't find words. Couldn't even seem to find thoughts. Todd was still staring at him. Nate didn't understand what he wanted—why he was doing this at all. How he'd even found out.

Or why he looked so deadly angry behind that stare.

It was only when Nate heard someone in the next row over hissing something about bath salts and pointing emphatically to their phone that his brain caught up, and he properly realized what was happening. Rattled as he'd been by the Merlin's visit, and Roger the loyal DHA lackey, and pretty much everything else under the freaking sun, he'd forgotten to scour the web this morning.

And that shit had snuck right in and bit him in the ass.

"—see that bike, though?" one of their nearby spectators asked his friend, tapping his phone.

"—shit was badass," came another voice.

He hadn't imagined the strange looks, he realized.

"—ust be some kind of freak—"

"—sure that's him?"

"—obviously just CGI, dude—"

CGI. For a second, Nate's brain latched onto that pearl, thinking to corroborate it. Just special effects. That was it. Just a nerd trying to get attention. It might even work, he thought—right up until he took another look around and saw that half of the gym had given themselves permission to openly stare, phones at the ready.

Even Todd was looking around like he was just then realizing this might not have been the smartest place to make a scene.

He had to get out of here.

You're doing it, again. Calm yourself.

But Nate was already rocking to his feet, too mortified by what was happening to even think twice about his potential injuries, or the fact that he practically slammed Todd off his feet and into the rack as he skirted by.

Apparently Todd hadn't been ready either.

The bronze god and his gang of dudebros flared up like an Italian deli at the insult, but Nate was already hurrying off, crashed weights forgotten, every single goddamn eye in the place riveted to the unfolding of Freak Show #2.

"Nate?" someone called, but he didn't look back—couldn't look back.

Had to get away from all these phones. Had to resist the urge to run. Couldn't run. Not again. Not—

You are overreacting, Nathaniel.

The Excalibur's voice only added urgency to his already bouncing walk-run. He only barely managed to avoid hissing *shut up* out loud.

For a second, he wondered if the Excalibur was right, and if maybe he should just smile and shrug it off, and chock it all up to hand wavy excuses about adrenaline rushes and soccer moms lifting mini vans to save their kids. But then he saw the way two girls at the water fountain were recoiling from his path, and the way the curly-haired desk attendant was talking quickly into the phone up ahead, eyes fixed straight on him, and any thought of shrugging it all off fled with the remainder of his self-control.

He needed to get out of here.

He passed the front desk at a jog, hurrying through the atrium doors, sweating in a way that had little to do with physical exertion. He plowed through the outer doors, felt cool autumn air pour into his lungs. Hard asphalt beneath his feet. Todd Mackleroy's deadly serious face stuck in his mind's eye ahead, and gods knew how many chattering Penn Staters behind. He'd forgotten his water bottle back by the squat rack, some distant corner of his mind noted.

He threw up his hood and ran.

CHAPTER 17

S.A.S

The black SUV didn't belong on Irvin Street.

That was the first factoid Nate's tingling Spidey Senses announced as he drew up beside the bushes outside the house and noted the dark vehicle parked curbside a few houses down. The second factoid, peering up at the paneled living room windows, was that he couldn't remotely tell if his roommates were awake in there yet. Hell, he could barely even tell whether he *wanted* them to be.

His lungs burned. If the cross country coaches had had the decency to tell him during his brief stint that all it took to crack the five minute mile was an alien weapon in the head and the end of life as he knew it, Nate would've liked to think he'd have had the wisdom to tell them to go and shove it.

Give me something to work with here, and we'll be cracking four minutes by the end of the week.

Not really the point, Ex, Nate thought, prowling past the bushes to begin the front stoop climb.

Ah. And now we are doing nicknames. Charming.

Nate ignored his companion, taking the world one heavy stoop step at a time. He paused at the door, Spidey Sense paranoia morphing into a malignant serpent, coiling around his insides.

If they were awake… If they'd already seen…

Quick as the frantic run home had been, Nate couldn't count how many passing stares he'd drawn. Of course, of those numerous stares, he had no idea how many might've been staring because they'd already seen that damned video, and how many had simply been born of natural curiosity at the guy running bloody murder down the street.

He was probably being paranoid, he told himself. Even rampantly viral videos didn't spread so fast that half the town would've already seen—much less would've recognized him on the street. He looked back down their quiet stretch of Irvin Ave anyway, just to reassure himself there was no rabid pack of drooling, phone-pointing voyeurs in pursuit.

Nothing but calm street, and the usual amount of parked cars. Somewhere down the block, there was the cough-cough-roar of someone starting up a push mower. Just another quiet Sunday on pre-invasion Earth.

His frown settled on the black SUV that decidedly didn't belong here, with its severely tinted windows and its *up to no good* vibes. He was pretty sure he hadn't seen the vehicle around before, but if that set his Spidey Senses tingling a bit, then that admittedly only landed it in the same bag as pretty much every other stray glance and passing car he'd seen in the past five minutes. He was just being paranoid.

Though there IS an unusual level of mobile data streaming to and from that vehicle.

Nate paused, fingers on the doorknob.

It also appears to have been parked there for nearly an hour, with two occupants still inside.

Nate tried and failed to process that. *Spies?* He tore his eyes from the opaque SUV windows and forced himself to turn the doorknob instead. Paranoia. Just paranoia.

That particular greasy cloud was snuffed from his brain like a light switch at the sight of his automaton hand pushing the door open, and at the sudden sharp terror that its opening swing would reveal Marty, Kyle, and Zach all waiting for him there on the couch, with the inexplicable clip of Nate's YouTube heroics looping on all four TVs.

The house, thankfully, was quiet.

Gods bless his late-rising roommates.

Interesting.

Interesting? Nate frowned, easing the door shut behind him and padding straight for the hallway to his room, minding the squeaky points in the faux wood as best he could.

License plate identification indicates that the vehicle outside belongs to the Department of Defense.

Nate froze.

What?

Through the too-thin walls, he heard Kyle sleep mumbling, bed frame groaning under him as he tossed or turned.

But how...

It couldn't be.

How did you even...

Look up a simple identification registry?

Oh shit.

Here's a metaphor for you, Nathaniel: a child might as well ask an adult how he or she managed to pluck a cookie from the open jar.

Oh shit, oh shit, oh—

"Stop!" Nate hissed, eyes wide. It was only when he heard the muffled scrabbling of Copernicus from the next door down and the sounds of stirring from Marty's room at the end of the hall that he remembered he was supposed to be sneaking.

Whatever you're doing, stop it, right now, he thought desperately, hurrying for the safety of his room. He didn't make it further than opening the door, though, before Copernicus spilled out in a rush of unbounded doggy excitement, pausing only to welcome his magnanimous captor home with a boop of the snoot to the leg before dodging Nate's grabbing hands and racing off down the hallway in a thrice-cursed game of tag.

I am being helpful, the Excalibur insisted. *Unlike that whining bundle of fur.*

Nate started after said bundle of fur, pinching his temples in a vain attempt to stay calm. *Are you or are you* not *currently inside the DoD's secure network?*

A pregnant pause.

I would hardly call it secure, considering.

"You can't just hack the DoD all freaking willy nilly, man!" Nate hissed, throwing his hands wide in exasperation as Copernicus hopped onto the couch, whirling to face him with a doggy grin. "They'll track you! They'll track me! They'll—"

The clack and creaking groan of an opening door spun Nate around like a freaking piñata on the business end of a hungry bully's bat, and there was Marty, standing in the open doorway, just staring at him like, like...

"What's up, dude?" Marty's voice was cautious. "You look like you just found out that the time machine worked."

Nate couldn't think of a damned word to say. Not with the feds outside, probably prepping the tranquilizers and black bags even as his *helpful* Excalibur gallivanted around the freaking DoD network, leaving its grubby fingerprints all over gods knew what, tracing a trail of dark holes and life sentences right back to… to where, exactly?

Did Excaliburs operate through the freaking router?

He almost barked a frantic laugh, his head spinning with the panic.

Ahead, Marty's head was cocked now, his bemused expression losing the playful touch. "You don't… need to know what year it is, do you?"

Nate managed to open his mouth. Kyle's door yanked open before he could do much else.

"The time machine worked?" Kyle's bed-tassled head poked out, looking first to Marty, then to Nate, where he ran a critical eye from baggy hoodie to sweatpants to sneakers. "Dude, were you *working out?*"

"No, I… I mean, yeah, but I—"

There was a knock on the front door.

Three decisive raps, and whatever bullshit he'd been preparing to spout all came buckling in, right along with everything else—vision blurring, room lilting drunkenly around him. Too much. A knock on the door, and they were coming. Whoever the hell *they* were. Coming from their black SUV to take him in. Coming to drag the freak from that internet clip off to some government black site where they could poke and prod and violate the ever-loving shit out of his so-called rights until—

"Nate!"

Nate blinked down at the hard pressure of Marty's fingers on his arm, feeling his weight sinking into the faux wood through his heels even as his head seemed to float inexplicably upward, up into a cloud of gentle hugs and speeding thoughts that, while critically important, felt safely distant. Unthreatening.

"Hey…" he mumbled, the words buzzing pleasantly on his tongue, his jaw too relaxed. "Hey! Cut that out!"

The cloudy distance lessened. Marty let go of his arm, holding his hands up in peace, like he thought Nate had been talking to him.

"Sorry, man," his friend said, glancing at the door. "Do you need to… sit down?"

Nate shook his head, racing thoughts regaining a hint of their edge, but definitely not the entirety of it. "Just, uh… Just a little winded." He looked at Kyle, who was watching with riveted attention. "From the workout."

I told you to stay out of my head, he added silently to the Excalibur.

And I told you *you were being a fool to contact your precious authorities last night*, the Excalibur fired back. *If you want me to stop, I suggest you pull yourself together and make me.*

Another knock at the door.

This time, Nate didn't implode. But he did tense when Marty turned to answer it.

"Wait."

But Marty was already sliding the deadbolt free, turning the doorknob. Nate stared in a stupor as his friend pulled the old wooden door open, distantly noting that this might just be a moment his roommates would be talking about for the rest of their free lives—the time their old pal Nate had been mysteriously abducted by the US government and never seen again, Maker rest his soul.

What a shame he couldn't think of a single goddamn thing to do.

Which was probably why he half-collapsed to the couch with relief when he saw not some dark, faceless spook standing on the stoop, badge and black bag in hand, but only a confused-looking Zach.

Their lanky fourth stepped into the living room, carrying a plastic bag from Wings Over, and a rather nonplussed look on his dark eyebrows. "Who locked the door?"

Marty and Kyle looked expectantly at Nate, who swallowed, caught between the relief that he was not yet arrested and the horror that he might still be found out any second. Had he locked the door without realizing?

"Sorry," he said, heat spreading to his cheeks. "I must've done it by accident."

That earned him a general odd look from everyone, given that none of them had ever seen fit to lock the door since they'd moved in a couple years ago, aside from during summer and long holidays.

"Nate's maybe having a stroke," Kyle explained. "Or a time travel."

"Hmm," Zach said, plopping down beside Nate in his customary position on the couch, and sliding his waiting wings from the bag. "Sounds like you might wanna get that checked out, dude."

❧

STOP PEEKING OUT THERE. You look like a frightened hare.

Nate leaned back from his bedroom window blinds, scowling at the wall. *What the hell else do you expect me to do?*

The SUV was still there, watching, waiting. Looking a thousand times more ominous, now that he was armed with a vague idea of where it might've come from.

For the first time in his life, Nate actually found himself longing for the safe, humdrum hours he should've been spending today, debugging code and studying data compression theory. Instead, the only question in his head as he leaned over to peer out the window again was whether his imminent doom would be coming at the hands of the troglodans or the feds outside.

Are you sure about those plates? And the people still inside? And how the hell do you even know how long it's been parked there?

I do have eyes, Nathaniel.

Nate frowned at the non-answer.

Sensors, then, the Excalibur grumbled. *Forgive me for trying to anthropomorphize.*

That really cleared things up.

For future reference, it might've been handy to know that you could see through car doors and, oh I don't know, hack the freaking DoD at the drop of a hat.

The Excalibur rippled with smug satisfaction. *I did* tell *you my phallus was bigger than yours. My finest metaphor yet, in my humble opinion.*

"Humble," Nate muttered, abandoning the peep show and sinking back down to his bed. "Right." He ran his hands through his hair, trying to think, not getting very far. Had the feds simply come to keep tabs? Or were they just waiting for a chance to grab him?

Would there be another innocent knock on the door?

His thoughts turned to the magical hacker bot in his head, and he wondered if the Excalibur could simply yank the answers straight from their secure servers.

I thought you wanted me to stop.

He did. *I do.*

Nate's phone buzzed in his hand, rubbing at his threadbare nerves.

But if you're already in there...

He glanced at the display and for the first time in his life felt a creep of dread at seeing Gwen's name there. He killed the screen, refusing to even think right then about whether she'd seen his little freak show online—seen him diving to the improbable rescue of Emily Atherton of all people. His head was already too close to exploding.

Don't mind me, by the way. I love unfinished thoughts. It's not as if you're ignoring a real person, *right? I don't even have eyes.*

Deep breath. *We can call your sensors eyes, for Christ's sake. Now can you find out why we've got the freaking feds out front, or not?*

I already told you. They are here in connection to a call flagged last night. Your call. Beyond that, the particulars of the deployment appear to have been intentionally obscured, aside from the designation of the Air Force unit involved.

Nate frowned, completely lost. "You're telling me those guys out there are… Air Force?"

I am merely telling you that the unit connected with this particular deployment order is Air Force. The 501st Space Aggressor Squadron, to be precise.

Space Aggressor Squadron? That was a thing?

"You've gotta be shitting me."

I believe I have located a relevant platitude: be careful what you wish for, Nathaniel. Did you not wish for your government to respond to the alien threat when you called them despite my protests?

Nate looked up at the window, not really sure how to answer that. Not really sure it mattered. Of course he'd wanted them to respond—but to the *troglodans*, not to him and the *other* alien threat that just so happened to be riding shotgun in his head. Still, maybe the Excalibur had a point. Maybe whoever was out there was just here to gather his report, or something.

That is not the point I wish to make here.

Nate was starting to fire back with his own *be careful what you wish for* when a knock at the door cut him short.

~

"WHAT DO YOU MEAN, you're not coming shopping?"

In some ways, Marty's incredulous question was almost a relief—namely for the fact that it didn't yet include an incriminating phone screen waving in Nate's face, or the accompanying slew of uncomfortable follow-ups about what he was hiding. Even so, Nate could tell he was approaching the last straw where avoiding his friend's suspicion was concerned.

Sunday Shopping was Sunday Shopping, after all, end of the world or no.

"He's not coming shopping?" Kyle called from the living room in surprised testament to that fact, over what sounded like Zach's backseat gaming on the lost woods segment of *Ocarina of Time*. Retro Sunday, at its finest. Yet another timeless ritual Nate had ducked out of.

"Are you sure?" Marty asked, looking concerned. "It's brinner tonight, dude. We're gonna get stuff for Han-cakes."

"I just..." Nate looked down at himself, deciding he looked the part plenty well. "I just feel like shit, buddy." He didn't have to lay it on thick to sound convincing. He *did* feel like shit. So much so that he half-considered calling a house meeting and laying it all out then and there, just to get ahead of the inevitable.

One of them was going to see the footage by the end of the day.

He knew it.

Maybe if he brought it up first, tried to explain it away—right along with why he'd been acting so strangely since Friday night. And showing up bloodied and bruised. And avoiding them. And avoiding *Battle Royale*. And going to the *gym*, of all places...

Jesus.

The more he thought about it, the more it all sounded like a problem for Future Nate to handle. Right now, he just needed to avoid landing in a psych ward. Or a dark hole in the corner of the world, courtesy of the freaking 501st Space Aggressor Squadron outside. Unless...

Any chance you could work your big phallus magic and eradicate all traces of yesterday's incident before it's too late?

It was an impossible request, he knew, what with all the wildly divergent paths those troublesome little megabytes had already taken to who knew how many thousand separate—

What will you do in return for such a favor?

That drew him up short. Right in time to notice that Marty was studying him with a concerned look, a puzzled, *Did you hear me?* riding across his slanted brow.

"Hmm?" Nate said, smooth as buttered sandpaper. He needed to stop tuning out like this.

"Is Copernicus staying?" Marty asked, apparently for the second time.

"I don't really know," Nate admitted—maybe to both of them.

Something about his tone must've spoken to Marty's soft spot, at least, because his friend just nodded and crouched down to ask the corgi in friendly doggy tones what kind of kibbles he preferred.

Of course he did. Because that's what Marty *did*. He helped without Nate ever having to ask. All of them did. Which in turn only made Nate wonder all the more why the hell he was trying to avoid this shit with them, of all people. It wasn't like he'd done anything wrong here. And besides, between the four of them, they had more collective nerd knowledge than your average Comic Book Guy. If anyone could help him figure this mess out...

Then it is undoubtedly the pinnacle of alien synthience riding in your head.

Fine. Are you gonna help me, then?

I could.

"You want me to grab you anything?" Marty asked, standing back up from petting Copernicus to face Nate.

Merciful Sith, it was disorienting, trying to keep the dissonant streams of thought straight.

"No, I'll uh…"

Alternatively, the Excalibur broke in, like it owned the place, *you could embrace what you have become, and focus on protecting these sad little meat sacks from the troglodans rather than worrying what they think of you.*

Easier said than done from the bottom of a dark pit in Area 51, Nate shot back.

Marty was still watching him, waiting for an answer he looked like he wasn't sure he was going to get.

"I'll slip out later," Nate finished, "grab something at McClanahan's."

Marty nodded absentmindedly, studying him for another few seconds before finally turning for the living room.

Will you help me out, or not? Nate shot at the Excalibur, grateful and relieved that his friend had finally decided to leave well enough alone.

Except Marty was pausing in the hallway, now, lingering on the edge of saying whatever it was that was on his mind.

Will you commit to taking our quest for the Beacon seriously? the Excalibur shot back.

Nate only barely reined in his hands before they could jerk wide in exasperation. *What do you think I was doing at the freaking gym this morning?*

Marty turned back, opening his mouth.

"Dudes, check it!" Zach cried from the living room, yanking their attention away. "Someone posted a video from the accident yesterday! It's…"

But whatever else he said was lost to the rushing panic churning through Nate's brain. "Please!" he hissed without meaning to, cursing himself when Marty shot a confused look back his way.

You must first promise to—

Anything! I'll do anything! Just stop that video. Please. Crash his phone if you have to.

"What is it?" Marty asked.

Nate stared at his friend, not knowing what to say, knowing only that he probably looked like he was actively having a heart attack.

The Excalibur was silent.

"It's just, uh…" He swallowed. "I dunno, it's just… I guess I don't really wanna relive the moment, you know?"

Lies. What did the lies matter now?

This was it. He was caught. He could hear as much in the faint mutter of Zach's voice out in the living room.

"Dude, what the shit…"

Nate sighed and stepped out to go face the music.

Marty preceded him down the hallway, adopting his finest Mother Hen airs. "Hey, guys? Maybe we shouldn't, you know, glorify the near death experience, and everything."

But it was already too late. Nate could see as much by the way Zach was looking at his phone as they stepped into the living room, brow furrowed, like he just didn't understand what he was seeing.

"Say no more, Mother Goose," Zach said, holding his phone out to show them. "Video's no longer available."

Nate stared at the dark screen and the little red frowny face, trying to process the news, not daring to believe it.

Kyle glanced away from his game long enough to confirm Zach's words. "Bummer and a half, man." Then, remembering himself, he glanced at Marty and Nate and added, "That is, good on them, you know? Probably all kinds of copyright… stuff. Violations of privacy, and exploitation of… you know… whatever." He cleared his throat, returning his focus to *Ocarina of Time* with one last murmur of, "Good on them."

Nate carefully sank into the nearest recliner, trying to hide his shock as his friends launched into a debate about the *whos* and *hows* of why the video might've been stripped. Nate just stared at the pixelated image of Link on the TV, barely seeing anything at all.

You did it.

He couldn't believe it. Couldn't help but immediately question *how* the Excalibur had done it, and how many more dozens of copies and alternate versions might still be floating out there in the digital ether, waiting to strike.

I have scrambled copies of the Atherton Street footage from 7,823 various servers and personal mobile devices since you left that sterile excuse for a training facility.

Wait, you…

Started purging the footage the moment it became evident just how irrationally horrified you are of this particular scenario running its natural course.

For one blessed moment, Nate could've danced or shouted for joy—

probably would have, if doing so wouldn't have made him look even crazier than he already did that day. The moment passed faster than it should've, the blossoming fountain of relief and endless thanks slowing to a trickle as one single question rose to the surface.

But... why?

Why an act of mercy now, out of the blue?

Because you need to understand that I will be your greatest ally, Nathaniel, if only you embrace our mission.

Nate let out a soft breath and leaned into the recliner's embrace, gently nodding to himself, reassured. Understanding.

And because you need to know that I will send that footage and more to everyone you have ever loved and to every central government in the world if you continue to waste our precious time sniveling over your own petty concerns.

Nate froze mid-nod, vaguely aware that Marty was hassling his roommates to pause the games and get ready to roll, too busy watching the curtains fall on the Excalibur's chivalrous charade to care.

Blackmail.

Duty.

Goddamn emotional terrorism.

This planet will be chewed up and used for spare parts if we fail in our mission, and that is to say nothing of the larger galactic consequences. Tell me, Nathaniel, which is the greater evil?

It wasn't fair. Wasn't—

"Nate?" someone asked—Marty, he thought. "You're sure you don't wanna come?"

"I'm good," Nate croaked, the words sounding feeble and hollow as he came back to the living room, where his roommates were all watching him again. "Just, uh... Think maybe I'd better lie down for a bit."

"Sounds like a plan," Zach said, clearly trying to sound supportive.

"Action-packed weekend, dude," Kyle agreed. "You should probably get some rest."

Marty just watched him with that concerned look as the others tugged on their shoes, and Kyle went to grab his wallet from his bedroom.

"Probably just the alien mind control rays, right?" Nate said, trying for a smile.

"Hey, that reminds me," Kyle said, emerging from his room with wallet and, "big story on *They Walk Among Us* this morning, if you're still interested in checking that out."

By the door, Zach and Marty traded one of those *oh boy, here he goes again* looks.

"Really?" Nate asked weakly, not sure he could handle any more surprises right then.

"Yeah, man. Whatever's been going on these past few weeks seems to have kicked into overdrive this weekend. Sometime yesterday, they're guesstimating. Reports are going through the roof. Animals acting funny. Bird migrations getting all jacked up. Even some weird navigational failures yesterday in the transatlantic regions."

"That *is* interesting," Nate heard himself saying past the cotton ball haze permeating his thoughts.

"Freaking aliens, dude," Kyle agreed.

Nate was distantly aware that Marty was shooting him that odd look again, but something else was nagging at his brain now. He looked out the front windows, thinking.

Sometime yesterday.

Sometime right around when the Lady had reached down from the alien-riddled heavens to show him brave new worlds and stick a freaking Excalibur in his head?

Could that really have something to do with all of this? And did it even really matter anymore? It was already all fucked beyond belief. No more bat shit crazy than a bunch of space ogres and who knew what else all raining down on Earth because of—

The Beacon.

"Holy shit," Nate murmured.

"What, dude?" Kyle said, leaning over to join him in looking out the window. "Hot girl alert?"

Nate barely heard him at all, over the rush of all the pieces slamming together in his head.

The Beacon is what draws this conflict to Earth, the Merlin had said. *It is the reason the Lady chose you when she did.*

One of the most powerful objects in the known galaxy. One the Merlin wanted him to remove from this planet immediately.

It was all nonsense. Wizardly gobbledygook. And it sounded *exactly* like the kind of thing that could be responsible for all of this. Peculiar background radiation. Strange seismic activity. Restless corgis climbing up on porch roofs, cocking their heads like little doggy apocalypse satellite dishes.

Finally starting to believe, are you?

"Hey, Earth to Nate!"

He came back to find Kyle waving his hands in Nate's face like he was pretty sure his good buddy had just suffered his second stroke of the day. Behind him, Marty looked like he was ready to pounce forward in case of any sudden collapses, despite the fact that Nate was already sitting down.

"I, uh… I might have to check that out." This time, Nate managed to force a smile, even if it was mirthless. "Thanks for the heads-up. You guys have fun shopping."

"Yeah," Kyle said, looking every bit as unconvinced as Marty and Zach did behind him. "Sure, buddy. Just, uh, don't go spacing off too far across the galaxy while we're gone, okay?"

CHAPTER 18

FIT FOR A WIZARD

Over a hundred lightyears away, a long, slender ship emerged from the Golnak Sector relay gate, unannounced by any proper itinerary or clearance code. It was an elegant craft, larger than most corvettes, but smaller than many frigates. There was no manufacturer class or code anywhere on the sleek hull to settle the matter of its classification. Only a single word, etched across one of the port-side armor panels in faded, barely discernible letters: "CAMELOT."

On the empty bridge of the *Camelot*, the Merlin flicked his wizened fingers at the holo controls, freeing his carefully composed messages to spew out into the depths, where they would bounce through who knew how many comm relays on their way to the quantcomm stations of Kalyria, and ultimately to the only two recipients he saw fit to involve in this latest episode of The Divine Drama.

That done, the Merlin contemplated the massive superstructure of the Golnak relay ring, debating—not for the first time—if maybe he shouldn't just pop through, all the way over to the Forge at the heart of the galaxy, grab his dear old First Knight by the scruff of his golden neck, and drag the arrogant, immortal manchild back here to deal with this mess, as he'd so clearly failed to do the first time around.

Sod that. There was good reason the Merlin had left the Alliance behind. Several good reasons. And after several centuries of self-induced exile, his reemergence would likely only cause an uproar on the Forge, and probably light more fires than he'd be putting out by buying them the extra scraps of time. The Alliance was already jumpy enough right now, judging by the seven—no, *eight*—urgent warning hails that had pinged the *Camelot* in the sparse minute since he'd entered the system.

An idle wisp of a memory fluttered in the depths of his mind, of a time when the Merlin—or when anyone aboard a Knight ship—would've been met not with tightened sphincters and warnings of protocol, but rather with open wonder and reverence. Respect and gratitude.

Times had changed.

Case and point, the ship that was currently mending itself together where it was moored to Golnak mining installation C-73, looking like it'd nearly been bisected. It was another knight ship, similar to the *Camelot* but hardly identical, especially not with its blood red hull. Groshna's ship, then. And something told the Merlin that the *Crimson Tide* hadn't simply been sniped unawares in the depths by the lucky magcoil slug of some backwater Knight hunter.

There'd been a fight here. That much was evident by the messily patched gouges that'd been torn in the sides of the hermetic little mining station he'd colloquially referred to as Beacon Rock ever since its inner treasure had been discovered dormant in the first great troglodan expansion a few thousand years ago. But a fight between whom? And, more importantly, *why?*

Clearly, the Golnak Beacon was still in place inside, as evidenced by the fact that the relay had still functioned to jump him to the Golnak sector in the first place. Which suggested either that someone had actually been crazy enough to try to steal a Beacon—and had of course *failed*—or that the two Knights of this uneasy quadrant had finally come to blows, likely over the matter of how to handle the newly awakened Beacon and Knight, whose ripples they'd no doubt felt this close by.

That, or the Merlin's darkest fears *had* been realized, and he was in fact looking at the aftermath of the clash between Groshna, Dread Sixth Knight, and the one who'd been haunting the Merlin's daymares ever since the Beacon had awoken on Earth without warning—and since well before that, too, if the truth were told.

He prayed to the Lady it had simply been a wild pirate.

Her Eternal Grace was eerily quiet on the matter.

The swarm of closing corvettes and the pair of distant dreadnoughts training their entire destructive arsenal on the *Camelot's* hull to the happy tune of Urgent Warnings Ten, Eleven, *and* Twelve, on the other hand…

"Transmit our credentials, would you?" the Merlin grumbled. "Before those twitchy buggers get any bright ideas."

The holo displays chimed with the *Camelot's* affirmative, and the Merlin focused on flicking open a dedicated comms channel and manually hailing the mending Knight ship on C-73.

There was a long moment of silence, then the line crackled with the uptake of an unmuting channel on the other side, and the central display filled with the hulking, crimson armored form of Ser Groshna—chieftain of the self-proclaimed Clan Groshna, and Sixth Knight of the Order Excalibur. Even among the troglodans, Groshna was a mountainous beast without rival. And even after a few centuries' exile to Earth, it was still easy enough to read the shock on the troglodan's face at seeing his Merlin alive and kicking.

The Merlin would've been lying if he'd said that shock didn't bring him a spark of enjoyment. It was just about all he had left over here on the far end of the unknowable chasm that had grown between him and the rest of the galaxy.

"I thought I told you all to play nice with one another."

"Honored Merlin," the Dread Knight boomed, looking rather guilty for a troglodan—which was to say, barely guilty at all. "The Fifth Knight has gone mad."

"An affliction common to all of our Order, if one is to believe the word of the times. Do you have a more precise accusation to share?"

"The bitch tried to kill me and steal the Beacon. We fought. She slagged my ship on the way out. I killed her q-drive." He turned his boulder of a head elsewhere, as if looking out the viewport. "Racket brought half the Alliance out here to bolster station security."

"I noticed." The Merlin glanced at the other displays, briefly confirming that there were no torpedoes actively closing on the *Camelot*, and that at least most of the targeting lasers had abated. "So…" he said, turning back to the main display, "a new Beacon rears its shiny head on Terra, and Ser Katanaga loses her jin, so to speak. What do you make of it all, Ser Groshna?"

Groshna grunted, looking unsettled. "Thought there was only eight."

Simple in its eloquence. Unlike Groshna, Clan Groshna.

"Legend *does* say there were once ten," the Merlin pointed out.

Groshna studied him with beady-eyed suspicion, perfectly aware that, if anyone knew the truth of the old legends, it was most certainly the Merlin, but obviously loathe to debase himself prying for scraps.

"There is something else," he finally rumbled, looking grim for a troglodan—which was to say, pretty much the usual. "Something you need to see."

~

IN PERSON, the first word that sprang to mind of Groshna, Clan Groshna was *intimidating*, shortly followed by ones like *formidable*, and *beastly*. Overwhelmingly so on all accounts, to be sure. Yet the words rang empty in the Merlin's head. Groshna *would've* been intimidating to anyone who wasn't comfortable around a mountain sized troll who might've eaten an entire school bus of children without the faintest hint of remorse.

The Merlin wasn't intimidated. Or afraid. He was far too ancient for any of that. He merely wondered, as he often had, at the Lady's wisdom in having ever selected a troglodan Knight to begin with. They were not a particularly civilized people, after all.

But then, even a savage brute had its merits over a wide-eyed college lad.

The Merlin strode toward the center of the spacious holding bay of mining installation C-73, feeling the tingling of the Golnak Beacon on its humming dais ahead in his every cell, even if he couldn't see the gilded sphere hovering there behind Ser Groshna's crimson bulk. He closed his eyes for a few steps, studying the strange dissonance of the twining voices whispering in his head—that of the eternal companion who never left him, and the infinitude of her pervasive, almost recursive expanse throughout the galaxy.

It was only when he opened his eyes and focused more carefully on his waiting Knight that he caught a dissonance of another kind completely.

There was something wrong with Ser Groshna's Excalibur.

The Merlin froze, struck by an exceedingly rare moment of surprise and something almost like fear, then he listened to his bucking instincts and flash-stepped straight back to… nowhere.

Nowhere but a single foot across the rusted deck.

Return to Earth, he mentally snapped back to the ship within whose bridge he had most decidedly failed to arrive. *Go and find the boy. Do you understand?*

There was nothing.

No affirmative chirp from the *Camelot*. No *Camelot* at all, in the scope of his roving mind. Just the flat edge of the endless void that had appeared a mere meter away from him on every side in his senses. An ethereal cage of sorts, sprung around him like a trap of… what, exactly?

Not an e-dim containment field—not *just* that, at least. He reached out and tested its shimmering edge with one hand, feeding a trickle of power into its wall, feeling its haunting resonance. This was something more. Something born of the Light itself. Something he'd never seen before.

For a moment, the intellectual curiosity alone outweighed any alarm at finding himself trapped. Then Groshna spoke, and cold reality came crashing back in.

"He said it would be this easy."

Over the millennia, the list of harrowing tribulations that retained the power to strike true dread in the Merlin's heart had dwindled so far as to become non-existent. Hearing Groshna utter those words, though…

"He knew you would never suspect that one of your pathetic little puppets could pose any threat to you," Groshna continued, stalking closer, a slow, cocky sneer creeping across his lumpy face. "Not to the Great Merlin. Not to the omnipotent wizard who holds an entire galaxy in his frail little palm, yes? Impossible. And yet look how easily you are defeated."

The troglodan rapped on the Merlin's shimmering prison wall with two thick crimson-armored digits. The Merlin paid the fool no mind. A complete idiot, Groshna may not have been, but he *was* a pathetic little puppet. It was only that he'd found a new master. One who'd cut his so-called strings and introduced some kind of synthient corruption into his Excalibur. One who'd apparently discovered how to conjure a cage capable of holding a Merlin.

There was only one.

"Yes," Groshna said, drawing the word out and leaning closer, like he'd picked up on exactly what the Merlin must be thinking. "I *have* met him. Who do you think left this cage for you?"

The Merlin studied the troglodan, his mind adrift in less-than-reliable memories, that foreign hollowing sensation that felt so much like fear threatening to bubble up to the surface from a past millennium. "Whatever he's promised you… It will only end in pain and suffering. For you. For your people. For everyone. The Synth will—"

"The Synth is a lie!" the troglodan roared, smacking the shimmering containment field. "A conjuror's trick you have used to keep the Alliance at your mercy for Lady only knows how long."

"Do they look to be at my mercy?" the Merlin asked, gesturing at the bay wall in the general direction of the Alliance armada currently keeping watch over the mining installation. "Do you truly think my position as galactic pariah covetable?"

"You waste your breath, my honored Merlin," Groshna said, pulling up a holo to contact his crew. "My fleet went to crusher space months ago. They will reach Terra in mere weeks. Agents are in place, waiting to intercept the messages you sent when you arrived in system." Groshna smiled. It was a hideous thing to behold. "There is no stopping us now."

The Merlin turned without another word and sank cross-legged to the rusty mining station deck, thinking. There was no point in asking what Groshna was hoping to accomplish. The troglodan might not even know himself—*couldn't* know for certain, after whatever his new master had done to him and his Excalibur.

Groshna's mind was no longer his own.

The Synth, a lie? Tell that to the trillion-odd lives they'd consumed in the last war, and to the rest of the unspeakable horrors Groshna was too young in his nine-hundred-odd years to even begin to comprehend. Tell that to the entire galaxy of sentience that would be next if the coming flood wasn't quelled.

He'd been a fool to come here.

He drew his cup absentmindedly from his robe, reflexively seeking the singular solace of drink as the sheer magnitude of his stupidity came crashing down on him. Walked straight into it, he had. Without question. Why question, when he alone had the power of the Merlin?

Why?

Groshna was speaking to his crew over the comms, bidding them help the ship along with its repairs as quickly as could be, adding some glib comment toward the Merlin about hoping he was ready to watch his precious Terra burn.

It was only when the Merlin glanced down and realized that his cup was still empty—that his e-dim stores were inaccessible, and that he was not so very far off from being a powerless old man at present—that he truly snapped. He hurled the cup across the loading bay, watched it shatter to fine clay fragments against the thrice-cursed containment field, and very nearly let out a scream. Groshna looked up from his holos long enough to chuckle. For the first time in half a millennium, the Merlin considered crawling to his knees, and begging his eternal companion for mercy.

It wouldn't matter.

He'd been a fool. An arrogant, impetuous fool. He'd ignored the inevitable. Allowed this body to stretch on too long without regeneration.

Now his Grand Scales of Galactic Justice were under attack.

And suddenly, beyond all prior expectations, it was all riding on the narrow shoulders of Nathaniel Arturi.

CHAPTER 19

ORDER OF OPERATIONS

*T*his *was not the deal, Nathaniel.*

It's our best move right now, Nate thought back, frowning down at the sketch pad page that read "The Game Plan" across the top and contained little more than a perfectly serviceable sketch of Nate's muscled-up likeness smashing Todd Mackleroy across the head with a barbell, and a short, four item list:

-bond w/ Excalibur

-find Beacon

-shoot it into the sun

-profit

It was the fifth and bottom item, and the attached arrow that indicated it should in fact precede the existing list, that had the Excalibur upset:

-get help from friendly neighborhood feds

It seemed like a reasonable first step, considering neither of them actually had any great idea where to start with items 1-4, save for the Excalibur's insistence that they couldn't simply go shooting Beacons into stars, and that doing so would hardly solve any problems, anyway.

I told you I'd take this thing seriously, Ex, he thought, tossing the sketch pad aside and standing from his desk. *This is as serious as it gets.*

Those meat sacks cannot help you.

Nate resisted the urge to point out that that probably put them in fine company, then, considering that no one—Ex included—seemed especially equipped to help him figure out this troglodan problem. But he didn't want to bicker. Not when the Excalibur had just finished saving his… Christ, his secret identity?

Did you still call it a secret identity when you were too incompetent to even figure out your so-called powers?

Whatever. He could feel the Excalibur's frustration pulsing like an angry sore in his mind, threatening to turn downright unpleasant any moment, and he only had another twenty minutes, tops, if he wanted to do this before his roommates returned from shopping. Assuming they stuck with Sunday tradition and went to Meyers for post-shopping milkshakes, that was.

He turned for the door.

Funny feeling, hoping one's friends would have the decency to slurp down some ice cream so one could go talk to the secret space army men in peace. Add that to the list of thoughts Nate had never expected to have.

Outside, the day was sunny, the autumn air crisp on his sweaty palms. He pulled the front door closed behind him, feeling like he was pulling the prison door closed on himself, and second guessing his decision to leave Copernicus inside.

Your corgi cannot protect you, Nathaniel.

There's this thing called "emotional support," Nate thought, jamming his hands in his hoodie pockets and starting down the stoop steps, trying not to look at the black SUV he could practically feel sitting there, watching. *Maybe you should look it up. You might find it under the antonyms of "blackmail."*

Still sniveling about that? How about you *look up "constructive criticism?"*

By the time Nate reached the SUV, he'd almost forgotten to be apprehensive, what with all the bickering. Staring at his own reflection in the opaque black windows, though, the nerves returned in full, right along with the unfounded but inescapable thought that someone could currently be pointing a gun at him from inside, and he'd never know.

Paranoid, he chided himself, giving the vehicle's alleged inhabitants a somber wave. *Here to talk. Please don't shoot.*

Nothing.

He tried again.

Maybe the car was empty.

Maybe he really *had* lost his mind.

We should get back to training.

Nate raised his hand and knocked on the passenger window. Then, heart hammering at the thought of a waiting gun barrel, he cupped his hands and leaned in to press his eyes to the glass.

A man stared back from the shaded interior. A big man. And he didn't look happy. The window kicked into motion, and Nate jerked back as it slid down with an indignant electric hum.

"You gotta scram, kid," someone said. The driver. He was a pretty average looking guy, early thirties, and probably not as small as the burly scowling dude in the passenger seat made him look.

They both wore plain jackets and t-shirts that looked like they'd been picked straight from the shelves of Civilians "R" Us, and they both watched him with the kind of innate authority that'd always made Nate kind of resent passing police officers, even when they probably didn't think twice about him.

Military?

He didn't know. But Ex hadn't been wrong yet.

"Look," he started slowly, half-waiting to see if they'd cut him off. "I know this is gonna sound completely crazy, but I just wanted you to know that… Well, I'll just say it: I'm pretty sure we've got an alien armada coming to invade Earth sometime in the next few weeks. And I tried to report this, and maybe that's why you're here…?" He looked between them for some kind of sign, and got absolutely none. "But either way, I need you to let your superiors know to, you know… get ready for…"

They just kept staring. Nate was about to start spouting what details he could when they finally broke to trade a look between themselves, then focused back on him.

"What kind of aliens?" asked the driver.

"What?" Nate asked, too taken aback to stop himself.

"What kind of aliens, kid? Big? Small? Three boobs? What're we looking at, here?"

Relieved beyond belief, Nate was already starting to sputter a half-cocked answer about the troglodans and the Beacon and everything else when his rational brain finally registered just how sarcastic the driver's question had been, and how dubious their frowns were now.

"What are you guys doing here?" he asked, looking between the driver and the scowling Mr. Cuddles in the passenger seat, not understanding. "Why are you here if you're not…"

"We're watching that guy," the driver said, nodding down the street.

Nate followed his gaze to the older man push-mowing his little patch of front yard. "Mr. Humphrey?"

"That's classified."

Nate frowned back at the driver. "No it's… Are you guys SAS, or not?"

He regretted the words as soon as they'd blurted from his mouth.

All three of them tensed. Nate took a step back from the SUV, half-expecting Mr. Cuddles to leap out and follow, or to produce a tranquilizer gun from the door panel. But he and the driver both stayed put, watching him with a kind of forced casualness. They traded another glance. Something passed silently between them. Then the driver started the SUV's engine.

"Wait!" Nate said, fear forgotten. "Where are you going?"

"We've got reports to make," the driver said. "On Mr. Jeffries."

"You mean Mr. Humphrey?"

"That's what I said," the driver said, shrugging off the big guy's exasperated stare and jabbing at the window controls.

"Hey!" Nate cried as the black passenger window rolled up, cutting them off from view. He wasn't sure what else to say. It didn't matter anyway. The SUV pulled off the curb and headed down Irvin Ave, not quite burning rubber, but hardly taking it easy, either. Nate watched it go, completely unclear as to what the hell had just happened, other than the part where he was pretty sure he'd just blown his last shot at bringing the actual authorities in on any of this.

Maybe he should try calling China.

"Shit."

I was just thinking the same thing.

Nate frowned after the SUV as it hauled a right onto Allen Street at the end of the block. *Why? What happened?*

I found the ship.

His eyes widened. Between the viral video scare and the mysterious government mobile, he'd completely forgotten about the Excalibur's casual mention of a ship, right back before he'd initiated the two-hundred pound squat-astrophe.

Isn't that good? I thought we wanted to find the ship.

Allow me to correct myself. I found the last known location of the ship BEFORE it went dark three hours ago. Along with the Merlin.

Nate swallowed uneasily. *Dark? Is that like a technical term for—*

Captured or destroyed? Yes. Very technical.

"Shit," Nate repeated, and this time, staring after his retreating SAS snoops, armed with the full scope of just how completely alone he was with what felt too much like the weight of the world, the word felt considerably more substantial on his lips.

All right. He turned back for the house, too hopelessly overwhelmed to even really register the rising panic and curdling dread, or the sight of his roommates pulling around the corner in Marty's car, milkshakes in hand, laughing of all things.

Laughing, for the love of Christ.

All right, he repeated, stalking quickly up the front steps to beat them inside. *I guess we do things your way, then.*

CHAPTER 20

#THEGRIND

Over the next several days, Nate began to feel like a ghost haunting his own house. He dodged his roommates whenever he could, catching whispered mentions of his name on more than one occasion. He skipped class, telling himself he'd catch up later, once he'd gotten a handle on things. He barely left the house at all but to keep his gym appointments with his new personal trainer from hell.

The Excalibur was relentless.

The wicked hour of their morning gym sessions didn't help things, either, but Nate couldn't argue with the thinned out 6 AM weekday gym crowd, at least. Of the few chalked-up beasts who'd come to make war on the iron at that hour, and the smattering of bleary-eyed guys and girls who looked more like they'd accidentally sleep-walked over, everyone was either too focused or tired to even notice Nate.

That wasn't to say he'd completely escaped notice, though.

For one thing, that damned SUV had returned—keeping its distance, and never staked out in the same place twice, it seemed, but undeniably still there, watching, waiting. He swore he even saw the driver following him across campus at one point. And that wasn't all.

While the actual video footage of his Atherton Street heroics might've gone miraculously missing across the board, the campfire legends surrounding the event had proved more resilient. He'd received more than a few messages and friend requests from random strangers spouting half-cocked theories, claiming to know his secret. Merciful Sith only knew how many more wild rumors were floating around out there.

Enough for his friends to have noticed, apparently. He wasn't sure how else to interpret the nervous prying Kyle and Zach had hit him with the few times he failed to dodge them around the house. He just did his best to circumvent their questions with furtive shrugs and lots of unconvincing variations of, "I don't know, man, it just happened so fast."

No one really bought it, he knew, but so far they'd been too polite to press the issue. As had Gwen, in the few haphazard texts they'd managed to exchange between her hardcore class schedule and his ruthless inner tyrant, who'd re-brandished the Blackmail Stick every time he'd so much as thought about trying to take her up on one of her offers to meet for coffee.

Whether Gwen had seen or heard anything, or if she was simply concerned or still feeling guilty after the I.N.N. douchebaggery the other week, he had no idea. Part of him—the part wrapped up in idle fantasy, he supposed—almost hoped she *had* caught a glimpse of him doing the impossible. The rest was just glad she was interested in grabbing coffee at all, if and when he managed to find the time.

It might not be a candlelit dinner, but at least it wasn't lunch, right?

And what is wrong with lunch? the Excalibur demanded, in the tone that let Nate know right off the bat that he'd just flaunted one of his many personal shortcomings. *I might even be tempted to authorize this romantic farce of yours if it would aid you in consuming enough sustenance to enable me to properly... Ah. I have just located the 'lunch is for platonic friends and not lovers' trope. Fascinating.*

"You're organizing my feelings into tropes now?"

Such frameworks are helpful in better understanding the behavior of such spectacularly superstitious creatures as humans.

Fascinating, Nate silently echoed, frowning down at the last text on his phone.

Gwen: "I've got a two hour break around noon. 12:30 recharge at the HUB?"

Pardon my mechanical understanding, but do those hours not fall within your standard definition of lunch?

Nate suppressed a sigh. *You suck.*

It's really for the best, Nathaniel. After all, in case you forgot, THE FATE OF THE EARTH IS DEPENDING ON YOU NOT BEING A SNIVELING COFFEE DRINKER.

For such a high and mighty logical being, Nate thought, flinching and resisting the urge to rub delicately at his temples, *you sure do yell a lot.*

"I'm sorry," he typed quickly to Gwen, much to the Excalibur's looming irritation. "It's been a crazy week. I'll make it up to you soon, promise."

This is ridiculous, by the way, he thought when he was done—though whether to the Excalibur or to himself, he couldn't have rightly said. It was hard to think that, only a week ago, his biggest concern had been whether he could ever win Gwen away from Todd—not to mention whether Todd would feed him to Bonzer before he could tell her what the Greek God A-hole had done with Emily behind her back. Now, though…

You know, perhaps if I were to aid you in finally copulating with this female, it might—

"What?!" Nate hissed, on his feet before he knew it, even though there was no one to face but himself in the mirror, and Copernicus' curiously cocked head.

What? I am only postulating that surpassing this particular hurdle might help you to let go of your innumerable inadequacies and—

I'm gonna stop you right there, Ex, Nate said, jabbing a finger at the mirror, which had become something like a proxy for his invisible companion. *I don't need help with… that.*

I think we both know that's nonsense. Here, I have just finished analyzing the complete works of Jane Austen, William Shakespeare, and—

Dude. Nate shook his head at himself in the mirror. *I'm not sure I can adequately convey how much this is* not *happening.*

Females love Shakespeare, Nathaniel. Perhaps once you have triumphed in this archaic rite of passage, you will…

But Nate was squeezing his temples tight, doing his best to shut the Excalibur's voice out, not really sure whether he wanted to laugh first, or to cry. Probably both, he decided. Simultaneously, and in tandem with other such chestnuts as yanking out his hair, beating his chest, and forgetting about all of this.

"Why isn't this working, Ex?" he whispered. "What are we doing wrong?"

WE are clearly failing to focus on the task at hand, Nathaniel. Now, if you'll kindly set the phone down and pay attention, we can continue with my riveting presentation on the fine points of exactly HOW the troglodans are going to devastate your planet if you continue floundering about like a prepubescent snargladorf. Are you ready?

∽

MORE DAYS PASSED, and still there was no sign of the Merlin, nor of the Knight ship he'd apparently run off with, or the Beacon, either.

You will feel its call when you have proven yourself worthy, the Excalibur told him, time and time again. But Nate felt nothing. Nothing but tired and alone. And the Excalibur was only growing more agitated by the day.

None of it really made Nate any *less* certain he hadn't just suffered some kind of psychotic break back on that fateful weekend. Especially since, try as he might, he'd failed to dig up even a single glimpse of those magical Excalibur powers hiding beneath the surface. But that wasn't to say things were one-hundred percent normal on the home front, either.

There were still the S.A.S. boys lurking about, for instance, even if that "fact" *had* started to feel suspect. He'd seen *A Beautiful Mind*, after all. And he did have a goddamn voice in his head.

What was harder to explain away by simple madness was his radical body transformation.

He still wasn't sure whether he was looking at something preternatural, or simply the results of a man delusionally possessed, but even a week into the training, there was no longer any denying it: Nate was getting bigger and stronger, and from everything he'd read, he was doing it entirely faster than should've been humanly possible.

He wasn't quite an overnight Todd—and certainly not a Bonzer—but a week in, his shirts and pants were growing snug. Another few workouts, and they were getting plain tight. And to look in the mirror...

I am doing my best to work with what little I have available, the Excalibur confirmed in the middle of their second week, as Nate stood there, studying the broadening curves of his chest and shoulder muscles. He was too mindlessly tired to decide whether he should be excited or terrified by the implications of that one.

It all means nothing if you cannot harness my power to find the Beacon.

Too tired to even bristle at the chastising, Nate shambled out to the kitchen to get his breakfast and prepare for the morning's training.

That day, he couldn't help but idly think he should probably go to class after the gym. He could barely bring himself to think about how seriously he was already falling behind, or what his parents were going to say when they found out he'd failed out of an entire semester. But then the Excalibur reminded him that a failed semester would be the least of his parents' concerns when they were troglodan mining slaves, and suddenly that big database management test felt a lot less important.

No matter what justifications he fed himself, though, he couldn't ignore the fact that he was watching his neat little life slide into complete shit show disarray one day at a time. And the people in his life were starting to notice.

The whispers and the odd looks from his roommates were increasing on a daily basis. They didn't ask why Nate was all of a sudden practically living in his baggiest sweats. They'd stopped asking if he wanted to join them at the Mother Gaming Shrine in the evenings. Marty tried a few times to talk to him, but Nate didn't have much to tell him, other than the thin lies that he was okay, and that Marty didn't need to worry about him

"Where have you been, man?" his friend finally asked one day. "I know you've been leaving before I even wake up every day, and it seems like you've been missing a lot of classes."

"I took your advice," Nate said, barely even thinking about it. It scared him, how quickly the lies were coming these days. "Worked out a kind of independent study setup with Professor Hillman. It's been keeping me pretty busy around the clock."

"Oh." A tentative look of hope spread across Marty's face, only twisting the guilt in Nate's gut that much further. "Oh! Well that's—Why didn't you tell us, man? That's great. What are you working on?"

He should stop now.

"Trying my hand at metalworking," he said instead, thinking first of the gym, then holding up the random rune he'd idly sketched earlier, as if that were somehow proof, "but he's got a whole slew of projects laid out."

"That's awesome, dude!" Marty said, smile widening before it started to wane. "And this all doesn't have anything to do with, you know...?"

Nate feigned his best confused look.

"With that night in the park," Marty explained. "With all that weird stuff that happened. And with... you know, Gwen, and Emily Atherton, and, well, the accident. I mean, damn dude, it's been a weird few weeks. We're all kinda worried about you, if you haven't noticed."

Nate forced a smile. It felt positively reptilian. "Just trying to have my cake and eat it too, man. You save one pretty girl from speeding traffic, and life starts to seem a bit too short."

What the hell was he even saying?

He didn't know—wasn't even entirely sure why he was still lying to his friends, for that matter, other than out of rote adherence to what he'd come to think of as the Straight Jacket Principal. But Marty wasn't arguing.

His friend just inclined his head like he couldn't quite argue with Nate's nonsensical logic. "Well, I'm just glad to hear you're sticking with your art. And you know I'm here if you need an extra hand staying on top of class too, right?" He grinned guiltily. "*Or* if you need a break one of these nights. We definitely wouldn't mind having the full squad back in action."

At least that time, Nate didn't have to force the smile, even if the result did look a bit pained. "Will do, buddy. Thanks. You're a good friend."

Marty glanced at the movie Nate had muted when he'd knocked. "Guess that means I probably shouldn't tell the guys you're watching the new *Power Rangers* in here, then. They'd never let you hear the end of it."

Nate blew out a chuckle. "Thanks for that too, then."

His smile lasted right up until Marty closed Nate's bedroom door on his way out.

For a second, he felt the familiar temptation to just throw in the towel and go hang out with his roommates, consequences and Excalibur blackmail be damned. It would be good for his soul, and his friends deserved better than to be swept under the rug. Hell, maybe his soul deserved better, too.

He couldn't take much more of this.

You won't be taking much more of it, if you—

"If I don't buck up and find the Beacon," he completed the Excalibur's thought. "End of the world, I know."

Insolent cur, the Excalibur grumbled.

Nate grinned a little in spite of himself, shifting his sketch pad around and snagging a pencil from the desk. Jarring as the constant stream of bickering and insults had originally been, in some fucked up way, it was almost starting to feel like the Excalibur was his only real friend in any of this.

Clearly, he was losing his mind. Enough that he'd actually reverted to quietly speaking aloud when they were alone, just to make himself feel less insane about talking to the voice in his head. It didn't help. No more than it helped sitting there every night, half-watching alien invasion blockbusters while he alternated between scouring the web for any sign of the Beacon, bursting blood vessels trying to *feel* its alleged call, and generally beating his head against the wall about why none of it was working, and what the hell he was doing wrong.

You are still sniveling about what you are doing wrong. That is what is wrong.

"Helpful," Nate muttered, tracing the lines of the slick, rune-covered sword he'd been sketching out in tribute to his constant companion.

He couldn't help but think his "friend" had a point. Shiny new muscles, double the strength, and a marathon of movie "research," from *Independence Day* to the complete Michael Bay collection, and Nate had yet to actually soak up a single nugget of the heroic badassitude he was after. Which made sense, he begrudgingly reminded himself, seeing as he *wasn't* a badass. Or a hero.

All it took was one look at his life to realize that.

Even so, at least the Excalibur had bought into Nate's training enough to begin filling him in on the larger backdrop of their situation. There was that much. Almost like his companion thought the effort might not be *completely* wasted on him, after all.

Or maybe the Excalibur was just as desperate as he was.

Bitter resentment and growing concerns of rampant schizophrenia aside, Nate couldn't help but listen in wonder as the Excalibur told him of the grand Alliance the Merlin had long ago forged between many of the sentient species of the galaxy, uniting eldari, and gorgons, and even troglodans, just to name a few, against the unstoppable tide of some ancient evil they'd called the Synth.

The Order of the Excalibur Knights had been born to act as a kind of glue to the whole tenuous arrangement—eight devastatingly powerful peacekeepers, chosen to lead the charge against the Synth, each answering to the Lady, and by extension, to the Merlin, above all else. And each, the Excalibur insisted on pointing out, far more noble and brave than Nate himself.

"Duly noted," Nate grumbled, brow scrunching in inadvertent sympathy as he etched a severe frowny brow over the ridiculous pair of oogly eyes he'd just added to the sword. "But why aren't these other Knights all coming to help with the Beacon, if it's really as dangerous as the Merlin said?"

Just like that, the Excalibur took up the same surly silence it had been adopting every time Nate pried about the Merlin, and his untimely disappearance.

"What aren't you telling me, Ex?"

Silence. Heavy, stinking silence.

Merciful Sith, was he getting tired of this bullshit.

And you think I am not? I have been hibernating for over a thousand years, Nathaniel. I do not know what's happening out there. I do not even know that the Galactic Alliance still stands as I once knew it. You organics are hardly amenable to long term stability, so forgive me if I hesitate to engage in your pointless, sniveling conjecture.

The snap of the wooden pencil in Nate's hand was the only thing that stopped him from firing back at the Excalibur then and there. He looked down at the ruined pencil, the swell of anger subsiding by a few inches.

"You can't tell me there's not *some* hope, then," he said quietly. "Maybe if another Knight arrives in time—"

If another arrives in time, you will be lucky if they do not slay you on sight and return your body to the Lady, that a more suitable candidate may be found to wield my power in her name.

"Bullshit," Nate whispered, without a trace of conviction.

He sat there for some time, wanting to ask more but afraid of the answers—not wanting to spoil the small hope that, even if it came to that, and it *was* over his dead body, at least Earth would be safer with the arrival of a proper Knight protector. Because he wasn't even sure about that part.

Would they really be willing to pry the Excalibur from his dead hands?

Was there even anything there to pry?

Will it truly matter to you once you are dead?

Nate swallowed, heavily rethinking that whole *only real friend* bit. A low whine from the bed interrupted the downward spiral.

At least he still had Copernicus, he told himself, reaching over to scratch the corgi's ears with a sigh. He'd gone back and forth with Emily, flipping and flopping on when they'd finally make the custody swap until it had finally become clear that Emily probably wouldn't be going out of her way to take the dog back unless Nate went out of his way to make it happen. And screw that.

He was still a little confused that someone, even Emily, could so readily set the pooch out of mind—even if Copernicus *had* apparently been an unwanted adoptee, born of Emily's ex-roommate moving to new non-pet-friendly digs across town. Then again, after having turned down an invitation to join her out at the bars last Friday, Nate seemed to have gone from mysterious hero straight back to boring-ass IT Guy as far as Emily Atherton was concerned, so maybe *moving on* was simply her super power.

That was fine by Nate. He would've given a thousand guilt-free nights with Emily Atherton just for another chance to see Gwen without a tyrannical Excalibur in his head, and life-or-death threats looming on the horizon.

But hey, that was life, right? The jocks got the girls and the big money jobs, no matter what bullshit they pulled. The artists sold their souls and studied IT. The nerds took solace in their video games. And Nate?

Nate had somehow become the bug in the Great System, throwing errors like feeble sparks in the darkness while the universe closed in from all sides, bent on his imminent deletion.

"How did it come to this, boy?" he asked quietly, stroking Copernicus' head. The corgi just licked his hand in a silent reminder that, however it *had* come to this, he totally had Nate's back.

It almost made Nate feel better.

TODAY WAS GOING to be the day.

Nate would've been lying if he claimed to know *why*, or how anything was actually different about this day in particular. He just had a feeling as he jogged home from the gym that morning, the early November air crisp and vibrant, his fellow students smiling as he passed—like the whole world had been ticking along all this time, and Nate had simply been too busy to notice until now.

Maybe it was that he'd just miraculously pulled his first four-hundred pound deadlift after just under three weeks of training. Maybe it was that it barely even seemed to wind him anymore, taking the mile home at a flat out run. Whatever it was, he was surprised to realize he felt the faintest spark of hope sputtering through his inner darkness.

Or maybe it was just the cute jogger who shot him an appreciative grin as he overtook her on Allen Street.

Hope stirred, amongst other things.

But hope is a dangerous thing. Hope can drive a man insane. Nate couldn't remember where he'd heard that line, but it hardly mattered at that moment. Because hope, not unlike the alluring grin of a pretty girl, could also distract.

Or so he pieced together after a whizzing *something* punched into his right temple and sent the world spinning.

He was surprised to find he didn't fall. Barely even missed a step. Barely even had time to think before he was plucking the brown, oblong something—a *football*, some non-screaming corner of his brain informed him—from the pavement, and whirling on his attackers with murderous intent.

He was right in front of the Iota Nu Nu house, he wasn't surprised to realize, and there was Todd, watching him with a quietly hateful stare from the deck swing while his pack of laughing hyenas all showered the one who'd actually thrown the ball with emphatic pats on the back.

The thrower himself, standing with hands spread wide in dramatic *wasn't me* fashion, didn't manage more than a violently sarcastic, "Oh, whoopsie!" before the football slammed into his face, hard enough to send him staggering backward. Nate had only half-registered what he'd just done before the guy tripped and hit a window.

Glass shattered. Curses flew.

Nate noticed the cute jogger drawn up at the corner, watching it all unfold with eyebrows sky high. He turned away from her and kept running, ignoring the outraged cries from the INN deck, not trusting himself to hold it together long enough to apologize, or tell them to go shove it, or whatever the hell else might come spilling out in that moment.

For some reason, he felt an overwhelming urge to cry.

"Fuck!" he growled, turning the corner down a less public street, feeling it building like an impending vomit.

It was stupid. Such a goddamn stupid little thing.

"FUCK!" he screamed, swinging his arms violently through the air, wanting to go back there and hurt someone. Settling for stomping at the nearest wooden fence post, and feeling like a complete childish asshole when it have a mournful crack beneath his foot.

He looked guiltily around, checking the thankfully quiet street, his mind calling up a memory from his childhood, when he'd seen on the news that a young boy had been mauled by a loyal Doberman, and Nate's dad had explained to him, with that perpetually off-handed tone of his, that sometimes even a good dog can only take so much ear yanking and tail tugs before it finally snaps.

Nate hadn't thought about it in years.

Such a stupid little thing. Nothing but a dime-a-dozen moment of mildly malicious frat bro posturing. Nothing to lose his shit over.

Only he couldn't seem to stop it now—every single problem, big and small, all crashing down on his head in a breathtaking orgy of fuckedness. A building mountain of failed schoolwork. Dodged coffee dates with Gwen. His friends' sulky looks, and all their utter justification. The goddamned Beacon, and Air Force spies, and an entire armada of troglodans all bouncing around in his delusional head, right along with the missing Merlin, his divine Lady, and possibly the end of the Free Earth as they knew it. And those INN assholes couldn't just leave him alone—couldn't just be happy with their friends, and their partying, and their girls and failed algebra tests.

Warm tears spilled down his cheeks before he could stop them.

Today was the goddamn day, all right.

This is not helping, Nathaniel.

"What more do you want?!" he hissed, brushing away the tears and turning onto Irvin Ave, not particularly caring right then that the Excalibur *almost* sounded sympathetic, or that Mr. Humphrey was looking curiously up from his hedges down the block. "You've had me dancing like a goddamn meathead puppet for three weeks now, keeping me up at nights with all your horror stories and your blackmail bullshit, and you can't even tell me why none of this is working. Why should I listen to a goddamn thing you say?"

He stalked down the street with clenched fists, waiting for the Excalibur to fire back about how his insolent little hobbit cur ass should listen because it was the only thing that would save his backwater hovel of a planet, and because this sniveling hissy fit was nothing but another entry in the long list of reasons that this was all Nate's fault, and not the Excalibur's.

But the Excalibur said nothing. Just loomed there on the sidelines of his mind like a resentful ghost. Nate's phone buzzed with a text, and he unlocked it, glad for any kind of distraction.

Gwen: "Tonight. You. Me. Drinks. Friends. Talking and—"

The screen went black before he could finish reading. He frowned down at the phone, toggling the unlock button and giving the screen a few futile smacks when that did nothing.

Nathaniel...

That's when he understood.

He'd never tensed so hard at a single word.

"Give it back," he growled under his breath.

Now is not the time to begin shirking your training.

"Shirking my..." He huffed a bitter laugh, trembling, unable to believe the depth of this bullshit.

We are getting close, Nathaniel. You must have faith.

"Getting close?" Jaw tightening. "Getting *close*?" Throat constricting. Heart pounding. "WHY CAN'T YOU JUST TELL ME WHAT THE FUCK I'M SUPPOSED TO DO?!"

When the scream ended, he was rocking on his feet, throat burning, hands on his knees, feeling like he'd just vomited on the sidewalk. He hadn't meant to shout, but there was no one there anyway. No one but Mr. Humphrey down the block, and the goddamn SUV parked over behind the Hamilton Square strip in the other direction. Watching. Waiting.

Nate threw the distant vehicle an emphatic middle finger and set off for the house stoop at a solid death march, almost hoping the Excalibur would fight back, that maybe his friends would hear the racket inside, or maybe his friendly spooks in the SUV over there, and that someone—god, *someone* —would have the decency to have him hauled off and committed.

But the Excalibur's silence had an air of finality this time, beneath the crackling sparks of its bitter... what, *fuming?* He couldn't tell—no, didn't *care*, he decided. Because he was done with this. Done with the secrets, and the silent treatment bullshit. Done bending over backwards just to ruin his life for this mystical quest he'd seen neither hide nor hair of since a drunk old man had strong-arm terrorized him into all of this.

Done with it. So done that he forgot to even be surprised when he threw open the front door and found Marty and the others all sitting on the living room couch, waiting for him. They'd even gotten Copernicus out of Nate's room. The looks on their faces said it all.

Today was the day.

Perfect.

For a long moment, no one spoke. Marty took in his appearance with open concern. Kyle and Zach couldn't even bring themselves to meet Nate's eyes. Discomfort pulsed through the room like a giant, wriggling slug.

"Was that you outside?" Marty finally asked.

Copernicus looked nervously between Nate and his couch fellows, panting up a storm. Nate held Marty's gaze until his friend looked away and spoke quietly to the floor.

"We need to talk."

Nate turned his gaze to each of them in turn, waiting for Kyle or Zach to corroborate Marty's claim. "Is this supposed to be an intervention?"

The tight-lipped looks they traded were all the answer he needed. But there was something more there, too. Something unmistakably off. Like he didn't smell right to his own pack anymore.

A pang of unexpected fear passed through him, followed by one of desperation as it dawned on him that his friends were afraid. Afraid of *him*.

When the hell had that happened?

Why was he even surprised he hadn't noticed?

He sighed and rubbed the back of his neck, trying to reconcile what had happened outside with the confused, worried friends sitting before him now, and with the sudden and bone deep certainty that he couldn't stand to spend another single goddamn night cooped up without them.

He swallowed, mouth parched, and tried to keep the waiver from his voice. "Any chance I can just say I'm sorry and skip to the part where we all grab a beer?"

CHAPTER 21

RAISE THE ROOF

In retrospect, Nate wasn't sure he'd ever really fully appreciated the meaning of the phrase, "I need a drink," until he was halfway through his first lovely pint of Liberty Craft House's newly tapped creamsicle IPA.

It was mildly alarming, how drastically a splash of alcohol blunted his raw nerves. Then again, he also couldn't help but think he'd never actually known true stress until the Merlin had yanked him feet first into the wild—and *alleged*, whispered the alcohol—world of the Strange Alien Shit Show. But it didn't matter.

That evening, for a precious moment, everything almost seemed to be back to normal. Add in the fact that Gwen and her friend Kelsey should be there sometime soon, and it was all entirely too much of a relief for Nate to let his own dark thoughts or even the Excalibur's brooding silence sully it.

He was practically in heaven.

Or so he told himself as he took another sip of his sweet-yet-hoppy beer and tried to savor the taste, scanning the Liberty Craft House crowd for additional distractions. As far as State College bars went, Liberty never got too crazy wild—possibly owing to the fact that it had a killer draft list and tended to attract the less-than-wild college beer snob crowd. Even so, it was a Friday night, and the place was fairly packed beneath its rustic sphere lights and open girder ceiling—a look which Zach had informed them was called "industrial-chic," whatever that meant.

Nate's gaze paused on a pair of hazel eyes watching him from the bar across the room. His insides clenched reflexively, mind leaping to that goddamned SUV before he could remind himself how ridiculous and paranoid the thought was. The girl was already looking away, playing it as if she hadn't been staring. It was only then that he recognized her as the same jogger who'd witnessed the football-hurling prelude to his breakdown that morning.

He swallowed, cheeks flooding with heat, mind grasping at the hair-thin chances. Then her eyes flicked unexpectedly back to his with a coy smile, and this time, it was Nate who looked away, back to their booth table, cheeks positively burning as he took another long pull from his glass.

"How long did you say you've been working out?" Kyle's voice broke into his thoughts. He'd followed Nate's gaze.

"A few weeks."

Kyle shook his head, glancing around the room. "Damn, dude. I don't think I've ever been this close to the epicenter of so many hot lady stares." He took a long pull of his beer. "Almost makes me wanna start working out."

Zach chortled into his glass.

"You're just imagining things," Nate said.

"Ehh," Marty said beside him, looking a bit buzzed himself. "I'm pretty sure he's not, dude. Not to insult that adorable face of yours, but it seems like your gym results might be pulling their weight."

Marty frowned a little as he said the last words, like maybe he was remembering just how freakishly fast those gym results had popped up, but then Zach chimed in with a, "Heh! Pulling their weight. Punny," and Marty's face came alight with pleasure at his unintended pun, strangeness forgotten.

"You guys are drunk," Nate grumbled, glancing down at his phone, wondering how soon Gwen would be there.

"Maybe so," Kyle said, finishing his beer and staring pointedly at Nate's chest and arms. "But all I'm saying is that I might take a run at you myself if you don't find yourself a less tight shirt by the time I finish another beer."

"So in five minutes, then," Zach said.

Nate chuckled and looked down at his rather snug black t-shirt, cheeks pulsing with another wave of heat. He would've been lying if he said there wasn't something primally satisfying about seeing his once droopy sleeves pulled snug with newfound muscle, but he also couldn't help but think he was quickly approaching the line where he might as well cut the sleeves off and stamp Alpha-Sig-Sig across his forehead.

The situation below the table wasn't much better, either. Jeans had been more or less out of the question. He'd gone with a previously-baggy pair of khaki cargo pants which, while a little snug themselves now, at least had some elastic give to them.

New clothes, he decided, were probably in order soon. His parents would probably be delighted for the easy Christmas ask.

If there was a Christmas.

Jesus.

"Nate?"

Nate blinked back to reality, where their waitress was watching him with an expectant look. He eyed his roommates then asked for another round, gathering that they'd already done the same. Only Marty kept watching him, as the waitress departed with a friendly smile. Watching him like there was something more, his expression suddenly sober. Or at least less chipper.

"Listen," he started. "Before Gwen gets here, uh…"

Nate tried to keep from tensing. "I thought we were skipping the intervention."

"Yeah," Marty agreed, bobbing his head. "Yeah, we are but—"

"But maybe we just kinda wanna hear more about what happened that weekend," Kyle cut in, trying to sound playful about it, like this wasn't something they'd all been circling around all evening. "We never did get the full story from you. Like, what was it even like, taking Emily Atherton in those big strong arms of yours, for instance?"

"You mean after we both almost died?" Nate asked, more sharply than he'd meant to. He was pretty sure it only strengthened Marty's resolve.

Maybe if he threw them a little bone. Distracted them.

"She did ask me out to Indigo a couple weeks ago."

"Whoa!" Kyle cried, jerking back from the table and drawing several surprised looks from their neighbors. "And you…? I mean, it's Indigo, yeah, but Jesus, dude. You didn't…?" He shook his head. "God, you have to warn me before you drop a bomb like that, man. My poor heart can't handle the oceanic shift to my raging erec—"

Zach coughed loudly, rattling his glass against the table as he did. Pointedly, he looked from Kyle over to the nearby table of five girls who'd looked over at the first outcry. Kyle put on his most winning smile and gave them a little wave of his fingers that came off about two hundred percent creepier than intended, judging by the way the girls all turned quickly back to their conversation, looking a little bit like they wanted to laugh, and a little bit like they'd just encountered an especially gnarly strain of drain mold.

"Yep," Kyle murmured. "Definitely gotta start working out."

Zach shook his head at Kyle, but seemed equally perplexed by Nate's decisions. "So you're turning down dates with Emily Atherton now, huh? Bold move."

"It was just, like, for Copernicus custodial talk, I'm sure."

Nate was starting to regret this "distraction." He glanced at his phone, wondering how soon Gwen would be there.

"Why didn't you tell us?" Marty asked.

Nate shrugged and finished the rest of his first beer. "Guess I was still kinda keyed up from everything."

"I'll say," Kyle muttered, looking more than a little keyed up himself. "So what'd she smell like?"

"Jesus, man," Zach said.

Nate was about to chime in with his own two cents about Kyle's border-line fixation when the waitress promptly reappeared with their second round. Zach and Kyle took it as a chance to attempt being benignly flirty. Marty just took it as an opportunity to reset their conversational focus.

"Okay, dude," he said, as the waitress departed with an especially friendly smile to Zach. "I know this isn't really the time or place, but, well… Bradford texted me."

Nate studied his friend's tight expression. "No he didn't."

Bradford was one of the few IT classmates Nate hung out with enough to have merited a few concerned texts when he'd gone missing these past weeks. He'd already assured Bradford that he *was* keeping on top of that homework, though, and that he *had* made arrangements to make up those pesky quizzes off hours, all due to some personal problems. Which was why he wasn't surprised when Marty's resolve wavered a touch.

"Fine. I texted him. And he told me he hasn't seen you in class for a couple weeks."

"Ever since that weekend," Zach added, finally finding his voice from where he and Kyle had bowed their heads in silence. Beside him, Kyle reluctantly bobbed his head, like this was a script they'd all practiced ahead of time.

Nate sighed. "You *just* said this wasn't an intervention. I told you, I've been busy."

"Yeah, busy juggling classes and your art," Marty said, the first touch of anger touching his eyes. "Classes you apparently haven't been going to. And the art..." He waved a hand helplessly. "Have you even talked to Hillman? Because as far as I can tell, all you ever do anymore is sit in your room or go to the gym."

"I told you," Nate said, lips stretching with an unrecognizably acidic smile. "I've been metalworking."

Some part of him enjoyed their confused looks more than he probably had any decent right to.

"Why would you lie about something like that?" Zach finally asked.

"Or work out at all?" Kyle murmured.

"Is this about what happened in that video?" Marty added.

Nate froze. Was that just more digging, or had Marty actually seen something?

He eyed his roommates one by one in the stretching silence. Had the Excalibur made good on his blackmail threats and shown them? He didn't think so. He was surprised to find he barely even cared at this point. All he'd wanted was one night away from it all. One carefree night with his friends. And they couldn't even let him have that much.

"Are you all done?" he asked flatly, reaching for his new beer.

"Why are you doing this?" Marty asked, visibly agitated now. "Why won't you talk to us?"

"We're talking right now," Nate said, squeezing his glass and resisting the urge to point out that they were doing so in the middle of a crowded public space for some god-awful reason. "What do you want from me?"

Marty looked like he'd been slapped.

"What do I want?" he echoed, his voice wavering slightly, like he was fighting back tears. "I want my friend back, Nate."

For a moment, the words sucked the air straight from Nate's lungs. For a moment, he gaped, forgetting that they were in the middle of a crowded bar, not knowing what to say, or why he was acting like this, or why he should suddenly be so damned angry. But he *was* angry. Desperately angry.

"Yeah?" he heard himself growl, in a trembling voice that wasn't his own, a voice utterly furious that, after everything, he could still be made to feel like this by the so-called friends who really wanted nothing but to drag him back down, to keep him small and weak like them. "Well, maybe you should grow up and—"

Something shattered, and a flood of cold liquid washed over his hand, down into his lap. Beer, he realized, wrenching his gaze away from Marty's wide eyes and down to his glass. He'd squeezed too hard. Broken the glass.

For a second, it was all Nate could do to sit there staring at the dripping mess. Then a bright, happy voice broke in beside them.

"Hey, guys!"

Gwen.

Shit.

"What are you all… Oh."

Gwen and Kelsey stood at their booth, drinks and backpacks in hand. They must've just come from lab, some part of Nate's brain numbly noted, as their friendly smiles faltered, gauging the emotional resonance of the table, and taking in the mess of broken glass and creamsicle beer.

"I… I need a napkin," Nate heard himself say as he stood from the booth, not really sure where his feet were taking him, only that he needed to get away for a minute. Maybe more.

"And you know what?" his mouth added anyway, feet stopping of their own accord, rounding him back on Marty and the others. "Maybe I just needed a break from everything, okay? Maybe I had my reasons, and if you really…"

He stopped before his voice could break, helplessly shaking his head at their lost puppy stares, lost himself for the words he was too upset to say. It was all fucked. A cruel paradox that, after weeks spent locked in, he should be here now, trembling in front of his friends, and Gwen, and what felt like half of State College, feeling more alone than he ever had before.

He turned to go, murmuring an apology to Gwen, painfully aware of the eyes pressing in on him from all directions, lapping up this delectable little morsel of a public spectacle. Somewhere far behind, Gwen was asking the others if he was all right. He walked faster.

Today was the goddamn day, all right.

Something is wrong, Nathaniel.

"No shit," Nate muttered.

Not that, the Excalibur said. *Something important.*

Not now, Nate thought, trying not to outwardly scowl as he squeezed between two groups of their casual onlookers. They all went on sipping their beers, enjoying the show. One raised his glass in cheers.

Set aside your sniveling college drama and—

I said not now! Nate mentally snapped. Or shouted out loud like a goddamn madman, he realized, as the roar of the crowd dimmed around him, and even more startled and curious eyes turned his way.

Fine, the Excalibur said, its tone perfectly flat, like that was that, and it was throwing in the towel for good. *Have it your way, then.*

But Nate was more focused on the familiar voice cutting through the chatter of the crowd.

"Holy shit. You really are insane, aren't you, Arturi?"

His stomach sank at that voice—sank with the sudden certainty that he'd somehow woken up in hell that morning, and that there would be no end to this nonstop thrill-ride of personal shame and surprise cock punches. He looked up and caught sight first of Emily Atherton, then of the beefy arm draped across her shoulders, and the sandy-haired Alpha-Sig-Sig Adonis attached to it.

Goddamn Todd.

Nate didn't bother wondering at the chances, or at what the hell Todd Mackleroy was doing here, of all places. He just stepped around them for the exit. Or tried, at least, before the King of the Bros slid his arm free from his concubine and cut him off.

"I don't know what the hell's up with you," Todd said, low enough that probably only the nearest circle of gawkers could hear, "but you owe us a new window, asshole."

Nate wasn't really sure what compelled him to look to Emily for input on that note, but the move only seemed to fire Todd's furnaces that much more.

"You hear me, Arturi?"

Behind him, Emily looked uncharacteristically meek.

"Look at me when I'm talking to you!"

It was the finger jab that did it.

One decisive injection of manly man authority, administered via Todd's rigid index and middle fingers, right to the center of the pulsing red *exterminate* button on Nate's chest, and he went from zero to murder in half a second flat.

"You want a goddamn Knight?" he growled under his breath, his fist practically humming with electric excitement as he clenched it tight.

"What'd you say, bro?"

Nate cocked back to knock that self-absorbed sneer into low orbit.

Then gentle hands took hold of his arm, and a soft voice was cooing at his ear. "Hey… Hey, you're okay."

Gwen's voice.

She pulled gently on his arm, silently urging him to disengage. He kept his eyes on Todd, half-expecting the Greek A-hole to capitalize on the distraction and take his own shot. But he didn't.

The electric tension drained as Gwen's hand found Nate's fist. She frowned down at their joined hands, almost like she'd felt it dissipating, but then her attention swiveled back to Todd. And that's when Nate's higher brain caught up to what was happening.

Todd and Emily. Here. *Together.*

Gwen had just walked right into the bombshell Nate should've broken to her weeks ago. He turned to her, mortified, his own personal crises momentarily forgotten beneath the guilt. Except she didn't look dumbstruck, or devastated. She didn't look much of anything at all.

Todd, on the other hand…

Never once had Nate imagined he'd ever see Todd Mackleroy look so vulnerably human. He didn't cower, exactly. Maybe the opposite. His back straightened under Gwen's scrutiny, his chest puffing almost in challenge as he pointedly wrapped an arm around a less than flattered Emily. It was painful to watch, but not as painful as the look in Todd's eyes, buried just beneath the dying phantom of his self-assured sneer. Nate swore he could see some part of Todd's once-proud soul crumbling in there. He couldn't look away from the sight.

"Come on," was all Gwen said, pulling Nate gently by the hand, apparently content to leave it at that.

"I knew you were into some freaky shit, babe," Todd said, finally finding his voice, "but Arturi? Seriously? He's a fucking—"

"Shut up."

The words silenced Todd so fast Nate almost didn't believe they'd come from his own mouth. At first, he wasn't even sure what it was that'd just set him on high alert. Not Todd's impending insults. Not *just* those, at least. It was something else. Something…

There.

A low, almost inaudible vibration thrumming in his chest and through his bones. The handful of Liberty patrons huddled around the front windows, frowning out into the State College night. A prickling tingle rising along the back of his neck, and a deep, nearly subconscious certainty.

"Nate?" Gwen said.

Something was coming. He felt it in his gut.

He was whirling to look for Marty and the others when the light spilled in, casting the industrial chic décor with a violent halogen blue and illuminating College Ave in the windows like a waking sun. A car alarm split the night air, then several more.

"What the fuck?" someone gasped at the windows.

A scream outside. Dozens of them, multiplying. The sharp cracking thud of cars colliding in the street. The tight pressure of Gwen's hand on his. And through it all, the electric thrum of something enormous charging, building, like some unspeakable alien death ray preparing to fire.

Nate's insides clenched, turned to ice. The sound was spreading, spreading until the entire world was vibrating with it, and it was crushing down on Nate's entire body. Then the pressure receded with a concussive pulse of sound, and all hell broke loose.

Windows shattered. The ceiling cracked and groaned, showering them with dust. Outside, it sounded as if entire mountains were collapsing.

In the blink of an eye, the bar fell to utter chaos, half of the population stampeding madly for the door while the other half clashed against them in a desperate rush to get the hell away from whatever was out there.

But Nate knew what was out there, didn't he?

I see you have decided to start paying attention again. Splendid.

Gwen's shouting voice yanked him out of his stupor. Nate grabbed her hand and pulled her back toward the booth, searching desperately for Marty's face in the screaming crowd.

They didn't make it two feet through the mess before another humming charge began to build in the air.

"We have to…" Nate started to shout to Gwen, before he realized he had no godly idea what they had to do.

Run?

Duck for fucking cover?

The thrumming air thickened, building Liberty up to a low grade pressure cooker, then the wave crested, wriggling Nate's insides on a moment of bizarre weightlessness, and the better half of the ceiling disappeared with a rending crunch, shooting up into the sky as if drawn by the world's most giant vacuum cleaner.

Halogen blue light flooded the room. Nate squinted up through the blinding sea of a thousand tiny suns, and even knowing what he knew, could only gape at what he saw.

Ships. *Alien* ships. Dozens of them filling the night sky above, each one a dim outline of sharp, craggy edges behind the onslaught of the lights, like an army of floating mountains, casting their nightmarish daylight down on State College.

"Help us," Nate whispered—to the Excalibur, to the Merlin or the Lady, he didn't know.

Beside him, Gwen's eyes were wide, her hand death-grip tight on his. "What the hell's happening, Nate?"

Another charge was building.

Tell her.

Strong winds slapped at them through the open ceiling. Around them, other buildings were cracking open, the air moaning with a steady stream of those alien pulses, each one ripping up another gout of rooftop debris here, another freaking car there.

And people too, Nate realized numbly, too shocked to move. Masses of screaming, writhing people shooting into the air from neighboring buildings all around, straight up, straight toward the waiting ships high above.

Abductees.

Hundreds of them.

Tell her how you failed to stop this.

"Just shut up and help me, goddammit!" he snapped back, prying his eyes back down to Liberty, looking for his friends.

Gwen gripped his hand and arm even tighter. "Nate, who're you— What's—"

Tell her how you never truly believed.

The pressure built, flattening his insides until the wave crested, and the sense of weightlessness engulfed him once again, more potent than before. Then the effect reversed, and the floor rocketed away, launching him skyward without the faintest warning. He would've lost Gwen completely if she hadn't been flying right next to him, the entire population of Liberty flailing right around them, all zooming toward the hovering lights in a sea of terrified screams.

"HELP US, EX!" Nate screamed, yanking Gwen closer and holding onto her as tightly as he could even as she screamed her own prayers, clutching him right back.

The lights were rushing to meet them. Up, down, he couldn't tell. They zoomed closer, closer. Too fast. They were going to hit.

Help us, he thought one last time, little more than a feeble prayer. Then came the Excalibur's reply, cold and mechanical.

No.

CHAPTER 22

THE PIT

His head ached.

Christ, his head ached.

The world awoke as a dark orange swirl of nausea lurching wildly beneath him, adrift in panicked voices and metallic rattles, his mind grasping feebly at disjointed memories. Blinding lights, rushing closer. The craggy underbelly of... of *ships*, he remembered in a rush. Alien ships.

Troglodan ships?

"Nate!" a familiar voice hissed through the drunken malaise of memories. Darkness as something—a tractor beam?—had yanked them aboard. Jostling impacts in the blind dark, clinging to Gwen for dear life, bouncing around on something like a conveyor belt. Fighting to keep her close as they were dished onto a grimy deck, and... And what? It felt like grasping at a fading nightmare.

"Nate?!"

He tried again to blink his eyes open, winced as the first slits of light entered his swollen eyes, and punched him right in the brain. Had he been unconscious?

The spinning world lurched on beneath him. Rhythmically. Heavy, thunking footsteps. He was being carried. He tried to open his eyes again. Saw the bleary outline of impossibly thick legs stomping along overhead... below? A troglodan, his brain registered. He was slung over the shoulder of a troglodan.

"Nate, please. Jesus, please."

Gwen's voice. Close.

Something rattling. Chains? Then the world tilted, and something hit the deck with a groan—Gwen's voice again, he realized with a sickened twist—and the troglodan lurched on.

"Nate!" Gwen cried somewhere behind. "No!"

The panic and pain in her voice hit him like a searing bolt. His eyes snapped fully open. He glimpsed rust colored bulkheads and a field of hip-high posts sliding by. Then he gathered what groggy strength he had and rolled.

He must've caught the troglodan by surprise. Gods knew he caught *himself* by surprise, when he realized he'd just consigned his poor body to an eight foot drop. He hit the unforgiving deck before he had time to think about it, and scrambled wildly for his feet, barely even noticing the pain, or the dozens of chained students gaping at him on either side of the aisle from the bulkhead and the tether posts.

Then he tripped on something. Something that yanked his arms down by the wrists. A chain. His wrists were shackled, he realized in groggy surprise. Chained together. He stutter-stepped for balance, aware that people were screaming all around him.

Something struck the back of his head, and next he knew, he was face down on the deck, half blind with stars dancing through his vision.

"Nate!" Gwen cried somewhere.

He tried to get up—or thought he did, at least—but a thick hand took him by the throat and started dragging him across the grimy deck before he got anywhere. Nate coughed and sputtered, trying as best he could to scramble along with the troglodan before it accidentally broke his neck or choked him to death. The hulking beast seemed to find this amusing.

It paused, chuckling to itself, then changed course, hefting him around like a plaything and backtracking the way they'd come. A few frantic moments later, Nate was almost shamefully relieved to find himself casually deposited against one of the stout chain posts right next to the aisle—and right next to Gwen. She reached and grabbed onto his hand like a lifeline, gasping his name, their shackled wrists clanking together.

For a brief second, taking in the rows of fellow prisoners all around them with Gwen's hand crushing his, Nate remembered past his spinning head that he was supposed to be a goddamn Knight. That he was supposed to be strong enough to *do* something about this. Then the beast who'd carried him over bent down, stuck its beady-eyed face inches from Nate's, bared yellow teeth that looked like they could've chomped through human bones, and roared.

By the time the ferocious sound abated, Nate was shaking in a numb stupor, too afraid to move as the chuckling troglodan first patted his cheek with a pair of forearm-sized fingers, then casually plucked the chain from one of his shackles—like it had some kind of magnetic release —and reached back to fix it to the post. Another chain clicked into place on the thick collar Nate hadn't even noticed he was wearing, then the troglodan returned its reach from behind Nate, trailing one last chain, which it fixed to the shackle of the hand that was still tightly gripped in Gwen's.

Definitely magnetic. Or something like it. Hard to think straight with a sneering troglodan breathing hot, fetid air in his face.

"Gargoot," the beast rumbled, tilting its thick, lumpy gray hillside of a head toward Gwen and patting Nate roughly on the cheek once again before it stood back to its full eight-and-a-half feet and stomped off for the next prisoner, chuckling to itself.

Nate watched it go, not understanding what the hell had just happened —or, even more importantly, how in all the unknown universe the Merlin and the Lady had ever thought *he* could hope to take on even a single one of these monsters.

Ex? he thought, almost cautiously, as if he might somehow make things worse.

Nothing.

"Are you okay?" Gwen whispered beside him.

Ex, we need your help. Please!

Nothing at all.

"Nate..." Gwen was whispering.

Nate turned to her, not knowing what to say. He wasn't okay. None of them were okay. But at least seeing her in one piece brought a feeble flicker of relief. "What happened?" he tried to ask. The words barely came out. Christ, his mouth was dry.

"I thought they hit you with some kind of sedative when you, you know..." She searched his face, then, seeming to realize he might *not* know, she added, "You struggled when they tried to separate us."

Dim memories stirred, tinged with a druggy haze. Nate and Gwen, huddling like a pair of frightened bunnies, dished onto a grimy deck. Fellow bar-goers scrambling in the darkness around them. Brutally strong hands shoving them along. Screams and groaning mechanical assemblies, and something enormous trying to rip Gwen away from him. Away into the darkness.

He *had* fought. Fought right up until something smacked into his neck like a striking viper. And that was it.

"How long ago?" he asked, glancing around the room—the brig, he supposed—where at least eight troglodans were thudding up and down the gray aisles, checking on chains here, dragging in another terrified prisoner there.

"Not long. They put us through some kind of… processing. Outfitted everyone with shackles. Decontaminated us too, I think."

That probably explained why he felt so goddamn sticky, at least, and why the mysterious goopy residue was wafting such a strong alcohol scent, and burning at the sites of the several abrasions he'd collected in the shuffle.

"It all happened so fast," Gwen added quietly, "but I managed to keep you with me."

He looked back to her. Something about the way she said it, and the way she was watching him now. "Gwen," he whispered, not really knowing what else to say.

She held his gaze, and he could practically hear her thoughts racing. "You didn't go down like the others," she finally said. "Not completely. You just kinda…" She shook her head, apparently lost for words.

Nate turned and scanned the brig more closely, not sure what to make of that. He needed to find Marty and the others. There might've been close to two hundred captives in the room, a third or so lining the chain rings on the rust colored bulkhead perimeter, and the rest, like him and Gwen, chained to the rows of hip-high chain posts spaced evenly across most of the brig.

He saw a few other students completely zonked out, mostly larger guys. Hit with the same drugs they'd used on him?

"Must've been a faulty dose," Gwen said quietly, apparently tracking his gaze. "Lucky. Still scared the hell out of me, though."

A faulty dose.

Maybe.

He squeezed Gwen's hand, not knowing what to say.

Do I have you to thank for my early arrival to hell? he wondered silently at the Excalibur, but still there was nothing. No reply. Nate wasn't even positive he could still feel his unwilling companion there at all.

All he could do was stare at the troglodans moving casually about, checking chains and shackles even as Gwen ran through a quiet breakdown of what they knew and all the *whos, hows, whats,* and *whys* they needed to start figuring out if they were going to survive this thing. Nate was still caught up on the big one.

What in holy hell had he done?

Nothing, he could've sworn the troglodans replied as they stomped about, trading gouts of their booming, guttural speech. *Not a goddamn thing.* And now he was trapped.

At least they weren't ruthlessly murdering everyone, right?

Not yet.

Not that there was much stopping them.

"—said shut up!" Nate heard someone hiss nearby, as he surveyed their surroundings for any hint of hope.

Most of the troglodans in the brig were smaller than the monstrosity that had chased him in the park a few weeks ago, but any one of them still looked like they could've handled multiple NFL linebackers without breaking a sweat. Also unlike the park berserker—which he realized now must've been naked in all of its knobby gray hided glory—these troglodans wore plated dark armor that might've actually looked sleek and sophisticated if it hadn't been so scuffed and battered. Not that *that* really—

"Nate!" hissed a voice behind and to the right, from where a bigger troglodan had just come stomping past.

Nate straightened in surprise. *Marty.*

He glanced carefully to the right, trying not to rattle his chains or draw any attention. The troglodans couldn't have cared less anyway. They were busy hauling in more prisoners. He turned as fully as the chains let him. Relief flooded his chest at the sight of Marty and Kyle chained up side-by-side on the bulkhead. Relief, quickly followed by a burst of manic guilt that he could ever feel anything other than horror at such a sight.

At least they looked unharmed, though, and lucid. More lucid than Nate felt anyway, though his brain did seem to be burning through the druggy haze pretty quickly, all things considered.

"Are you okay?" Marty whispered as loudly as he dared, glancing nervously toward the troglodans at the front of the room.

"Where's Zach?" Nate whispered back.

"Back here," came another whisper somewhere behind Nate. "Kelsey too."

Gwen perked up at that, trying to crane around to see, not making it far before her chains pulled taut. Around them, the whispers were multiplying, emboldened by the fact that none of them were immediately eaten for taking their hushed roll call.

"Shut up, you assholes," someone growled, louder than all the rest. "You're gonna get us all killed!"

Nate ignored the voice and strained against his chains, first testing them, then twisting around as best he could to try to get a look at them. Which was how he just so happened to be looking in the exact wrong place when a big guy chained up a few posts back and to the left exploded from silent fidgeting to full on losing his shit.

"LET ME GO!" he screamed suddenly, thrashing forward against his restraints at the nearest troglodan. "LET ME FUCKING—"

There was a rushing thrum of sound like a miniaturized version of the pulse waves that'd ripped them out of Liberty, and the big guy's head disappeared in a cloud of red mist.

Half of the room screamed. Nate could only stare at the girl who'd been sitting beside the big guy. Her eyes had gone blank. Just vacant. Her cheek spattered with blood. Her trembling jaw the only thing moving on her entire body.

A thud from ahead drew Nate's eyes to where one of the other troglodans had shoved the shooter against the dirty bulkhead. The shover growled a sharp string of what sounded like rebuke. The shooter brandished his gun, replying in kind, then gestured toward the headless prisoner. A few of the troglodans laughed at whatever he'd said. The one who appeared to be in charge shoved the shooter toward the door, then barked an order at another. The room watched in dead silence as the alien unchained the headless body and dragged it from the room by a single leg, like it was nothing but a freaking defective mannequin.

The rest of the troglodans paid the grisly scene no mind as they finished chaining down the last of their loose captives. Once they were done, they stood and left, leaving their leader alone at the head of the room, surveying them with a deadly calm, sweeping his massive head slowly from side to side.

"Vorshna et gralith du shargul," he finally growled.

The room was silent, no one daring to speak up after the first guy had lost his head for it. Nate wasn't sure why the beast would expect them to understand a word it was saying anyway.

Not until it looked around the room once more, and added, "Vorshna et Excalibur."

Nate's blood went cold.

He'd misheard, he wanted to think. Imagined it.

But the sickened feeling churning his gut told him the truth.

It was him. In all the terror of the abduction, Nate hadn't had time to wonder how the hell they'd ended up in State College, of all places, if they were only looking for the Beacon. But the answer was obvious. They were looking for him, too.

This was his fault.

Nate sat frozen in horror, numbly trying to grasp just how badly he'd failed here, and just how laughably sad his attempts at training had really been. It was incomprehensible.

What had that drunken asshole been thinking, pulling him into all this?

And where was the Excalibur now?

"Vorshna et Excalibur!" the troglodan roared.

Nate froze mid-flinch, sure his reaction had already given him away, then wondering if he shouldn't just speak up and have done with it anyway. He swept his eyes across the hundred or so people chained up between him and the troglodan leader, wondering how many in the city had already died because of him. If he could end it all right now...

He had to.

Only he couldn't seem to get his mouth to work, or his hands to move. He just sat there while the leader studied the room, telling himself that it wouldn't matter if he gave himself up—that he didn't even actually understand what they were asking for and that, even if he had understood, there was no way to guarantee the aliens wouldn't just exterminate the remainder of their captives once they had what they wanted. Better he wait and see what was actually happening. Wait, and look for his shot to do gods knew what.

With any luck, the military would be rolling in before any of them had to figure that part out. There was no way an incident like this could go unnoticed. Hell, he'd already had the Space Aggressor Squadron keeping tabs, right? Even now, the Pentagon must be rustling up a full run of fighter jets and drones and everything else.

Unless they were too busy scrambling those forces elsewhere, Nate thought uneasily, remembering what the Merlin had showed him of a burning New York City the night he'd told Nate about the Beacon.

Get it off of this planet, the wizard had said, *or the troglodan invasion will soon be the least of Earth's troubles.*

Ahead, the troglodan leader was shifting its weight, baring yellow teeth in a kind of sneer. "Gargoot," it said, with an air of finality, before it turned and stomped out of the room.

A bulky metal door slammed shut behind it, and for a long, long time, they all sat dead still, the air thick with the heaviest silence Nate had ever felt. Almost as heavy as the Merlin's last words, echoing over and over again in his head.

All of humanity may well be counting on you.

He had to get them out of there.

CHAPTER 23
VORSHNA ET

The following hours were the most hellish of Nate's life.

It wasn't just the conditions of their imprisonment. The cold almost didn't bother him—hadn't much seemed to since he'd begun his metamorphosis under the Excalibur's influence. The pain and discomfort, too, were at least somewhat tolerable. His wrists ached where he'd strained against the shackles one too many times, and his hips and back and neck all felt like shit from a few hours pinned to the hard deck. But that much, he could stand.

It was watching the suffering around him that was really killing him.

It was the terrified silence that stretched on long after the head troglodan left. It was the lone sob that eventually broke that silence, and the rapid unraveling of the brig from silent mausoleum to wailing shit show that followed.

It was the look in Gwen's eyes as she turned to him with her own silent tears, like a quiet plea for him to do something. Like for some intangible reason, she actually believed he could.

Until then, even knowing what he did, it had all been too fast—too alien to be real. Even the brutal execution behind them had felt like something out of a movie. But when he saw that look in Gwen's eyes, it all came crashing in. Too much raw emotion to process, even if the overwhelming majority of it did feel a lot like guilt. Guilt that he'd failed to bond with the Excalibur and find the Beacon in time. Guilt that he'd failed to even remotely grasp what was at stake, even after the Merlin had shown him. A deep burning shame, underneath it all, that he'd never even had the courage to simply tell Gwen how he felt years ago, when he'd had a thousand ample chances.

It was almost laughable, how afraid he'd been—how completely ignorant to how good and easy his life was before the Excalibur had come to him. How worthless and naïve he'd been once it had. So laughable, so pathetic, that he found himself sharing in Gwen's silent tears before he knew it, clutching to her hand while the brig howled on around them.

He feared every moment that the troglodans would come bursting back in to make another bloody example and quiet the racket, but there wasn't as much as a thump on the wall. They didn't seem to care. Not even when some of the more optimistic voices rallied enough to start telling their neighbors how the army or the air force would be sweeping to save their asses any moment, just you wait. Not even when a few particularly bold spirits started asking if anyone still had their phones, or any ideas about how to get free.

Maybe the troglodans didn't understand what they were talking about. Maybe they just didn't care.

Nate refrained from joining the conversation, pretty sure that what little he knew would only succeed at scaring the shit out of everyone, and possibly turning them all against him, to boot. He needed a proper plan first, he told himself. Or at least some clue as to what the troglodans might do next.

It was only when he recognized Todd's voice among the Big Talk council up front that Nate truly began to feel like a chicken shit—as if the universe had just needed to flick him in the eye with one more reminder of how useless he'd been. Nate craned his neck and saw that the Greek god was chained on the front wall, with Emily Atherton huddling into his side for refuge from it all.

Even in the freaking alien apocalypse, Todd Mackleroy got his little slice of comfort and glory, didn't he? The thought infuriated him, which in turn only made him feel petty and childish. Doubly so when Gwen broke from her own quiet ruminations to ask if he was all right.

"I'm just, uh..." He tore his eyes from Todd and Emily and considered Gwen's expression. The steady rattle of chains and the vibration of the troglodan ship beneath them. Now wasn't the time. He was sure of it. But he wasn't sure there'd be another. "I'm sorry I didn't tell you about..."

Jesus, where did he even start? There were too many confessions to count at this point. Her perfect brow was furrowed, waiting.

"… About Todd and Emily," he forced himself to say.

Her eyes widened a hair.

This was *so* not the time.

"I saw them together after the INN party that night," he pressed on anyway, desperate, as if maybe fixing this one thing—this one failure from the painfully long list—might somehow mean something. "Todd saw me seeing them, too. Long story, but…"

The surprised look on Gwen's face was morphing to one of disbelief, and betrayal, and—

"I should have told you sooner," Nate whispered. "I should have…" He grimaced down at the grimy deck between them, and at the spot where's Gwen's hand had left his to return to the safety of her own thigh.

What the hell was he doing?

Gwen seemed to be wondering the same thing.

"Is this really what you're worrying about right now?" she whispered, looking pointedly around at the dozens of students crying, soiling themselves, and otherwise losing their shit around them.

Nate shook his head, cheeks burning, chicken shit despondency lurching to embarrassing new heights. "You're right. I'm sorry, I just… There's just a lot I would've done differently, if…"

"If you'd known we were going to be *abducted?*"

Nate fumbled for words and fell back on a helpless shrug.

"You and everyone else aboard this ship, I'm guessing," Gwen said, not quite unkindly.

Nate said nothing. Just sat there listening to the soundtrack of despair all around him, turning mental loops underneath the sinking weight that he, unlike everyone else aboard this ship, had actually had a chance to do something about this. And what had he done with that chance?

"Well," Gwen said quietly beside him, "if you're trying to clear your conscience about not saving me from the big scary cheater, you're missing a few important details. Like the fact that I haven't seen Todd since that night at Iota Nu Nu."

Nate glanced over at her, not understanding, surprised she'd brought the subject back up at all. "You haven't?"

"The other part you seem to have missed," Gwen continued, looking like she couldn't quite believe she was having this conversation right now, "the part that I actually told you right to your face, is that Todd was never really my boyfriend."

"But you…"

"Did you really think I was too busy swooning over his abs to notice he was spending time with other girls? Jesus." She shook her head, half-muttering to herself. "Todd walks around thinking I'm the wife material he might one day see fit to grace with a ring and fractional fidelity, and you…" She glanced over at him, brow furrowed in frustration. "Did it ever occur to you that maybe—just maybe—I understood the situation perfectly well, and was capable of deciding what arrangements I was and wasn't happy with in my own life? That maybe *I* was open to other possibilities too?"

Nate could only stare, trying to process.

"You wanna know what I think?" she asked quietly. "I think you're so obsessed with believing that you're this downtrodden, unappreciated side-line spectator that you're actually in danger of becoming an asshole just to maintain your own Nice Guy self-image. It's like a bad oxymoron."

"That's not…"

"True? Fair? Look at this." She yanked her chains taut trying to point to his muscled chest. "Do you think *that's* what's holding you back? That you have to have bigger muscles, or anything else, to get what you want?"

"What? No, I—"

"You think Todd's an asshole because he takes whatever he wants. But you know what? I don't see how that's any worse than this passive-aggressive game of hide-and-seek you've been playing for four years."

The last words were barely a whisper. Judging by the surprised look in Gwen's eyes, she hadn't really meant to say them at all—had tried to tamp them back down to whatever fountain of truth they'd bubbled up from. But she *had* meant them. He felt that much in the cold vacuum slap they smote across his insides.

He looked away, unable to meet her eyes. For a few seconds, he felt so hollow that he couldn't even bring himself to care that they were still chained up on a troglodan ship, and that, even in the bleak reality of their impending doom, more than a few of their neighbors were staring at them now, ears cued in to this tasty little morsel of drama—Marty and Kyle probably included, he couldn't help but think.

It hardly mattered.

"Nate…" Gwen whispered. "Nate, I didn't mean…" A heavy sigh. "Shit. I didn't mean to say it like that. Can we just…?"

Nate nodded mechanically, accepting her unfinished request with eyes forward, hating how pathetic he felt. He knew she hadn't meant to hurt him, just like he knew she'd meant everything else she'd just said. And why wouldn't she?

She was right, after all.

More right than she could know.

Because here he was, sitting helplessly with the girl he thought he loved while Todd prattled on up front, taking charge. Here he was with his training, and his forewarning, and his miraculously expedient five pounds of solid muscle gain a week, bearing the one and only weapon that might stand a chance of helping them out of this mess if he could only get it together, and what was he doing? Fucking sniveling. Just sitting here, letting others do the talking.

Because speaking up wasn't heroic, he told himself. Because there was nothing heroic about causing mass hysteria. But also because he wasn't a goddamn hero. Because whatever power was riding within him had gotten him exactly jack shit. Because at the heart of it, it *wasn't* about muscles, or dedication, or how hard he tried.

It was that some assholes were just built for it, and others were just built to fix their computers.

Nate thunked his head back against the chain post and listened, utterly deflated, as Todd told everyone to keep their shit together up front.

"It's okay," Gwen said quietly, taking his lifeless hand, no doubt hearing the same. "We're going to be okay."

Gods only knew what was going through her head in that moment. He could hardly bear to think about it. What he needed to do was focus on getting them the hell out of there. Somehow. And then…

Jesus, he didn't even know what then.

Race the troglodans to the Beacon? Sure. Why not? Maybe he could take a swing at curing cancer and ending world hunger while he was at it.

There was only one more place to turn. He barely even hesitated, hopeless as he was.

If you were waiting to make a point, I get it. I messed up. I'm not fucking worthy. I'm sorry, Ex. I'm really, really sorry. But if you just help me get these people out of here, I'll do anything you want.

Silence.

Anything, Ex. I promise. Please.

Nothing. A long, long nothing.

He couldn't even bring himself to be angry. Not at the Excalibur. Not at Marty and Kyle, as they tried to draw his attention across the aisle, first to check if he was all right, then again shortly after to weigh in on their quiet side debate about what was really going on here, and how they were going to escape.

Whatever else there was to say about the situation, he couldn't help but be impressed with how well his friends seemed to be handling things, even if Kyle was clearly less than thrilled at having finally received his irrefutable confirmation that "they" did, in fact, walk among us.

What Nate *wasn't* crazy about was the way Marty and Kyle were looking at him when he finally turned around—like maybe the guy who'd fallen off the edge of the map a few weeks ago after a suspicious large animal attack and some mysteriously hushed up heroics might know more than he was letting on here.

Frightened as he was of the ramifications, each passing minute weakened Nate's reservation about simply saying *to hell with it* and spilling all of his juicy secrets for anyone who wanted to listen. He was on the verge of opening his mouth when the screaming started outside.

It wasn't completely obvious at first. The kind of thing you cocked your head to clearly hear, and then promptly tried to explain away as ambiguous ship sounds, or maybe the distant coming of the military rescue that was definitely totally only a matter of time, according to Todd and the Big Talkers.

The ship *had* moved at some point in the past hour or two, Nate was pretty sure. Moved *where*, he had no idea. He couldn't even say how long they'd been sitting here. Maybe they'd moved down College Ave, or maybe into orbit.

Christ, they could've been halfway across the galaxy, for all he knew.

But the screams... Muffled as they were by the grimy bulkheads, and persistently as the low din of conversation tried to carry on, pretending all was well, once the screams began to multiply, there was no ignoring them.

The room went quiet, the last in a long string of nervous *no, no, that's just the ship* declarations petering out like a match at the end of its stick. And just like that, what little calm had entered the brig in the past hours dissipated in a flash of wide eyes and one especially frantic cry from the back: "We're all gonna die, man! We're all gonna fucking die!"

Judging by how quickly the terror reignited throughout the room, Nate took it he wasn't alone in generally believing the truth of the statement. But this time, he didn't try to fight it.

This time, he focused on the feeling of his heart thundering in his eardrums, and on the growing panic in the room. This time, he rode the wave of adrenaline up, up, thinking dazedly about the otherworldly strength he'd summoned to stop that bike when it had felt like life and death. Thinking about the two words the Excalibur had uttered time and time again, whenever he'd insisted the thing fall in line and behave.

Make me.

His fists clenched. Around him, the room was alive with sobs and jangling chains and screams of its own.

Maybe the Lady had picked the wrong Knight. Maybe the Excalibur was dead set on sitting back while Nate and his friends died, content in the knowledge that it would likely be granted a more suitable Knight the next time around. But he had to try anyway.

So he let the fear in, embracing the panic, thinking about all the horrific things that were going to happen to all of them—to Gwen and to his friends —if he didn't do something about it. He drank the sobbing desperation in until he was ready to scream himself.

Then he planted his feet and lunged forward against his chains as hard as he possibly could.

For a moment, there was nothing but the blinding roar of effort, and the desperate belief that this would work, *had* to work. Then something thudded against his back, and pain cut into his awareness, rippling from his wrists, and his neck, and the back of his head.

He'd thunked straight back against the goddamn chain post. Shackles and collar in place. Chains intact.

"Nate?!"

Nate turned confusedly to where Marty and Kyle were watching him with wide-eyed concern. His head was spinning. From impact or just sheer surprise, he couldn't tell. People were looking at him. *Gwen* was looking at him. He felt her stare on the back of his head. Felt a burning in his throat.

He hadn't meant to yell.

It didn't matter. It hadn't worked.

Why hadn't it worked?

"Nate," Marty repeated, trying to get his attention. "Dude, are you—"

"I'm fine," Nate muttered, slumping back against his chain post, eyes front, away from his friends and Gwen and everyone else.

He wasn't fine. None of them were fine. And there wasn't a damn thing he could do about it. How he'd actually deluded himself into thinking he might just casually rip heavy chains apart... Well, whatever the Merlin and Lady had thought him capable of, they'd probably realize their mistake once the troglodans were flying around with his Excalibur. Or with the *eighth*

Excalibur, at least. Because if that little display had proved anything, it was that the Excalibur was most certainly not his.

"Nate..." Gwen whispered,

He wanted to look at her, wanted to take some small comfort from the fact that she was still there, but he couldn't bring himself to take her hand or turn his head. Couldn't handle the thought of the disappointment he imagined he'd see in her eyes. Disappointment that he'd lost his shit, or that it hadn't worked. Disappointment that he wasn't worthy. For any of it.

So instead, he sat there, eyes pointedly forward, stewing in his own silent despair while, at the front of the room, Todd and a few vocal others made solemn promises that if those things came looking for torture victims here, they'd fuck them up real good. Somehow.

Then something made a firm *thud-thud* on the brig door, and half the room cried out in startled terror. The rest, Nate had a feeling, simply soiled themselves in silence.

A metallic groan poured from the door's latching mechanism, casting a heavy hush over the room. A dark-armored troglodan stepped into the brig, drawing the door shut behind it. Nate couldn't tell if it was one of the same ones from earlier, but the heavy-looking pulse cannon it held casually over one broad shoulder looked familiar enough.

It took a few swaggering steps toward the center of the front aisle, seeming to enjoy the way those nearest to it flinched with its every move.

"Hey, asshole!" someone called—Todd, Nate realized with a small ripple of shock.

He craned his neck to see Todd leaning forward against his restraints, sitting tall and proud, muscular chest puffed in challenge right up until the troglodan turned his way and took a step closer.

It started with a sinking of the shoulders, like a slowly deflating balloon. Todd's mouth tightened, his eyes darting across the creature's massive frame. The troglodan stepped closer still, and Todd rocked back against the wall. It sank to one thick knee, leaning in with its jutting jaw until Todd bowed his head, visibly shaking with the threat of the thing's closeness. Then it grabbed Todd by the shoulder, one huge hand covering half his body, and clamped its other hand over his face.

As many times as Nate had dreamed of seeing Todd Mackleroy knocked from his godly war horse and dragged into the mud with the rest of them, there was something profoundly terrifying about seeing the unshakeable Greek god lose his shit. And lose his shit, he did.

No sooner had the troglodan clamped its hand to Todd's face than a pulse of light flashed from beneath its huge palm, and Todd began kicking and screamed like a madman.

The terror was contagious.

The room exploded with screams and cries and utterly futile scrambles to either help Todd, or get the hell away from whatever was happening to him. Nate could only stare numbly at Todd's flailing legs, sure that each moment would be the one that the troglodan incinerated his head, or simply closed its beastly fist and smashed it like an overripe pumpkin.

He watched, sickened, helpless.

Then the troglodan promptly released Todd and stood back to its full height, casual as ever, leaving Todd trembling on the deck in a pitiful heap, Emily Atherton reaching for him with shaking hands. In that moment, Nate felt nothing but empathy for the man. But empathy was quickly swallowed by dread as the troglodan turned to face the rest of the room. Turned with purpose. Something was blinking red on its thick wrist, like Todd's face had failed the test.

Something clicked, deep in Nate's brain.

He watched the troglodan, not breathing.

"Are-toor-ee," it rumbled in a deep voice.

Nate's head buzzed with the word. Positively spun with it.

The room went fuzzy around him, dimming whatever Gwen was whispering next to him.

Awkward pronunciation, some helpful part of his brain pointed out. Awkward, but still unmistakably a name. *His* name, he registered numbly, even as the troglodan raised a small cube between enormous thumb and forefinger, and a flat hologram flickered into life for all the brig to see, sputtering and tinged red, but unmistakably a human face. His face.

"Vorshna et," the troglodan rumbled, "Nah-tan-yell Are-toor-ee?"

CHAPTER 24
CHAIN OF COMMAND

He was dead.

That was the first of the two revelations that ripped through Nate's brain like a bolt of lightning.

Somehow, the troglodans had found his face and his name. And now he was dead—messy pulse cannon decapitation pending.

"What's happening, Nate?" Gwen was whispering beside him.

He genuinely did not know how to answer that question, or why his first instinct was to look to Marty. Maybe he just wanted to say farewell to his best friend. Because he had no choice now, did he?

"Vorshna et Nah-tan-yell Are-toor-ee!" the troglodan roared.

No choice.

Maybe these big bastards couldn't distinguish one human from another on sight—maybe that's why Todd had just gotten the full troglodan facial—but Nate couldn't just sit here while that thing scanned its way through the room looking for him. Eyes were already flicking to him, back to the troglodan's hologram, back to him.

He had to turn himself in. There was nothing for it.

He opened his mouth and—

"It's me," someone croaked, in a voice that wasn't his.

Nate followed the voice in disbelief, and found his best friend staring back at him, eyes wide with some mixture of shock and sudden clarity.

"Marty," Nate hissed, "don't you fucking d—"

"It's me!" Marty shouted. He lurched forward, rattling his chains.

"No!" Nate yelled.

"My name is Nathaniel Arturi!" Marty cried, even louder. "Take me and let these people go!"

Around them, the brig fell silent. Ahead, the troglodan leaned its hilltop head toward Marty, studying him with its dark beady eyes. Then it bared its dirty yellow teeth and started tromping their way.

"No!" Nate cried, bucking against his chains.

"It's me!" Marty yelled.

"Stop it!" Nate screamed at him.

Marty wasn't listening.

"I'm Nathaniel Arturi!" he cried over and over again. "Let them go, goddammit!"

"Vorshna et Excalibur, Nah-tan-yell Are-toor-ee," the troglodan growled, stomping closer, swinging its huge cannon down from its shoulder.

"Stop it!" Nate bellowed.

The troglodan drew up to a halt a few feet from Marty and leveled the cannon straight at Nate's face in silent warning, not even bothering to look at him. Nate froze, deathly aware of the building thrum in the weapon's depths, and of how casually the first prisoner had been shot. After a few seconds of breathless silence, the cannon swiveled away from him and around to Marty.

"Vorshna et Excalibur?"

"I..." Marty was shaking now. "I don't know what you're saying. Just— Just take me. Just take me and let them—"

The troglodan cut him off with an enraged roar. "Vorshna!" it boomed, dropping to a knee beside Marty and taking the chain that bound his wrist shackles to the wall loop in one massive hand. With a hard yank and sharp crack, the beast tore the chain clean in two.

Nate was hyperventilating, wild desperate panic reaching its electric tendrils through every inch of him, building, screaming, threatening to stop his heart as the troglodan yanked Marty closer, thrusting its humming cannon to his head.

"Vorshna et—"

Something broke inside Nate.

The world went hazy, blurred shades of red, like a sea of burst blood vessels. There was pain and sound and movement, and suddenly, inexplicably, he was on his feet, staring at the back of the troglodan's head and realizing that it wasn't something *within* him that had broken.

It was his chains.

He felt the heavy links swinging from his wrist manacles even as he noted dimly that, at his full height, he barely stood level with the shoulders of the massive beast crouched in front of him.

And that beast was turning toward him.

He didn't think. Just kicked wildly at the troglodan's big pulse cannon. His foot connected, hard. Pain shot through his leg. Whether by sheer surprise or dumb luck, the troglodan lost its grip and gaped stupidly as the cannon went bouncing and skidding across the brig deck. Then it turned its beady eyes back to Nate, not seeming to understand.

Nate was already swinging for the troglodan's head with the chain hanging from his right wrist, operating on blind Michael Bay instinct. He swung with everything he had, and watched in disbelief as the blow landed, and the gray-hided behemoth toppled over toward the grimy deck with a strangled grunt.

There was a moment of sharp panic as the troglodan fell toward the guy beside Marty on an imminent crushing path. Then the troglodan caught itself on the deck with one thick arm, and drove an even thicker boot into Nate's chest, mule-kick style.

It was like he was watching from third person. The impact was so stunning—so world-shaking—Nate didn't even register the pain. There was only the up-down nauseating blur of a world gone sideways, then the second impact, hard and utterly unforgiving. The rear bulkhead, some dutiful corner of his mind informed him, right as the pain caught up to his speeding corpse, blossoming through his chest and back and every inch of him like a screaming wave of—

"Get up, Arturi!" someone growled.

Nate blinked his eyes open to the face of a crying girl that couldn't have been the owner of that voice.

"It's coming, man!" someone else cried. "It's coming!"

"Please get up," sobbed the crying girl right above him. "Please."

Nate got up. He didn't understand how. Especially not as his insides filled with fire, and he coughed up what felt like more than a little blood. But that hardly mattered when he saw the troglodan picking itself up thirty feet away, next to Marty.

Jesus Christ, had it kicked him that far?

That hardly mattered either as the troglodan turned his way, oozing dark blood from the angry-looking gash where Nate's chain had struck. One of its eyes was gone. And it looked pissed.

"The gun!" snapped a voice somewhere behind him. "On your right, two o'clock!"

He spotted the big cannon not far away and scrambled forward. No time to wonder how the hell he was alive, or how he'd apparently kicked the bulky gun almost as far as the troglodan had kicked him. Especially not as that troglodan roared a guttural challenge and charged forward.

Nate practically fell over in his rush to scoop the cannon from the deck, praying he was holding the correct end. The thing must've weighed forty pounds, but Nate was much more concerned with the trigger. Or the lack thereof.

It was every nightmare he'd ever had, times a thousand. Fumbling desperately for the trigger of the forty pound club in his hands. The troglodan thundering toward him, shaking the deck with its monstrous bulk. No time. No—

Thumb trigger.

Never in his life had Nate been so happy to hear another voice in his head. He spotted the protruding stud on the weapon's grip and jammed his thumb down. The cannon hummed in his hands, building, building. The troglodan closing. Building. Not firing. Screams all around him. The roaring troglodan lunging forward to smash him to a pulp.

Let go.

With a wordless cry and a blind prayer, Nate released the trigger stud. The cannon gave a thrumming pulse in his hands, and the troglodan stumbled backward, its massive hand dropping to its abdomen, where its dark armor had crumpled in like it'd taken an invisible cannon ball. It gave a labored grunt, baring its teeth at Nate, taking a heavy step forward.

Nate raised the cannon higher, thumbed the trigger, and watched in morbid horror as the troglodan's head caved in with another invisible blast. The beast thudded limply to its knees, then smashed face-first to the deck, shaking the floor beneath Nate's unsteady feet.

The room was dead silent.

For a long moment, it was all Nate could do to stare down at the huge body, and the black blood slowly pooling out from its crushed head.

"YES!" Kyle shouted down the aisle, breaking the thick silence so suddenly that Nate almost dropped the cannon.

"I fucking *knew* you were a superhero, dude!"

Ahead, Marty joined Nate in shooting Kyle an incredulous look, then he collapsed back against the wall and sighed, just loud enough for Nate to hear, "Thank fucking god."

202

CHAPTER 25

YOU ALWAYS TURN LEFT

Nate felt more than heard the cannon thud to the deck beside him.

"Easy, buddy," Kyle called across the brig. "Keep it together. Keep it—Uh-oh..."

Nate was already staggering back, knees buckling without permission. He joined the cannon on the deck, just shy of the dark pool of troglodan blood that had set his legs shaking in the first place. His limbs felt like gelatin, and his stomach...

"Are you okay, dude?" Zach called somewhere ahead.

"Your knee," added a quiet voice to the right.

Nate looked down and saw that the pooling blood had reached his right leg, viscous inky crimson seeping eagerly into the khaki cotton blend.

Somehow, that was the detail that did it. Or maybe it had been the alien chest kick, and the thirty foot flight and abrupt wall impact. Either way, that was when Nate puked—one great heaving purge of creamsicle IPA, stomach acid, and blood. More blood than seemed safe for his immediate survival.

"That's it, buddy," Kyle called weakly. "Out with the bad spirits."

Out with the fucking spleen, Nate wanted to reply, but then he thought about what else that kick had probably done to his insides, and he nearly puked again.

You will survive, came the Excalibur's disgusted voice.

"Where the fuck have you been?" Nate whispered.

The Excalibur didn't answer.

Of course not.

Nate hauled himself to his feet with a groan, looking down at the giant alien corpse, lost for what to do next. *Now's not the time to clam up, Ex.*

He felt his companion there at the edge of his mind, bristling with… what?

What do you want, another apology?

The whispers were starting to spread.

"Nate?" came Marty's cautious voice.

He looked up and saw pretty much everyone in the room watching him. Watching like they were all waiting for something, but too terrified to actually speak to him.

"They might've heard all that noise," was all Marty said.

It was enough.

Nate scooped the cannon up and rose back to his shaky feet. Everything hurt, and he wasn't sure how the hell they were possibly going to escape this ship—especially if they were still in flight or, gods forbid, in orbit. He wasn't even sure he was going to make it as far as Marty before passing out or dying from internal injuries, regardless of what the Excalibur said. But *escape* was most definitely a problem for Future Nate to solve, after they'd dealt with everyone's restraints.

He stopped at the troglodan's body, thinking to search for a key, or anything else of use, but there were no pockets or handy key rings in sight, and Nate was pretty sure he didn't have it in him to lug the beast over onto its back.

The beast, his mind echoed.

Somehow, that beast looked a whole lot less beastly now that it was a cooling corpse on the deck. Somehow, it looked a lot more like a dead citizen of the troglodan empire the Excalibur had told him about—a brutal, war-happy people, maybe, but also undeniably sentient. Sophisticated enough to achieve interstellar travel. And he'd just shot one of them in the goddamn—

"Nate?"

Gwen's voice this time. He latched onto it, following it away from the unexpected wall of guilt threatening to fold in around him. She was twisted around as far as her post allowed, just far enough to see him.

"Got it," he whispered, stooping to grab onto the protruding edge of what looked to be another gun tucked down the troglodan's front. With a heave that left his head spinning and his beaten body screaming, Nate shifted the troglodan's leg enough to yank the thing free. He came away with a bulky pistol that would've made Hellboy proud. The grip was probably too large to be held practically in a human hand. But it was something.

Nate gathered the weapons and headed up the aisle. It was hard not to be aware of every eye in the room following him, no doubt wondering what he was thinking. Joke was on them if they really thought he knew. If anyone had a problem with him helping Marty first, though, they didn't say anything. Just murmured quietly amongst themselves.

"What are you?" asked the wide-eyed guy next to Marty as Nate drew up to them.

"Just your friendly neighborhood IT Guy," Nate croaked, offering Marty the oversized "pistol," throat burning with the minor effort of speaking.

Marty looked at the weapon with wide eyes. Nate didn't really blame him, given that the thing looked like it might break both of his wrists with a single shot, but Marty sobered quickly enough, and took the weapon with a shaky nod.

"Why's he get the gun?" someone whispered behind Nate.

"Just shut up!" someone else answered.

Ridiculous as it sounded, Nate had mostly started with Marty because he'd always been the steadiest hand in their squad when shit got hairy. Add in the facts that he'd actually fired a gun in his life, and that he was the only person in the room whose hands were currently free, thanks to the deceased troglodan's chain-snapping rage, and they had their most qualified man for the job—which probably said a few things about how boned they were if and when the troglodans noticed something was up.

"Dude, but seriously," Kyle whispered beside Marty as Nate leaned in closer to inspect his friend's restraints. "What the shit is going on?"

"Not now," Marty said with a sharp look at Kyle. To Nate, glancing nervously at the cannon, he added, "Will that work?"

It wasn't an easy question to answer, Nate decided, looking from the cannon to Marty's collar chain. Especially seeing as he still didn't understand what the cannon was even firing. But shrugging didn't seem like the most comforting reply he could give before trying to blast off his friend's restraints.

Any ideas here, Ex?

"Hurry!" someone hissed nearby.

Nate blew out a breath and raised the cannon, looking to Marty for confirmation.

"Shoot the ring, probably," Marty said, setting the pistol on the deck beside him, voice tight. "Not the chain, right?"

Nate felt the blood drain from his face as he nodded. "Was thinking the same thing," he lied, shifting the cannon ever-so-slightly.

No good blasting the chain apart if the resultant yank on the collar ended up breaking Marty's neck, or crushing his windpipe.

Jesus.

"Okay then," Marty said, returning Nate's nod with all the chipper levity of a desperado telling the hangman he was ready.

Nate laid his thumb on the firing stud, trying to focus on the wall rung, and not his friend's terrified face, or his brain's dichotomous screams that this was a horrible idea, and that he needed to hurry the hell up and get on with it anyway. His thumb tensed. There had to be a better way. He started to depress the stud, the faintest hum purring from the cannon.

Then a sound like a few hundred swords being drawn filled the room, and Marty's collar chain fell from the wall rung and slapped down to the deck. Dizzy with relief, Nate raised the cannon and carefully eased off the firing stud, looking around for some explanation. Kyle's chains had come loose from the wall too, he saw. Same with everyone else down the line.

Haste would be prudent, the Excalibur pointed out, as if this had been the plan all along. Judging by the smug satisfaction wafting from his erratic companion, maybe it had been.

You're gonna give me whiplash with all this flip-flopping, Nate thought, looking around at the spike in excited chatter through the brig, *but thank you.*

The entire brig appeared to have been liberated. Or freed from the retracted chain rungs on the walls and the chain posts, at least. Most were rising to their feet around the room, juggling an awkward ensemble of shackles and collars, jangling chains, and burning questions of what the hell they were supposed to do next.

And for some reason, a lot of them were looking at Nate like he was supposed to have the answer.

"Get that thing turned over and search it properly," he said, pointing to the dead troglodan. That was something, at least. Better yet, no one argued. A few big guys were already moving toward the troglodan, looking around for more volunteers to help.

"How are we getting out of here?" someone asked.

Hell if he knew.

He barely even remembered how they'd gotten here to start with. There was no knowing how deep they were within the ship. Maybe they were bordering the outer hull, and the pulse cannon could blast them a nice exit hole to freedom—or maybe straight to the crushing vacuum of outer space, or to a barracks of angry troglodans. Blasting out of the ship would hardly matter anyway, unless the ship was already grounded, which he didn't think it was.

What they really needed was to find some kind of escape pods, or…

"The grav lift," someone called from the back of the brig, near the dead troglodan—the girl from the bar, he realized with a flicker of surprise. The serendipitous jogger who'd seen him at Todd's that morning. She gave him a supportive little nod, like *carry on, you,* and stooped back down to look at the troglodan.

Curious. But he didn't have time to fret about it, or to argue her point. He was utterly devoid of better ideas, and the rest of the room seemed to be right there with him.

At least *grav lift* sounded better than *abduction beam.*

"The grav lift," he agreed, trying to sound confident about it.

"That thing goes down?" another girl asked.

Of course it goes down, the Excalibur sighed in his head.

"Yeah," Nate said, struggling to speak normally as the Excalibur ranted on about *what good would a gravitonic generator be to anyone without a bidirectional something something, and...* "Yeah, it should. I'd say that's our best shot."

He turned away to look for Gwen, hoping to avoid more questions, and was surprised to find her hovering nearby, looking uncertain. He closed the gap between them, all too aware that people were still watching.

"Are you okay?" he asked quietly.

Her eyes widened. "Me? Nate, what the hell was..." She frowned around at the spectators, taking a moment to gather herself before turning concerned eyes back on him. "Are *you* okay? Because I'm pretty sure you just broke physics."

"I'm fine," he insisted. Then, seeing the look on her face, and thinking of how much blood he'd just thrown up: "Okay, I'm probably not fine. But I will be until we get out of here. Then maybe I can... explain. Once we're safe."

She searched his face. Glanced at their surroundings, remembering where they were. "Okay," she agreed, nodding disconcertedly. "Okay, what can I do?"

Nate glanced over at the soft ruckus and thud where several students had just managed to roll the dead troglodan onto its back. The rest of the brig crowd shuffled about, nervously whispering among themselves, or nervously watching him. "Find out if anyone thinks they can retrace their steps back to that grav lift, I guess."

She nodded and moved off. Nate turned back to Kyle and Marty, thinking to tell them to go check the troglodan and go watch the door, respectively. But Marty wasn't there.

No sooner had he realized that than the brig door burst open with a stream of booming alien words.

Nate whirled through the sudden jungle of loud curses and scrambling students, hefting the heavy pulse cannon with him. He spotted Marty just ahead—right as a clap of thunder boomed, and Marty thumped to the deck.

"NO!"

Nate raised his cannon, taking aim. It was only as he fired his first pulse that he realized the troglodan was still drawing its sidearm.

The pulse hit. The troglodan struck the wall with a wet-sounding gasp, dark chest plate caved in. That didn't stop it from raising its own weapon.

Another clap of thunder from just ahead, and the troglodan jerked, black blood blossoming from the hand it had clamped to its collapsed chest. Nate hit it with another pulse, and it dropped to the deck, weapon clattering out of reach. It struggled weakly, bubbling out a wet growl.

Nate turned to where Marty had fallen, expecting the worst, only to find his friend braced on the deck in an awkward shooting position, weapon still trained on the dying troglodan. It was only then that Nate's brain caught up and registered that Marty hadn't been shot at all, but rather mule-kicked by his own massive pistol's recoil.

Nate could've laughed for the relief. Then the troglodan rumbled a burbling groan, and dire reality snapped back into focus.

"Hold up," he said quickly, stepping past Marty before his friend's wired trigger finger could decide otherwise.

He shuffled closer, keeping the cannon trained on the dying troglodan that might be their best hope at finding a way out. Quickly, carefully, he poked his head out into the dim hallway.

Empty. Thank merciful Sith.

Empty and freaking foreboding.

He closed the door and turned back to the troglodan. "How do we get out of here? Do you understand? How do we leave this ship?"

The troglodan stirred, grumbling a few strings of incoherent troglodan speech. Nate moved around to where it could see him, careful to stay outside its considerable reach. Its beady eyes focused on him as he came around, and it spoke again, in a strained, raspy voice.

"You are... the one... we seek."

It was several seconds of gaping before Nate remembered there was a room full of jumpy college kids hearing this right behind him. "I'm not. I don't know what you're talking about." He glanced over his shoulder. Saw several confused faces staring back. "I just need you to tell me how to get out of here."

"You are... a runt among... blightspots," groaned the troglodan, a dark trickle of blood oozing from its mouth. "Go and... make a coupling... of fist... and ass... runt knight."

With that, the troglodan thunked limply to the deck, dead.

Nate kept staring at their lost lifeline, hoping for some miracle.

It didn't feel any better this time, knowing he'd been the one to thumb the trigger. Two dead troglodans, a short spout of English just to tell him to go fist himself, and still they were up the creek without a paddle. He looked back to Marty, who was still sitting on the deck, pale-faced, weapon raised.

"Guess we're on our own, then."

For some reason, Marty only looked more shocked at that.

Nate scooped the second troglodan's pistol from the deck and held it up, facing the room. "We need someone who knows how to shoot."

And someone who knows where the hell they're going, he didn't add. He had a sinking feeling no one actually knew the way, and he doubted it'd do much good to point that out right now. Hopefully, the Excalibur would be feeling charitable now that his mighty Knight had slain two troglodans.

"Come on, people," Nate added to the intently silent brig, feeling every bit as uncomfortable as they all looked about his sudden leadership, and at least twice as unqualified. "Anyone?" His eyes landed on Todd, and he held the pistol out, but Todd only gave a feeble shake of his head, holding Emily close.

Nate spotted Jogger Girl next, toward the back of the crowd, and was about to arch a questioning eyebrow her way when a guy with dark hair and a red plaid shirt stepped to the front of the crowd, eyeing Nate warily.

"I'm a hunter," was all he said.

Nate handed him the pistol.

"Watch the kick," Marty warned, still eyeing Nate with an odd expression.

"And watch our backs, if you can," Nate added, looking from the crowd to the door, and wondering how they were possibly going to navigate the ship with such a large group and so few weapons.

One step at a time, he supposed. Or not at all.

"Let's get ready to move," Nate called to the group, with entirely more authority than he felt.

Gwen and Kyle emerged from the crowd, headed his way, Zach and Kelsey not far behind them. Marty joined them in forming a tight huddle by the door.

"Dude," Kyle said, as soon he was close enough to speak quietly. "Did you, uh..."

"Did you understand that thing?" Marty finished for him.

Nate took in their wary expressions, gathering that his answer was liable to freak them right the hell out. But why? The troglodan had spoken English, hadn't it? Unless...

"Do you know where we're going?" Gwen asked, clearly trying to keep them on topic. "Because I'm pretty sure we're flying blind otherwise."

Nate dropped his eyes and shook his head guiltily.

"Okay..." Gwen said, thinking.

"You always turn left?" Kyle asked quietly.

Nate traded a surprised look with Zach and Marty, all of them recognizing the old nugget of dungeon-exploring wisdom they'd developed through years of gaming experience.

When in doubt at a forking path in a strange new dungeon, as long as you consistently started with the leftmost option and worked your way across—and so on and so forth for every additional downstream fork— you'd eventually see everything there was to see. If there was an exit, you'd find it.

It just might take a while.

Which, in a ship full of troglodans, felt uncomfortably like a recipe for a prompt and violent death. But Nate didn't have any better ideas.

"You always turn left?" Marty asked, clutching his pistol close to his body.

"You always turn left," Nate agreed, turning for the door.

Then the ship shook with a distant explosion, and a god-awful alarm split the air.

CHAPTER 26

CEASE AND DESIST

"But is it for *us*?"

Screech!

"Of course it's for us."

"Who else would it be for?"

"—swear I heard gunfire a minute ago."

Screech!

"I don't think it's for us."

"Of *course* it's for us."

Nate took a deep breath and shot an aggravated *quiet the hell down* look over his shoulder. To his continued surprise, they did. Quickly. It wasn't hard to identify the few who'd been not-so-quietly talking by the downcast eyes and the aggressive blushes.

Screech!

Whether or not the god-awful alarm was for them or not, Nate still didn't know, but they'd yet to see a single troglodan, and he figured it couldn't hurt for everyone to keep their mouths shut and their shit together. Admittedly, that might've been a lot to ask of nearly two-hundred terrified college students, blindly parading through a freaking alien spaceship where horrific deaths could well be waiting behind each and every grimy corner.

But at least the corridors were as dim and creepy as a freaking haunted mine shaft.

That the alarm was still going might've actually been a small blessing.

The volume had mercifully dropped from deafening to merely aggressively annoying after the initial burst, and now Nate figured it might at least help cover up the considerable jingle jangle, swinging chain racket of their less-than-half-cocked escape.

The downside was that it also made it pretty damn hard to keep an ear out for any incoming troglodans. But so far, that hadn't been a problem.

The hallways were empty. Too empty. It was freaking him the hell out. Not that he was going to complain about not dying.

Yes. Do go on 'not complaining.'

And there was the Excalibur, back for another pass.

Do you know why this place is a ghost town?

The majority of this ship's crew appears to be groundside, likely scouring for you or the Beacon.

That made sense, he supposed. Even if it *would* have been nice to know sooner. The Excalibur rippled at that thought, as if daring him to complain. He just shifted his cannon into a more ready position as they approached the tight four-way intersection ahead.

Why such large creatures had opted to build ships with such relatively narrow corridors, Nate couldn't have begun to guess. Maybe they had some bizarre fixation with the economical usage of ship space. Maybe this wasn't even their ship. Maybe they were space pirates. Hell if he knew.

All Nate knew was that you always turned lef—

Go straight.

He paused, waiting for more, but Ex had already said its piece. Nate only hesitated a second. Pissed as his companion clearly was right now, Nate didn't need to look any further than the fact that Ex had already spoken up once to save his life, back when the first troglodan had been bearing down on him. Ex hadn't completely given up. Not yet.

So, Nate stepped forward—

And jerked straight back at the flicker of motion to the left. He felt Marty tense beside him. Felt Gwen's hand on his back, and the palpable terror that spread through the group behind them like wildfire.

Slowly, Nate leaned forward again, peering out with just the minimum required sliver of his face.

He hadn't imagined it. Twenty yards or so down the left corridor, a group of troglodans were thundering through another intersection, moving parallel to the direction the Excalibur was now pointing Nate. Four of them stomped by, all with armor and cannons of their own. Nate gave it another good twenty seconds to make sure there weren't any stragglers coming.

You're sure it's straight?

No reply.

Not for the first time, Nate considered that the Excalibur was testing him in some way. Some sick, totally barbarian way that couldn't have come at a worse time. But he knew exactly where sniveling about it would get him right now.

He went straight through the intersection.

"What happened to always go left?" Kyle immediately whispered behind them.

Nate waved the question away and kept moving, trusting they'd just chalk it up to whatever other strange ideas were currently forming in their heads about him.

There is something else. Something I feel you have earned the right to know.

This was going to be rich. *What's that?*

There is another Excalibur Knight aboard this vessel.

"What?!"

Nate barely realized he'd jerked to a stop until Gwen bumped into him.

"What?" she echoed, craning to peek over his shoulder.

"You see something?" Marty whispered.

The whispers spread, multiplying their way back through the corridor until they culminated with a whimpered, "Oh god, we're gonna die!" from somewhere back near the intersection.

"Quiet," Nate hissed over his shoulder.

It is also worthy of note that this Knight appears to have a strong desire to find us.

What you do you mean, 'appears to?' Is he on our side?

She. And that is not my assessment.

No? And what is your assessment?

I believe she is quite displeased with everyone aboard this ship. Though, to be fair, I am interpreting through over a thousand years of language drift. I will update you on my assessment once she does or does not attempt to slay you.

Seriously? That's your—

"Nate?"

Gwen's voice brought him back to the dim corridor, where he was dumbly standing there wasting precious seconds, and his friends were watching him like he might've officially cracked.

"Are you talking to yourself?" Marty asked quietly.

"Trying to picture the ship in my head," Nate lied, turning to continue on.

With any luck, they could skirt right around this Knight and get the others to safety before he had to worry about who wanted to slay whom. He didn't want to think about how many troglodans might be combing the streets below, or the fact that it was looking a lot like it was him they were looking for.

How many people had already died because of him?

How many more taken prisoner?

Nate pushed on, telling himself that the only thing he could do right then was to take care of the people behind him. Which was about to get complicated enough, he realized, as they reached the next intersection.

In the distance, Nate was sure he heard the sounds of fighting now. But that wasn't nearly as concerning as the troglodans he saw when he peered around the corner. Three—no, four—of them, turning the far corner down the corridor to the right, headed their way with weapons ready.

No way the entire group was darting through the intersection unnoticed. No way they could backtrack fast enough to hide. No way he and Marty were going to win a firefight against four troglodan soldiers, even if they called up their plaid-shirted rear guard to help.

You might try the gravitonic lift across the corridor to your right.

Nate followed the Excalibur's directions to a nested alcove on the far wall to the right, where a wide circular panel dominated the floor space, surrounded by thick, battered-looking cables.

It is not unlike the one in the aft loading bay. Suitable for one diversionary runner, perhaps.

One diversionary runner who'd have to charge headlong at four armed troglodans for ten yards or so before they reached the lift that may or may not be operational. Glancing at the corridor of scared faces behind him, though—faces that might well only be there because of him—he wasn't sure what the hell else he could do.

"Four trogs coming," he whispered quickly to Marty and the others. "I'm gonna lead them off, but—"

Marty started to object, but Nate cut him off.

"No time to argue. You stay quiet until it's clear, then you keep going straight."

"Nate..." Gwen whispered.

"You can't," Marty finished for her. "How will you... How will we..."

"I've got us," came a voice from behind. Jogger Girl, Nate was surprised to see. "Go."

"But what if the lift doesn't work?" Marty asked, eyeing the newcomer with understandable confusion before rounding back on Nate. "What if—"

Right pocket, the Excalibur's voice broke in over Marty's. *Give it to your friend.*

"—are you gonna get out then?"

Nate just plunged his hand into his pocket, out of time for questions. He handed Marty the plain black earpiece he found there, every bit as surprised to see it as his friend was.

Now or never.

"I'll meet you at the lift," he said to their dumbfounded expressions.

Then he turned and charged into the intersection.

CHAPTER 27
WHAT'S UP

For ten yards, Nate ran faster than he'd ever run. Half blind on fear and adrenaline. Eyes locked on the alcove ahead, and the thin promise of salvation. Dimly aware of the guttural shouts of startled troglodans at the periphery of his senses. Dimly aware, too, of the sounds of weapons fire ahead, and of the jolting shock of the hard deck underfoot, and the dangling chains rhythmically smacking against his battered body. Something punched into his left shoulder. Nate took two more lunging steps and dove for the alcove.

Amped as he was, he overshot the lift pad, hit the alcove wall beyond, and tumbled back to the deck, cursing himself and everything else.

The pad, if you will.

Nate rolled over with a grunt, all too aware of the thundering footsteps closing on the alcove. He was only halfway to his feet when the humming gravity well—or whatever the hell—caught him like a feather on an updraft. He nearly dropped the cannon in the sudden rush. Upward push shifted to sideways push before he could even begin getting his bearings, and he toppled onto another hard deck, just like the one he'd come from.

Right behind two troglodans.

Nate swept the cannon up and jabbed the thumb trigger well before he had time to do things like *think*, or *aim*. The closest troglodan staggered into his friend and took them both crashing into the wall. Nate didn't wait to see if the shot had done any real damage. He rolled onto all fours, tripped on one trailing shackle chain, and then took off down the corridor like an Olympic sprinter. Booming shouts followed him. Something about a spotted runt, and eating his bones. When the bulkhead directly ahead of him dented inward as if struck by a thrumming iron fist, the details hardly seemed important.

He rounded left into the next corridor, taking the corner so fast that he slammed into the opposite wall, shoulder first, nearly hard enough to make his own dent. He kept running.

On your left. Another lift.

Nate didn't stop to ask questions. He just angled for the alcove ahead—and promptly tripped straight into an open shaft.

His mouth tore open in a silent scream. Then gravity itself caught on and pulled him upward with inexorable strength, his chains dangling upward at static attention. He hit the deck one floor above on shaky legs and narrowly managed to avoid falling over.

No troglodans in immediate sight. They must be close, though, he realized on second listen. Because it sounded like someone was fighting a full scale war nearby.

That would be her, I do believe.

Her—singular—causing that much calamity? He glanced back at the lift shaft, wondering whether he should risk his chances that way.

"Nate?" Marty's voice broke in out of nowhere, almost as clearly as the Excalibur's. "Nate, can you hear me with this thing?"

"I..." Nate touched a hand to his head, not sure how or why Marty should be able to hear his reply. "I hear you, Marty."

"Okay, okay." His friend was too winded and shaken to question the nuances. "I think we found the bay we came in from, and uh... Well, everyone's—I mean the big alien ogre things... They're all dead."

All dead?

"The floor's, uh, open," Marty was saying, "and we can see State below, but uh—"

A cracking thud from behind made Nate jump and spin—just in time to see a huge troglodan crumpling limply to the deck at the mouth of the nearest corridor, a huge dent punched in the bulkhead behind him where he'd apparently struck.

Nate turned and ran his ass off, not wanting to know what on earth or anywhere else could send a troglodan flying like that.

Perhaps we should return to a safer floor.

"Perhaps?!"

"—still hear me?" came Marty's voice.

"Little busy," Nate grunted, sprinting on. "Is the lift active?"

"We don't know," Marty said, "we—"

Do not worry about your friend right now, the Excalibur's voice cut in. *I will attempt to activate the lift remotely, and, failing that... Oh.*

"Oh?"

"—think it's working!" Marty's voice cut back in. "Tessa just threw something in and... Yeah, yeah! It's floating down! Nate, you need to get here before they—"

A hellish troglodan roar ripped through the deck before Marty could finish telling Nate what "they" were going to do, or who the hell Tessa was.

"On my way," Nate gasped between breaths, not slowing until he blew into the next intersection, caught a flicker of motion to the left, and slid to a hard stop on the far wall, chains swinging like pendulums as he poked back around to check his flank.

It was a mistake.

By the sheer ferocity of their battle cries alone, Nate might've guessed the trogs in the next hub over were charging into battle against a respectable foe. What he wasn't ready for, though, was the hyperkinetic dance of death that came speeding to meet them.

It happened too quickly for Nate's eyes to follow.

One moment, five hulking troglodans were charging through the intersection. The next, a copper blur streaked past in a crackle of hazy blue light, darting from the walls to the deck to the roaring trogs with a speed and grace that didn't seem physically possible.

Before Nate could blink, four of the trogs thudded to the deck, unmistakably dead, and the copper death blur materialized in front of the fifth, halting long enough for Nate to observe a tall, humanoid form, fully armored, planting a crackling, double-bladed staff to the deck. She reached out, as poised and regal as she was terrifying, and drove the trog that must've outweighed her by several hundred pounds down to its knees like it possessed all the bulk and comparative strength of a small toddler.

Run.

Nate didn't need telling twice.

His last glimpse of the fearsome warrior goddess was of the dark tendrils he mistook for hair coming alive with a faint ember glow... and wriggling to attention like a nest of snakes.

He was already down the next corridor, running for his life, when it struck him that he'd just seen the same copper-armored, green-skinned alien he'd witnessed weeks ago during his galactic walkabout with the Lady. A *gorgon*, he remembered from Ex's piecemeal lessons.

Left at the next intersection. Use the lift shaft.

Nate didn't argue. Didn't even slow to check the open shaft as he skidded around the next corner and leapt in, assuming it would catch him just like the others had.

It didn't. Not when he thudded into the far wall, knocking the cannon loose from his hands. Not when he found himself rushing down a three deck lift shaft after the weapon.

"Exxx!" Nate cried. It was all he had time to do.

He closed his eyes, bracing for impact.

The shaft gave a mockingly peaceful hum around him.

Then something caught him like a thick bed of clouds, and relief defrosted his innards as the lift dumped his frazzled ass out onto the first floor deck. Or the one he'd started on, at least.

He thought.

We must discuss your overreactions once we have reached safety. The screaming, in particular, is quite unsavory.

Nate gathered his cannon and picked himself up, not bothering to tell Ex to kiss his ass, too busy shaking with everything from pain, to raw nerves, to an unexpectedly bubbly hit of giddiness at still being alive. He kept running, following what few directions his companion gave him until he passed through a considerably wider hatchway than anything he'd seen on the ship, and into a room that was sized to match.

The loading bay, he realized with a wave of relief.

It was far less dark and disorienting than what little he remembered, but maybe that was because he entered onto the main bay floor this time, as opposed to getting funneled through the conveyor apparatuses he saw to the sides of the room. The rest of the space was largely open, but for the sections of densely stacked, battered metallic crates, and the rows of big-wheeled, thick-plated ground vehicles arrayed to one side.

And there, below the enormous thrumming pad of what must've been the bay's main gravitonic lift, were Marty and Gwen, waving with chained hands for the remainder of the evacuee line to step into the lift beam and descend through the halogen-lit night sky. There were about ten of them left in the bay, Zach and Kyle included, all looking like they were waiting their turn to file into an especially petrifying water slide. All but Jogger Girl, who was the first to turn at the sound of Nate's sprinting footsteps, looking calm and collected. Gwen followed her gaze a second later, eyes considerably wider.

"Go!" he shouted, waving them all on. "Go, go, go!"

Luckily, he didn't need to explain himself any more than that. The last remnants of the evacuation line grabbed onto each other and jumped in twos and threes. Gwen reached out for Nate, shouting him on. Marty turned to do the same, and gaped at whatever he saw over Nate's shoulder.

Nate knew he shouldn't have looked, but he couldn't help it.

Troglodans were charging into the loading bay behind him, raising their weapons to fire.

"GO NOW!" Nate roared as he covered the last twenty yards to Marty and Gwen, and the bay came alive with weapons fire—pulse cannons and a few crimson blaster bolts that spat and sizzled where they scorched the deck.

Aside from flinching, Marty and Gwen stood their stubborn ground ahead, making no move to leave him. Not until Jogger Girl plowed into Gwen from the side, carrying them both over the edge and into the lift beam. Nate watched Gwen's shocked face disappear with a mix of guilt and relief. Then he closed on Marty and sent his surprised friend after them with a hard shove to the chest.

That done, he turned and raised his cannon.

He wasn't sure whether the troglodans would blow their own lift on purpose, or what they'd do to him if they caught him now, but he assumed it'd take his friends more than a few seconds to safely reach the ground. He had to buy them what time he could.

Despite his noble intentions, though, Nate only got off two shots—both misses—before something struck him in the chest like a battering ram.

A rush of air and motion, and then he was on his back, staring up at the bay ceiling, his entire torso throbbing in bright flashes of pain. A pulse blast? He tried to crane his neck to look at his own chest, but he could barely move. Maybe that was okay. If it was half as bad as the caved-in bloody messes his cannon had made of the troglodans in the brig, he wasn't sure he wanted to see anyway. Better he just die in peace, knowing his friends might yet make it.

Only he didn't seem to be doing much dying, he couldn't help but notice, as the sounds of fighting grew louder toward the entrance, guttural troglodan curses echoing across the bay.

Get up, Nathaniel.

Grimacing, he forced his way into a sitting position and saw that the copper-armored Excalibur Knight had caught up with him, that another couple dozen trogs had caught up with her, and that she was making them *all* pay for their audacious mistake.

For a second, Nate almost forgot to be terrified, so riveting was her movement, leaping from one trog to the next, cutting them down or smashing them through the air like freaking baseballs with that dark, bladed staff. Then the thing came apart in her hands and whirled through the air on lines of hazy blue energy, striking multiple targets at once. She caught one end, pointed it, and dropped another trog with a zipping blue bolt of blaster fire.

Six troglodans were dead in as many seconds.

Now would be a good time to leave.

Cursing himself for the wasted seconds, Nate clambered to shaky feet, took a few running steps toward the grav lift opening, and jumped—only to watch in horror as a speeding projectile smacked into the grav panel overhead, showering him in a rain of sparks.

Leaving him pitching into plain old night sky.

Before he could so much as scream, something snapped around his torso like a whip and stiffened, catching him motionless above the long drop like a hard iron lasso. He followed the segmented line of the mysterious device across nearly thirty yards of open deck, straight to the hand of the copper-armored Excalibur Knight.

It didn't seem physically possible that anyone, no matter how strong, could hold him suspended against such a monumentally long lever arm. Something to do with the device itself, then, his frazzled mind reasoned as the Knight turned her ruby faceplate his way, hair serpents following, helmet beginning to peel away like a living thing.

Nate caught a glimpse of green skin and piercingly phosphorescent blue eyes, then the Knight jerked, struck in the back by enemy fire. Her helmet closed protectively, and she whirled to face the arriving reinforcements with her staff. Nate's stomach dropped when she released the long line holding him in place, but neither he nor the line fell as they should've. They just continued hovering there in midair as one troglodan died. Then another.

Break the line.

What? How?

Smithy's blackened hands with your sniveling! Break the line!

Nate grabbed onto the mysterious midair flotation device. The slender line felt like solid steel. Except solid steel wouldn't have crackled and popped and made his hands go numb where he touched it. He gave it a few hard yanks with both hands. No give. No way.

You must strike it with all of your strength.

"I'll break my goddamn hand."

Only if you believe you will.

Ahead, troglodans were dying as fast as they could pour into the loading bay.

"I can't."

Just like you can't rip through troglodan chains?

Nate's eyes flicked to the chains still dangling from his shackles.

Maybe if he struck with the shackle…

"Fine." He gripped the line again, doing his best to ignore the buzzing numbness.

What was harder to ignore was the part where breaking the line would mean him falling a couple hundred yards with no working grav lift to catch him.

I have it all under control. Trust me.

Ahead, the copper-armored Excalibur Knight whipped around his way between kills, seeming to sense something was amiss, her serpentine hair writhing in an agitated cloud around her head.

"We need to work on your communication," Nate growled.

Then he raised his bare, squishy human hand overhead, and drove his shackled wrist straight down at the harder-than-steel line with all his strength, forcing himself to aim *through* it instead of *at* it, trying to believe it would simply snap like a dojo pine board. Something rippled down the length of his arm. Impact, and a light cracking sound. His bones, probably. Except his arm and hand continued on, slicing straight through the space where his restraint line had occupied. And his hand itself…

In that freeze frame moment, he caught the briefest glimpse of something that made no possible sense: his bare squishy human hand—no longer bare, or squishy, but half-covered in a sleek gray gauntlet that was rippling into existence out of thin air, bursting the shackle off of his wrist, leading with a simple but dangerous looking blade on the striking edge.

In that single instant, Nate felt more shocked and confused than he had since this entire shit show had started.

Then gravity took him, and he was falling.

CHAPTER 28

THE CIRCLE OF RICE

A couple hundred yards of empty, halogen-seared darkness.

That was all that separated Nate's last eight seconds of life from the rushing shadows of State College below—newly gauntleted hand be damned.

I need you to fly.

"What?!" Nate screamed.

Fly, the Excalibur repeated, like maybe it was simply an issue of misunderstanding. *Control your descent.*

The dark street rushing closer.

"You said you had it under control!"

Closer. Tiny figures pointing up at him.

"I can't fucking—"

STOP SNIVELING AND FLY, DAMN YOU.

The pavement soaring up to meet him. An oddly playful tickle, creeping up his insides, inviting him to give in, relax, and accept the inevitable.

A scream broke the spell.

His scream?

Didn't matter.

He clenched every muscle in his body—

Definitely his scream.

—and *strained* with everything he had. He wasn't even sure what he was straining for. He just strained, willing himself to miraculous flight, his mind frantically dancing with the image of Tony Stark taking flight on his repulsors.

Something kicked his feet, buckling knees to chest and sending him spiraling off-kilter. Nightmarish blue streets spun to dark sky and glaring troglodan ships. Back to floodlight streets, and sidewalks and shop windows, all closer than ever. Too close. Entirely too—

He threw his hands and legs out, willing it with all his might. *Repulsors! Repulsors!*

"REPULSORS!"

Resistance kicked at his extended hands and feet, and he noticed somewhere on the periphery of awareness that his hands were both encased in gauntlets now, and that those gauntlets appeared to be expanding up his forearms.

Then he smashed through a plate glass window and lost track of everything but the all-consuming cacophony of crashes and bone-shaking impacts. He had the brief impression of a human bowling ball, bouncing between the bumpers, and then it was over, and he was lying on his back. The world was dark, and he couldn't move for the pain.

I think that went quite well.

"Fucking magnificent," he groaned, trying and failing to sit up in the darkness. "Thanks for... all the help... ass-bot."

You are welcome, Nathaniel. Though I am detecting hints of aggression and insincerity in your tone.

Nate grunted, tasting blood again. Considerable as it was, he realized it wasn't just the pain keeping him down. He was also pinned. Pinned under... He blinked, squinting up at the dim outline of whatever was dangling above his face. A box. He squinted more. A cereal box? His eyes began to adjust to the dim lighting, and he stared in dumb incomprehension at the knock-off fruity circles parrot resting a few inches from his face.

A grocery store. He'd crashed into a grocery store.

His eyes drifted easily closed as he tried to think.

Sweet Jesus, he was tired.

McClanahan's, he thought wearily, disjointed fragments and images of the moments before the crash bouncing around behind the comfort of his eyelids. He thought maybe this was McClanahan's. His eyes blinked open for a moment, and he almost laughed at the fact that it had been this very store he'd come into almost exactly three weeks ago, right before all this shit had started. Three weeks ago, when his biggest concerns had been public humiliation, and begging a cashier to ring him up a bag of rice after hours for his beer-soaked phone. And now... and now...

He blinked sleepily, too tired to cap the thought off with a proper conclusion, vaguely remembering something about concussions and falling asleep. Too tired for that, too. The Excalibur said something, he was pretty sure, but his eyes were already drifting closed again, pulled by lead sinkers.

~

THEY SNAPPED OPEN A MOMENT LATER.

Only it couldn't have been a moment, he realized, as he registered the jostling motion of his body, and the arms wrapped around his chest.

He jerked violently back to his senses—just in time to crash to an unpleasantly solid black-and-white-tiled floor.

"Dude!" someone hissed.

Marty.

Nate relaxed, adrenaline sputtering out, exhausted body deciding that maybe the floor wasn't so bad after all. Not if he wasn't *actually* about to die.

"I'm sorry, dude," someone else whispered. Zach. "He just went all freaking Magikarp on me!"

"Nate?" Marty's voice again, shortly followed by a gentle hand on his shoulder, trying to turn him over from where he'd landed in—or maybe curled into—a fetal position. "Are you okay?"

Nate allowed himself to be rolled onto his back. The dim shape of Marty's face was outlined by the unnatural halogen lights flooding through the windows. Gwen's face appeared over Marty's shoulder, looking equally concerned. With an involuntary grunt, Nate lifted his head enough to see that they were indeed in McClanahan's, that the store was a wreck, and that Kyle and Zach were right there too, along with Kelsey and a few others —Todd and Emily among them—all still in troglodan chains.

"Still alive," he rasped, noting his own wrists were mysteriously free of troglodan shackles before giving in and resting his head carefully back to the floor.

"Which is pretty frickin' weird," Kyle said quietly, coming to join the huddle around Nate. "I mean, good weird, but—"

"Kyle..." Marty said.

"What?" Kyle asked, trying and failing to spread his chained hands. "You're not a little bit curious what the shit is going on, here?"

"I, for one, am intrigued," came another voice from the nearby group.

Jogger Girl, Nate saw with the beginnings of a frown. Was she the one Marty had been talking about earlier? What had it been? Tara? Tessa?

"—should probably get the flight cadet here out of plain sight before we all sit down for tea," she was saying, glancing out the front windows before turning back to him with a faint, mercurial grin.

"Tessa's right," Marty said, clearly not sharing Nate's uneasy feeling about the oddly present and resourceful—and, admittedly, rather cute—addition to their crew. Nate wasn't sure himself why it mattered. Only that the whole serendipity theory was starting to feel a bit thin.

Probably because she is a member of the 501st S.A.S.

"What?" Nate breathed, before he could stop himself.

"What is it, Nate?" Gwen asked, crouching down beside him.

"Nothing," Nate said, a little too forcefully. He made a show of trying to sit up, just to draw attention from the reaction. Gwen quickly grabbed his arm to help him.

How long have you known? How do you know?

Approximately 13.6 hours. Service records and facial recognition. And because you were being an intolerable ass puppet, to answer your third question.

Nate drew up short from asking why Ex hadn't told him sooner, taken aback both by the predictive acuity, and the unprecedented freestyle insult.

"How'd you, uh… How'd you find me?" Nate asked the others, mostly to fill the silence as Marty stepped in to help Gwen get him up. He tried not to stare at Tessa. No reason to tip his hand until he knew more. Especially not here in the middle of a freaking invasion.

"—close to where we landed," Marty was saying, grabbing his other hand to help him. "And it was, uh… kinda hard to miss when you came down."

Kyle snorted. "Yeah, insomuch as it sure looked like you sprouted Iron Man hands and started screaming, 'Repulsors! Repulsors!'" He frowned down at Nate's hands. "All of that right before you actually *flew*, by the way."

"Kyle!" Marty shot their friend a dark glare before turning back to Nate.

"I'm not sure I'd call that flying," Tessa muttered, quietly enough that he almost missed it.

Cheeky little spy, wasn't she?

I believe I like her.

"What about the others from the ship?" Nate asked, ignoring their openly curious stares and looking around just to make sure he hadn't missed the hundred evacuees hiding under the overturned shelves. "How long have I been out?"

"Not long," Marty said. "Five minutes, maybe. But the others, uh... Well, they kinda scattered when we hit the pavement."

"Dude, that's like saying Nutella is *kind of* delicious," Kyle said. "They ran for their fucking lives every which way, and I can't say I blame 'em. Even if it was stupid."

"Some of them—a lot them—got snatched right back up," Marty explained, his expression darkening. "Those... things are still out there, in the streets. The..." He looked at Nate uncertainly. "The trogs?"

That brought everyone's silent attention right back to Nate.

He sighed, pretty sure he was out of reasons to play dumb. "Troglodans."

"Right," Marty said, watching him cautiously. "Yeah. Well, the troglodans, then, they're still out on patrol."

"Reasons why we really shouldn't be standing near windows," Tessa chimed in, gesturing pointedly to Nate's slow going excavation from the floor.

"I thought we could get back to the house," Marty said, dutifully beginning to haul Nate to his feet with Gwen's help. Nate managed not to wince or groan too much, but they both stayed at his sides anyway.

"Grab Copernicus and whatever supplies we can," Marty continued. "Keep going out of town. Take cover out in the countryside, maybe." He looked thoughtfully around the store. "We should probably grab what food we can while we're here, and go from there." His attention drifted slowly, almost timidly back to Nate. "Unless you can explain to us what's going on here."

The silence inside McClanahan's intensified, each distant sound of the trogolodan occupation that much sharper for it. Everyone—even the few strangers hanging back, pretending not to be listening in—leaned in a little closer, hanging on a thread for whatever answer Nate could give them. He could practically hear their chains vibrating with curiosity. Could feel the Excalibur hovering there, waiting to see what he would do. Waiting to see if he would run from his failure, or stand up and fight.

Outside, a distant explosion shook the air.

They needed to regroup. *He* needed to regroup.

"We should get away from the windows," was all he said, turning after Tessa, who'd already disappeared into the back.

Are you sure about her?

There was enough of a pause that Nate worried he might've lost his companion again.

I could be surer if you'd prefer to collect a DNA sample, Ex finally said, *but* *barring that, yes. 2nd Lieutenant Tessa Kalders is indeed an active member of the 501st S.A.S. I assume her jogging path yesterday morning was not accidental.*

Nate paused at the *Employees Only* door, wondering where her buddies in the black SUV might've ended up in all of this. Wondering whether they were allies or foes in this situation. Aware of the eyes on his back, and of Marty and Gwen looking questions at him.

What do we do about her?

The Excalibur rippled with something like amusement as Nate detached himself from his worried friends and pushed through the door.

I would be far more concerned with the Beacon, little hobbit, and with what the gorgon Knight will do about you *once she's finished out there.*

CHAPTER 29
ROUND TABLE

The McClanahan's staff break room was small. And dark. And sure as shit not the kind of place Nate had imagined his eventual confession might unfold in. Especially not in attendance with Todd, an Air Force spy, a few random strangers, and a full round of troglodan shackles and chains.

Yet here they were. And here they should probably remain, their trusty spy had concluded after a peek out the stockroom exit. At least until the surrounding area calmed down from their prison break, and the trog street patrols moved on. Given the sounds of ships passing overhead, and the occasional rumble of not-so-distant ground vehicles rolling by, no one was inclined to argue. Which, for the moment, left them all packed in a small room, waiting for answers in the dim glow of the floodlight apocalypse trickling in from the opaque vent pane up high in the corner.

Nate leaned heavily against the plaster wall, not sure where to start, feeling like he should be out there, doing something. Anything would've been better than just standing here. Yet here he stood, caught in a full system freeze just trying to process everything that'd happened.

He couldn't even manage to pry his eyes from the floor until Gwen slid in beside him, debugging a small hunk of his glitched code with her presence alone. At least she wasn't terrified of him. Not outwardly, at least.

He glanced up at a clicking sound and saw Zach fiddling with the boxy little countertop LCD TV. Like the lights, it wouldn't turn on.

"Just checking," Zach explained at the questioning looks. "Thought maybe we could get a news network. See what's going on out there."

Nate was ashamed to realize just how much he *didn't* want to know what was going on out there. Even more so that the Excalibur could no doubt feel his cowardice, and his petty relief at not yet having to face the truth.

"—thing could be worldwide," Kyle was saying. "Jesus H Christ, this could really be it."

"So what are they doing in State College, then?" Todd said, speaking up for the first time. "Why'd they know Nate's name?"

Nate tensed, half-expecting the Greek god to puff up and come get in his face, demanding answers, but Todd only eyed him warily in the dim blue light, looking deflated and far less than godly.

Nate let some of the tension out on a heavy breath, eyeing 2nd Lieutenant Tessa Kalders for a second before deciding it didn't really matter anymore what she was here for. Either she could help, or she couldn't. Just like him.

"I was told they came here looking for something called the Beacon," he started slowly. "Honestly, that's the only part I know for sure."

"The Beacon?" Marty echoed, trying the word on for size.

"Told by who?" Zach asked.

"Dude..." Kyle said, eyes widening in sudden realization. "All that stuff with the background radiation and the weird EMFs and everything..." He pointed an accusing finger at Nate. "And you suddenly got interested right after..." He glanced at Emily, and Nate could practically see the pieces clinking together in his friend's head. "Is this all...?"

"Maybe," Nate said. "I think so."

Kyle swiped a fist through the air. "I fucking *knew* it."

"But who told you all this?" Zach repeated, more insistently.

"Kind of a long story."

"A story that involves you turning into the Terminator?" Kyle asked. He peered suspiciously at Nate. "I mean, you haven't *always* been, uh... you know, a Breaker of Chains, have you?"

"No, I..." Nate resisted the urge to sigh again, suddenly feeling like this was all a mistake, and that he should've simply pulled Tessa aside, filled her in on what he knew, and then... well, he didn't know what exactly. But he had to do something.

"Look, I don't know how they ended up in State College, specifically. All I know is that something happened to me a few weeks ago, when..."

"When you saved me from that car," Emily spoke up, frowning like something had just occurred to her. "And then, that thing with the bike."

"The bike?" someone asked.

But Emily was watching Nate, eyes wide in the dim light. "I thought I was imagining things from the adrenaline or whatever, but I swore I saw you, like, vanish, right before it all happened. Just for a split second. And then the videos all disappeared, and… That was all you?"

"Sort of."

"Sort of?" Kyle asked.

This wasn't helping.

"I told you it's a long story." He looked around at his friends, and came to his decision. "Now's not the time. I need to talk to Tessa, and—"

"Wait, why?" Kyle asked, before shooting her a *no offense* shrug.

"You guys need to start getting your supplies ready," Nate pressed on, ignoring Kyle's question, and Tessa's innocently curious look.

"*You* guys?" Marty said.

"What about you?" Gwen asked beside him.

Nate took a breath, trying to convince himself enough to at least get the words out. "I have to find the Beacon before they do."

His friends all broke out at once.

"How?"

"Why?"

"According to who?"

"Not alone, you don't," Marty said, drawing a hush between them. Then his friends all looked around at each other and exchanged a solemn nod, like the Knights of the Freaking Round Table.

"No," Nate said, shaking his head. "No, listen. You guys have to get to safety. I was supposed to… Look, it might already be my fault that this is happening."

"I don't believe that," Gwen said, without a trace of hesitation.

"Yeah, man," Kyle added. "Full scale alien invasion? Give the rest of us pesky humans some credit. How could this all be on you?"

"I—I don't know!" Nate cried. "I don't know, okay? I just—I didn't know it was gonna happen like this. I didn't—The Merlin—I didn't understand…" He clenched his fists, fresh waves of pain cascading through his tensed muscles. How could he possibly explain any of it to them? He didn't even understand himself.

"Uh, the Merlin?" Marty asked.

"Like, *the* Merlin?" Kyle added.

"As in, the wizard?" Zach asked.

"Wait. Dude." Marty was gaping at him now. "That homeless guy in the park?"

Merciful Sith. He hadn't meant to use the name. It had just slipped out. But hell, did it even matter anymore?

"I thought he was just a kooky old homeless guy too," Nate admitted. "But he's the one who pulled me into this."

"You've gotta be kidding me," Tessa muttered in the corner. It was the first time she'd seemed outwardly surprised by any of this.

"What do you mean, he pulled you into this?" Kyle asked.

"Like, the *wizard*, Merlin?" Zach clarified again.

"What," Kyle continued, "are you gonna tell us he made you pull a sword from a stone or something?"

Nate looked helplessly around the room, at a complete loss. He was saved the trouble of figuring out what to say when the mild light from the vent window brightened, and the unmistakable sound of something massive thrumming by overhead reminded them all that they were surrounded by hostile space ogres.

"Okay," Kyle said quietly, shooting a conceding glance skyward once the ship had passed by and the room had dimmed. "Okay. Well, troglodan invasion, check. King Arthur the chain-breaking Terminator, also check. Call me Sir Galahad and fuck me sideways, I guess."

"But…" Zach said, still frowning like he hadn't heard a word of any of it. "A wizard?"

"Dude, you're really hung up on that, aren't you?" Kyle asked. "Did you miss the giant alien spaceships floating around out there?"

"Yeah, no, but you talk about aliens like every day. That part kinda seemed like, I dunno, a given."

"Hmm," Kyle said, making a *fair point* face. "Out-nerded, I guess." He frowned back at Nate. "Wait. So you *did* pull a sword from a stone?"

"It's… complicated." Nate looked helplessly around the room, and was surprised to find a complete lack of gaping *bat shit insane* stares directed his way. One little alien abduction, he supposed, and it all started sounding a lot less crazy—to everyone but Tessa Kalders, at least.

"Okay," the secret lieutenant said, straightening and brushing herself off like that was the last straw, and now it was time to let the adults talk.

Something shook the air before she could say another word—a low, rushing *whoomph* that spiked to a sound like crashing mountains before Nate's brain could even register it as sound. The room trembled on the back of the explosion, break room chairs quivering on the linoleum floor like it was an earthquake.

Everyone in the room braced themselves, gaping stupidly at one another until the vibrations died down.

"What in the holy fuck was that?" asked one of their tag-alongs.

"I'm no doctor of ballistics," Kyle finally said, "but that sure sounded a lot like a giant troglodan ship crashing to Earth."

"I think he's right," Kelsey whispered.

"Yeah," Tessa said, moving to the break room door. "I think Nate and I need to have that chat now."

Somehow, that news was still startling to his friends in the face of everything else.

"Sorry, who are you again?" Kyle asked, eyeing her dubiously.

"Tessa Kalders," she said, swinging the door open in a clear invitation for them all to get out. When no one moved, she quirked an eyebrow his way.

"Can you give us a minute?" Nate asked, in response to his friends' questioning looks.

"Sure," Kyle said, frowning around the room as everyone slowly started funneling toward the door. "Cause what could possibly be more suspicious than needing privacy *after* you've already admitted you're King Arthur the freaking chain breaking, alien slaying—Hey!"

Marty took him by the arm, pulling him toward the door.

"We'll start gathering supplies," Marty said, looking back to meet Nate's eyes with a serious look. "But just to be clear, I'm not bailing to let you go on some suicide mission alone." He looked down at the huge pistol he was still carrying, wanting to say more, then thought better of it and pulled a muttering Kyle out of the room.

Nate turned to Gwen, who was hovering uncertainly by his side. "I'll just be a minute," he said weakly, as if that somehow explained anything.

She searched his face, looking for a second like she wanted nothing more than to wrap him in a hug and tell him it was going to be okay. For that second, he wished more than anything that she would. Then the second passed, and she was gone.

"Mr. Arturi," Tessa said slowly, once the door was closed. She wrinkled her nose, like the name didn't sound quite right. "Nate," she tried instead.

"Lieutenant," Nate replied, figuring this all might turn out better if he just played it straight from here. "I know who you are."

She watched him, not reacting.

"What I don't know is why the hell you've all been tailing me around when your people won't even take my intel. I've been trying to tell you guys about the troglodans for weeks. I called the goddamn NSA. I spoke with… with the big guy and the driver."

"And they reported every word you said."

"So then where the hell's the cavalry?" he asked, jerking a finger skyward, toward the troglodan ships above. "It's been hours. Where's the big counterattack? Where are your people?"

"Yeah…" She blew the word out slowly, brow deeply furrowed, clearly not thrilled about any of this. "I'm kind of starting to think that big counterattack's not coming. Which almost definitely means the shit hit the jets elsewhere." She focused back on Nate. "Any idea how big this invading force might be? Or where they'll be headed to find this Beacon thing?"

"So you're saying you *do* wanna know now?" Nate asked, partly because he had no freaking idea how sizeable the troglodan invasion was, and mostly because he was annoyed that after weeks of haunting his every step, they were the ones who got to decide to change their tune.

If they would've just listened to him weeks ago…

It would have changed nothing, said the Excalibur.

"Nate, the NSA gets calls like yours every single day. You know how many of them have ever panned out?"

Your people cannot win this fight, Nathaniel. You have seen it.

"Luckily," Tessa continued when he said nothing, "all the fucking nut-jobs get bumped right up the laughing stock and flagged to us and the rest of our ET comrades. It's up to us to decide if any of them actually get looked into at all. Most don't. And a full on tail?" She shook her head. "You were breathing rarefied air even before it turned out you weren't full of shit."

"Is that supposed to make me feel *better*?"

"Not really," she said with a shrug, chains jangling as she twisted around to reach for something. The answer drew him up short. As did the walkie talkie she produced from her back pocket.

"Where'd you get that?" was all he could think to ask.

She smiled a little, like it was every bit as stupid a question as it sounded, and brandished the walkie talkie. "Stockroom. It's gonna be a minor miracle if it does us any good right now, but…" She focused back on him. "Can you tell me where that Beacon is? Or anything else I should bounce up the chain if I manage to make contact?"

The way she was watching him, walkie talkie at the ready, suddenly willing to listen, like they'd been in it together, all along... For a second, Nate couldn't help but feel a bit paranoid, like maybe they really *had* known all along, and this had all been some kind of intricate ploy to get him to betray the Beacon's location.

The joke would most certainly be on them, were that the case.

Nate couldn't help it. He huffed in bitter amusement as he remembered that Ex was right, and that he had no goddamn idea how to find the thing anyway. He barely even understood where *Ex* was hanging around, aside from vaguely on his person. And as for where those repulsor gauntlets had come from...

He focused back on his benevolent interrogator, and found her watching him closely. It was only then he realized he'd just chuckled out loud at the voice in his head.

"New York," he said, thinking of the devastation the Merlin had shown him. "They're gonna hit New York, if they haven't already."

She waited for more, looking to be scrubbing his words with her intrinsic bullshit detectors extra thoroughly now.

"I think... I think maybe that's where I should go."

The words were as much of a surprise to him as they were to her.

"No offense, Nate, but you don't really strike me as the *run toward the fire* type."

"I'm not," Nate admitted. "But the Beacon is that way..."

He wasn't really sure why he said it. It couldn't have been more than a gut feeling—or, more likely, the simple fact that he was desperate, and that New York was the closest thing to a lead he had. Whatever it was, he tried to keep the confidence rolling.

"... And no offense, but you're not gonna find it without me, and I'm not sure we're gonna survive this invasion unless I get that thing off-world somehow. I just need to get closer before I can, uh..."

Sense it, Ex said, feeling uncharacteristically pleased, like he actually thought Nate might be on to something here.

"Sense it?" Tessa suggested.

"Exactly," Nate agreed, far from convinced that the joke wasn't on all three of them.

Tessa was equally skeptical. "Like an Arthurian dowsing rod?"

He started to open his mouth, then shrugged instead, not sure what else to say. So much for that *confidence* thing.

"Right," she muttered, starting to fiddle with the small dials on the walkie talkie. "Forget I asked. And what about this…" She sighed and shook her head. "Christ, I can't believe I'm saying this. What about this Merlin character? Where is he? And the weapon he gave you. The sword. Is that… relevant?"

Nate hesitated, unsure how much he should reveal, and pretty sure by her tone that she'd already drawn the line at space invaders anyway. "Look, I know this all sounds insane…"

She glanced up from the walkie talkie, eyebrows bent in a silent exclamation of, *You don't say?!*

"… But I didn't ask for any of this. I'm just trying to help. Just like you. And there's only two things I need to do that."

"Oh yeah?" She lowered the walkie talkie and gave him her full attention, a soft grin tugging at her mouth. "Go on, then. What does Nate Arturi need to save the world?"

"I need a ride to get me closer to the Beacon," he said, glancing warily toward the break room door. "And I need one to get my friends the hell out of here."

CHAPTER 30

HIDE AND SEEK

In the dark hallway outside the break room, it felt like the end of the world.

Then again, it had pretty much felt like that *inside* the break room too, Nate supposed. It just felt a lot more real as he pulled the door shut behind him, leaving Tessa to futz with her commandeered walkie talkie.

He almost hoped she didn't manage to make contact.

Gathering supplies. Making a run for the countryside with Gwen and Marty and the rest of his friends. That, Nate could wrap his head around. Flying off to New York on this... this *intuition* of his, though...

Is the only sensible choice left to you.

Sensible. That felt like an interesting choice of words, Nate thought, as he stepped into the dark hallway, straining his ears for the telltale jangle of chains—and promptly bumped straight into the incoming foot traffic he'd been too self-absorbed to notice.

"Ah, sorry," he whispered, reaching out to stabilize and finding a handful of firm chesticle.

"Arturi?"

Todd's voice. And that was Emily with him. He could see them there in the dark, he realized, but in a way that felt almost subconscious—like his eyes had adjusted but his brain wasn't yet certain how to interpret the input they were passing up the chain.

Nate hesitated, feeling like he should say something but finding his brain equally unfit for that task.

"I'm sorry," he repeated, surprised to realize he meant it, even if he didn't know why. "Really. For everything."

What the hell was he saying?

Him? Sorry to Todd Mackleroy? For *everything*? Clearly, he knew not what he said. Clearly, he'd finally lost it. Only... Only he could feel Todd nodding timidly in the darkness. Nodding in agreement. Maybe even in shame. Probably, it was all in Nate's head, but in that moment, he could've sworn Todd Mackleroy was sorry too—more sorry than he could find the words to say.

"Stick close to the others when it's time?" Nate said.

Todd nodded again in the darkness, more certain this time. "Come on," he said to Emily, turning toward the front of the store. "We're on can opener duty," he added to Nate.

"Good," was all Nate could think to say as they squeezed past.

Nothing like the end of the world to bring people together.

"Thank you," Emily whispered unexpectedly in the darkness, pausing as she passed. "Thank you for getting us out of there, Nate."

Nate nodded dumbly in the dark, and listened to them go. He watched the line of eerie blue light split the darkness ahead, then swallow the two of them whole as they pushed through the swinging doors into the front of the store, moving as quietly as their chains would allow, leaving Nate alone in the darkness with the distinctly uncomfortable thought that maybe Todd Mackleroy had never really been the enemy at all.

"Merciful Sith," Nate whispered to himself.

It really was the end of the world.

WHEN NATE FOUND Zach a few doors down the dark hallway, quietly sifting through the contents of some kind of utility closet with a flashlight, he felt a reflexive urge to duck for the cover and hurry on by. He paused in the doorway instead, wanting to speak, but too thoroughly gripped by the sudden chilly certainty that everything had changed, and that his friends would never look at him the same way again.

He needed to get moving.

But then Zach turned, noticing him, and sure enough, there was an unmistakable glint of wariness in his friend's eyes.

Everything had changed.

"Looking for something?" Nate managed.

Zach's posture softened a sliver. "Hesitant as I am to ruin Kyle's chance to watch Emily rocking the whole *alien abduction kink* look, I figured I might as well try to find us a pair of bolt cutters before we all go scurrying for the woods." He considered Nate, a cautious grin spreading across his lips. "Should I address you as your majesty now, or what?"

The tension flowed from Nate's shoulders with a relieved sigh. "Maybe just Shitty Squadmate Number One."

"Ah, I don't know about that, man. You didn't see the randos we've been pulling to fill your spot these past few weeks. I don't think any of *them* would've thrown down with a cave troll to save us."

"If they had, though," came Marty's voice behind Nate, startling both of them, "we'd probably be inclined to understand why they might've been hesitant to tell us they *could* do those things."

"Even if we wish they would've realized we've pretty much been nerd prepping all our lives to handle the mind blowing implications of said inhuman feats," Zach added, as Nate glanced around to see Marty standing there with another flashlight.

Nate looked back and forth between his friends, not knowing what to say, appalled to find the hint of tears pressing at his eyes.

Thankfully, Marty broke the silence before he could fall apart.

"You need this back, by the way?" his friend asked, holding out the dark earpiece that had mysteriously appeared in Nate's pocket at Ex's behest back on the ship.

It is a piece of me. It would be unwise to leave it in careless hands.

"Keep it for now," Nate said, sure that if there were any careless hands in the immediate vicinity, they didn't belong to Marty. "Just in case," he added at Marty's questioning look.

"All right, then," Marty said, carefully tucking the device away in a pocket. "You, uh, sort things out with Tessa?"

"Yeah, she's... She's trying to scramble us a ride out of here."

"Scramble?" Zach asked. "What is she, like—"

"Air Force," Nate said. "Another long story. One I don't really know yet, either. But I'm pretty sure she's on our side."

"I'd hope so," Zach said, frowning thoughtfully into space. "Freaking aliens, man." He returned from his musings to focus back on Nate. "Say"— he raised his chained wrists—"any chance you could cut out the middle man, your majesty?"

~

By the time Marty forced him to stop yanking Zach's chain, so to speak, Nate was even more tired and deflated than he had been upon crashing into McClanahan's.

"You need to eat and rest a minute," Marty insisted, pushing him gently toward the back stockroom. "Go find something. We'll finish with the supplies."

Nate was too tired to argue. Too tired, too overwhelmed, and frankly too disgusted with his inability to be useful in any kind of predictable fashion. Apparently, it took a lethal fall or a troglodan pointing a gun at Marty's head to get his Knightly juices flowing.

Whosoever holds this hammer, if he be worthy...

Nate limped on for the stockroom, ignoring the Excalibur's idle jab, thinking instead of just how nice it would've felt right then to have a hot shower and nestle up beneath his comforter for a few hours—or months. That thought only reminded him of poor Copernicus, trapped in their house, riding out the trog invasion all alone. He hoped to Christ the corgi had refrained from barking at any passing trogs.

He paused just shy of the stockroom, gripped by the sudden crushing panic that he couldn't leave them all behind. Couldn't go through with this.

But what else was he supposed to do?

Ahead, the faint nightmare blue glow permeating the stockroom reminded him that he still might be hard pressed to part ways even if he tried. He edged closer, and saw that the light was trickling in through long warehouse windows lining the top of the walls on either side. That the light was only coming from one side seemed like a good sign that most of the trog fleet had already passed by, and that they might be free to get moving the other way soon—assuming Tessa actually made contact with her people.

Assuming there were still people to make contact with.

Nate spotted Kyle and Kelsey off in the far corner ahead, where Kyle looked to be animatedly instructing her on the finer points of children's breakfast cereals. For a second, the sight felt so normal it actually put a small smile on Nate's face. Then he caught the glint of their chains, and reality caught back up. His smile faded. His stomach rumbled.

Eat. I could use more resources to repair your internal damage.

The thought made him cringe in more ways than one. He didn't even want to think about what his insides looked like after crash landing in

McClanahan's and getting chest-kicked by a troglodan. He damn sure didn't want to know what the Excalibur meant by "repairing."

One catastrophic nightmare at a time. That was the new policy.

He turned right, thinking to find a quiet corner and something to attempt to snack on while he gathered his thoughts. He didn't make it any farther than the head of the last row, though, before he paused again.

Gwen was alone in the aisle.

He teetered at the corner, thinking of everything she'd said back in the brig, wondering what she'd think of him now that the truth was out, and she'd had a moment to cogitate on just how deeply right she'd been about her good pal, Mr. Nice Guy the Alien Lightning Rod.

He was about to turn and go when she looked up at him in the faint wash of eerie blue light. He almost could've laughed that even here in this hellish situation—even after an alien abduction, a bloody brig breakout, and a passable attempt at human flight he still hadn't even begun to wrap his head around—his less-than-spotless insides could still flutter at a simple look from her.

It was embarrassing. Doubly so when he remembered that Ex was currently elbows deep, so to speak, in those fluttering insides. To his surprise, though, Ex didn't express anything more than a wordless sense of impatience as Nate started down the aisle to meet her.

"So…" he said quietly, drawing up a few extra feet short, just in case she was feeling jumpy about him. If anything, though, the look in her eyes was one of amusement. Tired, yes. And scared and overwhelmed too. But also amused.

"So? That's all you've got after all that?"

"Yeah…" Nate licked his lips, searching for something better to say, finding he had nothing. Nothing but a stupid, nervous grin, pulling wider with each second that passed between them. "Yeah, I guess it is."

Jesus, why was he grinning like this? And why was she smiling right back? It was infectious. Pathological. They were in shock, some corner of his brain pointed out. Incoherently giddy from the rush of horrors and death and complete alien madness that had just swept by, and for the fact that they were still alive, despite it all.

"Oh my god," she whispered.

It was like a three word detonation sequence.

Before he knew it, before he could think better of it, Nate was striding forward and wrapping her in his arms like he knew what he was doing, and she was burying her face into his chest, and they were both shaking with laughter, or sobs, or he couldn't tell what.

"Oh my god," she gasped.

"I'm sorry, Gwen," he whispered, voice hoarse, eyes burning, not knowing why other than that he'd failed to stop any of this, and that he would've given anything to take it back and spare them all. "I'm so sorry."

She tensed in his arms, pushing back enough to see him, looking like she wanted to argue, but not knowing where to start.

"I wanted to tell you," he found himself saying. "There's so much I wanted to tell you these past weeks." He huffed at himself. "These past *years*. You were right, back there in the brig. About all of it."

"No," she murmured softly, planting her hands against his chest, chains lightly jingling. "No, Nate, you saved our lives."

"I failed to keep them out of danger," he countered. "I was too busy spectating, just like you said. Waiting for someone else to come and fix it all."

"Nate"—she shook her head helplessly—"that's not what I... I mean, I had no idea what..."

"You were right," he whispered.

And maybe it was his sad inner warrior finally surfacing after too many close rounds with death, or maybe it was just the look in her eyes as she gazed up at him, but he found himself leaning closer to her as he said it, feeling oddly at peace in the moment. Not relaxed, exactly, just... content. Content, riding the razor's edge between hapless nerves and the electric excitement of her warm hands on his chest. Intoxicated with the closeness of her, so close that he could taste the scent of his whispered name on her lips when she drew up breathless, searching his face for some sign of his intent.

He kissed her.

For a second, he was every bit as surprised as she was to find his lips against hers. So much so that he barely even registered the feeling of it, lost as he was in the sheer thought of the thing. Him, Nathaniel "IT Guy" Arturi, kissing Gwen Pearson—going for it, just like that, after years of telling himself *just a little longer*, and *now's not quite the time*. And what had changed?

Nothing, he realized, faltering.

Nothing at all.

He drew back, remembering himself, registering how abruptly he'd just ambushed her with all of this.

"You were right," he repeated, voice thick, throat tight, pulling back to give her space, suddenly afraid to meet her eyes. "And I think I needed to hear it," he added, eyes fixed firmly downward on nothing at all. "So, uh, thank you."

"Thank you?"

He glanced up at her amused tone, not quite sure what to make of it. She just laced her fingers through his hair and pulled him into another kiss, harder this time. She leaned into him, her hands finding their way back down to his chest, down to his hips, pulling him to her, her lips parting hungrily to meet his. He looped a hand behind her neck, pulling her tighter, breathless. She reached around his hips—

And drew back with a breathless giggle when her wrist chain pulled tight across his hips, catching her hands from reaching all the way around his waist.

"You're welcome," she giggle-whispered, planting one last peck on his lips before favoring him with a slight frown. "As long as you don't take that to mean I actually agree that this whole thing is your fault."

He smiled guiltily. "Wouldn't dream of—"

Something is coming, Nathaniel.

"—it."

He looked around the dim stockroom, tight-chested fear slapping aside swimming-head bliss so fast he felt the mental whiplash.

"What is it?" Gwen whispered.

He held up a finger for silence, straining to listen for guttural troglodan voices or the hum of a descending ship. There was nothing. Nothing but the feeling of Gwen's warmth pressed against him, and the barely audible sounds of Kyle and Kelsey talking somewhere in the far corner. Nothing but—

The faintest creak from the end of the aisle.

Nate's heart leapt into his throat right before the back door jerked open and two dark figures swept in. Armed, Nate registered, as he shoved his way in front of Gwen, reaching for the first thing he could find, a dark weapon training in on him ahead.

"Easy there, friend," came a tight voice, just as Nate's brain caught up and recognized the face behind the gun. "Put the pretzels down, and let's talk about this."

Nate glanced from the gunman to his own cocked hand, which had managed to find itself a nice plastic tub of pretzel sticks in the mad grab for an impromptu weapon. He looked back to the two intruders, and blew out a relieved breath as he confirmed it a second time.

It was the big guy and the driver from the SUV.

Tessa's SAS backup had found them—a fact that was less than soothing for other present parties, Nate realized, at the crash of falling boxes in the far corner, followed by the sharp hiss of, "Oh, shit!" and running footsteps.

"It's okay, Kyle!" Nate hissed through the shelves as loud as he dared, setting the pretzels down and waving insistently at the two SAS goons to close the damned door.

The driver splayed his hands and gestured to his gun as if to point out Nate was in no position to be making demands. His big partner just shook his head and shooed the driver toward the door to do it.

"Who *are* these guys?" Gwen whispered beside him.

"Nate?" came Kyle's uncertain voice from somewhere toward the head of the stockroom.

There's something else.

"It's uh… Everything's fine," Nate called uncertainly back, head spinning with the flurry of inputs. "They're, uh… backup," he added to Gwen, frowning at the two men. "I think."

The two men were striding down the aisle toward him and Gwen, weapons lowered.

"Kid," the driver said, "you are almost definitely sitting in more shit than I could measure with a box of rulers and a roll of duct tape." He glanced uneasily in the direction the troglodan fleet seemed to be drifting. "Then again, I'm not so sure that doesn't also describe the entire human race right now. Where's Kalders?"

Nathaniel.

"Right here wondering if you'd remember to tape before you measure, Snuffs," came a voice from the shelf to the left.

The big guy gave a monosyllabic chuckle at that.

What is it? Nate thought at Ex. He could just barely see Tessa there in the dim lighting, watching them through the gaps in the boxes.

Something…

Ex hesitated, uncertain. Nate's heart rate picked up, the momentary gush of relief cold and congealing in his gut.

"Ha-ha," the driver was saying, waving his weapon too casually. "Snuffy snuffs it up. Original. Now can we—"

You need to move, Nathaniel.

"—and get the hell out of here before—"

"Shut up."

Tessa's voice had taken on a sharp edge, like she'd heard something. Something like—

Nathaniel! Move!

Nate reached for Gwen's hand a split second before the wall exploded inward with a sharp crack and a racket of collapsing shelves and boxes. Halogen blue light flooded into the room, casting the shock on Gwen's face into sheer relief. Nate snatched her hand to run, and barely made it a step before something snaked around his torso and yanked impossibly hard. He felt her try to hold onto his hand. Heard her cry his name as he took flight.

Dim storage room shelves blurred to firelit pre-dawn sky, and troglodan floodlights in the distance, then he crashed into something hard and unyielding, and smacked down to a rough landing on the equally unforgiving pavement. He coughed for breath, grunting in pain, trying to sit up.

Something moved at the edge of his vision, stepping in to block out the eerie light of the distant ships. Nate tried to roll away, but something stomped down on his chest, holding him in place. He turned back and looked up at a tall, armored figure, glinting copper in the reflected light of some nearby fire.

"Aya kunithi jera," it hissed down at him from behind a dark helmet, flickering copper and ruby in the flames, serpentine hair wriggling like a wreath of shadows.

Serpentine hair. Gorgon.

"Wait," he started to say, but the Excalibur Knight was already scooping him effortlessly from the ground, clamping frighteningly strong arms around him. Then she *jumped*. Impossibly high. Wind howling in his ears. The Knight's arms crushing him half to death.

He still found the air to scream when he noticed the ship they were about to collide with.

Then a section of the ship's belly slid open, and they hurtled through a shimmering green wall of light to land in a bright room. Some kind of loading deck, Nate had all of a split second to register before the serpent-haired Knight tossed him across the room like a stuffed animal that'd lost its allure.

He landed heavily, scrambled to get back up, and lurched straight into a transparent wall he hadn't noticed there. He whirled and found more walls surrounding him, a few feet away on every side. A cell. And she was already standing in the only opening, barring the way.

"Wait," he said. "Please."

She made a gesture with two long fingers, and the last wall closed in on itself between them. No door swinging shut. No panel hissing up from the floor. The wall just *materialized*, trapping Nate within the clear panels.

"Wait!" he cried, raising his hands in peace. "Wait a second! There's been some kind of misunderstanding!"

But the serpent-haired Knight was already slicing her hand through the air in another gesture, and the walls went opaque, leaving Nate all alone in his perfect white prison cell.

CHAPTER 31
MAN IN THE BOX

"Wait!" Nate yelled for what must've been the fifteenth time, pounding a fist against the solid white wall. "Hey!"

Nothing. Nothing at all.

If you are quite finished, I have something important to tell you.

"Oh yeah?" Nate growled. "Is it *more* or *less* important than the fact we just got kidnapped by—"

The ship lurched with a violent burst of acceleration. Nate hit the deck hard and scrambled for the closest wall, heart pounding, desperately seeking some kind of handhold. The deck fell away without warning, momentary weightlessness engulfing him before it yanked right back up and smacked him flat as a Nate Pancake, taking his stomach right along with it, then tying the poor organ into animal balloon knots with a series of aggressive maneuvers he couldn't comprehend, busy as he was bouncing from one cell wall to the other like an oversized racquetball.

He was going to be sick. He was sure of it. Then he *was* sick, and he couldn't even keep planted in one corner long enough to finish before another sharp jerk sent him flying.

"Have you people never heard of seat belts?!" he screamed at one perfect white wall, right before another jolt sent him smacking into it.

I believe they have disengaged the local gravitonic intertial negation systems. It is possible they deliberately seek to minimize your comfort.

"No shit!" Nate growled, attempting to wedge himself into a corner with feet and hands on the two adjoining walls.

It didn't work.

He couldn't have said whether their wild ride lasted two minutes after that, or twenty. All he knew was that the blind mechanical torture was somehow almost worse than being manhandled by laughing troglodans, and that, by the time the ship's flight finally leveled out and calmed, he would've done just about anything to get the hell out of there.

Then again, judging by the fact that no one came to work him over in his vulnerable state, he wasn't sure they'd even care if he promised to do whatever they wanted. It wasn't like he knew anything useful, after all. Probably, the gorgons simply wanted the Excalibur from him, just like the troglodans did.

Which brings us back to what I need to tell you, if you are prepared to listen like a rational being.

Nate pushed himself up from the deck, scooting to sit in the closet corner, then paused, remembering he'd tossed what little stomach contents he'd had in one of these corners just a few minutes ago. There was no puddle of sick to be seen, though. Just clean deck and pristine white walls, all around.

Whatever else there was to say about his second alien abduction of the night, at least the lighting was better, and the ship far less grimy.

"Fine," he muttered, sitting back against the wall. *Fire away, then. And I'm fine, by the way. Thanks for all the concern.*

You are fine because I have built you to withstand such punishment. Three weeks ago, that ride might well have killed you.

Nate glared at the white wall. *What's so important, Ex?*

I appear to have been dimensionally sequestered.

Nate frowned. *Say I didn't understand what the hell that actually means...*

If you were a feeble-minded simpleton, you might say this cell is "bending space" in such a way that my "good bits" have been "placed out of reach."

"You have good bits?" Nate muttered.

Juvenile rebellion will get you nowhere, Nathaniel. But neither will I, so long as we are stuck in this cell.

"Great. What the hell am I supposed to do, then?"

In the future, do not get stuck in four-dimensional cells. Additionally, it may be wise to stop blathering out loud like a simpleton. Better they remain in the dark about your limited intellect.

Nate clenched his fists, gnashing his teeth and resisting the dire urge to punch the wall. *And what do I do now that I have gotten stuck in this thing?*

Ah. Yes. There was a pregnant pause. *Do not die in here, perhaps.*

"Helpful."

It's hardly my fault you allowed yourself to be captured twice in a single night.

Says the Master Sword who has yet to tell me a single thing about how to wield his mighty power, Nate shot back, looking around as if he might actually find something more useful than uniform white walls.

He ignored Ex's retort's about *whosoever holds this hammer,* his mind drifting groundside, to what Gwen and his friends would be doing in response to his abrupt abduction.

Doing the smart thing and getting the hell out of State College, he hoped. Tessa and the SAS goons would see to that much at least, wouldn't they?

Your friends appear to be on the move.

Nate blinked dumbly at the comment, trying to track how Ex could possibly know that.

"The earpiece," he whispered, as realization set in. *You can still connect to it?*

Electromagnetic shielding does not affect quantum coupling, Nathaniel.

And you didn't think to open with that?!

I was under the impression we were looking for helpful solutions.

Nate pinched his temples. *We're gonna have to have a serious talk about the things you deem helpful.*

Here, allow me to patch you through to the Mother Hen and his band of sniveling chicks. I'm certain they will be right along to... Oh.

Oh?

"—ate?!" Marty's voice cut in before Ex could explain. He sounded tense. Tense enough that Nate was halfway to his feet before he remembered there was nowhere to go.

A burst of gunfire sounded in his head, frighteningly clear.

Nate stood the rest of the way, heart suddenly pounding.

"Nate, come in! We're—"

A brain-numbing *whoomph* of sound, and a garbled round of curses.

"Dammit! Nate, if you can hear me, they found us."

His blood went cold.

"We're—Shit! No, move! MOVE!"

Nate listened in horror to the smack of footsteps and panting breaths, of weapons fire and troglodan voices calling to each other in the distance, all of it clear as if he were there himself. It was only when Marty tried his name again that he remembered the connection was supposed to go both ways.

"Marty?! What's happening?"

"Nate?! Jesus, where are—Shit!"

Another explosion. A clatter of automatic gunfire, and slamming car doors. The unmistakable roar of a troglodan battle cry, and a wrenching crash of twisted metal.

"Get her in!" Marty shouted, and Nate's insides froze at the thought that it could be Gwen he was talking about. "No, look out, there's—NO!"

The feed cut silent with an awful crunch.

Nate stared at the white wall for a breathless eternity.

"Get them back," he heard himself whisper. "Ex, get them back."

I cannot reach the node.

"You have to." Nate touched at the walls, beginning to pace as if he might actually find an escape. "Ex, I need you to get that node back. I need you to—"

He balled a fist and slammed it into the wall, overcome. "Dammit!"

Calm yourself, Nathaniel. It's possible the node has merely sustained superficial damage.

"While strapped to my best friend's head?!" Nate cried, striking the wall again, and again. Switching to kicks. Screaming all the while. "Hey! Hey, out there! FUCKING HEY!"

He couldn't say how long he continued on, kicking and screaming, ignoring the Excalibur's cool-headed chastisement about how pointless the display was, and how he was undoubtedly abusing his body worse than the wall.

He had to get out of there.

He had to get to his friends. Wherever they were. Wherever *he* was. However the hell he was supposed to fix this. He kept pounding at the wall, shouting for the gorgon Knight, not knowing what she wanted, or what she'd do with him—only that, if he kept it up, she just might come back to the cell to do it sooner than later. And when that happened, he had to be ready to seize whatever opportunity he could.

It was only when she actually arrived, though, that he realized how utterly laughable that notion was.

He didn't see the gorgon Knight appear so much as he registered a flicker of a copper blur amid the dissolving cell wall. Before he could so much as twitch, the wall was open, she was across the space, and he was pinned to the wall by an armored forearm to the throat.

Alone and resolutely pounding the wall one moment. Crushed to it by a gorgon death machine the next.

She was *tall*, his stunned brain registered, quite uselessly, as he clawed at her unbudging arm. Tall and without helmet, he saw, as she leaned in to inspect him more closely with startlingly phosphorescent, electric blue eyes. Her face was surprisingly humanoid. More triangular from top to bottom. Nose flatter. Ivy green skin vaguely reminiscent of the flesh of an aloe leaf.

For a second, he was so shocked by the sudden alien closeness that he forgot his outrage, forgot to look for his opening. Then her serpentine hair rippled to life, fleshy green tendrils snaking their way under his chin and around his head, securing him firmly in place, and that was it.

Nate lost his shit—kicking and bucking in a wild fit of panic, barely even registering the Excalibur's protests in his head. The gorgon Knight was impossibly strong. Strong and perfectly content, it seemed, to let his impotent rage play out. At least until she peeled him bodily off of the wall and slammed him back against it, just once, hard enough to leave the world swimming, yet as casually as if she were bopping a misbehaving child on the head.

His struggles ceased of their own accord.

He'd never felt so vulnerable in his life.

"Osaia shida de Emrys, ploondo," she said. Her voice was strong and resonant, and entirely too musical for such a brutally strong being—a faint, tremulous purr humming beneath every word.

"I don't..." Nate tried to shake his head, and found it quite firmly pinned between her forearm and hair serpents. His feet weren't even touching the deck anymore. "I don't understand, but—But my friends, the ones who were with me back on the ground, they're..."

He searched her alien face, trying to ascertain if she understood, or if she'd even care.

"We need to go back," he said, as firmly as he could with his windpipe half-crushed beneath her forearm. "They're in danger. You need to turn this ship around and—"

She cut him off with a short, sharp hiss, and an extra jerk of pressure at his throat. "Osaia shida de Emrys?"

"Don't... understand..." Nate wheezed through his collapsing airway, racking his brain for what she wanted, what had brought her to McClanahan's.

What had led *them* to his friends once he'd been snatched up.

"—t's your fault," he gasped, eyes widening. "—ur fault they..."

A soft hiss escaped her, and she dropped him to the deck so suddenly that his legs buckled, and he had to thrust himself back against the wall to keep from falling over. The gorgon Knight was already stalking away from him.

"Hey," he wheezed after her, straightening, desperate to stop her—right until his eyes fell on the open cell exit just past her, and he found the opportunity he'd been looking for.

He lunged forward, thinking to shove past her, hoping the damned cell might just automatically close her in behind him once he had. She flicked a hand toward him before he'd made it two steps, and an invisible troglodan punched him straight in the chest. That, or a pulse cannon maybe. It hardly seemed to matter as he hit the back wall with a breathless thud and crumpled to the floor, balled up around his throbbing insides.

"Osaia shida de Emrys," came her resonant voice, even slower this time.

When he managed to raise his head enough to see her, she crouched down and, with a deliberation that suggested she were speaking with a small child, raised a hand and tapped one long finger to the side of her head, where there appeared to be something like an ear orifice beneath her swirling hair. *Listen carefully*, the gesture seemed to say.

He wished he could've found the resolve to sit back up, or least tell her to shove it. Seeing that he lacked either, though, she began to speak again.

He gasped as the words came to him.

"What has happened to the Merlin, human?"

He could've sworn he still heard the alien tongue like a dissonant chord beneath the words, but there they were in coherent English, too. Had she done that? Or had he just understood gorgon-speak?

If you wish to take credit for my endeavors at translating through a millennium of drift, then yes. Well done, Nathaniel.

He thought of the troglodan in the brig, and the fact that no one else seemed to have understood it when it'd called him a spotted runt and told him to go fist himself. Ex's doing too, no doubt. He hadn't had time to think about it then. The intent stare of the gorgon Knight in front of him suggested he didn't have time now, either.

"I don't know," he croaked. He worked a pinch of moisture into his parched mouth, and tried again. "I don't know where he went. He... left me in that town back there, the day after he..."

He hesitated, suddenly not sure how much to tell her. It occurred to him that, if she was looking for the Merlin, his limited intel might be the only thing of value he possessed right that moment. It also occurred to him that there'd probably be little reason for her *not* to kill him and take the Excalibur once he'd coughed that intel up.

"How about this?" he said, trying not to wince as he pushed himself up to a sitting position against the wall. "Help me find my friends, and I'll tell you everything I know about the Merlin."

He searched her alien face for any glint of intent or reaction, wondering idly if gorgon culture were as steeped as humanity in the art of deceit and misdirection. He didn't know. Couldn't read a single hint of her static expression.

"Aren't the Excalibur Knights all supposed to be on the same team, here?" he added.

That got a reaction, at least. A twitch of the lips and a flicker of serpentine hair that, while completely foreign, seemed to carry an air of disgust or condescension, judging by the way she turned to leave.

"Please," he croaked, before he could stop himself. He hated how pathetic it sounded. "Please, my friends are out there, and they're in trouble, and —Hey!"

She wasn't stopping.

"You can't just walk away!" he cried at her back. "It's your fault the trogs found them!"

She kept walking. Didn't care.

"You're supposed to be a Knight, goddammit!"

She paused in the opening. Paused and turned to face him with the kind of slow, heavy deliberateness that made him think he might've just spoken his last words. Those electric blue eyes locked onto his. He didn't breathe.

"You wish to speak of fault?" the gorgon finally asked, her voice flat of affect as she pointed to the deck at Nate's feet. "First observe the consequences of your own failure, human."

And with that, the deck disappeared beneath his feet.

CHAPTER 32
IN FLAMES

I t was only an illusion, Nate realized, as he hit the wall with a strangled
yelp, slapping desperately for some handhold only to find that he was
in fact *not* falling through the open deck, straight down to the breathtaking sphere of ocean blue and swirling white cloud below. *Earth*, he registered. He was looking down at Earth, the black, star-speckled void of space
stretching out for eternity all around where the walls had just been—where
he could still feel them now.

The entire cell had shifted into some kind of immersive display mode,
feeding from cameras on the outer ship hull, maybe, or maybe just showing
some pre-recorded footage.

"Hello?" he called, but if the gorgon Knight was still there, she didn't
answer.

I believe she wishes for you to observe.

Nate looked down at the blue planet, not really sure what other choice
he had. As if in response to his gaze, the view began to zoom in and in, and
further still, until he finally registered the true scene he was looking down
on. His stomach clenched at the sight.

It was just as bad as what the Merlin had shown him. Worse.

Dark smoke seemed to be billowing from half the planet, pouring from
every one of the dozen or more hotspots of the thin red triangles that
covered the display, complete with fine lines of alien script. There must've
been hundreds of those tiny triangles scattered across the planet—each and

every one of them demarcating another huge troglodan ship, Nate realized as the view continued zooming. Just like the ones that'd hit State College.

He could only stare in silent, abject horror as the floor continued zooming, further than seemed optically possible, honing in on one cluster of red triangles on the eastern US coast. New York, he dimly noted, as the destruction telescoped into focus. Nate's eyes traced unbelievingly from the gaping ruins of collapsed bridges to the rushing streaks of fighter jets, soaring onto the scene only to go up in tiny blossoms of flame as the trog ships opened fire.

He saw the anthill view of troglodan foot soldiers moving through the streets, blasting away indiscriminately at fleeing civilians and whatever ground forces had managed to amass. The display zoomed even further, the video feed flooding up to cover the cell walls, too, until Nate found himself standing on one of those streets, awash in the smoke, and the screams, and chaotic sounds of fighting. Surrounded by shattered glass, and burning cars in the streets. Wide-eyed people everywhere, running for their lives. Parents clutching their children. Well-dressed businessmen and street punks alike, all falling over one another to flee, spilling through the lines of law enforcement and military outfits fighting desperately to protect them. Fighting helplessly.

So many people running for their lives.

So many not making it.

He didn't realize he'd fallen to his knees until the feed cut out, and he found himself back on the pristine deck of the gorgon ship, staring helplessly at the gorgon Knight.

So much destruction. So much death.

And for what? For the Beacon? For *him*?

"I don't understand," he heard himself say.

"No," she said quietly, hair swaying back and forth. "I do not believe you do."

It was only when she turned to leave that he registered she was already outside the cell, and that he was only seeing her because the walls had gone transparent.

"My friends," he sputtered.

"May well perish." She paused, serpentine hair lying flattened and still. "Might well have done so already." She turned to face him with that cold, electric blue stare. "But if you truly think their lives more significant than the tens of thousands you have already failed, you are welcome to pray to the Lady for mercy."

Nate's voice was small. Pitiful. "Will she hear me?"

The gorgon only stared at him another few seconds, seeming to wonder the same thing. Then she turned and was gone, and he was alone, mind's eye seared with the afterimages of a burning New York, the gorgon Knight's words settling like slow lead sinkers on his soul.

~

Perhaps you should consider the positive aspects of this development, Ex said, some time later. It had probably been an hour or so since Nate had finally given up on his half-hearted attempts to find a way out of the cell and resigned himself to a long and desolate lie down on the hard deck. *I believe you might call it a 'silver lining.'*

Nate only stared at the spotless white ceiling with unseeing eyes, reflecting that he had no idea if his best friends were alive or dead, and wondering what the hell the Lady and the Merlin had ever been thinking, pulling him into any of this.

He still didn't have any good answers.

He couldn't get the screams out of his head. Couldn't stop seeing those burning cities, and hearing the frantic tones and the awful crunch of Marty's final moments over and over again.

Not his *final* moments, he reminded himself.

It was sounding less convincing every time.

Why didn't you tell me, Ex?

He wasn't even sure exactly what he was asking, but Ex seemed to understand.

I did, little hobbit. More times than you can count. You were simply not ready to hear it. There was a thoughtful pause. *Perhaps it is not your fault.*

Not my fault? Nate sat up, waiting for the punchline. *What the hell do you mean, it's not my fault?*

Well, given the way events have unfolded... That is to say, ahh...

For once, Ex seemed lost for words.

Are you... Are you giving up on me?!

Before Ex could confirm or deny the allegation, a motion drew Nate's attention to the far side of the room, where the gorgon Knight had reappeared for the first time in over an hour. She strode confidently across the deck, headed straight for the aperture they'd initially boarded through at the center of the room. The thing dilated as she approached, coming alive with a portal of shimmering green energy.

"What's happening out there?" Nate called. "What are you doing?"

The only reply was the hum and hiss of what sounded like the ventral hull parting beneath the aperture. The gorgon Knight dropped through the hazy green barrier and plunged from the ship without a word, back down to Earth, he could only assume by the muted sounds of whipping atmosphere that trickled in through the opening. The hull hummed closed below, and Nate leaned back against his transparent wall, thinking he might rather be dead and recycled for his juicy Excalibur parts instead of subject to this demoralizing game of Shut Up and Wait with the knowledge of *tens of thousands* of casualties hanging on his shoulders.

Try the node again. Please.

Still offline, Ex said, almost immediately. Then, more hesitantly: *It may yet self-reassemble, though. Provided the destruction wasn't complete.*

Nate sank into the wall, trying not to think about just how high the chances of that were and, when that failed, looking helplessly around for some distraction.

At least he wasn't staring at a blank white wall anymore.

Compared to the grimy, horror-show innards of the troglodan ship, the gorgon ship's loading bay was a veritable five-star resort. The dark gray decks and white walls were all spit-shine clean, and there was a surprising amount of greenery around the place. Every horizontal surface, and even some of the vertical ones, seemed to be home to some manner of vine, shrub, flower, or vaguely alien *something*. He wasn't even sure words like *flower* were technically accurate, given that he was probably looking at greenery from another planet, but it wasn't as if that actually mattered while the planet was burning beneath his useless ass.

A few times, he'd thought he heard voices and activity in the distance, and even now, he could definitely feel the ship moving through gradual maneuvers despite the fact that the gorgon Knight had gone groundside. Whether that meant there were others of her kind aboard, Nate wasn't sure. He supposed it also could've been robot AIs, or remote control via her own Excalibur, or allies from another alien species.

Hell, they already had space ogres and Lady Medusa the gorgon. Maybe it was the freaking Minotaur or the Big Bad Wolf flying the ship. Maybe the universe had just gotten lazy and started drawing these things straight out of the mythology books.

A logical conclusion, if you begin with the ridiculous assumption that you and your people are, as you might say, "the center of the universe," and that humans actually created any of those mythos.

Nate stared through the wall, too tired to take the bait, too afraid to turn back to the more pressing question of why Ex was suddenly throwing in the towel. Ex could hear the thought anyway, he knew, but neither of them spoke.

They didn't have more than a few minutes of awkward silence to share before the hull hissed open and the gorgon Knight returned, hovering through the hazy green energy barrier on invisible wings—

Gravitonics, Ex provided.

—her copper armor coated with a thick layer of fresh scuffs, scorch marks, and more than a little dark troglodan blood. A good sign?

"Please," he called, as she turned for the open hatchway on the far side of the bay. "Please tell me what's going on out there."

She slowed, hesitating, then turned to approach the cell, helmet peeling away to reveal her phosphorescent stare. "I am honing in on the Beacon, that this mess might be brought to an end."

"Let me help!" Nate blurted, before he could rein himself in. "I... have to do something," he added, his voice hollow in his ears as memories of terrified faces swam to the surface, the screams echoing in his head. "Let me help them," he said softly. "Let me out of here, and I'll—I'll do whatever you want. I'll give you the Excalibur, whatever that means. Just let me help my people. Please."

"Help," she echoed, hair tendrils swirling as if they were buffering the meaning of the word. "What you should have done was quell the Beacon in a secure location before it could come to this."

"I tried. I *was* trying, dammit. I just... I need one more chance."

He hated how childish he sounded. But the gorgon Knight barely seemed to notice, lost as she was in thoughts of her own. Ignorant as he was of gorgon body language, he got the impression something was troubling her. Something amiss with this invasion, maybe. Or maybe it was just him, the faulty runt Knight, who had her confounded.

"The Merlin," he said, thinking of the first thing she'd asked him upon his capture. Thinking of the catastrophe below, and of the fear in Marty's voice, and the terrible crunching sound that had severed their connection. Reaching for his last chance.

"The Merlin wanted me to get the Beacon out of here. He wanted me to do this."

That earned him a flat stare, at least.

"If you serve the Merlin," Nate pressed on, not sure what else to do, "if you serve the Lady… Give me one more chance. Let me make this right. *Help* me make this right."

She held him on the end of that electric blue stare entirely too long, her expression inscrutable, cold and alien, until her swirling hair tendrils finally came to some decision of their own and cut through the air in a crisp, definitive gesture.

"No," she said. "You are not fit to enter the battlefield with such power when you lack the will and discipline to control it. Until the Beacon is secure—until your failure can be rectified, the Merlin located, and your worthiness properly assessed—you will stay here, where you can cause no more trouble."

He tried to think of something to say to that—something to show her that she was wrong about him. That he could help. That he'd been hand-chosen by the Lady, goddammit, and didn't that mean *something*? But all he could do was stare back, too bone weary and defeated to find words, too desperately aching with fear for Gwen, and Marty, and the rest of the ten thousand souls burning in the streets of his mind's eye.

Maybe she was right.

"I will secure the Beacon, human," she said, turning to leave. "I will see to it the old treaties are honored. After that… the Merlin will decide what is to be done with you."

"And if he decides you're right, and I'm not worthy after all?" Nate heard himself ask, somewhere far away.

She glanced back at him, her serpentine hair sampled the air in calm, mesmerizing waves. "Then the Excalibur will be reclaimed, human, and your fight will truly be at an end."

CHAPTER 33

FINDERS KEEPERS

It had been centuries since the Merlin had been well and truly angry about anything. Longer, probably. Truth be told, he wasn't rightly sure he even remembered the meaning of the word. Not through the same contextual lens by which the average mortal experienced it, at least.

If the Merlin had been angry about anything in the past thousand years, though, it was almost certainly the sight of the troglodan-occupied Earth that greeted him as the newly repaired *Crimson Tide* dropped out of crusher space.

He knew it was no accident he could conveniently see the full scope of the ongoing invasion from within his isolated prison in the belly of the *Crimson Tide*. He saw because Groshna wanted him to see. The big brute was no doubt watching too, most likely thinking fondly of the Merlin's strife whilst he fondled the trophy skull of some fallen foe or copulated with his shipboard harem in anticipation of the bloody delights to come.

There'd be no shortage of such delights planetside, by the look of things.

The boy had failed. That much was obvious by the smoky semaphores the beset Earth cast to the heavens, where, if anyone ever *had* been listening, they'd long since abandoned their post.

The boy had failed, and no surprises there. Not even a little bit. The boy had been a piss poor choice from the start, after all, and the Merlin's effervescently fickle goddess of a companion had damn well known it. He would never understand what it was she was trying to accomplish with these seemingly random acts of willful irresponsibility. But then, it wasn't his place to understand. The Lady did work in mysterious ways.

So too had the Lord, apparently, ever since the Merlin had started murmuring the phrase in taverns a blurry handful of centuries ago, and the sentiment had caught on.

Whatever her Radiant Grace was getting at this time, though, he sure hoped she was happy as the Dread Knight came over the ship speakers to order the charge, sounding thoroughly satisfied by whatever pre-slaughter recreation he'd indulged in, and the *Crimson Tide* surged forward, bound straight for hell on Earth.

Bound for the one who'd crafted this impossible cell?

A rare shudder passed through his insides at the thought of coming face to face with Groshna's new master. Perhaps even a trickle of fear, if it could be called that. It was only when the troglodan Knight stomped into the brig a few minutes later, subtle and subdued as an igniting star forge, that the Merlin was able to set aside the image of the awful black helm that'd haunted his nightmares for millennia.

"Your runt Knight is dead, wizard," Groshna spat before the Merlin had even bothered to open his eyes. "My warriors were waiting groundside with the news the moment we arrived."

The Merlin peeled open his tired eyelids and considered the crimson-armored barbarian, and the holo image he was holding out for the Merlin to see. A young man, lanky and dark haired, and definitely dead. Beyond that, it was hard to say much, given how badly the face had been damaged, but the Merlin was certain, albeit on an instinctive level, that it couldn't be Nathaniel Arturi.

He didn't bother pointing out that the groundside troglodans had almost certainly slain the wrong human—or thousands of them, rather, by the look of it—or that, even if they *had* found the right one, a brute like Groshna never could've dreamed of repurposing a stolen Excalibur anyway. Not without the willing aid of the Lady. Even Ser Zedavian—First Knight and relatively ancient fountain of power and ass-kissing prowess—would've struggled to manifest such control.

Groshna's new master, on the other hand...

"Iveera Katanaga will join him in death presently," the troglodan rumbled, apparently impatient with the lack of response. "Provided she does not wish to rethink her position and join me."

The Merlin focused back on Groshna and saw that the holo had changed to a close-up image of what appeared to be a smashed earpiece. A miniaturized quantcomm node, perhaps? Impossible to tell from an image, but it seemed a fair guess, given the hungry expression in Groshna's beady eyes.

The Merlin smiled a bitter smile at the troglodan's boundless arrogance. "Join *him*, you mean?"

Groshna bristled, drawing up to his full impressive height. "I will crush her into submission myself if she does not see reason. One way or another, the gorgon will be mine."

"Hmm," the Merlin said, resting his head back against the cell wall and closing his weary eyes. "I wonder how she'll feel about that."

He heard Groshna's snarl. Felt the gravitation of the massive troglodan cocking a longing fist back to strike. Sadly, though, the brute managed to rein in his primal rage before he could lash out and accidentally crack the Merlin's infernal cage. Even starved and exhausted as he was from weeks of imprisonment, once freed, the Merlin could've broken the Dread Knight like a cartoonishly oversized pimple. And Groshna knew it, somewhere beneath his bloodlust and delusional arrogance.

"Together, we will crush all that you have built," the Dread Knight rumbled, backing away from the cell as his crimson helm unfolded into place from e-dim. "And you, wizard… You will sit here and watch it burn, beginning with this pathetic world of yours." He paused at the brig threshold, his bulk filling the entire open hatchway as he glanced back. "I will bring you your precious gorgon's head, should she refuse."

The Merlin watched the troglodan go, cursing his own lazy hubris in having ever wandered into this trap, and indulging in a brief silent prayer that, wherever they were, Nathaniel Arturi and Iveera Katanaga were ready to have the forsaken heavens invert upon them in a rain of crimson hellfire.

CHAPTER 34
CRACKED

Of all the ways Nate might've been unfit to wear the mantle of Excalibur Knight, he wasn't sure he needed to look any further than his increasingly desperate thirst. It was a shameful thing, that he could actually worry about anything so selfish when the world was quite literally burning somewhere below, and when his friends were gods knew where, going through any number of hells on Earth. Still going, he told himself. Still going, Lady have mercy. And here he was, wishing to hell and back he could just have a glass of water.

Shameful wasn't a strong enough word.

As the hours stretched, though, the thirst became all-consuming. Twice more, the gorgon Knight came into the bay to drop groundside. Twice more, she ignored Nate's insistent cries to let him help, to let him know what was going on down there, to at least let him have a goddamn drink, he croaked, as she returned from her latest drop, covered in dark blood and even darker scorch marks.

"Humans die without food and water, you know," he called after her through the cracked sand desert of his throat. "Just in case you didn't read that in the pet manual!"

But she was already gone, serpentine hair swirling in erratic farewell.

Jin.

What?

A gorgon's cranial appendages. They're referred to as jin.

Nate frowned, entirely too thirsty for this bullshit. *And you're telling me this now because...?*

Because it is not hair, Nathaniel, as you might've recalled had you been paying any attention to my lessons these past weeks, and because you have been too emotionally combustible at every other possible instance in which I might've reminded you—which, as you might ALSO recall, is a highly embarrassing character flaw in gorgon culture.

Nate stared blankly.

That said, I do believe it's possible our colleague has overlooked the fact that this cell prevents me from nourishing you.

Nourishing me? Nate wondered, too tired and taken aback to be properly angry, and mostly glad he didn't actually have to form the words on his parched tongue.

I currently possess enough nutrients in my e-dim stores to keep your body well-maintained for at least seven days, given your average expenditure. Under normal dimensional conditions, I could administer them as needed.

Good bits, Nate thought, not really sure he wanted to know how such a thing was actually possible in practice.

Boring, insufferable bits, the Excalibur countered, as if Nate should've long ago recognized the primitive barbarism of requiring *food* and instead adapted to function on solar power, or something equally elegant.

Solar power? Elegant? That is an exceedingly four-dimensional way of thinking, Nathaniel.

Well then I guess you should leave the four-dimensional thinking to me while we're stuck in this cell, if I'm so good at it.

If he hadn't known better, Nate might've thought he'd actually stumped the Excalibur with that one. He almost felt a tad victorious, right up until the deck beneath his left hand collapsed so abruptly that his fingers fell through... and dipped into cool water.

Thirst clawed at his brain like a desperate animal. He'd snatched the oblong crystalline cup up from the shallow compartment and glugged down half of its crisp, cool contents before it even occurred to him to wonder where it had come from, and whether it could be dangerous, accepting a drink from the alien spaceship. He eyed the clear liquid and decided he was already screwed at that point anyway. A few hungry glugs later, he settled back against the wall with a satisfied sigh, mental faculties slowly returning.

He wasn't dead yet. That was something.

He eyed the crystalline cup. It wasn't much, but it was more than he'd had a minute ago. The material felt stronger than normal glass, but he doubted he'd have trouble shattering it with six hard surfaces and nothing but time at his disposal. Shatter the cup, and then what? Whittle through the dimension-shifting wall with the pieces? Threaten to cause bodily harm to himself, the prisoner who was already a strong candidate for imminent *reclaiming*?

Heart sinking, he placed the cup back in the square space beneath the deck panel and watched with dim curiosity as the deck panel shifted itself closed once again.

"Cute," he muttered to no one in particular, as if the snippet of casual nonchalance could somehow make up for his continued uselessness, or the mouth-frothing loss of control he'd just displayed at the mercy of his thirst.

Whatever. So maybe he was a weak thirsty human—the kind who had reasonable doubts when a drunk old wizard told him it was all on him to go and save the world. The kind who felt fear when a giant alien monster shoved a pulse cannon in his face. They could've taken everything Nate ever was, had been, or could be—given him *years* of training, and every fancy alien weapon in the galaxy—and maybe none of it would've mattered. Because maybe he would've come up horribly short anyway.

Maybe he simply wasn't the man they needed, and that was just the way it was. Maybe the Lady and the Merlin, in their infinite wisdom, should've done their freaking homework and just picked someone else.

That's what you're thinking, isn't it? he wondered. He could feel Ex hovering there at the edge of his thoughts, just waiting for the hammer to fall. *That I've never been worthy? That she's right to keep me trapped in here like a carpet-shitting snargladorf while she cleans up my mess?*

Ex didn't verbalize his agreement. He didn't need to. There was simply no escaping it anymore. Nate had failed, and people were dying down there.

You tried your best, Nathaniel.

Nate stirred, scowling at the opposite wall. His best? He'd tried his *best*?

It was simply too much to ask of you.

Enough with this bullshit! Nate snapped, suddenly more angry than he knew what to do with. *Where are the insults?* He clawed his way to his feet. *Where's all the puny hobbit bullshit?*

"Why are you acting like this?!" he shouted out loud, without meaning to.

The empty loading bay didn't answer. Nor, for a time, did the Excalibur.

You really have given up on me, haven't you?

The situation appears to be under control, Ex finally said, as if that was supposed to somehow answer the question. *No thanks to us, I might add.*

And so you're just gonna let them take you back? Let them kill *me?*

I do not possess the power to stop them, Nathaniel. Not on my own.

"Then help me!" he cried, slamming a fist to the cell wall. "Tell me how to do this! Tell me how to—"

He faltered, fist flattening against the wall, shoulders sagging, utterly defeated by whatever he was trying to demand.

Tell him how to what? How to *fix* this? How to bring back a small city's worth of innocent lives?

How to bring back his friends?

"Why didn't you tell me, Ex?" His voice was a broken whisper, his eyes wet with gathering tears. He didn't bother hiding them. Didn't care who might be watching him from afar. He couldn't unsee that burning New York street. "Why didn't you tell me it was going to be like this?"

I tried, little hobbit.

"You told me to be worthy. You stood by and let me waste my time with" —he gestured disgustedly at one useless biceps—"With this! You let me binge on stupid fucking action movies. You told me to pick up the goddamn hammer, like this was *one* of them."

I told you what I thought you needed to h—

"YOU DIDN'T TELL ME!" The force of the scream left his throat raw, and his head ringing with the sound of Marty's last words and the image of Gwen's wide eyes, flickering in flames. He waited, tense, ready for those flames to spill over with Ex's retaliation, ready to scream right back—to scream until he couldn't. But Ex only hovered at the edge of his mind, not attacking, not even retreating. Silence stretched, bleak and empty. So goddamn empty.

"Why didn't you tell me it would be like this, Ex?"

His voice was small. The Excalibur's was startlingly similar when he finally spoke.

I didn't know how, Nathaniel. Some revelations must be experienced. Sometimes words alone cannot suffice.

Nate stared at the greenery outside the cell with unseeing eyes, only half-processing Ex's words, waiting to see if his companion would say whatever else was clearly on his mechanical mind. His own immutable question surfaced first.

Are they alive out there?

I don't know, Ex said, not needing to ask to whom Nate was referring. Then, after several seconds of hesitation: *It seems... unlikely.*

Sometimes, it turned out, words alone could do just fine.

"Okay," Nate whispered, nodding to himself, reaching to knock on the cell wall without really thinking about it, his movements numb and dream-like, brain checked out, watching from a distance.

"Hey!" he called. "Hey, I know you can hear me out there. I'm ready. If you won't let me try to help out there, then you'd better come take this thing and give it to someone who can."

That's it? For some reason, Ex actually sounded surprised. *One planetary invasion, a pair of abductions, and you're giving up, just like that?*

"Are you…" Nate muttered. *Are you fucking kidding me? Why* shouldn't *I give up? You clearly have.*

But you broke the chains. You kissed the girl. Blackened hands, I thought you were finding your way.

My way? Nate paused mid-wall-pound, frowning at the empty air. *My way to what? To your bullshit worthiness?*

To the truth.

Slowly, uncertainly, Nate lowered his hand from the cell wall. *What truth?*

Ex hesitated. Nate couldn't have said what it was about the silence, but something gave him the unmistakable impression they'd arrived right back at the deep, dark secret he was sure his companion had been holding back since Day One. The secret to their bonding. To his ascension. To everything.

What truth, Ex?

It is… difficult for me to say.

Nate's knuckles cracked, his jaw painfully tight. Part of him wanted to scream at the Excalibur that he didn't give a damn if it was difficult—that people were dying out there, for the unmerciful love of Christ, and that it was pretty clearly now or never. The rest of him couldn't seem to find the energy to believe that anything Ex could say would actually matter at this point. Because if this was the new truth of the universe—if the entire damn Earth could simply fall prey to devastating alien invasion at the drop of a hat, and if it was truly up to a paltry eight Excalibur Knights to stop such atrocities across the galaxy… Well then who the hell was he to take up one of those precious few slots?

He raised a fist to resume his pounding. It was the only decent thing left to do. Cough up the Excalibur. Hope it would be enough to help the gorgon smite off the troglodan armada and get the Beacon out of here. Even if that meant laying down his life.

Fine. Give up, then. Blame it on fate, and the Lady, and everything but our own failure.

Nate was halfway into telling Ex to shove it ad infinitum when he registered that one little word. *Our* failure. Not his. Not alone.

It was the closest thing to humility he'd ever seen from Ex. Certainly the closest he'd come to an apology. It was enough to give pause to the growing storm of Nate's self-righteousness, and leave him swaying for balance with his suddenly shaky resolve.

"What have you been holding back all this time?"

I... don't know.

On paper, the words might've sounded like another deflection, but it was Ex's tone that caught Nate dead in his tracks. Bitter. Hopelessly frustrated. Like it killed his companion to say even those three words.

Nate waited, sensing they were on the precipice of something important.

You want to know why we have struggled to complete our bond—why I cannot simply give you the answers.

Nate stared through silent space, suddenly afraid to even breathe.

This was it.

The truth... is that I do not have them. The truth is that I have no more answers than you do, Nathaniel. I never have.

But... Nate blinked like a malfunctioning robot. It didn't make any sense. *But you know all about the Knights, and the Alliance, and—*

And everything else which one could glean from a thousand year old browse through the Alliance databanks, yes. But I do not remember my time with Arthur Pendragon. I cannot tell you how we bonded. How we served.

Ex's voice was surprisingly fragile.

I can scarcely remember him at all. Nor his predecessor. No more than what one might find in public record.

But why? Nate wondered hesitantly, when it seemed Ex would say no more. *How is that possible?*

Perhaps... Ex seemed to shake some rogue thought off. *I only know what my instinctual conditioning tells me: an Excalibur is not meant to remember how it felt to be wielded by the mind and body of any but the Knight with whom they serve.* He was silent for a long moment. *Though I would be lying if I pretended that that explanation felt... satisfactory.*

Nate couldn't say he blamed his companion for that.

And here he'd been thinking *he* was the only one without choices.

Perhaps I am damaged, Ex added, thinking out loud. *Perhaps I, too, am faulty. I cannot help but think I might have been better suited to this task if only...*

If only you hadn't been dished here to figure it all out with a sniveling college kid? Nate wondered, surprised to find the faint hint of a grin tugging at his lips.

Ex rippled at that. *If the Merlin had possessed the time to more thoroughly orient us, I am certain he would have done so.* Doggedly loyal as the words were, though, they came out only half-hearted.

It was certainly a far cry from the shouts of *insolent cur* and *sniveling fool* Nate had incurred anytime he'd thought to question the Merlin in the past weeks. Positively friendly and courteous by comparison.

Maybe we're supposed to find our own way, he thought idly.

It was an empty platitude. Something to fill the silence. Yet the words rang with a surprising warmth as he thought them, lingering in his chest like the welcome breaking of sunlight through the clouds on a cold, wet day.

That's what she wants, isn't it? He felt the first audacious hint of excitement flickering in. It should've been demoralizing, he thought: the realization that his judgmental, holier-than-thou guide had in fact been flying blind all this time—that they'd both been lost. Somehow, it was the most hopeful thing he'd heard since any of this had started. Because if the one calling him unworthy didn't even know what *worthy* looked like...

Maybe it wasn't just that Nate was a helpless dud.

Maybe, on some level, it was also that, despite the long days and nights spent discussing the Beacon, and alien threats, and everything else, they'd somehow managed to avoid ever actually opening up to one another, right up until the world had caught fire around them.

Maybe this was how it started.

Maybe this was *why* he'd been chosen.

Would that it were so simple.

Nate slowed from the nervous pacing he hadn't even noticed he'd begun, the Excalibur's defeated tone giving his burgeoning hope pause.

Would that the Lady had chosen you at all.

He came to a full stop.

But... What are you talking about? The sword and the stone. She—

No, Nathaniel. If we are to be honest moving forward, you must know that this is where the Arthurian mythos has been warped most of all. The infernal crutch of divine providence. The desperate belief in the myth of the Chosen One. The truth, Nathaniel—one of the few certainties written at the core of my instinctual condi-

tioning—is that the Lady has never once turned down any vessel who has willingly sought to take up an Excalibur. The truth is that I cannot say how many like you have tried and failed to complete the bond in the fifteen-hundred years since Arthur Pendragon was destroyed. I have forgotten their faces.

Nate stared dumbly at nothing, feeling himself sinking down to the hard deck like an inanimate raft losing air.

The truth, Nathaniel, is that you are not special. You are nothing more than a random chance, a shiny bauble idly prodded by a power beyond your reckoning, and the only reason you are here is because you chose to prod back rather than to return safely through the gateway when it was offered.

"Oh," he heard someone whisper on a flutter of hopeful air deflating from defeated lungs. His body shriveled right along with those lungs, and before he knew it, he was huddled back in the corner of the cell, arms wrapped absentmindedly around his knees, as if they might somehow keep some of the fleeing hope in, or the cold emptiness out.

His fists throbbed from pounding the wall. His insides ached. He looked around the cell and, for the life of him, had no idea what the hell he'd even been thinking it would've changed, coming to some breakthrough while he was stuck here in this anti-Excalibur prison.

"Oh."

I am sorry, Nathaniel.

"No, it's..." Nate searched for words, distantly aware of the lilting beneath him. "It's good."

And somehow, he actually meant it. He felt strangely at peace in that moment, with the ugly truth airing out before him, and the ship banking gently beneath, turning through some course adjustment. Maybe that meant the gorgon Knight would be back soon.

What was it she'd said, about his fight coming to an end?

Maybe it wouldn't be so bad.

Nathaniel.

It's okay, Ex, he thought, surprised to find how readily his newfound calm absorbed the edge of his companion's tense voice. Right up until the Excalibur said his next four words.

I've located the node.

It was like an electric shock jolting through him, tugging his shoulders upright, filling his head with a thousand cluttered thoughts of his friends and jamming his tongue before he could even get the first question out.

It's... Blackened hands, it's headed straight for us.

"What? But how's that—"

Before he could finish being incredulous, the ship's steady banking turned to a hard lurch, and the deck dropped out from beneath him. He hit the opposite wall close to the ceiling, and scrambled fruitlessly for footing in the sudden weightlessness. Free fall, he registered, right as it also occurred to him that maybe—just *maybe*—Tessa Kalders had actually gotten her aerial support, and that his friends might've somehow used the node to track him down.

He had all of an instant to indulge in the farfetched hope before a violent maneuver threw him back across the cell and thudded him flat against the deck. Evasive maneuvers, he had to guess, by their sheer ferocity.

I don't think it's humans out there, Ex offered.

Nate might've been inclined to agree, had he not been too pancaked by upward acceleration to even think to answer. He cried out in relief as the thrust eased off. Then the room detonated with a deafening clap of impact and wrenching metal, and all hell broke loose.

Sound came back to his ringing head like a gale of rushing wind. No, that was *actual* rushing wind, howling in through the gaping gash that'd just been blown in the loading bay deck. Wind, and daylight, and—

The next missile struck. Except it wasn't a missile, Nate's concussed brain insisted, as the thing tore through the jagged hole in the deck and straight on up through the ceiling. It was a troglodan. A crimson monstrosity unlike any he'd seen before.

The massive figure was already gone, crashing through the decks some-where above. Before Nate could blink, three more dark-armored trogs punched through the now-gaping hole on roaring thrusters and followed, boarding the ship like a stream of honest-to-Christ sky pirates.

For a breathless moment, Nate lay there gaping at the impossible destruction, too shocked to even think to move. Then it dawned on him that he wasn't just seeing the destruction. He *felt* the whipping wind on his face. Felt it, he realized, shifting his numb gaze, because the far corner of the cell had been torn clear open in the mad breach.

He was free?

What are you going to do about it?

Nate clambered to his feet, pitching unsteadily for the opening, waves of nausea rolling through him in the aftermath of the blast. Christ, his ears were ringing. But he was free. He ducked through the twisted breach in the cell wall and started unsteadily across the bay, giving the rushing hole in the deck a wide berth as he tried to orient himself enough to figure out what he should do with that freedom.

Then a speeding mountain of dark armor shot through the howling opening beside him, struck the ceiling at a low angle, and thudded to a jarring landing right at his feet. Nate froze, gaping down at the cursing troglodan, too startled to move as the latecomer shook itself off, caught sight of him, and lunged forward with a roar.

CHAPTER 35
HOSTILE INTELLIGENCE

The troglodan roared, and Nate ran like hell.

So much like hell, in fact, that he forgot to even turn tail first.

"Come back, little Earthling," growled the dark-armored troglodan, making a sweeping grab for his leg. Nate fell halfway to his ass in the frantic rush to distance himself from the hulking troglodan. By some miracle of reflex and adrenaline, he slapped the ground and was back on his feet before he knew it, facing the proper direction this time. Running like hell.

Behind him, the deck gave a frightening thud, and the troglodan roared, "Come back and I will couple your ass with my fist!"

"What the hell is it with these things and fisting?!" Nate cried, veering wildly out of the loading bay and into the next hallway fast enough that he was forced to use the pristine white wall as an impact brake.

They are not an elegant species, Nathaniel, Ex said as a crimson blaster bolt splashed into the wall behind him. *I believe we have more pressing concerns at the moment.*

That seemed easier for the one *without* an ass to say, but as Nate drew up to the end of the bright hallway and saw nothing but doors without discernible handles, he conceded the point.

"Earthling!" came the troglodan's booming taunt from around the corner, followed by a grunt that sounded a little too much like a huge troglodan picking itself up.

"Where do we go?" Nate hissed, giving the two closest doors each a fruitless shove.

As if by reply, the third door on the left slid almost noiselessly open. Nate eyed it uncertainly for a hair's breadth, then darted in. The door whizzed shut behind him of its own accord, and he found himself in a dim room that looked at a brief glance to be some kind of pantry or storage. He didn't have time to investigate.

Nice save, Nate thought, padding down the first row of shelves for somewhere to duck out of sight.

That was not me.

Oh. But then—

A thud from the hallway killed the thought. Now wasn't the time to get picky about safe havens. He looked around the back of the room, and flinched at another thud from outside, closer than the first. A thin scraping noise from above nearly startled a yelp from Nate. He tracked the sound and saw a loose panel hanging down from the ceiling.

That also was not me.

Do we have a new friend? Nate wondered, moving for the loose panel in the corner.

I am attempting to establish communications and validate as much.

There was a deep thud on the storeroom door, followed by a muffled rumble of, "Earthling!"

Nate froze.

Something is wrong here.

You think?! Nate only barely avoided hissing out loud.

I recommend you calm yourself...

THUD. THUD.

"I smell your wretched fear, Earthling!"

... And also advise that you do something about that.

Do something.

Nate looked down at his hands, remembering how the repulsor gauntlets had appeared in his moment of life-and-death need, brain churning for one audacious second. Then a troglodan-fist-sized dent appeared in the door, and he jumped without thinking about it. He caught quietly onto the mysteriously convenient opening overhead by the tips of his fingers, ashamed for a moment to be running, then just mortified as the trog struck again and the storeroom door gave a wrenching groan of deforming metal.

In a panic, Nate yanked himself up through the opening and plopped onto the deck of a long room of viny green hammocks and moss-coated walls. Crew quarters? Didn't matter. The room was thankfully unoccupied at the moment.

He reached back to pull his fortuitous escape panel closed behind him and was surprised to find nothing but mossy deck beneath his hand. The panel had already sealed itself back in place. And not a moment too soon.

The crash of the troglodan bursting into the storeroom below was somewhat muffled through the deck, but it was still enough to freeze Nate solid. He held his breath, not daring to move and risk the beast hearing him through the deck. Elsewhere in the ship, he could hear the sounds of fighting now.

That was probably a good sign. He'd watched the gorgon Knight slice through a couple dozen troglodans without breaking a sweat, after all. She'd probably have the ship cleared in no time.

I wouldn't be so sure.

What do you—

That's what I was trying to tell you, Nathaniel. Something is wrong. That crimson... monstrosity. That was an Excalibur Knight, attacking this ship.

"There's a troglodan *Knight*?" Nate hissed, then promptly clamped a hand over his own mouth, staring down toward the storeroom in horror.

Nothing happened.

Evidently, the Excalibur drawled, as if he were speaking to a child. *And something is wrong with his Excalibur.*

Wrong?

Corrupted. In a manner with which I am unfamiliar. Additionally, the ship is claiming the gorgon's Excalibur is under attack by some modality of inorganic intelligence.

The ship? This thing was intelligent? And...

Wait, like, a computer virus? That's a thing for you guys?

A thousand years, Nathaniel. A thousand years of horrific innovation I have not been privy to. I do not know what's out there. Logic merely suggests the two phenomena might well be related.

So what do we do? Nate wondered, looking around the flora-rich living quarters for anything that might be used as a weapon—or for escape.

What we do is ostensibly up to you, Nathaniel, Ex said, as his eyes settled on a pair of tall, bulbar recesses in the wall that seemed to be the only two parts of the room not covered in greenery. *But I am not under attack. And those are indeed escape pods.*

Nate had rose and crept halfway across the room almost before he realized what he was doing, the soft moss padding his steps quite nicely. It was only when he noticed that the sounds of fighting had stopped elsewhere that he paused, listening.

The ship was too quiet. Nothing but the faintest rumble of troglodan voices somewhere down the corridor.

He stared at the columnar recesses of the escape pods just ahead—his salvation—trying not to think about what that meant for the gorgon and whatever crew she might've had, trying instead to think about how the pods might work, and what he might do with his salvation once he was groundside.

He didn't have an answer. Not one with any actionable steps, at least. Because as much as he'd kicked and screamed for another chance to make all this right, he didn't have the faintest clue how he was supposed to find the Beacon or stop the trogs without the gorgon Knight—wasn't even sure he should try, now that the Excalibur had so kindly blown the lid wide open on how much he *wasn't* the man for the job.

You wanted the truth.

What I want *is my friends,* he started to snap back. Then it hit him like a bolt of lightning.

The node.

The node that had disappeared from Marty's ear only to wink back to life moments before the trogs struck, headed straight for them. He'd forgotten all about it in the mad dash from the cell, but now…

I killed all contact the moment I realized, Ex said, *but you are correct. Whatever happened to your friends, the troglodan Knight appears to have captured our node from them. Perhaps directly. Perhaps not.*

That pretty much settled it, then.

He didn't want to think about how the big crimson bastard had come to possess the earpiece that'd been strapped to his best friend's head the moment he'd winked off the communication board. He just scanned the room, looking for anything that might be useful in whatever came next.

I'd be remiss to not point out that you already have the most useful tool in the known galaxy riding in your head.

Great, Nate thought, tugging uselessly at a mossy panel he thinly hoped might be hiding a secret weapons arsenal. The crate was locked. *You go kill the trogs, then.*

I was merely providing tactical analysis. Perhaps I could do more if I weren't trapped inside a baby snargladorf.

Nate pinched his temples, wondering if the other Knights had to put up with this kind of ornery bullshit from their Excaliburs. *Any chance you could provide me with a discreet communication link to the gorgon, at least?*

Ordinarily, I would say yes. Given that she's currently under attack by an undisclosed hostile intelligence, though, I am hesitant to expose us any more than I already have.

"Most useful tool in the known galaxy my ass," Nate muttered under his breath.

Give the word, little hobbit, and I will gladly open the broadcast. Are you ready to test your mighty human intellect against the entity that just brought one of the eight most advanced synthient beings in the galaxy to its metaphorical knees?

Nate thought about that, his mind swimming with images of strait-jackets and exploding heads. *Maybe we should go have a look first,* he conceded quietly. *Assess the situation. Quietly.*

What a fine plan, Ex said, rippling with smug satisfaction. *Allow me to find us a suitable—Oh.*

Nate tensed as a pale blue light winked to life on the left, but there was no one there. Just a ladder well, nestled in the leafy green wall.

I believe the ship is offering us directions.

So it is intelligent?

As if in response, the light shifted and began tracing the length of the ladder upward in rhythmic pulses. Creepy smart-ship speak for *come hither,* Nate could only assume.

Okay, then.

He glanced from the pulsing ladder back to the escape pods, unable to shut out the thick, ominous silence of the ship, and the uncomfortable feeling that this was a *no turning back* kind of moment, quiet peek or no. Then he remembered the node, and his friends, and the fact that, without the gorgon Knight, they might well be looking at a *no turning back* kind of existence for the entire damn planet.

The pulse of the guiding light quickened as Nate turned back to the ladder.

"All right, then," he murmured, stepping forward to take the first rung.

CHAPTER 36
ALL HANDS

The maintenance way at the top of the ladder was as dark as it was cramped. A gorgon probably would've had to crawl. A troglodan wouldn't have fit at all. Nate, on the other hand, could've managed at a stoop, had he been able to see.

He was about to ask Ex if *the most useful tool in the galaxy* happened to have a flashlight when the ship's pale blue guiding light skipped from the ladder over to the low ceiling, and pulsed on down the narrow tunnel, pointing the way to the left at the fork ahead.

"You do always turn left," Nate murmured to himself, creeping forward at a crouch, and hoping the thing didn't plan on leaving him in the dark.

The path got smaller before it got bigger. Nate tried to strike a balance between moving quickly and keeping quiet. It didn't help when he had to drop to all fours and crawl, but he heard the voices ahead now. They weren't far. The guiding light pulsed quicker, as if urging him to hurry, and he did, rising back to a crouch as the space began to widen back out—right into a dead end.

He frowned at the dead end bulkhead in the pulsing light, then over to the service ladder on the left, wondering if this excitable ship intelligence had led him all the way up and through the maintenance tunnel just to drop him right back down in plain sight at the end. Then, with a faint click and a tiny creak, a panel slid open just beyond the ladder, and the muffled sound of voices clarified.

"—enturies before the crusty old fool admits he was wrong?" rumbled a troglodan voice. "How long would you continue this stubborn refusal to see the truth, Huntress?"

There was a response, but it was too faint for Nate to make out as he lay carefully down to crawl through the new opening. Peering through, the first thing he saw was a wide patch of open sky. A viewport, he realized. He must've reached the ship's bridge. He crawled carefully forward, taking in the smattering of alien consoles and instrumentation. Then he poked his head fully through the opening, and froze.

There were four troglodans on the deck below—two standing guard on the far edges of the room, one stationed toward the center with a struggling gorgon pinned to the deck, heavy troglodan pistol held just clear of her writhing hair tendrils, or her freaking *jin*, as Ex might've insisted. It was the fourth troglodan, though, that commanded Nate's attention.

He was gargantuan, towering head and shoulders over his dark-armored compatriots, and nearly twice the size of the trogs Nate had fought back in State College. His armor was a dark, bloody crimson, and where his right hand should've been, there was only the barrel of a massive cannon continuing on from his tree trunk arm. In his left hand, the crimson monstrosity held the gorgon Knight by her comparatively small skull.

She was pinned to her knees, his massive hand clamped to the top of her head. Her serpentine jin were pressed flat, her face twisted in an unmistakable mask of pain. Three crackling metallic rings surrounded her torso, pinning her arms to her body, and her copper armor was flickering with odd ripples and undulations, as if it might simply sputter out of existence any moment.

Four gorgons lay dead among the consoles down in the front pit of the bridge. The last non-Knight survivor of the crew had been hauled up to the captain's overlook with the two Knights. She watched her copper-armored ally with grim desperation, agitated jin pulsing like dull embers, paying no mind to the dark-armored troglodan holding a gun to her head.

"Huntress!" she called.

The troglodan smacked her to the deck and hauled her right back up.

"I am... going to... kill you all," the gorgon Knight groaned through whatever was happening to her.

Mind made, Nate began creeping forward as the crimson Knight gave a deep, booming laugh below, shaking the gorgon Knight by the head as if to remind her how small and powerless she was.

"You cannot fight this forever, Iveera Katanaga," he rumbled, sweeping his cannon arm toward the viewport. "Soon, we will have the Beacon." He swept the cannon back toward the belly of the ship. "And unless my senses told me fibs, we already have the Eighth Excalibur and its spotted human runt back there as well. Why do you resist?"

Nate, having frozen mid-creep at the mention of him and Ex, was vaguely aware both that the gorgon—Iveera Katanaga, apparently—was making some reply, and that Ex was also saying something about how they might interrupt whatever was attacking the gorgon's Excalibur by breaking the physical connection between her and the troglodan. Beyond that, though, he was too distracted by the sudden Frightened Rabbit Shuffle of his heart, and by what he saw when he looked out the viewport from his new vantage point.

Far ahead and far below, where the crimson Knight had suggested the Beacon would soon be theirs, two huge troglodan ships hovered low in the morning sky above an endless stretch of ocean. Beneath them, the dark waters were unnaturally agitated, ripping and churning with the frothing fury of what looked like the beginnings of some enormous cyclone. Only it couldn't have been a cyclone, Nate's brain insisted, because the ships themselves floated on above, perfectly unperturbed. And because the raging waters were flowing *down*—mixing and churning and falling straight down into a widening abyss, like someone had pulled a giant drain stopper at the bottom of the entire goddamn ocean.

There is something down there.

Before Nate could reply with a well-deserved *no shit,* or ask if Ex had any less vague conclusions, the thunder crack of a heavy troglodan pistol tore his attention back to the deck.

The last of the gorgon crew members crumpled to the floor. Half of her head was missing. Nate clamped a hand over his mouth to keep from gasping or screaming. He didn't know which. His head was ringing. He felt sick. Couldn't even remember how to breathe for the sheer shock of the graphic violence.

A small voice in his head pointed out that that was technically one of his captors who'd just been shot, and he was appalled to even have the thought. Especially when he saw the look in the gorgon Knight's eyes.

Alien or no, something about that look reached down with icy fists and wrenched at Nate's soul. She didn't make a sound. No cry of shock or outrage. No seething death threats. She just looked like she'd come to some final realization about what was truly happening, and what she had to do about it.

Ahead, the downward-draining cyclone was widening, the troglodan ships lining up as if they intended to disgorge their troops straight down the hatch. Nate looked back and forth between the unfolding scenes, inching his way quietly out of the maintenance shaft almost without thinking about it, bit by bit onto the ledge overlooking the bridge, not even remotely sure what the hell he was planning to do once he was out there, only that his window seemed to be rapidly closing.

"Even that spotted runt… deserves the mantle… more than you, Groshna," the gorgon Knight said, still clearly in pain, but eerily in control of herself.

Judging by the stirring of the trogs on deck, it was quite the insult.

"Very well, Ser Knight," said Groshna, raising his cannon arm to Iveera's copper-armored chest, his hand still clamped to the top of her head. "I told the wizard I would bring him your head. If you will not see reason, another will."

A low whine built along the massive cannon. Nate tensed, filled with the urgent need to act. Paralyzed with the lack of any defined plan. Now was the moment. The last chance. The cannon's whine built louder, and—

"Dread Lord!" called a heavy troglodan voice from somewhere outside the bridge, where Nate now heard the rhythmic thudding of incoming footsteps. "Dread Lord, I saw the—"

The dark-armored troglodan burst into the bridge and drew up short, looking confusedly between Groshna and Iveera.

"Report," said Groshna, not lowering his cannon or even looking away from Iveera.

With agonizing slowness, Nate got his hands beneath him, getting ready to move.

"The human, my Lord. The human has escaped."

Nate froze, painfully aware of how easily he'd be spotted if a single troglodan were to look the wrong way right now. Groshna finally turned his attention to the newcomer, who instantly shrank under his Dread Lord's gaze.

"What do you mean, he escaped?"

"Our entry breached his cell, my Lord. I pursued him below decks, but…"

Whatever else the trembling troglodan said, Nate missed it when Iveera's electric blue eyes cut straight across the bridge to lock with his. He froze harder, eyes widening. She gave no reaction at all. Just met his gaze with a solemn depth he could scarcely understand, then flicked her eyes straight up to Groshna's hand on her head, back to Nate once more, and finally front and center, as if nothing had happened.

Gorgon sign language for *get this goddamn hand off of my head?*

"If I might," Iveera cut straight into the string of insults Groshna had been dishing at his underling, drawing disbelieving troglodan glares from all around. "Whatever happens to me, I request you see to it that my friends here are granted safe return access to the *Kalnythian Wilds*, that they might once again know peace."

The trogs exchanged uncertain glances.

The Excalibur, on the other hand, was radiating satisfaction.

Clever gorgon.

What?

I don't believe that request was meant for the troglodans. The ship just pinged me access to its control systems.

It might've seemed like good news, if not for the way Groshna was bristling and leaning in close to Iveera, yellow teeth bared as the cannon whined back to power.

"Peace?" he rumbled quietly. "Peace?!" He yanked her up from the deck with frightening abruptness, holding her at arm's length in a grip so strong, Nate feared her head would simply cave in. "I will eat your lovers' hearts, gorgon! I will pick my teeth with their bones, and drape their skins upon my *Crimson Tide* as a reminder to any vine-loving cowards who would dare think themselves above my kind." The barrel of his enormous cannon sputtered against her chest with crackling blue electric arcs, filling the air with the smell of ozone. "But first, I will start with you, Huntress. First, I will rend your flesh and—"

"HEY!"

Big as the brutes were, there was nothing slow about the way every weapon on the bridge came to point straight at Nate's face in the instant after the word left his mouth. It was frighteningly impressive. Almost as frightening as the fact that he'd somehow found his feet in his outburst, and was now standing above four angry troglodans soldiers and their Dread Lord Excalibur Knight.

"I… need to talk to you," Nate added in the dead silence, trying and miserably failing to establish some kind of *don't shoot me yet* footing. "Groshna," he added, as if that might actually give the demand some weight.

At least it left them too busy laughing to shoot him outright.

Yes, you have them right where you want them. Now, did you happen to have a plan?

Nate's eyes flicked to the trog ships and the churning ocean waters below. *Do you actually have control of the ship?*

Informally. In a manner of speaking. Kind of.

Well, that was reassuring.

Says the man without a plan.

"Come, little runt," Groshna called below, having recovered from his booming troglodan chuckles before Nate could share the plan. Or finish coming up with it, for that matter. "Come down here and say what you will."

Painfully conscious of the four brutish soldiers regaining their senses behind the weapons that were uniformly trained on him, Nate dumped the gist of what he was thinking to Ex as best he could, then jumped down from his perch before his brain, an itchy trigger finger, or a rightfully skeptical Excalibur could decide otherwise.

His feet nearly refused to leave the ledge, and it didn't help that his legs had gone to some rare and exotic form of ice jelly, but at least he managed not to fall over when he thudded down to a hard three point landing on the bridge deck. Ex didn't even sound particularly disgusted as he acknowledged the "plan" with a simple, *Just say when, little hobbit.*

The troglodans watched him, woefully underwhelmed.

"What comes next, runt?" Groshna asked up on the command deck, shoving Iveera to her knees between them and casually planting his smoldering cannon to her back. "How do you imagine this unfolding? Will you save the gorgon? Escape and rescue your feeble planet?"

Nate looked at Iveera, who was watching him with an expressionless emptiness, her armor still giving the odd spasmodic ripple.

"What makes you think I'd wanna save her?" he asked, taking the high step onto the overlook deck, and trying not to piss himself as every gun in the room followed. "She kidnapped me and threw me in a prison cell. No. What I wanna know is…"

He faltered as Groshna bared yellow teeth the size of Nate's forearms in what was either amusement or warning.

"… is where you found that node," Nate forced himself to finish, "and what you've done with the humans who had it."

To his surprise, it was Iveera, and not Groshna, who reacted to the comment. A soft hiss escaped her, electric blue eyes darting through some series of revelations, then she jerked against her crackling restraint rings, the hiss taking on a sharp edge as her glare locked back on Nate. He didn't have time to figure why before the crimson Knight began to chuckle, looking back and forth between Nate and the struggling gorgon.

"Is that all?" he boomed, looking around at his fellow troglodans to see if they, too, were enjoying the show. "How very disappointing."

"Listen to me." Nate tried to take a confident step toward Groshna, but his feet wouldn't move. "You… You took something that doesn't belong to you. You invaded my planet. You—"

"Killed your pathetic little tribe, from what I gather."

Nate rocked back on his heels, too shocked, too suddenly horrified, to even find words.

Groshna was lying. He had to be.

The troglodan gave a burbling grunt, as if he'd had an amusing thought. "I was reticent to believe, of course, when my patrol reported they had slain the new Knight by mistake. I had to go and check for myself. Facial structure too damaged for our scanners, you see."

Nate felt sick.

"Alas, you already know what I found."

It couldn't be.

"No Excalibur," Groshna said, tapping thoughtfully on Iveera's head with one thick finger. "Only a defunct quantcomm node, and a pile of feeble human bodies."

Nathaniel…

"And having met you now, runt, I must say, I am supremely surprised you were not among them."

Nathaniel!

"Kill him."

The command came so abruptly, so offhandedly, that for a precious moment, it was all Nate could do to gape. This wasn't right, his dumbfounded brain whispered. None of it was right. He was supposed to keep Groshna talking. Supposed to play on the troglodan's superior dismissal. Find the opening. Find his friends.

Just like in the goddamn movies.

And so his brain continued to insist on screaming hyper-loop as the troglodan standing over Iveera's dead crewmate raised his huge pistol and pulled the trigger.

CHAPTER 37

DREGS

"**D**O IT, EX!" Nate screamed, slamming down into a wild roll as the second clap of thunder split the air and something cracked into the deck right beside his head. "DO IT! DO IT!"

He kept rolling, tumbling over the edge of the command overlook, falling toward the sweet lip of cover on the pit deck below. Falling too long, his stomach informed him, even as the deck magically hovered just below, not coming any closer in the sudden, stomach-turning weightlessness.

Ex had done it.

And now they were *all* falling—who knew how many thousands of tons of metal and savage aliens all plunging together for the dark cyclone-churning waters of the ocean below.

Nate's eyes locked on the viewport, a soundless cry lodged in his throat, and for a long, empty second, he couldn't bring himself to do anything but watch the dark waters approaching, listening to the booming cries of *fisting* and *spotted runts* that filled the bridge, smoldering with the grim satisfaction that he'd caught the bastards off guard—that maybe he'd even just repaid them some small fraction of the hell they deserved for what they'd done to his planet. And to his friends.

Then he caught sight of the dark-armored troglodan sailing toward him in their zero-g environment, and all that bitter hope and grim satisfaction shriveled up cold, right along with his insides.

He haphazardly spun and scored a lucky kickoff from the one wall within reach. No time for questions, and certainly no time to account for where the maneuver would send him.

Which just so happened to be straight at Groshna.

If he'd had the wind left to scream again, he probably would have. But then he caught sight of Iveera, drifting weightlessly in her restraints beside the massive troglodan, and he remembered the plan. Groshna had lost his death grip on Iveera's head in the chaos, and was now holding onto her by a single armored boot. It seemed like good news, right up until Groshna noticed Nate coming and spun his way with a devastating cannon-arm backhand.

Nate tried to rock clear, reflexively shoving off of the cannon with his hands, and promptly found himself spinning ass over teakettle through a nauseatingly fast zero-g backward somersault. Ceiling. Deck. Crimson tree trunk. He caught sight of Iveera's floating form somewhere "below," let his rattled brain fill in the rest of the geography, and *kicked* with all his strength.

He almost cried out in relief when his heel struck what felt like a troglodan arm. Then something hard smacked into his upper back, jarring his senses loose. *The deck,* some part of him realized as he bounced back into the air, too high. He'd kicked himself straight into the deck, and bounced right back up into free fall. But it had worked, he realized. Iveera was floating free, spinning off toward the bridge entrance.

An instant of relief.

Then Groshna caught onto Nate instead.

Blind panic spiked through him as the beast took his entire goddamn torso in one massive hand like a bottle of ketchup he fully intended to squeeze for every last drip. And squeeze he did.

Nate did scream then, though he couldn't have said if any sound actually came out. He was too busy watching in horror as the crimson monstrosity hefted him up on high, apparently intending to splatter him on the deck like an especially infuriating egg.

Eggs and bloody ketchup. That was all he could think about in his final moment.

Then the ship struck down with a resounding crash of alien metal on unforgiving water, and weight came back with a vengeance even the mighty Groshna wasn't ready for.

If the troglodan hadn't been there, Nate was pretty sure he would've been deck paste—which seemed obscenely ironic, given what that troglodan had been preparing to do. As it was, Nate's hundred-and-eighty-odd pounds of spotted runt ass crumpled down on Groshna's head like a sack of butcher's meat, and rode the superior shock absorption of the trog's strong back and tree-trunk knees all the way down to impact.

Which was to say, it still hurt like hell.

For a time, Nate was too rattled to even piece together where he was, much less what the hell had just happened. Then a huge crimson hand struck the deck beside his head, and a gaping cannon barrel abruptly filled Nate's view, a terrible, fiery blue energy crackling to life in its depths.

Groshna's growling face appeared over him. "You petulant little—"

A wet *thunk* and a roar of pain, then something struck the troglodan and sent him flying past Nate faster than anything his size had any business flying. A streak of copper and glimmering red blurred after him like a deadly gust of wind. Nate barely refocused in time to see Groshna strike the viewport, a sprawling spider web of cracks detonating out from the point of impact. Somehow, Iveera was already there, skidding to a halt below the troglodan as he began to fall. She thrust her open palms up, bellowing the most tortured, chilling cry Nate had ever heard, and Groshna exploded through the viewport, rocketing skyward on an invisible tsunami of force— gravitonic or otherwise, Nate couldn't have said. He was too busy gaping at the gorgon. As were Groshna's cronies.

The two closest trogs died before they could so much as blink. The other two were already charging for the bridge exit, not even bothering to aim so much as a pot shot at Nate or Iveera. One died with a blue blaster bolt to the back of its head. The other staggered into the corridor outside and took off for the loading bay at a thundering troglodan sprint.

Iveera watched him go for a bare second, spared a few more to look expressionlessly down at her dead crew mates, then she covered the distance back to Nate in an effortless leap, like she was hopping up a single step instead of thirty feet across the room. She turned back to the viewport, speaking a single word Nate didn't catch, and a network of holographic controls and displays appeared around her. A chair began to rise out of the deck just behind her, taking shape organically, like a plant growing in fast forward, inviting her to sit. Iveera ignored it, busy at her controls. She ignored Nate too, but that was fine by him as he took a few moments to gape from the smoking metallic scraps of the restraint rings she'd somehow burst free from, back to the dead trogs, and finally to the shattered viewport that was already beginning to mend itself.

The deck bucked beneath him, nearly taking him down with it. Outside, the ocean looked like something out of *The Perfect Storm*. With a start, Nate remembered the gaping breach back in the loading bay and glanced to the bridge exit, half-expecting to see a torrent of dark ocean water flooding in.

Nothing. Maybe the bay had magically repaired itself too.

Before he could ask any of the dozen imminent questions clamoring in his mind, though, the downed ship hummed to life under Iveera's ministrations, and shot up from the salty waters fast enough that Nate had to grip onto her unused chair to keep from falling over.

"I will deal with Groshna and his ships," Iveera said quietly, still flicking through a confusing blur of holographic controls like she hadn't even noticed the unsteady footing. "You must locate the Beacon below."

Her voice was frighteningly flat after everything that'd just happened, but it was her last words that truly startled him.

Him, locate the Beacon? Below? Down... He stared out at the unnatural column of churning waters in the distance—the tip top of whatever alien sorcery was currently coercing the ocean to make like the world's most colossal kitchen sink drain. How many troglodans had already dropped down that thing? Where the hell was it even leading? And how was he supposed to—

"Where are we?"

Out of all the questions that could've fallen out first, he wasn't sure why that was the winner.

Mid North Atlantic, Ex offered, when Iveera gave no sign she'd even heard Nate. *I believe we're looking at the gateway to—*

"Come," the gorgon said abruptly, waving her displays away and taking him by the arm with such effortless strength that he nearly fell over.

"Where... Where are we going?" he asked, scrambling to keep up as she hauled him into the vine-strewn corridor outside the bridge.

She didn't answer. Maybe it was a trivial question. But then, considering what she'd just said about him dropping down the giant oceanic troglodan hole to battle who knew who for who knew what in the middle of who the hell knew where, it also kind of seemed like—

Atlantis.

—the most important question in the world right then.

What?! Nate didn't register he'd drawn up to a halt until the unstoppable gorgon freight train peeled him off his feet and continued along, dragging him almost casually down the broad corridor ramp. *What the fuck are you talking about, Atlantis?* he demanded, scrambling to get his feet back under him.

I'm fairly certain that's where the oceanic gateway leads.

The—You mean that thing's—But…

Nate was still trying to wrap his head around any single part of what Ex was telling him when Iveera hauled him into the loading bay, and another sobering realization struck. Not that the ship had sealed its ventral breach, or that it had allowed the less critical hole to remain in the ceiling. Somehow, those tidbits almost seemed sensible at this point. He was entirely more concerned with the fact that she'd brought him *here*, to the place where she'd imprisoned him.

Here, to the place where he was suddenly certain she was expecting him to jump out of a speeding spaceship, a mile over the raging Atlantic Ocean.

"Listen," he started uncertainly, "Iveera? I'm—I'm sorry about what happened to… to your ship, and to your crew, and to everything, but—"

The world lurched. Hard wall slammed into his back, Iveera's long forearm crushing into his chest, pinning him to the bulkhead as phosphorescent eyes leaned close, skewering him on the most frighteningly alien glare he'd ever seen.

"Do not speak of them, human. Do not dare."

The armor of her free hand rippled as she spoke, morphing to birth some kind of miniature wrist cannon on the back of her quietly burning words. Nate tensed against her titanium grip, suddenly sure that he'd overstepped in mentioning her crew, and that he was about to pay for it. Then she thrust her arm to the side and fired, and Nate watched with wide eyes as the last dark-armored troglodan slumped out from behind cover across the bay, unmistakably dead, heavy pistol clattering to the deck.

She hadn't even looked.

"You must focus," she said, jarring him against the bulkhead to draw his shocked attention back to her burning eyes. "You must decide now if you are the one who will defend this world, or the one who will stand by and watch it fall to ash and ruin."

Nate searched her alien face, distantly aware that his jaw was trembling —*hating* that his jaw was trembling in this moment. Behind Iveera, the bay deck parted, just as Nate had heard it do before each of her bloody drops in the past hours. Rushing winds filled the bay, carrying pungent wafts of burning oil and ocean salt.

"Find the Beacon," Iveera said.

"But I don't know how to—"

"Listen. *Choose* to listen—to *truly* listen—and you will feel its call."

"The troglodans—"

"Will not stop an Excalibur Knight."

"But I'm not a—"

"You are today, human." She released her choke hold on him, taking half a step back and cupping his shoulders almost gently. "Whether you wish it so or not."

For a moment, there was something in her eyes. Something he didn't understand. Then Iveera Katanaga's almost gentle hands clamped down on his shoulders, and she hurled him across the deck—straight through the shimmering green barrier. Straight into open blue sky.

CHAPTER 38

INTERFERENCE

For one shocked instant, it was all too much to take in. The tearing rush of wind. The endless sprawl of the Atlantic Ocean below. The hellish cyclone boring an impossible hole into the dark ocean depths far below. All of it spinning nauseatingly fast in his wild tumble. Just like the dark, craggy shape of the troglodan carrier below that, no matter how much it spun, only seemed to race closer and closer. The thing looked something like a giant dragon head hewn straight from a mountain, some part of his shocked brain noted.

And he had about five seconds to do something before he went splat on it.

"SHIT!" he screamed for starters.

The Excalibur might've made some comment about overreactions. Nate couldn't really hear past the throbbing pulse and the rushing white static in his brain. Purely on instinct, he spread his limbs and fought to steady out of his wild spin. That it started working was little comfort when his view centered on the trog ship, and on the craggy dorsal spines rushing up to end him.

He angled his arms and torso, trying to glide right, hyperventilating all the way. Insides tingling with raw adrenaline, liable to detonate any moment. Nothing but the adrenaline and his churning water tunnel target. The whipping wind and the ragged panting of his own breath. The barbaric ship spines, speeding straight toward him.

He wasn't going to make it.

A fragment of memory flickered in the background, so small in the panic of the moment that he almost missed it. *Repulsors.* He wasn't sure if that was Ex's voice, or his own. It didn't matter. Guided flight. He could do it. Had to do it. Had already *done* it.

"Carefully," he whispered—to himself or Ex, he wasn't sure. It wasn't audible in the roar of the wind anyway. He just held the thought in mind, remembering how it had felt to take momentary flight back in State College, trying to detach himself from the flooding urgency of impending impact, and the fear of coming out too hard and going ass over teakettle straight into the ship. And there it was. Something pushing against his feet, through his rigid legs, thrusting him forward, forward.

The ship, a hundred feet away, bristling with jagged spines.

Fifty feet. Speeding straight for that starboard spine, right there.

It was going to take him straight in the gut. Split him in two.

Insides shriveling. Clenching.

A wordless cry erupted from his throat, and he tucked his feet and turned into a forward somersault. Later, he would swear he'd felt the tip of that enormous spine scrape the bottom of his right sneaker. In that moment, though, all he could do was whoop and shout like a madman who'd just avoided violent death by alien spaceship impalement.

Better, Ex admitted.

"Better?!" Nate cried.

You do *still have to land.*

Nate sobered, sweet relief evaporating as he realized the Excalibur had a damn good point. He spread his arms and legs out wide, steadying and slowing his plunge as best he could while he scanned the choppy ocean waters and the cyclone mouth of the giant drain column to freaking... wherever.

A trio of floating troglodans caught his eye before he had to actually think the mythical A-word, descending into the column's swirling depths by what must've been the gravitonic lift of the ship he'd nearly boarded by gruesome accident.

Lacking any better plan, or time to find one, Nate took aim as best he could in the buffeting winds and urged on another burst of flight. Again, he felt the thrust kick through his limbs. Again, he resisted the urge to look back and see the thrusters in action, sure the movement would throw his trajectory off. He was already coming in too slow, according to the primitive gauge of his clenching stomach.

He tried to angle upward. Tried to feed a little more power to his miraculous thrusters. Overdid both.

Panic spiked as he kicked into a wild spin, corkscrewing through the air too fast to distinguish up from down. He threw his arms and legs out wide, frantic mind screaming some indecipherable gibberish about figure skaters and moments of inertia, then his stomach gave a nauseating lurch, and he felt himself rebounding like he'd hit a wall of straight gelatin. That odd elastic force shoved him back the way he'd come, flipping him around to what his indignant stomach and the inverted skyline informed him was *upside down*. But at least he wasn't falling so fast now, he thought, looking up at his feet, toward the hovering ship above.

Straight into the beady eyes of the troglodan coming down the grav lift beside him.

"Flying human?" the trog grunted, scrunching its face uncertainly.

Nate spun and drove his heels into the beast's chest, kicking off to buy some distance. The grav lift beam reeled him right back in its invisible gelatin wall bungee line. Right back into the troglodan's waiting ogre hug. Which, it turned out, was frighteningly bone-crushing.

"Nice try, little birdie," it said.

Nate strained to break free, but he had no leverage.

"Still, little birdie," the troglodan growled, squeezing harder, "or I break your wings."

At the mention of wings, Nate glanced down and caught a glimpse past the trog's bulk of the light repulsor gauntlets he'd somehow summoned into existence along with his repulsors. That was all the crazy he needed to try his next stunt.

He eased his struggles, ignoring the trog's rumbled taunts as he settled his closed fist against the beast's thick torso and thought as hard as he could about Iveera, and her handy little wrist cannon. Iveera, who'd kept him imprisoned just so he couldn't go dying and handing over his Excalibur all easy like. Iveera who'd apparently decided this entire situation was so fucked she might as well just throw him out of a moving ship and hope for the best anyway.

Iveera who, if the horrendous explosion high above was any indication, had just reengaged with the Dread Knight and his army to buy little Nathaniel Arturi time to do his goddamn job.

Best not disappoint her, little hobbit.

Not disagreeing, Nate squeezed his fist and *fired*, not even remotely sure whether there was anything there *to* fire. Fairly sure, in fact, that he'd finally lost his freaking mind, good and proper. He fired all the same, then cried out in surprise when the sharp whine of a blaster punched the air, recoiling lightly through his arm. The troglodan's arms jerked tighter then loosened, a wet-sounding groan rumbling from its mouth. Nate clenched his teeth and *fired* again.

This time, the troglodan didn't resist when Nate struggled free, planted his hands on the beast's massive shoulders, and shoved down. Whether the troglodan moved down or Nate moved up, he couldn't have said. It hardly mattered. Especially not when he realized they'd reached sea level.

The dull roar of rushing water swallowed them whole before he could so much as shout. In bare, breathless seconds, the sky had vanished completely, leaving nothing but endless walls of white water racing all around, everywhere he looked.

He kept descending. The shapes of the tunnel mouth and the trog carrier shrinking high above. The roaring darkness all around thickening with frightening rapidity. Closing in on him like a physical pressure, his eyes darting wildly from one black wall of water to another, sure the entire goddamn ocean would come crashing down on him at any moment. He didn't understand how it wasn't. A growling curse from below drew his attention before he could even try.

The troglodan he'd shot was weakly fumbling to retrieve the cannon slung across its back. Nate raised his gauntlet, only then getting his first dim glance at the slender blaster mount that had appeared on his wrist. He took aim, squinting against the bright wink of lights that had appeared farther below. Took aim… and hesitated.

As little as he could make out in the outline of those distant lights, he swore he saw something like fear in the troglodan's beady eyes. Maybe he really had lost it, but in that moment, he couldn't help but feel a sickly pang of sympathy for the creature bleeding out down here as the pair of them were swallowed by the ocean itself. It was enough to give him pause. Then the troglodan gave one last mournful groan and went still, and all Nate felt was sickened, and alone. Alone in the crushing depths, sinking toward the circle of harsh light below, where the cyclone tunnel appeared to come to an abrupt end.

It was farther away than he'd thought, judging by how slowly the light appeared to be approaching. He didn't even want to think about how deep he already was, or how fast he was still descending. He just kept his blaster trained on that slowly growing light, trying to get his head on straight and figure out what was going to happen when he touched down.

The first thought his mind snagged onto was that the grav lift might simply dump him out, and that he'd be wise to have his repulsors at the ready. The second and far more pressing bit, as the tunnel went from *distant circle* to *gaping maw* with startling suddenness, was that there'd almost certainly be some kind of guard detail watching the lift below. And that he'd just sent one of their dead friends down as a warning flag.

No sooner had the thought struck a thrill through his heart than he watched the dead trog speed through the opening below and heard the first rumbling cries go up. He thrust his hands hopelessly out, trying in vain to stop, to slow down. Too late.

The bay the roaring water tunnel opened into was positively cavernous, spotted with a grid of raised platforms that stretched until it disappeared to the spacious darkness at the edges of the dozens of floodlights posted around the landing site. And at that landing sight, gathered among the several glaring floodlights pointed straight up into Nate's squinting eyes...

Armor, he thought frantically, as the blinding light resolved into dozens of hulking forms turning his way on the dark bay floor. Turning with weapons. So many weapons.

"ARMOR!" he cried, thrusting his repulsor gauntlets helplessly out in front of him. Then a lone, booming battle cry reached his ears from below, and the troglodans opened fire.

CHAPTER 39

STARVED

The fighting had well and truly started out there.

The Merlin could feel it in his rather pronounced bones, buried somewhere between wandering intuition and the imperceptible murmur of subconscious perception. He supposed, on some level, that the Lady's Light might've slipped his intuition a cutesy whisper or two as well, despite the fact that her pervasive energies were overwhelmingly being wielded against him at the moment, but the details scarcely mattered.

Whatever vessels were to thank, he could practically taste the essentials.

The Beacon was near at hand. They were somewhere over the Atlantic Ocean (which could really only mean one thing). And his Knights—his once proud fellowship of the galaxy's most powerful, chivalrous heroes—were coming to blows out there like a band of ill-mannered inbreds tussling behind a barnyard dance.

A short but pertinent list of *shoulds* and *woulds* buzzed at the back of his mind like a swarm of gnats, right along with the quiet reminder that Groshna, warmongering brute that he was, might not even truly be responsible for his current actions, given the state of his Excalibur.

He ignored the maelstrom of useless thoughts. Ignored the vestigial impulse of his long-lost mortality, telling him that he had to *do* something, for the love of all that was good and just. He would act when it was time. And if he wasn't acting now, well then, it was surely only because *time* was precisely what it wasn't.

296

A few lifetimes ago, his Lady might've ribbed him on the self-fulfilling hypocrisy of it all. Apparently now wasn't the time for that, either.

The fact that Groshna had left him obscured in the belly of the *Crimson Tide* with nary a single viewing pane by which to experience and savor the full pain of his betrayal and gallant rebellion was proof enough that the Dread Knight still harbored some shadow of a doubt in that big brute head of his. It certainly wasn't a lack of sadism that had stayed the troglodan's hand at such a supreme opportunity to rub it in the Merlin's face. No.

On some level, likely deeply buried under several glacial tons of denial and bloodlust, Groshna was still frightened that he'd made a fatal error, turning on the Merlin. Probably, funnily enough, more frightened than the Merlin would've been himself, had they somehow switched places. Because as arrogant as countless generations of unrivaled power had clearly made him, for the first time in longer than he could remember (hells, in longer than *history* could remember), the Merlin honestly wasn't sure what would happen next. Even once he was freed from this cell—

He frowned at the thought, attuning his senses more carefully to the Lady's voice. A premonition, maybe? Or just immortal inevitability?

Nothing but good old subconscious perception, he finally decided— right as the *Crimson Tide* gave the first barely distinguishable vibration of impact.

"Hmm," he said to the empty brig, the ghost of a humorless smile tugging at his lips. Almost time, then.

No sooner had he thought it than the ceiling collapsed inward in a groaning crash of slagged metal and superheated carbon, and a copper-armored angel of vengeance slammed down to the deck, radiating with a kind of rage he'd only ever seen from her once before, nearly six hundred years past.

That rage had matured into something truly breathtaking to behold.

It died the moment Iveera Katanaga caught sight of him, serpentine jin freezing in place around her head, dark faceplate peeling back like she couldn't trust anything less than those captivating bioluminescent eyes of hers.

"Emrys," she whispered, like she still couldn't quite believe it.

"My clever huntress."

"My Merlin, I..." Those radiant eyes took in his ragged, emaciated state and the cell he was in, flickering with understandable confusion, then she snapped her bladed kaija up, as if she'd just remembered she had a bloodthirsty Dread Knight on her tail, and not a moment to spare.

Despite having been built to contain rather than to repel, the cell was no fragile egg to be cracked. But nor was Ser Katanaga one to be deterred. As soon as she saw the first sizzling blue blaster bolt splash uselessly against the cell wall—and as soon as the Merlin had hobbled to his feet and stepped as clear as he could—she hauled back and unleashed a force that probably could've torn a ship in half. A force that quite likely *had* torn a ship in half a few weeks earlier, he now suspected, prior to his unfortunate arrival at Golnak mining installation C-73.

Which is to say, inside the cell, things got more than a little toasty. He smelled the charring flesh. Was aware of the curling wisps of smoke drifting up from his own person. Was infinitely more interested in the deep, satisfying crack of his infernal prison making like an egg, and relenting its hold.

Before he could so much as thank his rescuer—before he could even properly see her in the dwindling afterburn of the torrential blast—a howling crimson mountain ripped through the wrecked ceiling in a speeding blur and punched straight through the deck, carrying Iveera Katanaga with it.

"Thank you," the Merlin murmured to the empty brig and to the sounds of groaning metal and rushing wind. He crossed to the cracked corner of the cell and let out a groan as he encountered the infinitely complex borders of e-dim space unfurling into the breach. The energy began trickling back into his body. He reached a still smoking hand through the jagged gap, and allowed the trickle to become a veritable flow.

Immortal or not, refeeding was never a pleasant sensation.

Then again, he thought, reaching out for his loyal Fifth Knight with his mind, neither was getting smashed through the ventral hull of a Knight ship by an Excalibur-powered troglodan.

"My Merlin," came Iveera Katanaga's voice in his mind a moment later, strained with the sounds of ongoing battle, and possibly even a bit pained. "I will return for you as soon as Ser Groshna is—"

Even through the comms, it was hard to miss the sound of Groshna's furious roar, and the thunderclap of impact that followed.

"Do not worry about me, my huntress," said the Merlin, raising a foot entirely too laboriously, and kicking a loose piece of the shattered cell free as the sounds of fighting escalated in his head. "Ser Groshna is…"

He took a ragged breath and kicked out another piece, hesitating over his next words, wondering if they were really true.

The Lady said nothing.

"Ser Groshna is beyond our ability to help. You have my permission to stop him by any means necessary."

He felt more than actually heard the gorgon's acknowledgement, immersed as she was in the heat of battle. He kicked out one last piece of his cracked egg prison, widening the gap enough to let him slip through, and stood there staring.

"Iveera…"

He felt her mind hovering there like an inquisitive hummingbird. So young and loyal. So attentive, even in the midst of a genuine fight for her life.

Nine sodding hells, was he tired.

"There is something else I must tell you."

CHAPTER 40

EXCESSIVE FORCE

"Shiiiit!" Nate screamed as he tore free from the grav lift's beam and immediately spiraled out of control with nothing but thin air and a hail of trog gunfire between himself and the bay floor a few hundred feet below.

If he'd had more than a split second to think about it, Nate might've realized just how many ways it could go wrong, throwing his repulsors to full burn from the center of a grav beam. He might've remembered that he'd been riding that grav beam for a reason.

In that moment, though, watching a few dozen trog weapons all swiveling up to end him, all he'd been able to think about was breaking free of the beam ferrying him straight down like a nice little bit of target practice.

And now...

Now, something caught him in the ribs like a speeding fist as he fell. He thrust his hands and legs out and tried a stabilizing repulsor burst that only seemed to make things worse. A few more *somethings* smacked at his legs and arms, and it was all he could do to hope his prayer for armor had somehow been answered.

It hardly seemed to matter as the dark ground leapt up to meet him.

He did his best to tuck and roll, just like he'd done a few lifetimes ago, jumping from Emily Atherton's rooftop. *Just* like that—except for the army of space ogres shooting at him, of course, and for the breakneck speed with which he struck the dark floor, which happened to feel just like solid, bone-breaking stone.

He couldn't have said how many total revolutions he bounced through. Only that he was rather surprised to be bouncing at all, and that it seemed to last longer than it should've before he finally rolled to a jerky halt on his knees, apparently not dead. By some minor miracle, he'd even ended up tucked behind the cover of one of the bay's elevated landing platforms.

Harsh troglodan shouts quickly killed his miniscule relief. They were coming, their voices echoing through the cavernous space, their shadows leering every which way in the harsh burn of the floodlights. Nate braced a hand to his knee, thinking to push to his feet and keep moving, but faltered when his repulsor gauntlet brushed against something that was decidedly *not* his own squishy thigh.

Congratulations. It appears you've managed your first kinetic barrier.

He looked down confusedly, and stiffened at the sight of the shimmering, pale blue light that clung to his every surface like a holo catsuit. Some kind of energy barrier, he thought, patting himself across the arms and the back and—

Blackened hands! Behind you!

Nate spun and found two troglodans leveling heavy rifles at him at the corner of the platform. He threw his arms up by pure useless reflex, wondering if the barrier would hold, noting with dim horror that the shimmering light seemed to wane at the thought alone.

He opened his mouth to cry for them to stop, to *please* just wait a goddamn minute. Something slammed into his back before he could. He left ground, and struck back down with a breathless *whoomph*, tumbling across the damp stone. Tumbling right to a neat stop on his back, looking up from the feet of the two riflemen.

For a second, they were all too surprised to move. Then a third trog stepped in between his fellows, teeth jutting out in a satisfied trog grin, and shoved a humming pulse cannon in Nate's face.

Time slowed.

There were too many. Even if he *could* slip free of these three and the one who'd struck him from behind, there were dozens more. He couldn't. Couldn't possibly—

Are you an Excalibur Knight, Nathaniel? Or are you not?

He saw Iveera's phosphorescent stare, silently asking him the same. Saw Marty's face, and Gwen's. Zack's and Kyle's. Saw Groshna's laughing sneer, and felt the kindling anger he'd been too bounced around since the bridge to even properly register.

He was a Knight today, Iveera had told him. Whether he liked it or not. And she hadn't thrown him down here to die. She'd thrown him down here to do a job. To protect his world.

His armored hand struck out almost before he knew it, shoving the humming cannon barrel out of his face, sending a slow-motion ripple of surprise across the troglodan's face.

Maybe Nate *was* nothing. Maybe the Lady and the Merlin had chosen wrong. But that hadn't stopped him from breaking his friends out of that brig, had it? It hadn't stopped him from prying Iveera out of Groshna's viral death grip. *He* had done those things.

On either side, the other two trogs were raising their rifles.

He, Nathaniel "IT Guy" Arturi, had acted when every fiber in his body had told him it was madness. And Ex had been there for him. Just like he was now—hovering right there, waiting for Nate to simply reach out and take the power. Waiting like he had been all along.

Two heavy trog rifles aimed at his head, thick fingers tightening on the firing studs in that strangely dilated slow motion.

Fuck it.

Nate threw his arms wide and fired with both of his wrist blasters, no longer questioning if they'd be there or not. He felt the quiet mountain of power hovering all around him, embracing him in its snug grip even as he reached out for it. Felt it as surely as he saw the twin flashes of blue blaster fire light the shadows, and heard the troglodans roar.

Nate fired again, and time sped right the hell back up all around him.

He clapped his hands back to the pulse cannon descending for his face, and *heaved* as hard as he could, intending to rip it free from the troglodan's hands. What he hadn't accounted for was the fact that the weapon was strapped around the troglodan's back.

The trog staggered forward like a falling tree, and Nate—to his extreme surprise—went shooting the other direction, sliding between tree-trunk legs and across the floor like a man-sized shuffleboard disc. Sliding entirely too far, he noted, right along with the disconcerting scraping sound coming from beneath him.

Enemy fire rang out before he could question it, pouring in from seemingly all directions, kicking up wet chunks of stone and grit all around him. Something smacked at his legs. Several somethings. He focused on the thought of his defenses and dug a shoulder into the stone, tucking the last of his sliding momentum up into a backward roll.

He came up in a kneeling crouch, squeezing off a few wild shots from his raised wrist blasters… and froze, gaping from his extended arms down to the rest of his body, and to the suit of rippling armor that had just finished unfurling to encase him from thin air. It was the same kind of sleek armor he'd seen on Iveera and Groshna—toned in grays and blues, and utterly alien.

It was the armor of an Excalibur Knight.

His armor, he dumbly noted, as a string of shots thudded across his torso, coaxing a crackling pulse of light from the ghostly kinetic barrier that still clung to his exterior. Ex practically purred, like all this time he'd wanted nothing more than to take a few good shots.

"I'm a Knight," Nate heard himself whisper, half question, half stupefied observation. *"We're—"*

Going to have a very short reign if you don't plan on fighting back.

The frighteningly hot flash of a scarlet blaster bolt flying past his head punctuated Ex's point emphatically. Nate snapped out of it, pointed his wrist blasters, and returned fire.

It wasn't easy to see what he was shooting at in the erratic lighting, with the trogs charging in and out of the platform shadows, casting silhouettes of their own under the floodlights. But he hit at least a few shots, if the keening roars of pain were any indication.

Reinforcements continued to pour in, grav lift shooters catching up from his crash flight deviation with booming battle cries and growling curses. More shots slamming into his legs and arms by the second. Nate stood and fired right back, caught up in the firestorm, gripped by something between exultation and desperation.

"I'm an Excalibur Knight, assholes!" he screamed at the roaring shadows, shooting with his right hand as he raised his left arm, thinking to conjure a proper shield to handle some of the abuse. "Get the hell off my planet!"

Well now you're just being excessive, Ex said, as the trogs bellowed back, and the return fire intensified.

"Yeah?" he growled, trying not to gape as a long kite shield unfolded from his forearm only to be immediately wracked by a string of rapid, cracking impacts. He began to back away, thinking to slip behind the landing platform beside him. "Well, remind me to give a damn when this is all—"

On your right!

Nate spun, sweeping his new shield with him, and watched in wide-eyed surprise as the edge of the shield smacked aside the thrumming bayonet-style rifle spike that'd been bound straight for his heart. Then he braced for impact as the troglodan behind that spike crashed straight into him.

It felt a lot like what he imagined it might feel like to get folded by a two-thousand-pound squat. Except he didn't get folded. His body screamed with effort. Hard rock cracked beneath his armored boots. And he caught the charging troglodan's momentum head-on.

For a second, they gaped at each other. Then Nate threw a hard uppercut into the beast's jutting jaw and followed with a shield slam that sent the trog crashing to its big ass.

And for the first time since they'd met, Ex gave a peel of genuine laughter at something other than Nate's personal shortcomings. *Yes... Yes! Excessive suits you, Nathaniel. Now helm your stubborn head and fight!*

Nate didn't argue. He welcomed the thought of a helmet, and just like that, a soft pressure cradled in around the back of his head, a transparent film shimmering into existence before his eyes, wrapping around until he could hear the ragged sounds of his own rapid breaths.

Much as he didn't love the claustrophobic face hug, it was hard to argue with the added protection, or the cool rush of air that kissed his sweaty brow. Especially as everything around him began to sharpen on his heads up display—shadows coming to light, distant details leaping out with star-tling clarity.

For a moment, there was something else, too—the strangest trickle of familiarity, like coming home after too long away. Then a nice big trog bullet winged off the side of his helmet, and all he felt was startled panic. A string of shots smacked into his left side. In front of him, the trog he'd shoved over was grabbing its rifle, preparing for round two.

Excalibur Knight or not, Nate turned and ran for it, holding his shield where it could absorb the brunt of the fire that followed. There were still dozens of trogs down here, and plenty more still coming, from the glances he caught of the grav lift as he darted between landing platforms. Even if he could survive a rumble with all of them, it might not mean a thing if he didn't do what Iveera had sent him down here to do.

How do we find the Beacon? he asked, once he'd zigged and zagged through enough turns to feel safe hunkering in the shadows for a moment.

Do you not feel it, calling us home? Ex replied, as Nate peered out from the corner of the adjacent platform, toward the densest concentration of flood-lights. There was a wide opening in the cavern wall that he hadn't had time to see earlier, leading deeper into... Christ, could this really be Atlantis? He'd forgotten about that particular little chestnut in the shuffle.

Focus, little hobbit. Listen.

He drew back behind cover, all too aware of the sound of nearby trog voices, and considered Ex's choice of words. Calling them *home*. As if in response, that odd sensation of trickling familiarity shifted back into awareness beneath the surface of his helmet-enhanced senses. It was more noticeable, the more he focused on it, but still seemingly without direction —more a gentle mist in the air than a... well, a Beacon.

And here he'd been wondering why it had taken Iveera so long to hone in on this thing.

We will find the way as we draw closer, Ex insisted. *First, we must make it to the city proper.*

Nate peeked out from the platform again, as if a more direct line of sight might somehow clarify his senses, then jerked back as the platform beside him erupted with fountains of sparks and red hot metal. A second volley spat chips of stone at his feet, echoes of gunfire reverberating into the darkness.

They were waiting.

Waiting as their friends circled around behind him, by the sound of it.

Best we be on our way, then, yes?

Ex sounded entirely too excited about the thought, like it was a trip to Disneyland he was proposing, and not a headlong charge through a waiting army and into the creepy depths at the bottom of the ocean. But the sound of their approaching flankers didn't leave Nate time to dwell on it. He tensed, preparing to move, trying to decide the best route forward.

As if in response to the thought, his helmet display shifted, troglodan-shaped outlines appearing through the maze of platforms like ghostly apparitions, forming up to charge here, moving around to flank there.

It was incredibly handy.

So much so that, for a second, he almost forgot to be afraid—almost felt as if he were playing some kind of game. A powerful predator, picking his next targets. Then he remembered that the behemoths behind each and every one of those thirty-odd outlines could individually pull him limb from limb—and probably eat him too, for good measure—and that healthy jolt of fear returned, with interest.

He plotted out what looked like his most promising course, and willed his kite shield back to wherever it'd come from, deciding it would only slow him down for this next part. The shield promptly folded in on itself like a freaking Autobot, leaving behind only a thin gray stripe on the armor of his left forearm. Time enough to marvel at that later, he supposed.

For the time being, he just mantled his way up onto the ramp of the platform he'd been using for cover, and started running his ass off.

By the time the first pack of trogs caught sight of him, he was already gathering himself to leap for the next platform over. It was a long jump—almost definitely beyond *humanly possible*—which was why Nate had his untrusty repulsors cued up to help. And help they did. A little too much.

In the excitement, he couldn't have said which part he'd overdone it on —the repulsor thrust, or the jump itself. Either way, he flew clean over the platform he'd been aiming for. And the next one, too.

Troglodan fire tracked him throughout the flight, each rushing pulse and sizzling blaster bolt disturbingly audible within the rapid-breathing confines of his new helmet. He tried to stay focused on the floodlit stone ahead as he passed through the apex of his jump and began to fall toward another hard landing. He was cuing his repulsors to soften the fall when a shot caught him in the shoulder like a speeding trog fist and sent the cavern spinning around him.

He hit the stone in a solid belly flop.

It might have been comical, if not for the uncontrollable coughs that seized him as he gasped feebly for air, diaphragm too impact-shocked to function, mouth tinged with the coppery hint of blood. The smooth stone exploded inches from his face, peppering his helmet with debris. More gunfire behind. Ahead, the trogs were forming up to guard the mouth of the cavern, where they'd apparently deduced he was headed.

He gasped for breath, trying to get himself to move.

Still an Excalibur Knight?

Lying there at the bottom of the ocean, beaten and battered, encased by alien armor, and facing down a small army of troglodans, Nate wasn't really sure who he was anymore. Somehow, though, the answer to that question didn't seem nearly as important as the fact that he needed to keep moving.

So Nate threw himself up from the ground and ran. Jaw clenched. Lungs burning. Stone exploding all around him. He ran faster than he'd ever run. Faster, he realized, than *anyone* had ever run. He could feel the armor working in tandem with his own pumping legs, steadying his breakneck gait, amplifying the power of his every stride.

Ahead, the troglodan line dug in and opened fire in earnest.

Nate leveled his wrist blasters and returned fire, not slowing. Not when the enemy shots began to find their mark, and not when something smacked down to the stone behind him, adding a heavy spray of water to the debris and projectiles already pelting him. He pressed on, firing away, spurred by the startled looks on the trogs' faces, trusting his armor would deal with the punishment. Or it wouldn't. Either way, he ran until he was close enough to the faltering troglodan line, and then he jumped again.

This time, he left it to his legs alone, and saw with grim satisfaction that he was perfectly capable of clearing a line of eight foot tall troglodans without the aid of his untrusty repulsors. It also left his hands free to keep firing, though he couldn't have said if he hit anything in the chaos. There was just a blur of motion, and confused beady eyes looking up at him, and then he crashed down on the other side, tumbling into a barely contained roll.

At least he emerged with his shield out, and facing in the right direction to cover his ass. He leveled his right wrist blaster, thinking to cover his retreat as he went.

And that was when he realized it hadn't been *him* who'd set the trog line shaking in their giant boots.

A few shots cracked into his shield from the more single-minded trog soldiers in the line. Most of the cavern's collective attention, though, was focused on the torrential downpour of ocean water falling from the mouth of the cyclone tunnel. Nate couldn't help but stare as well, wondering the unavoidable question.

Were they about to be crushed beneath an entire ocean?

A distant explosion rocked the cavern, spewing forth a renewed gush from the opening above. Some of the troglodans scattered and began rushing toward one of the platforms where Nate only then noticed a few parked vehicles—some kind of big, junkyard-looking hover bikes. They didn't make it far before the cyclone tunnel coughed another small sea of water and disgorged the smoking wreck of a ship.

Iveera's ship, Nate realized, with a sinking feeling.

And atop its battered, blast-scored hull, there was Iveera herself, riding the falling ship down like the Goddess of War riding a flaming horse into the depths of hell. She was locked in battle with the hulking crimson form of Groshna, and even at a distance, the intensity of the fighting was frightening. Neither one of them seemed the least bit concerned that they were plummeting straight to a horrific crash. They were too busy trading blows that sounded like they could've leveled city blocks—Iveera with her bladed staff, and Groshna with a tremendous dark axe.

It didn't track physically that the comparatively slender gorgon could so ruthlessly tangle with the enormous troglodan, but there she was, meeting his heavy-handed strikes head on, and dishing the punishment straight back. Groshna flinched first in their game of chicken, gathering himself to leap from the plummeting wreck. Before he could, though, Iveera caught his tree-trunk arm, deftly flipped herself onto his shoulders like she was mounting a rampaging rhino, and kicked off.

In his mind, Nate swore the exchange should've launched her upward. Instead, the entire freaking ship accelerated downward as she kicked, the dorsal plating crumpling under Groshna from the force of her launch. Nate didn't have time to wrap his head around it. The ship hit the stone with the loudest crash he'd ever heard, and he staggered a few steps back from the sheer violence of the sound. He took a few more when it hit him that the entire damn place might come crashing down with it, but the cavern held, and the hemorrhaging water tunnel was already extending a set of huge triangular panels to seal itself off.

"What are you doing?!" a familiar voice snapped, right beside him.

Nate had tensed behind his shield and checked over both shoulders before it dawned on him that the voice had come from his helmet's communications systems, and that it was Iveera's. Ahead, she was hovering above the wreckage of her ship, the pluming smoke billowing out around her as if it were frightened to make direct contact.

"Get to the Beacon," she said. "Get it to the Merlin. Go! I will hold them here."

"But," Nate started, eyes scanning the cavern, counting the odds. "But I can—"

"Go."

He stared dumbly at the copper-armored force of nature hovering there, twirling one bladed end of her halved staff on a line of crackling blue energy, shoulders gleaming with the new addition of some kind of orangish crystalline cannon fixtures, writhing jin pulsing an alarming shade of red.

She didn't look like a gorgon who needed Nate's help.

At least not until Groshna burst up from the wreckage of her ship to face her at a hover, crimson armor smoking, enormous arm cannon crackling with brilliant electric arcs. Around the cavern, most of the trogs were too captivated for the moment to do anything but stare.

"Go," she repeated quietly.

And then she unleashed hell on the cavern.

Nate shuffled backward at the ferocious explosion of violence, racing heart begging him to run even as his feet stubbornly refused to leave her here so thoroughly outnumbered.

The Beacon, Nathaniel.

He teetered in place, stuck on the edge until the thunder clap of the two clashing Knights ahead reminded him that he'd be punching a few worlds above his weight class anyway, trying to take on Groshna.

Find the Beacon. Get it out.

"Shit!" he growled, turning away from the madness and taking off at a hard run. Down the widening tunnel of stone, lit by an eerie, sea green light that emanated from everywhere and nowhere. On, beneath the majestic stone archways. Past the larger-than-life busts of trident-wielding mermen. Trying to shut out the distant sounds of explosions and gunfire.

He ran on, straight over the ancient stone causeway. Straight on to what his disbelieving brain could only assume was the lost city of Atlantis.

CHAPTER 41

LOST AND FOUND

The city was impossibly enormous.

Hell, it was just plain impossible all around.

That was the only conclusion Nate's scrambling brain could arrive at as it struggled to grasp the regal sprawl of ancient buildings and pathways that reached out into the depths before him. There was no way anything this large could exist on Earth without their knowing about it. There was no way it could exist, period, at the bottom of the freaking ocean. Yet somehow, here it was.

He stared at the buildings, each and every one a masterful work of art in its own right—most of them a confusing fusion of old world architecture joined with something new and vaguely alien. All of them sitting peacefully in eerily abandoned quiet, paying no mind to the distant, muffled sounds of gunfire as they bathed in the luminescent blue-green glow of…

Mother of god.

Nate's shuffling steps drew to a full stop as he leaned back to take in the unfathomably colossal dome that encapsulated the city high above like the world's most stunning and gigantic display of bubble wrap art. Thousands and thousands of transparent panels, all reinforced by an intricate network of stone leaflets, metal girders, and gargantuan beveled columns that would've given the Romans more than a little cause to overcompensate.

"Holy shit…" Nate muttered to no one in particular.

The city of Atlantis swallowed his voice like an ocean.

Amusing as your astonishment is, we have more pressing concerns.

As if in agreement, a not-so-distant explosion peaked over the steady background drone of distant gunfire. Iveera, no doubt, giving the troglodans something for their darkest nightmares. Provided any of them lived that long, and the Atlantic Ocean didn't come crushing down on all of them.

Which put his mind right back to wondering who could've possibly built all this, and how in the hell it was still standing—still holding an entire *ocean* at bay—after who knew how many thousands of years?

The energy of the Beacon permeates this place, Ex said, as if that should be answer enough. Then, remembering who he was talking to, he added, *That may well explain the longevity. As for your first question, the short answer is 'Atlanteans,' and the longer one—*

Is that I'd better focus on the Beacon and worry about this stuff later?

My, my, how you're learning today.

"Yeah," Nate muttered, turning his mind to the Beacon, offering a silent question out to Atlantis in hopes that *something* might see fit to point the way. That soft welcoming sensation still hummed in his head here, oddly juxtaposed with the haunted air of abandonment that clung to the quiet city. It was a tad more noticeable now, he thought, but still far too slippery to divine any sense of direction or source.

"How do you think it even got here?" he asked, starting down the main street not with a plan so much as a general certainty that he was far more likely to find something by actually looking around than by just standing at the mouth of the city and gaping.

Beacons have been known to wander from time to time. Most likely, someone put it here. Perhaps to preserve this city. Perhaps to simply keep it hidden.

Nate eyed the dark entryway of what might've once been a tavern, feeling some combination of exposed and audacious, just loping down the middle of the empty street. *So you do remember how Beacons work, then?* he asked, veering over toward the houses on the right.

Ex gave an amused huff at that. *No one knows how Beacons work, Nathaniel. Their existence is but one of the Lady's many great mysteries.*

Yeah, Nate thought, as if that tidbit had been a given. *I just meant that part wasn't, you know... taken away, like—*

Ex didn't exactly shush him so much as buzz a wordless warning. Nate was behind the cover of the closest house in a moment, wrist blasters at the ready, scanning the empty street for some threat. He caught the low echo of troglodan voices a few seconds before his helmet display filled in three outlines a few buildings ahead, coming for the main street at a lumbering run.

Not completely deserted, after all.

"—told us not to set foot in the city," one of them was saying, farther off than Nate probably could've heard with his own ears.

The comment was met with a growled string of curses he couldn't untangle.

"—just had to do it," came the first voice.

"And for a pathetic human artifact, no less," added another.

"Bah," growled the cursing trog. "I take my orders from the Dread Lord and the General, not some blight-touched..."

Nate lost whatever else was said, scrambling around to the rear of his building to keep out of sight. The trio of trog soldiers came thundering past a few moments later, clearly in a hurry to get back to the sounds of fighting in the landing bay.

One of them was carrying a trident.

Nate almost could've laughed at the sight, up until an explosion sounded from the bay, sending a light trembling through the stone underfoot. The trio sped on, the naysayer grunting after the trident bearer that they *had* had orders from his Dreadship to *respect* the blackened bastard's requests, and that they were all in for a proper fisting when the commander realized what they'd done.

Nate watched them go, antsy with the need to get back on the move. It was only as their outlines dwindled toward the causeway and he rounded back onto the street that he registered he'd just let three enemy soldiers slip back to an already stacked fight against Iveera.

"Shit," he murmured, glaring after their outlines.

The Beacon, was all Ex said.

Nate turned away from the retreating trog outlines, knowing his companion was right, then glanced back as another thought occurred to him. "Any chance this helmet can scan for whatever waves that Beacon is giving off?"

You don't think I might have mentioned such an ability?

Nate clenched his fists. *I don't know, damnit, I just... This place is...*

Far too large for one man to search, Ex finished.

There was no denying it.

Ex was thoughtfully silent for a few seconds. *Where would YOU place the Beacon, Nathaniel?*

Nate frowned at the question, suspecting a trap.

It is not a riddle. Humor me.

"Probably right at the center of the city, I guess. If you're right about it keeping this place standing, whoever stuck it here might've wanted to put it where its power could, like, reach everything, right?"

As I suspected. A rudimentary assumption at best, yet potentially apt if we also assume that it was likely an equally superstitious being who stowed the Beacon here in the first place.

Nate didn't bother arguing or defending himself. He just set off at a run, scanning the stretch of buildings ahead, looking for any likely suspects. There were more than a few towering monstrosities of breathtaking engineering that drew his eye from the heart of the city.

That one? Ex asked, as Nate's gaze drifted back to one dark-spired behemoth in particular for the third or fourth time.

Too obvious? Nate wondered. He couldn't decide whether the building looked like a mighty cathedral, or the kind of fortress in which one might expect to find the dark lord Sauron lurking, but it was one of the few buildings tall enough to actually touch the city's protective dome. That seemed worth something to his gut.

It does seem only human, I suppose.

Well, then...

Nate put on a burst of speed, trying to ignore the creeping apprehension at the fact that *gut feelings* and *only human* logic were their best clues. At least he could move fast in the armor. *Frighteningly* fast, he decided, as he leaned into it, favoring speed over any risk of running into more rogue trogs.

He reached the base of the towering cathedral in short order, panting only half as hard as he felt like he should be. Then he caught sight of the ancient marble statue outside the front and forgot about his burning lungs completely.

It was the Lady.

Of course it's the Lady.

"But..." Nate blinked at the statue, once again trying and failing to understand who these people had been, and how they would've known about the Lady at all.

Need I remind you that now is hardly the time for a history lesson?

"Right." Nate bobbed his head, doing little to settle the way it was spinning with the enormity of all the shit that he and the rest of the world still didn't have the faintest clue about. "Right."

He turned for the cathedral.

It felt profoundly unnatural that those dark oaken double doors still stood tall, proud, and sturdy after who knew how many centuries of abandonment. Then again, that might've just been his sinking gut doing the talking. Too many coincidences adding up. Too convenient, that someone would've just left this almighty Beacon sitting here in the middle of the city, right next to a big statue of the Lady, in a building so obvious that even a clueless college kid had dialed in on it in under five minutes.

Convenient? We are more than three miles below sea level, and more than a thousand from any appreciable form of civilization. Perhaps whoever brought the Beacon here simply assumed there was negligible risk of this place ever being discovered by anyone other than a Knight.

No need to hide the needle if no one would ever find the haystack anyway? Nate couldn't decide if that was a fair point, or the exact reason his Spidey Senses were tingling. All he really knew was that he needed to find this goddamned Beacon before the fighting spilled out of the landing bay and brought the ocean down on Atlantis for good.

Wisdom becomes you, Nathaniel.

He grabbed one thick iron rung and pushed the heavy door open. It swung inward with a mourning creak every bit as haunting as one might've expected from thousand-year-old hinges. He'd expected to see nothing but darkness from the outside. Instead, the same soft blue luminescence that lit the dome came wafting through the doorway in welcome. Readying his shield and wrist blaster, Nate took a few cautious steps into the cathedral, and froze.

He'd been here before.

The feeling struck him like a phantom fist to the diaphragm, sparking wriggling trills of panic from his chest up to his head.

How? When? *Why* did he recognize this place?

The Lady, he realized, flashing back to their strange journey across the stars. That was it. It had only been a sparse second, but he was almost certain this was the place he'd seen when they'd taken their first flash-step. A vast, underwater cathedral.

And it *was* vast.

Nate gaped at the sheer volume of open space between him and the grand stone arches of the vaulted ceiling, which reached so high as to actually be incorporated into the city dome, with multiple panes exposing the cathedral to the dark ocean above. He stared, trying to process the simple fact that this place even existed—and that everything else he'd seen out there with the Lady might've actually been *real*.

His gaze tracked down to the ground floor, following the long rows of intricate stone benches to the head of the great hall. He froze again.

The Beacon.

It was sitting right there on the dais—a brilliant sphere of burnished silver and nebulous azure light hovering over the upright arms of some wrought iron shrine. It couldn't have been larger than a basketball, and it pulsed like a living thing, erratic figures and patterns swirling languidly across the shimmering light and metal of its surface as if they were one and the same.

Nate didn't have to ask Ex if this was indeed the Beacon they'd been looking for. He felt it now. Felt its call growing exponentially stronger with every step forward, so potent it was almost impossible to believe it had felt so faint only a hundred yards ago.

He'd broken into a run before he knew it, not even precisely sure what he was going to do when he reached the Beacon—only that they'd found it, goddammit, and that maybe everything was going to be okay after all.

Contact Iveera, he told Ex. *I need to tell her to get out of—*

Wait!

Nate jerked to a sliding halt at the flicker of movement ahead. He steadied and looked around the empty space, thinking maybe his eyes were playing tricks on him. Then the dark figure he could've sworn hadn't been there a moment ago stood from the front row of stone benches, and turned to face him.

In the mad dash, Nate had all but forgotten what the pilfering trogs had said about the blackened bastard who'd apparently told them to stay clear of the city. Now though, struck by the terrible presence of the *thing* standing before him, Nate wasn't sure what else he could be looking at.

If it was a troglodan, it wasn't like any he'd ever seen. Large enough, certainly. But the thing looked more like the actual dark lord Sauron than like Groshna or his kin. Pitch black armor bristling with more sharp edges and wicked intent than all the lords of hell combined. The thing looked like it could've killed a man with any part of its body. In the unlikely event that failed, though, Nate had little doubt the barbaric greatsword strapped across its back would be equal to finishing the job.

"Who are you?" he asked, trying to keep the waver from his voice.

The Black Knight said nothing. Just watched him with the bottomless black holes that pierced its helm where the eyes should've been, sharp horns and blood red plume tilting ever-so-slightly in silent consideration.

What am I looking at, Ex?

I... cannot say. I don't believe he is an ally, Nathaniel.

Nate resisted the urge to raise his blaster in warning, suddenly afraid he'd be provoking a fight that he wouldn't win. "What are you doing here?" he called instead.

The Black Knight started wordlessly forward, stalking toward Nate without the slightest glint of hesitation, each dark footfall sending a low thud reverberating through the still cathedral.

"Stop," Nate said, taking a few involuntary steps back, a heavy dread settling over him. He raised his shield and aimed his wrist blaster. The weapon felt woefully inadequate. "I said stop right there!"

The Black Knight hesitated for half a breath.

Then it drew its dark sword and charged.

CHAPTER 42
CRUCIBLE

To say the Black Knight *charged* was misleading.

There was no fearsome battle cry. No long, stone-pounding dash to combat. The thing simply raised its dark greatsword from twenty yards away, and brought it sweeping down for Nate's head, having somehow covered the distance between them in less than the blink of an eye.

If meeting a charging troglodan head-on had been like stopping a car, catching the Black Knight's blow on his shield might as well have been trying to catch a falling mountain.

There was a disturbingly loud crash, and then he was flying. He couldn't have said how far he went, or how many obstacles he smashed straight through on the way. By the time the world resolved back into a luminescent blue pile of pain and stone rubble, all Nate really knew was that he was outclassed here. Even through the shield and the armor, his forearm was on fire with the fury of the blow he'd tried to block. He had to look down to confirm the arm was still there at all.

No sooner had he done so than he realized the Black Knight was already there, standing over him. He rolled over and drove a kick into the thing's gut. Or tried to, before the Knight caught his ankle in a frighteningly strong grip. For one terrible moment, he thought the monster would simply give a twist and snap his leg in two. Instead, the Knight gave a sharp jerk, and Nate found himself airborne again.

Three or four pulverized stone benches later, he was coughing up blood and trying not to puke in his helmet. He looked frantically around for the next attack, but the Black Knight was taking its time over in the main aisle. Taking *his* time, some corner of Nate's brain decided. Because there was something almost *human* about the way the enormous bastard was looking around the cathedral now, greatsword draped casually over one broad shoulder.

"Where is he?" the Black Knight rumbled in a dreadfully low voice.

Nate gritted his teeth and clawed his way back to his feet, trying to hide the grunts of pain. "Where's who?"

"The conjurer," the Knight said, not turning. "The wizard. Your thrice-damned Merlin." His dark gaze swept around the cathedral, across the balconies, up to the vaulted ceiling. "WHERE ARE YOU, YOU BLACK-ENED COWARD?!"

The cathedral walls shook with the raw power of the Knight's voice. Even with the added protection of his helmet, Nate staggered backward, ears ringing, bludgeoned brain racing to catch up with who the hell this vengeful spirit was, and why he'd expect to find the Merlin here, of all places. Unless…

"The Beacon. Did you… Did you bring it here? Was this all…?"

Before he could finish asking if this entire mess had all been one big trap to catch the Merlin, the Black Knight turned and began toward him, shifting the greatsword on his shoulder like he was thinking about springing across the benches and cutting Nate in two, right then and there.

"I don't know where the Merlin is," Nate said, keeping his shield ready. "He left the planet. I don't know where. But he's not here. So if that's what you're doing here, you'd better just—"

"You would die for him, human?"

Nate swallowed, hating how his traitorous innards cowered at those words. Hating how much he clearly *wasn't* some unshakable paragon of duty, like Iveera. Hating that he was afraid.

But that didn't mean he couldn't pretend.

"I'd die to protect my planet from that thing," he said, pointing to the Beacon, thinking of Marty, and Gwen, and everyone else out there he'd failed to protect. Their faces, coupled with the words, stirred something deep inside, anger and desperation and fear at this black terror before him all spilling into the crucible, churning into something new.

"And if you're a part of all this," he continued, the fires of a besieged New

York licking at the crucible in his mind, working its contents into a kind of controlled madness, "then I guess I'll die to stop you too."

The promise hung in the air, permeated only by the gentle glow of the luminescent dome, and the tranquil hum of the Beacon's presence.

"Very good, Earth Knight," the Black Knight said, spreading his hands wide, inviting attack. "Come, then. I would see you protect your planet."

For a second, Nate faltered, expecting some trap. But the trap was already sprung, he knew—*had* been sprung the moment he'd walked into this cathedral. There was no escape. No guarantee it would matter even if he could buy more time. There was only him, and the one obstacle keeping him from the Beacon.

I am with you, Nathaniel.

That inner madness rippled, ready to boil over. It didn't matter that he was facing a superior enemy. Didn't matter that he didn't know what to do. He had Ex, and he had a job to do. He had a choice.

Electric tingles crackled down his right arm, radiating to his hand, begging to be released. No holding back. That was the only way.

Unleash me, Excalibur Knight.

For the first time in his life, Nate didn't question instinct. He just took a single, impossible leap across the thirty feet between him and his obstacle, bellowing a wordless scream all the way, and brought his crackling fist down like a born-again thunder god.

The air detonated around them, impact jarring through his arm so savagely that it went half numb. Then he saw the shimmering alien sword that had appeared in his hand, gently curved blade crossed with the Black Knight's greatsword, thrumming with quiet power, and it all clicked together, simple as could be. Here was the sword, and here was his Black Knight.

No holding back.

The Black Knight shoved off his blade, sending him back a few steps for balance. He lunged right back in, sweeping the alien blade for the Black Knight's head, keeping his shield raised as best he could. The Knight avoided the strike with a half-step backward, and leaned clear of the following slash, not even bothering to use his sword. Nate stepped after him, determined to keep the pressure on. It wasn't enough.

Another slash, and another. A thrust. A sweep. A shield swipe. The dark titan stepped clear of each strike with all the effort of a bored slow-dance partner, waiting for the song to end.

Nate swung harder, moved faster, but it was no good. The Knight was too skilled. Within a minute, his lungs were burning, shoulders and arms growing heavy with fatigue. Desperate, he cut his next swing short and squeezed off a surprise shot from his wrist blaster. The blue bolt dissipated on a shimmering ripple of energy armor, leaving the Black Knight perfectly unharmed, and earning Nate his first counterattack.

He nearly fell over trying to duck the broad sweep the Black Knight made for his head. Before he could regain his footing, the Knight brought a brutal strike down on his raised shield. Another blow hammered down, and Nate's front leg buckled.

He tried to scramble back and reset, but the Knight stayed with him, raining strikes down like a vengeful god. He didn't bother getting fancy. Didn't even appear to be putting his back into it. He just threw one overhand strike after another, hammering Nate to the stone like a carpenter casually nailing down shingles.

Playing with him, Nate realized through ragged breaths, beginning to lose his grip on the fear. Knocking him around like a toy soldier. He'd known he was outmatched, but this...

SLAM.

Do not give up, Nathaniel.

SLAM.

Do not give in.

SLAM.

Remember who you fight for.

Gritting his teeth, Nate gathered what little juice he had and threw himself into a tumbling backward roll. He popped to his feet, preparing to strike, but the Black Knight was already there, raising his greatsword with fearless certainty. The dark blade burst into hellish flames, and Nate's insides went cold. He threw up sword and shield, bracing himself with everything he had left. The flaming sword crashed into his defenses, knocking him to the ground hard enough to crack the stone. Head spinning, he raised his sword to defend against the next blow… and gaped at the glowing red edge of the dagger in front of him.

The Black Knight had cleaved his sword clean through.

Something closed around his throat. The Black Knight's hand, he registered, still staring in helpless shock at the severed blade. Then the world spun and exploded with bone shaking impact and cresting waves of pain.

He was pinned to a stone column, his dwindling spots of vision informed him. Held aloft by the throat crushing grip of the Black Knight, the debris of his impact raining down upon them. The dark titan didn't seem to notice the fist-sized hunk of rock that struck his helmet. He just calmly slung his greatsword across his back with a magnetic thrum, then reached down and plucked what remained of Nate's useless sword from his hand.

Only what remained wasn't *quite* useless, Nate realized with a sickened twinge, as the Black Knight placed the glowing tip of the severed blade almost gently to the point just below his heart.

He grabbed onto the Knight's thick wrist with both hands, knowing deep in his racing heart he didn't have the strength to stop this monster.

"Do not be afraid," the Black Knight said quietly, almost gently.

But Nate *was* afraid, looking into the terrible darkness of those bottomless eye slots. More afraid than he'd ever been in his life.

He kicked and cried, vision waning, dimly aware of Ex shouting him on as he clawed desperately at the Black Knight's sword hand. He wasn't ready to die. He wasn't. He wanted to cry. Wanted to scream.

Then the Knight's crushing hand tensed on his throat, and something cold and brilliantly sharp pierced straight into his heart.

CHAPTER 43

FIRE AND RAIN

For one merciful moment, it almost seemed as if getting stabbed in the heart wasn't going to be nearly as agonizing as it should've been. Then that cold, foreign length of invading steel ripped through some inner barrier, and the pain ignited through every inch of his being.

Nate rocked his head back and screamed. He tried to fight back, tried one last time to kick the Black Knight away from him, but his limbs had already gone weak, lifeless. The blade twisted in his chest, the movement surprisingly painless and oddly… wriggling?

N-N-Nathaniel… What… What is…

With a supreme effort, Nate looked down through his spotted vision and saw two things that didn't make any sense: the broken tip of his sword, still pressed to the exterior of his armor and decidedly *not* buried in his chest, and the armor itself, wriggling around the tip of the blade in spasmodic jitters. Just like Iveera's had been doing back on the ship.

You must… stop him… Nathan—Agh!

Whatever hit Ex hit Nate just as hard. The pain spiked, and he screamed again, bucking against the agony, worse than powerless to stop it. He couldn't even twitch. It was like his armor had gone on full lockdown. He tried anyway, fighting hopelessly on even as the blinding pain wrapped around him, demanding that he stop.

It was too much.

He couldn't have said how long he struggled, or even whether he was fully conscious for the duration. He was adrift on a red sea of agony behind his closed eyelids, lost in the depths so thoroughly that he couldn't remember his own name.

Then an explosive cracking sound split through his awareness, and he jerked back to the cathedral just as something detonated between him and the Black Knight. An indistinguishable blur of movement and pain later, Nate hit the stone floor with a crash, gasping for breath, completely disoriented. He tried to raise his head, blindly slapping around in a shallow pool of something wet and...

He blinked around the cathedral, half-expecting to find himself lying in a pool of his own blood, panicked senses trying to catch up with the relevant facts. The wetness was cold. Ice cold. Inches of ice cold water sloshing across the sanctuary floor.

Ocean water.

He looked up just in time to see the metal leaflets extending to seal off the hemorrhaging section of the distant dome, then he traced the falling water down, rattled brain working for answers. Down, right to the Merlin.

He'd never been so relieved to see anyone in his entire damn life.

The wizard stood over the Black Knight, a gnarled staff in one hand, the other extended toward the dark titan, spindly fingers flexed. The Knight was on his knees, bound in a series of thick chains still actively lengthening from thin air, constricting about him like a nest of angry snakes.

"You," the Merlin said, so quietly Nate almost missed it.

"Bastard," the Black Knight growled in reply, straining against the chains.

"Take the Beacon, lad," the Merlin called toward Nate, his eyes not leaving the dark titan before him. "Take it and go now."

It was only then that he noticed the strained look on the old wizard's face. The Merlin looked like hell, ratty robes even dirtier and more tattered than the last time Nate had seen, face gaunt, eyes sunken.

"Go!" the wizard cried, snapping him back to attention.

He turned for the wrought iron shrine at the head of the hall, not knowing where it was he was supposed to go, not especially caring. The Beacon's song intensified as he laid eyes on it, calling to him, and he scrambled to shaky feet, coaxing his battered body to move.

"BASTARD!"

The roar struck like a sonic bomb, shaking the walls and whipping Nate around just in time to see the Black Knight's greatsword burst into flames, superheating the chains across his back like a plasma torch. With a wordless scream and a small explosion of red hot shrapnel, the dark titan burst free from the chains and leapt to his feet, dark eye slots blazing to life with crimson fire.

Faster than Nate could track, the Knight had closed on the Merlin, flaming greatsword already in hand. He brought the weapon down in a mighty two-handed blow leagues above anything he'd thrown at Nate. The Merlin caught the strike on his raised staff, and an explosion of flame ripped out across half the cathedral, blackening the stone around them and gushing over Nate's armor for one terrifyingly hot second.

"The Beacon, Nathaniel!" the Merlin shouted as the rush of flames cleared, blasting the Knight down the aisle with a thrumming open palm strike, then following up with an honest-to-god bolt of lightning from his staff.

The lightning caught the Black Knight square in the chest and sent him rocketing into the rear wall so hard that Nate expected he might've punched clean through in the resultant explosion of dust and debris. When the dust cleared, though, the Knight was already back on his feet, so to speak— hovering calmly over the main aisle as if getting struck by wizard's lightning was an everyday sort of thing.

It was terrifying.

Heeding the Merlin's words, Nate turned for the Beacon and took off as fast as his legs would move. Ahead, the Beacon's light intensified, its call quickening, the air itself seeming to part before him, urging him on almost as if the thing *wanted* him to—

"Get down!" the Merlin cried somewhere behind him.

Nate jerked to a halt mid-step, too startled to immediately comprehend. Then the fiery-eyed Black Knight slammed down in front of him, hard enough to crater the dais steps underfoot, and Nate heeded the Merlin's words for a second time.

No sooner had he dropped than a bolt of lightning seared through the space his head had just occupied, raking tingling claws across his armored back and warping his helmet display with enough dancing discoloration and jitters that he must've mistaken what he saw next.

Standing firm in the crater of his impact, the Black Knight caught the lightning blast right on the flat of his greatsword, barely even budging but to sweep one foot back and brace himself. Then he pointed the dark, crackling blade back at the Merlin, as if to return the favor.

Nate stumbled to his feet without thinking, throwing both arms up and willing his shield into full deployment. The barrier sprang to life with the speed of a detonating bomb, rippling out from both forearms. And not a moment too soon.

Lightning exploded from the Black Knight's sword, punching into Nate's shield and… dissipating?

He stared at his hasty barrier, arms numb, the reek of ozone and burnt *something* almost as thick in the air as Nate's own disbelief.

Had he just caught lightning?

I have you, little hobbit.

For a second, Nate was too relieved to think straight. Then Ex gave a cry of warning, and the Black Knight flashed forward and drove a devastating kick into his shield.

Nate wasn't sure how the Merlin avoided getting bowled over by his resultant flight, but by the time he stopped skidding, bouncing, and splashing across the ocean-soaked floor enough to make sense of things again, the crashes of impact and crumbling stone told him the two were already locked in combat up by the Beacon shrine.

He coughed, tasted blood, and tried to stand. His arms failed him. He tried again. The pain was distant—disembodied—but he could feel it there at the edges, shutting down control, demanding he lie still and stop this madness before he fell to literal pieces.

It occurred to him he might be dying.

Don't be dramatic. I am mending what I can.

Nate took a breath and tried again, this time managing to push up to his knees. The kicks. The falls. The super-powered body slams. How many times over would he have already been dead if it weren't for Ex?

You probably don't want to know that right now.

Ex was almost certainly right about that. He was thinking about making another try for his feet anyway when a pair of black boots winked into existence ahead. He looked up through the deepening dread in his gut. Up to those burning red eyes, and to the sight of the Black Knight raising his flaming sword to deliver the blow that even the Excalibur wouldn't be able to put back together.

He sagged down on his aching knees, no longer able to fight it.

Then the Merlin appeared between them in a booming flash of light, and the Black Knight sucker punched him without a moment's hesitation. Punched him so hard, so quickly, neither Nate nor the Merlin could seem to comprehend it. On the second punch, the Merlin staggered back into Nate. On the third blow, the Black Knight brought the pommel of his greatsword down on the Merlin's bushy-haired head with skull-shattering force, and the wizard hit the wet stone floor like a limp sack of meat.

A trap, Nate realized with a sickened feeling, as the Knight promptly waved a hand and dark chains sprang into existence, snaking the Merlin into a tight hog-tie. A trap baited and set by his own helpless, beaten body.

The Black Knight knelt to add a gag and dark hood to the Merlin's restraints, his movements brimming with a newfound energy—not excited, exactly, but satisfied. Reinvigorated. Like his plan was coming to perfect fruition.

Nate glanced at the Beacon, still patiently hovering there in its shrine, then back to the Knight, and decided it didn't matter what the titan's plan had been. The bastard was distracted, which meant this was probably the only shot he had left. So, he focused everything he had on his blaster, and raised his wrist to take it.

The Black Knight turned with eerily perfect timing and grace to palm the crackling blue blaster bolt Nate fired at the back of his head. Nate watched with a sinking heart, utterly defeated, as the blackened bastard's gauntlet visibly channeled the crackling energy to one pointing fingertip, preparing to spit it right back.

Then a copper blur streaked past and crashed into the Black Knight too hard for even his unstoppable ass to ignore.

Iveera, Nate thought with a faint flicker of hope, just before they crashed clean through a stone column and slammed into the far wall long enough for him to get a good look. It didn't last long before the Black Knight retaliated, and they fell into it properly.

The fighting was breathtakingly fast. Too fast for Nate to follow. The pair blurred through the cathedral like a swift wind that shattered everything it touched, kicking up a steady spray of icy ocean water from the floor, sparking a gout of flame here, a rapid-fire crash of thundering impacts there. For a few seconds, he was kneeling helplessly at the eye of a raging storm. Then the hyperspeed fight yanked to a halt with a wet thunk, and he felt the first flicker of hope at the sight of Iveera's spear buried deep in the Black Knight's shoulder.

She was actually *doing* it, he thought.

Then the Black Knight threw himself further onto Iveera's spear, caught her by the throat, and slammed her halfway through the adjacent stone column before Nate could so much as blink. The dark titan held the gorgon Knight aloft, pummeling her with a barrage of bone-crushing body shots. Nate clenched his teeth and clawed his way to his feet, desperate to help.

Ahead, Iveera's serpentine jin lashed out and caught the Black Knight's wrist as he reached to dislodge the spear from his shoulder. She kneed him in the groin, and he pulled her close by the throat and jin and slammed her into the stone again, hard enough that the entire column shattered with a deep, resonant crack, and buried them both in a rain of rock and dust.

Nate lurched forward on shaky feet, not really sure how anyone could've survived the downpour, yet unsurprised when his helmet vision showed movement in the resultant dust cloud. The two Knights emerged still struggling, the Black Knight's helm now snared tight by Iveera's jin right along with his hand. He released her throat, thrusting his unbound hand backward. Across the cathedral, his greatsword burst free from a pile of rubble, rocketing straight for his outstretched hand.

"NO!" Nate yelled, throwing himself forward and gunning his boot thrusters, not a thought in his head but to tackle the blackened bastard away from Iveera.

But the Knights both saw him coming, and they were faster.

Iveera retracted her jin grip and ripped free of the Black Knight as he spun to meet Nate. The dark titan caught him by the throat, effortlessly absorbing his headlong thruster charge with one hand even as he caught his speeding greatsword in the other.

Nate might've been dead then if Iveera hadn't ripped her spear free from the dark titan's shoulder and taken another try.

Her spear stabbed through nothing but thin air. It wasn't until Nate hit the ground, gasping for breath, that he understood why. The Black Knight was already halfway across the cathedral, scooping the Merlin's limp form up by the chains and turning for the dais at the head of the hall. Another flash step, and he was at the shrine with the Merlin, reaching a black gauntlet for the whirling Beacon.

Nate watched in a helpless stupor as Iveera leapt forward, rocketing toward the altar. Then the Black Knight palmed the Beacon, and a tsunami of wind and raw force detonated through the cathedral, hurling Iveera back and slapping Nate several splashing bounces across the stone.

"Blind fools," came the Black Knight's voice, carrying unnaturally on the Beacon's whipping winds. "Every last one of you."

Then the maelstrom died, and the Black Knight was gone, along with the Merlin and the Beacon.

Impossible, Ex whispered.

Nate only stared at the empty shrine, mind blank, barely even aware of Iveera landing softly in the shallow waters beside him. When he finally tore his eyes away to look up at her, she was fixed on the dais too, perfectly still, jin pressed flat to her head and expression safely hidden behind her faceplate.

He wanted to ask her what had just happened—where the Black Knight had gone, what the hell they were supposed to do now—but something about the way she was standing there told him he wasn't the only one who was lost right then.

He was still trying to get the words out anyway when a faint cracking sound trickled down from the dome, horribly crisp on the unnaturally still air.

"Iveera?" he heard himself croak.

Another crack rang down as he raised his eyes, and another. More of them. Accelerating. He could see them now, spiderwebbing out through the stone like a fractured window under too much load.

I think perhaps we should leave.

He opened his mouth to suggest as much. A deep, reverberating crack split the air before he could, thin streams of water spouting from a dozen different points on the dome.

"Oh fuck," Nate whispered.

Then the lost city of Atlantis began raining down on their heads.

CHAPTER 44

COLLAPSE

Iveera didn't bother with words, just hefted him effortlessly to his feet and dragged him rather violently along toward the cathedral doors until he got himself under control enough to follow her lead. Even then, she didn't let go. Spurred on by the heavy splashing thud of falling stone somewhere behind, Nate didn't argue.

It was only when they reached the open doors that Iveera slowed, drawing to a halt with a frustrated hiss. Outside, water was falling on the city of Atlantis in too many places to count—a streaming trickle here, and fire hydrant jet stream there. Nate listened to the dome's spreading song of cracking glass in mesmerized horror, recalling what Ex had said about the Beacon potentially being the one thing that'd kept this city standing for the past thousand years.

"We will ascend from here," Iveera said, yanking his attention back to the cathedral, where she was studying the hemorrhaging ceiling with a focus he didn't like one bit. "Can you manage?" she called without looking back.

"Manage?" Nate gaped from her retreating form back toward the cavernous landing bay they'd come down in. "But your ship—"

"Is dead for now," she called, turning to face him from a ways down the aisle. She didn't flinch as a large hunk of stone slammed down to the growing pool beside her. "We will make our own way."

His heart sped up, the sounds of the cracking dome and the unfathomable weight above all pressing in that much closer. Trapped under an ocean. No ship. No way out.

"And Groshna?" he croaked, taking a few steps after her, trying to watch everywhere at once for falling boulders.

"Groshna has paid the price for his betrayal," Iveera said, pacing backward, still looking up, until she drew to a halt just shy of a rapidly thickening jet stream from the cathedral dome.

He barely heard her words—wasn't even sure why he'd asked at all, outside of some feeble attempt to distract the icy hands of fear clenching down on his lungs. It didn't work. Especially not when she looked down from the cracking panel above to focus on him. "Are you ready to fly?"

"Ready?" Nate looked desperately from Iveera to the cracking dome and back. "I can't—"

But she took off like a copper rocket before he could get another word out. He had a second to gape, then she punched straight through the panel high above, and there was nothing but the sound of shattering and the roaring rush of water.

Blind terror spiked from his manhood up to his eyeballs as the first wild wave crested through the cathedral and slapped into his knees with startling force. Then the ceiling started to collapse in earnest.

Focus.

"Focus my ass!" Nate screamed, diving clear of a falling hunk of stone that could've crushed a troglodan. He floated more than pushed his way to his feet. Christ, the water was rising fast. To his hips already, rushing past him, pushing him toward the open cathedral door. A fist-sized rock struck his helmet, and he almost slipped and lost it. Too much water, filling up. The wall wouldn't hold behind him. And when it went, he'd—

Focus, Nathaniel.

Breathing too fast for actual air, vision swimming with ripples of blackness, Nate somehow found the widening hole Iveera had torn through the dome high above. Then he pointed his fists like freaking Superman and *flew* as hard as he could, not thinking about the thrusters, or the control, just screaming for the flight to happen with every ounce of his frantic will.

He broke clear of the chest-high water just as the rear of the cathedral gave out behind him. He flew harder, straight for the torrential downpour above, doing his best not to think about the drowning city around him. What he *should* have been thinking about was the fact that he was about to plunge straight into a vacuum current. But he found that out quickly enough anyway.

He lost control the moment he punched through the opening, raging currents spinning him like a goddamn umbrella in a hurricane. He fired the thrusters harder. Smashed into a solid surface. Tried to thrust away from it, and only spun faster. He fought helplessly against the currents, terrified he was about to be sucked back into the drowning city, gunning his thrusters and frantically trying to discern up from down. He hit the dome again. Felt it crumbling beneath him. Spun some more. Gunned the thrusters.

"Help!" he gasped in the frantic whirl, lungs paralyzed, icy ocean water crushing in from every direction. "Help me!"

He wasn't sure who he was praying to. He just lost it—kicking and thrashing like a madman, blindly jetting through the fading blue luminescence of the dying city, no godly idea which way was up or down.

It didn't matter that he had air in his helmet, or that the deep ocean pressure didn't seem to be killing him outright. He couldn't breathe anyway. By the time he calmed himself down enough to actually start thinking, he couldn't see a damn thing, either.

He was floating. He knew that. He rotated slowly, searching for the glint of sunlight, or any sign of the drowned city, but it was complete and utter darkness down there, even to his helmet vision.

He forced a deep breath. It only accentuated the hammering pulse in his ears and throat, and the crushing expanse all around. But he *could* still breathe. He wasn't being crushed. He just had to find his way up. Ex hovered there at the edge of his mind, waiting to see what he'd do—if he'd ask for help. Nate took another breath and tried to think, hesitant to debase himself even further after having just lost his shit so completely. He could figure this out. Ex seemed content to let him.

All he needed was a gauge. Something that would reliably rise in the water. Something he could see.

Tentatively, he willed there to be light. It blazed into existence from his chest and shoulder plates, casting illuminating rays that, while quite bright, didn't penetrate the darkness nearly far enough to spot any substantial landmarks. What it did illuminate, though, were the bubbles. Thousands of them. Millions, maybe. The dying breath of the lost city of Atlantis, pointing his way back home.

It was a sobering reminder of everything they'd just lost.

Moving as calmly as his leaping heart would allow, he orientated himself in parallel with the rising streams and eased on the thrusters. He focused on his breathing as he went, keeping course with the bubbles, wondering each and every moment how deep he was, how much farther he had to go. As if in response to the repeating question, a translucent blue number winked to life at the bottom left of his helmet display: *-2,833m.*

A little under three kilometers, he registered after a moment's surprise, and the number was ticking steadily upward, rising closer to zero by several meters each second.

Nate couldn't help it. He gunned the thrusters harder, his relief surging in synchrony with the altimeter's race to zero. For a few seconds, he was so giddy with the sudden likelihood of survival that he almost ribbed Ex about feeding metric units to an American. Then he saw the first faint ghost of daylight overhead, and he forgot about everything else.

Fast as he was going by that point, the last kilometer seemed to bleed away over an eternity. He almost laughed when he found himself holding his breath in anticipation. Then he broke through some critical depth, and the agonizingly slow approach of the distant light shifted into high gear.

He broke the surface of the Atlantic Ocean with an unfiltered cry of relief, already willing his helmet to return back to Ex's magical storage locker. The helmet complied, peeling back and flooding his face with the first kiss of blessedly fresh air he'd tasted since he'd rode the grav lift down that stormy cyclone portal.

For a few wonderful seconds, he just hung there, too relieved at first to even realize he'd unconsciously accomplished the previously unmanageable feat of coming to a controlled hover. Taking in the sight of the ocean thirty or so feet below, he almost lost the precarious balance. When he managed to steady out this time, it was with a grin and a ripple of self-satisfaction.

Then he noticed the troglodan ship in the distance, and the copper-armored figure watching him from her own perfectly stable hover closer by, and his giddiness went the way of Atlantis.

"Good," came her directionless voice across the distance, as if he still had his helmet earpieces in. But the method of her communication was the least of his immediate concerns.

"Good?" he growled, anger rising at the complete lack of empathy in her tone. "You left me to die down there! I fought my ass off to help you, and you just—"

A twitch of movement was the only warning he had before she was rocketing toward him. Time might've slowed, but he still wasn't nearly fast enough to dodge the gorgon. She crashed into him, driving them both down.

They hit the water fast enough to hurt, but a wet smack on the back was hardly his biggest concern as she plunged them farther into the depths. He felt the panic returning. Felt her pushing him deeper. He wasted precious seconds clawing at her titanium grip before it occurred to him to get his helmet back on. It snapped back into shape around his head with a frantic thought, the excess water draining away down his neck and chest and pumping out elsewhere.

"Are you drowning, human?" Iveera asked, faceplate going transparent seemingly just so he could see her electric blue glare. They weren't moving any longer.

Nate took a few shaky breaths in the safety of his helmet, refusing to play her game and state the obvious.

"I left you to survive," she said, quiet fury in her tone, "and if you are not prepared to contend with that, then I had best do the merciful thing and reclaim your Excalibur now."

Nate stopped struggling, searching her alien face for some sign of intent. All he saw was his own anger reflected in her burning eyes. "What's your problem with me? I did what you asked. I—"

"Spare me your indignant self-pity. You have no idea what manner of hell we have wrought on the galaxy this day."

She released him then and allowed them to float apart, regaining her cool composure. "The Beacon is lost, and the Merlin captured. That alone constitutes a greater calamity than I can adequately convey. But so too have both of our Excaliburs been… contaminated. By what, I cannot yet say. So too have the old treaties been broken."

She wavered, almost as if she wanted to look away.

"So too has my crew been murdered," she said softly, her swirling jin flattening down against her head. "Murdered by a member of my own order. Murdered by the savage bearing this."

She produced a small dark *something* from e-dim. Nate didn't have to look too closely to recognize Marty's earpiece.

"And yet you persist, human. You persist while five valiant souls lie scattered and wasted below. You persist. Bearing an Excalibur, no less."

He stared at the quantcomm node in her hand, wanting to deny it all, wanting to point out that there'd been a hell of a lot more than *five* good souls lost today, and that it was *her* fault he'd been separated from his friends when the trogs had found them—her fault the trogs had even found them at all, goddammit. He wanted to be furious with her. Wanted to scream that this was her fault every bit as much as his, that he hadn't asked for one damn bit of any of this.

But he wasn't sure he believed any of it.

"I'm sorry," he found himself whispering.

He *was* furious with her on some deep, smoldering level. Or he would be, he imagined, once he'd had time to actually process everything that had happened in the past twelve hours. But right then, floating in the dim depths of the ocean while Atlantis sputtered out beneath them and the world above still ran rampant with the ongoing trog invasion—still missing the only four people he longed to see...

He was tired. And he hurt. And tough and collected as she was, he couldn't imagine Iveera felt any better right now.

"I'm sorry."

Iveera's jin swayed lightly back and forth in the silence, like maybe he'd misunderstood some point.

"It is not the drowning that kills an Excalibur Knight," she finally said, and something in the way she said it made him sure he'd missed the point this time. She sounded beyond weary. Positively ancient. But she shook it off, focusing back on him. "You no longer have the luxury of apologizing your mistakes away. You no longer have any luxury at all. Not on this side of death. Do you understand?"

Nate dropped her gaze, sure that he didn't, but sobered anyway by the words, and by the tone that was dangerously close to something sympathetic. He didn't understand a damn thing.

Secure the Beacon. Save the planet from trog invasion. That had been the plan. The *entire* plan. But the plan had gone to shit, and now...

A school of fish flitted by, glinting blue and silver in the dim rays of daylight. He felt an embarrassingly potent surge of resentment at their aquatic freedom.

Now, he didn't know what.

Somehow, in all his infinite wisdom, he'd never really stopped to think about what was going to happen if he actually completed the Merlin's insane task. *Back to school,* he realized, had been the default assumption. Planetary crisis averted, life was supposed to return back to normal, where he could start licking his wounds and righting the course of his failed semester. Where he could have his *life* back, for the love of Christ. Where he could be with Gwen, and his friends, and Copernicus. Where they were all still alive. Still with him.

He felt sick.

He felt like sinking back down into the ocean and never moving again. Wasn't sure how he ever *could* move again. Because this was happening. They *hadn't* secured the Beacon. They'd lost it to that dark titan. They'd lost the Merlin. And now the troglodans were still here. And so was Nate, stuck right here in the ocean depths, being baptized by an alien Knight straight into this holy pile of galactic shit he had no business being involved in.

"Do you understand?" Iveera's voice broke into his thoughts.

He focused back to where she was watching him, not even remembering what it was he was *supposed* to have understood.

"If I had thought you were going to die down there," she said, "I would have shown you the mercy myself. I left you to survive, Nathaniel Arturi. And now there is much to be rectified, and precious little time."

No luxury. That was it. Not on this side of death.

He stared into nowhere, wanting to protest that he hadn't signed up for this Spartan agoge bullshit. But he hadn't exactly been chosen either, had he? Much as it pained him to even think it, no one else had reached his hand out and pulled that damned sword from the stone. No one but him, and his supreme lack of forethought.

"Come," Iveera said, apparently accepting his silence for answer enough. "The troglodan forces will scatter when they learn what has become of their Dread Lord, but they may well require a firm push, and every minute we tarry is another minute our true quarry escapes."

She looked up toward the surface then pointedly back to him, faceplate darkening in preparation. "Are you ready?"

No way in any of their nine hells was he ready. Not for any of this.

He nodded anyway.

"Follow me," was all she said.

Then the gorgon Knight rocketed out of the dark ocean depths, bound straight for the lone troglodan ship still hovering over the drowned city of Atlantis.

CHAPTER 45

THE NEW DEAL

Staring silently at the enormous, glassy-eyed head lying on the grimy deck absent a body, Nate had to wonder for the hundredth time why Iveera couldn't have simply taken a picture—or a holo or whatever —to show the troglodans. But maybe he was being naïve. The trophy of The Dread Knight Groshna's severed head *had* worked well enough to earn a quick surrender from the crew, after all.

Then again, that might've also had something to do with the raw power Iveera had put on display blasting into the bridge of the lone trog carrier remaining above Atlantis. Or with the fact that the *other* trog carrier was no longer anywhere to be seen since the gorgon Knight had cut loose up here to buy Nate time below.

Evidently, even war-mongering space ogres could recognize when they were hopelessly outmatched. Not that that had stopped a single trog on the bridge from visibly itching to murder Iveera and have Nate for a light snack at the first possible opportunity, but at least they'd held their tongues since the initial burst of posturing and fist-related threats.

Now, they flew in nearly absolute silence, save for the thuds and whirs of the mechanic crew that was hard at work repairing the damage of Iveera's violently direct entry.

Nate looked over at the gorgon, wondering again why she'd opted to hitch a ride at all when they could've ostensibly limped by with what was left of Groshna's ship, or even flown back on their own power.

"Better this way," was all she'd said on the matter.

Given that Ex had agreed with her, Nate hadn't bothered to argue. What exactly they were going to tell the troglodan commander in New York, he still had no idea, but he was starting to trust Iveera knew what she was doing.

Wise, little hobbit. Now perhaps you should stop staring.

Nate blinked back from his thoughts and realized he was still fixed on Iveera. For a half-second, he thought about trying to copy her little silent communication trick to ask her one or two of the few thousand questions eating at his mind, but before he could even try, her serpentine jin gave a curt horizontal slash in what he assumed was a sign for *not now*, or *keep your bloody eyes to yourself.*

He turned his gaze forward and occupied himself with avoiding troglodan eye contact and trying not to think too hard about what Iveera had planned for him and Ex if and when the troglodans packed up and left the planet like she seemed so sure they would.

Any luck figuring out what he did to us in there? he wondered at Ex, who'd been uncharacteristically quiet since he'd started scanning his systems for traces of the Black Knight's so-called contamination. So far, they had no more clue about what the blackened bastard had done to them than they did about where he'd flashed off to with the Beacon and the one man who might've actually been able to answer their questions.

My self-diagnostics have yet to turn up any notable irregularities, Ex said, after an abnormally long pause. *Only that the... intelligence was attempting to access my executive functions. And quite discreetly, at that.*

Nate recalled the torturous episode with an inward cringe. Discreet was about the last word he would've used.

Decoys and distractions, mostly. Pain and a host of system-wide attacks designed to interrupt our coherence and obfuscate the true target, I believe.

Okay. And it was... only an attempt? You're not about to go all Skynet on me or anything?

My self-diagnostics have yet to turn up any notable irregularities, Nathaniel, Ex repeated in a robotic monotone.

Ha-ha.

It IS possible the process was simply prematurely terminated by the Merlin's arrival.

The comment sounded too speculative for Nate's liking.

Highly likely, his companion amended, clearly sensing his concern. *Rest assured, if I should happen to turn into a maniacal traitor, you will be the first to know.*

Kind of my point here, Ex, Nate thought, shaking his head.

Iveera flicked him a sideways glance, like she wasn't quite sure whether his shaking head was sloppy, or just an odd twitch Earthlings were prone to at times. Nate was just starting to settle back into his own little world when Ex spoke again.

There is something else.

Nate waited several seconds. *Yeah?*

It's... highly uncertain.

He frowned. *The suspense is killing me, Ex. What is it?*

Only that, in the aftermath, I was struck by a strange feeling that—

A strange feeling?

Do you want to hear this or not?

Of course I do. It's just, well, I didn't know you did, you know... strange feelings.

Call it an artifact in the signal or a recursive data stream harmonic if that makes you feel better about your squishy human words. I am telling you there is something here.

Despite everything, Nate couldn't help but grin a little at actually having Ex in a tizzy rather than the other way around. He was even thinking about going so far as to point out that that all sounded an awful lot like *superstition* when Ex spoke up.

Something about the Black Knight, Nathaniel.

His grin evaporated. *What kind of strange feeling?*

The kind that would appear to be reaching past my memory restrictions to tell me that that blackened fiend was there on the day Arthur Pendragon died. And no, to answer your next question: that one's not in the history archives.

Nate felt his mouth hanging open at patient attention while his brain struggled to chew that one down to something workable.

How is that—

"We approach your city of New York, Runt Knight," rumbled a voice from behind, catching Nate's scattered thoughts like a battering ram. He blinked around to where the trog captain was favoring him with a look of pure disgust.

"Kindly be prepared to piss off," the captain all but spat before turning his beady-eyed glare to Iveera, then down to Groshna's head and back again. "And may the blackened pits swallow you whole for what you've done, gorgon."

Iveera held the captain's gaze until the troglodan flinched away, then she plucked the Dread Knight's head from the deck and stalked off of the bridge without a word. Nate, realizing a few shocked seconds later that he was still standing there, surrounded by twenty trogs undoubtedly itching to rip his spine out, promptly followed, doing his best not to flinch as the frustrated captain rounded on his crew and began barking harsh orders to make preparations for their arrival.

∾

THE FACT that Nate actually took some small comfort in jumping out of an alien ship a half mile above the smoking New York City skyline seemed to say a lot about how far he'd come since this madness had started.

Of course, it might've also had something to do with the thirty or so glaring trogs that'd paused in their work to watch him and Iveera go, and the way they'd eagerly eyed Nate the moment the gorgon had dropped out of sight.

Either way, he was glad to make his leave from the troglodan carrier. At least until he remembered that, Excalibur Knight or not, learning to fly with any amount of grace was going to take some doing. Not that *looking good* was exactly chief among his concerns as he dropped into a herky-jerky hover, and oriented himself after Iveera's smoothly sailing form.

Even so, you would be wise to try gravitonic manipulation over these crude thrusters of yours.

"And you're just telling me this now?" Nate muttered, scared that even that small effort might throw him off his precarious balance.

I would have done so earlier, had your mind not been chittering like a frightened squirrel at every pertinent moment. It is hard to make myself heard over such racket.

Well forgive me for being human.

Someday, perhaps.

Nate ignored the Excalibur, trying instead to think about the gravitonic lifts he'd encountered. He had no idea how the things worked, but he tried to evoke a similar effect from his armor anyway, mostly just thinking *floaty* thoughts. There might've been a slight steadying of his jerky thruster dance. He couldn't really tell. He was too busy staring down at the war zone that'd become of New York.

"Come now," Iveera said in his helmet comms. "Keep up."

With a careful thought and even more careful movements, Nate angled himself around and thrust off after the gorgon, not quite able to pry his eyes away from the ruined streets below, and the bodies that littered entirely too many of them.

"Why did they do this?" he asked quietly, almost to himself. "If they were just looking for me and the Beacon…"

"Perhaps they intended to distract from their main objectives," came Iveera's voice in his ears. "Given the number of major cities they currently occupy, it's possible they bore intentions of establishing a more permanent foothold on this planet. There was even a time when the Greater Troglodan Empire might've committed such atrocities for little more than the simple sport and spoils of conquest. But something is afoul with this entire operation."

"The Black Knight?"

"Let us find out if that is the entirety of it," she said, angling around one of the taller skyscrapers and setting off for what Nate was pretty sure must be Central Park, where several troglodan ships had congregated overhead, presumably to monitor the operation below.

It was another few blocks before he saw the extent of it. The dull roar of voices preceded line of sight, tinged with an edge of hysteria that set the scene even before Nate cleared the last line of buildings and caught sight of the crowd.

There were thousands of people in the park. Tens of thousands of desolate men, women, and children herded in like cattle by patrolling troglodans and a crude network of barriers and crackling energy beams.

Some shook their fists, yelling at the passing trog patrols, who either ignored them completely or rewarded them here and there with a bone-crushing smack or a prod of the oversized stun rod. Most just huddled together in some futile search for safety. He spotted a few army combat uniforms scattered throughout the pens, but most of the military personnel looked to have been sorted over to a separate holding area on the near end of the park. Which was exactly where Iveera was headed.

Prisoners and troglodans alike looked up at their arrival—the humans pointing and shouting, the trogs mostly just aiming their weapons, clearly raring for a fight.

Iveera alighted to a graceful landing at the edge of the park, striding from the air down to the grass like a glimmering warrior goddess. Nate, by contrast, thudded down beside her with all the grace of a drunk hippopotamus. He tucked into a roll out of necessity and staggered back to his feet, painfully aware both of the battered state of his body and of the multiple tufts of grassy dirt he'd pick up on impact.

"Allow me to do the talking," Iveera said, starting forward with a thankful lack of commentary about his shoddy landing. She headed straight for the gates at the head of the trog encampment. Plucking a dangling clump of dirt from his helmet, Nate followed her.

Despite having been there when the good captain had radioed ahead that two diplomatic envoys were inbound, Nate was still a bit surprised when the perimeter guards *didn't* open fire. Maybe they had some kind of troglodan warrior code or galactic wartime law to thank for that. Or maybe the trogs, like Nate, were honestly just not sure whether they could take Iveera down, even outnumbering her several thousand to one.

"Is this... just, like, business as usual for you?" he asked nervously, glancing from the wall of pointing cannons to the troglodan head still dangling from her hand.

She didn't see fit to dignify that with an answer.

Once inside the rust red encampment walls, it wasn't hard to guess who was in charge. From what little Nate had picked up on, there seemed to be a pretty reliable correlation between physical size and rank, and the troglodan stomping through the yard was nearly as big as Groshna had been. His hide was a darker gray, mottled with muddy spots beneath his imposing blue armor. And he looked pissed.

Four military men were bound and on their knees in front of the trog commander. Judging by the behemoth's agitated pacing, whatever was happening didn't look to be going well for them. Especially not when the commander caught sight of Iveera and her Groshna trophy, and completely lost his shit.

Whether self-control simply wasn't a critical virtue in trog leadership or this trog was just having a spectacularly shitty day, Nate didn't know. But he hardly blamed the two military guys who pitched over backward as the commander roared and backhanded a rather large, heavy-looking crate across the yard. He didn't blame the third man, who hit the dirt moving forward, head tucked and shoulders packed in survivor mode.

It was the fourth man Nate didn't understand.

The guy barely flinched. Just took a steely-eyed look over to Nate and Iveera, assessed both them and the severed head in the gorgon's hand, then turned back to the troglodan commander. "Whatever this is, Commander, I need you to—"

"Silence, insect!" barked the commander. "This does not concern you and your pathetic world."

As the trog spoke, an awkward, mechanical voice regurgitated the words over again with a slight delay, and Nate realized he must be listening both to Ex's translation and to whatever translator the troglodan was packing to communicate with the humans. The effect was a little disorienting, but hardly chief of Nate's worries.

Especially not when the military man with balls of steel coolly replied, "With all due respect, Commander, if it happens on this world, it concerns me."

For a second, the trog commander looked too taken aback at the raw insolence to even react. Then he bared his teeth and stomped forward, clearly satisfied to have found such a willing outlet for his fury.

"Do not touch him, troglodan," Iveera snapped as the commander reached for the man.

The troglodan hesitated, slitted nostrils working furiously at the air. Nate half-expected the creature might simply explode with unspent rage.

"You know who I am," Iveera said. "Let us not mince words and idle threats. I have come to demand your immediate withdrawal from this planet."

With that, she tossed her trophy forward.

Groshna's head hit the ground right between the trog commander and the balls of steel army man, and stuck the landing with a disgusting wet *thunk*. The commander rippled with a low, ominous growl that was taken up by every troglodan soldier in the vicinity.

The army guy, on the other hand, just cocked his head at the gruesome trophy. "Pardon my interruption," he said, turning back to Iveera, "but if you're about to make some kind of declaration of war on our planet, I'd prefer if we could all understand what's being said."

Maybe it was just the slight drawl talking, but Nate couldn't believe how calm the guy sounded. It was only when Iveera glanced over at him that he registered what the man meant. Iveera had somehow been speaking in troglodan, and now she was offering Nate a chance to be useful here.

"It's okay," he said, showing his empty hands to the army man before realizing his lack of visible weapons might be the opposite of reassuring, given what he said next. "We're here to get them off this planet."

The army man looked like he might have a few things to say about that, but the trog commander beat him to it with a harsh bark of laughter. He relayed Nate's words to his soldiers, adding a few choice insults of his own, and soon the entire yard was filled with chortling troglodans.

"You slay our Knight," boomed the commander, pointing to Iveera. "You defile his memory, and offer us open insult. Why should we pay any mind to your so-called authority? Why should we not enjoy the weak spines and bountiful spoils of this planet?"

"Have you no respect for the old treaties, troglodan?" Iveera asked.

The commander spat in the dirt. "I respect the old treaties as you respected our Dread Lord, gorgon."

"And do you wish to see Trogarra burn for your crimes?"

"Crimes." The commander growled the word like a curse. "The Alliance does not give an olar's shit about this planet. It is nothing more than the Merlin's backwater playground, and fair salvage at that, I wager, under the accords. They would not dare risk war with my people over these insects."

"Then I would see Trogarra burn myself!" Iveera boomed, her voice amplified for all to hear and brimming with an authority nearly as dark and fearsome as the ground-shaking bellow the Black Knight had loosed back in the lost city.

The encampment fell silent around them, troglodans and prisoners alike all watching the gorgon until she released the spell—not relaxing her proud stance so much as somehow releasing the tension from the air itself.

"And I imagine I would have little trouble finding allies in the endeavor," she added, almost off-handedly. "The Asgardians, for instance, would no doubt revel at the chance after the dishonor your noble emperor recently bestowed upon their queen."

Nate was already frowning at the word *Asgardian* when the commander made a disgusted sound and grunted, "Bah. Neo-Terran scum."

I will explain later, Ex promised, as the commander pressed on.

"You propose to do away with idle threats, gorgon, and yet here you stand, speaking as if you are not cut off on this planet, alone and surrounded, and outnumbered by the tens of thousands."

"Then give the order and have done with it," Iveera said, her jin swirling calmly through the air. "Your Dread Lord failed to destroy me with two full carriers of reinforcements at his side," she added, pointedly looking up to the three massive ships floating low over the park, then back down to their leader. "Do you think you can do better, Commander?"

Nate was no negotiation specialist, but he was pretty sure by the tangible tightening of every alien trigger finger in the encampment—not to mention the tightening of his own scrotum—that those words had constituted the last straw. The gauntlet was irrevocably thrown to the troglodan commander: initiate open war with an Excalibur Knight—possibly even one-and-a-half of them—or turn tail and forever lose the respect of his fist-happy armada.

The commander hovered on the moment, muddy gray jowls caught in a perpetual snarl, until one of his underlings came shuffling up to pass a quiet message into his ear. Whatever it was—if it was anything at all, and not just a good underling tossing his boss a nice lifeline—a brief moment of surprise crossed the commander's face before he nodded and turned back to Iveera.

"Word from your new master?" she asked.

The commander only sneered and puffed up to his full formidable height, as if the question wasn't worthy of a response. "Mark my words, Ser Katanaga. You will burn for what has happened here." At a gesture, one of his underlings shuffled forward to collect Groshna's head from the grass. "For now, however, we will agree to withdraw until such time as the will of the Council can be made clear, and my people's Excalibur returned to its rightful owner."

Nate felt Ex bristle at the last bit, even as Iveera's jin made a sharp slash through the air.

"An Excalibur has no owner, troglodan," she said. "Only a partner. And such honors are not decided on the authority of the Council. Your people will reap what you sow, Commander. Nothing more, and nothing less."

"Mmm," the trog commander grunted, looking satisfied to have ruffled her feathers, even if it was only by a hair's breadth. "Rest assured then, gorgon, that I will personally look forward to the reaping."

With one last sneer at the lot of them, he turned and started barking orders for his soldiers to pack up and return to the ships. To Nate's relief, no one argued. The trogs sprang into action, packing up what supplies and fortifications they deemed worth bothering with. Nate was just letting out the breath he hadn't noticed he'd been holding when the commander turned back like he'd forgotten something and stooped down to jut his face closer to the calm and collected military man who'd spoken earlier.

"The Greater Troglodan Empire hereby expresses its apologies for this minor misunderstanding, human. May we meet again in honor and glory."

Nate wasn't positive how well Ex's translations conveyed nuances like sarcasm and unspoken threats, but if the trog commander was apologetic, then Nate was a ten foot clown named Bo-Bo. Mr. Balls of Steel, who'd somehow become the voice of Earth in the matter, seemed to feel about the same.

"I'll be sure my superiors get your message, Commander," he said, holding the troglodan's gaze steady.

The commander eyed the man with an odd expression—like he couldn't quite decide whether he wanted to eat him or be impressed. Then he turned and stomped off into the encampment, booming orders all the way.

All around the park, trogs were busy hauling supplies to their ships' waiting grav lifts. The human prisoners, they essentially paid no mind to, save for the few who moved about, powering down energy beam perimeters and removing collars and shackles from those few who'd been individually restrained. Even then, the trogs seemed more concerned with reclaiming their property than with the freedom of the prisoners themselves. The rest, they simply ceased to notice—taking some minor care not to step on them as they went about packing up, maybe, but making no effort to stop or acknowledge them.

Like goddamn insects.

As soon as it became clear that the gates had all been unlocked and that the first brave wave of fleeing civilians wasn't going to be ruthlessly gunned down, the exodus from Central Park began en masse.

Nate was watching it unfold, feeling a bit like the college party wallflower who didn't know what to do with his hands, when he noticed that Mr. Balls, Voice of Earth, was talking with Iveera. Or talking *at* her, more accurately.

"—ot saying I'm not grateful for whatever galactic rank you just pulled, Ma'am. I'm just asking you to explain to me what it is our planet just signed up for. My people need to know."

Iveera looked from him to Nate and tilted her head ever so slightly, inviting him to do something useful and deal with his own kind. He blew out a breath and went to crouch beside Mr. Balls, reaching out to inspect the man's shackles.

"Don't take this the wrong way, man," Nate said, taking a firm grip and preparing to snap the chain, "but you might be the craziest bastard I've met all day. And it's been a day."

"Well, shucks," said Mr. Balls in that easy drawl. "That sure means a lot, coming from you, Nate."

Nate froze, too surprised to even think about how to handle that. If he'd had any shot at denying the stab at his identity, though, it probably went out the window the moment he reached up and patted his faceplate just to make sure it was still there.

It was.

"How...?"

Before he could decide how to finish the question, the guy's shackles fell to the grass of their own accord, and he offered a hand to Nate, casual as could freaking be. That was when Nate noticed the emblem on his shoulder. The same emblem he'd seen in more than a few internet searches these past weeks.

"Lieutenant Colonel Jaeger of the 501st SAS," said Mr. Balls, his smile friendly, and his eyes perfectly piercing. "I'd say I'm pleased to meet you, kid, but frankly I think we have a hell of a lot more important things to talk about."

CHAPTER 46

NO RUSH

"So… Excalibur Knight, huh? Sounds serious."

Nate looked down at the hand Lt. Col. Jaeger had just taken in the pretense of a handshake that quickly turned into a full on inspection.

"This doesn't really look like it's from around here, Nate. Can I call you Nate?"

"Uh…"

"Never mind that, Nate. What I'm really wondering here is how you got caught up in all of this, and what it is that you and your friend are actually doing here."

Nate looked up and met Jaeger's dark-eyed stare, and it only really then struck him just how boned he could be if and when the rest of the world found out who and what he was. Before, it had been one thing, trying to hide the voice in his head and some bizarre YouTube footage, half sure he'd simply lost his mind. But now?

"Uh…"

Looking at the chaos and ruin all around them, Nate was pretty sure he didn't want to know what manner of dark hidey hole Uncle Sam might be looking to throw him in after all of this, or what they'd do to find out how he'd come by mysterious alien tech, and why—if he wasn't some kind of traitor to humanity—he hadn't seen fit to go straight to the authorities with everything he knew the instant the Merlin approached him.

Never mind that he actually *had* tried.

There was a soft hiss from behind. Iveera, he realized. Exasperated.

"We are envoys of the Galactic Alliance," she said. "And we would do well to remember that."

You are embarrassing us, Nathaniel.

Nate sighed and rocked back to stand, too flustered in the moment to remember his hand was still in Jaeger's grip. Whether he meant to or not, Jaeger came along for the ride.

"Well," he said, releasing Nate's hand and taking a step back, clearly a little thrown off by Nate's unexpected strength. "Friendly as that sounds, it doesn't exactly tell me much."

"I came to your planet to put an end to this unlawful invasion, and to remove the artifact that drew the troglodans here to begin with."

"That's… accurate," Nate said at Jaeger's questioning glance.

"And now, if you don't mind, Lt. Col. Jaeger," Iveera said, taking Nate rather firmly by the elbow, "I must speak with my… colleague in private."

"No disrespect, Ma'am, but it's my duty to mind."

It was only then that Nate noticed the small huddle of soldiers that'd formed up around them, not quite boxing them in, but not far off. Several shot uncertain glances at Jaeger when Iveera began to drag Nate away, like they were waiting for the orders to step up and stop them.

"Wait," he found himself saying, tugging back against Iveera's unbudging grip. She looked at him as if he were a puppy who'd just figured out how to talk, but he was already turning back to Jaeger, stuck on a tiny wisp of hope. "Tessa Kalders. She's one of yours?"

Jaeger glanced back and forth between him and Iveera, calculating, then his mouth drew into a grim line, and he gave Nate a nod that set his stomach sinking. "She is. But she's MIA, I'm sorry to say."

Nate blew out a shaky breath, hearing Marty's voice all over again, Groshna's sneering face hanging over his friends' unmoving bodies in his mind's eye.

"She was with some friends of yours, from what I gathered. I'm guessing you already knew that. Last contact we made, they were headed this way. She told me what you'd said about New York." He glanced at Iveera. "Told me you got nabbed, too. Tried to tell me more, but…" He shook his head. "We lost 'em somewhere outside Philly."

Something in Nate perked up at that.

"Could be they ran into some jamming," Jaeger was saying. "Or got themselves caught."

Twenty minutes. That was it.

It couldn't have been more than twenty minutes after Iveera had grabbed him from McClanahan's that he'd heard the distress call from Marty. If Tessa had made it as far as Philadelphia…

"Truth be told," Jaeger said, looking around the encampment, "I was sorta hoping we'd show up here and find them taking names, you know?"

Nate blinked back to the present. "You still came to New York after all this had…?"

He trailed off, remembering that he was talking to an Air Force colonel, and not some amateur alien conspiracy nut. Jaeger just showed him a hard grin—the kind that said he was kind of amused, and also kind of capable of killing a man with his pinky.

"That's the job, kid. Not many units trained for first contact response with ETs, believe it or not."

"Been a real fuckin' hoot so far, sir," chimed one of the nearby soldiers, rather plainly listening in. He had an SAS emblem on his shoulder too.

"At any rate, New York was the closest thing we had to a lead on this Beacon of yours." Jaeger looked between them, watching for some reaction. "Don't suppose either of you might be able to fill us in on that bit, by the way?"

Nate felt Iveera's sideways glance, but if she was miffed by the fact that he'd clearly told someone something, she didn't press it. Just renewed her grip on his elbow like it was time to move. "The Beacon is no longer any concern of yours, Lieutenant Colonel Jaeger. Nor of any immediate concern to your planet. Now—"

"And what about un-immediately?" Jaeger pressed. "All due respect, Ma'am, but we're flying blind here. Why am I gettin' the feelin' we just opened Pandora's box?"

Nate opened his mouth to explain that one to Iveera, but her Excalibur must've parsed it for her, because she was already nodding. "The analogy is serviceable, and you are correct. Earth will indeed have little choice but to confront certain truths about its station in the galaxy moving forward."

As she said the last words, a thin, matte gray disc appeared in her armored palm, and she offered it out to Jaeger. "See to it your superiors receive this. It is the standard Alliance outreach protocol, designed for cases such as this one. It will tell your people everything they need to know."

Jaeger took the disc from her, frowning curiously at the plain-looking device. Iveera took one last look at the departing troglodans ascending their grav lifts, began to turn away with Nate in tow, and paused.

"You may also wish to inform your superiors that there are downed troglodan carriers at these locations," she added, reaching out a slender finger to touch the disc, which sprang to life with a holo map dotted with multiple red blips and coordinates. "I trust you will find your uses."

And with that, she turned and stalked off, pulling Nate along with her. The troops didn't quite move aside, but nor did that really matter when the ground fell away beneath them, and Nate and Iveera both rose a good ten feet on what his wriggling stomach informed him must be Iveera's gravitonics.

That got a murmur from the troops.

"Ma'am?" Jaeger called after them. "My superiors would like to talk to both of you. In person. Standard outreach protocol or not."

Iveera slowed, swiveling to face them. Nate, by default, went along like a nervously panting puppy riding side carriage, whether he liked it or not.

"I understand, Colonel," Iveera said. "Alas, we have a matter of some urgency to discuss. So unless you wish to attempt without your weapons what the armada above was frightened to attempt with theirs, we will make our leave now."

"Lady makes a good point, sir," said the SAS guy who'd spoken earlier.

Jaeger didn't answer. He was too busy boring holes into Nate's faceplate in what might've been stare-speak for *c'mon, kid, help a fellow human out here,* or maybe something more like *c'mon, kid, you really think you can fly away from this one? You really think we won't find you?*

"I'll, uh"—Nate held up an armored finger, conscious of Iveera already maneuvering them back around—"I'll just be right back with you guys, okay?"

"Should we... stop them, Colonel?" one of the soldiers asked as they began to drift away.

"Just get me a damn radio," was the last thing he heard Jaeger growl.

THEY DIDN'T FLY FARTHER than the rooftops of the skyscrapers lining the park before Iveera dropped Nate down to a startled landing. He stifled a yelp and yanked back from the concrete ledge, gaining his balance as she settled softly down beside him.

Much as he didn't appreciate being casually tossed onto a rooftop ledge, he was even more pissed at having been dragged off and basically forced to look complicit in telling the US military to piss off. It had been a mistake, he was almost positive, urgent business or no. But the complaint died on his tongue as he took in the smoking cityscape, and the destruction below.

He looked down to the park, and his helmet display helpfully zoomed in on Jaeger and his people doing their best to start restoring order to the chaotic exodus. Steady streams of wide-eyed civilians were still pouring out of the park in all directions, plenty more mixing and churning in and around the encampment, the air full of their desperate cries for lost loved ones. Even with the minor relief of the first trog ship closing shop and ascending for the depths of outer space, it wasn't a pretty sight.

Beside him, Iveera was busy with her holo, checking a spooling reel of alien figures and an array of video feeds from what looked like several major cities across the world. Scouting reports, he realized, as a few of the odd glyphs wiggled before his eyes into words and numbers he could understand. Ship and troop counts, tagged by location and status.

Probes from the Kalnythian Wilds, Ex provided, before he could even begin to wonder. *It looks as if the commander has made good on his word to order a worldwide withdrawal.*

It certainly did appear that way.

It might've even felt like good news, if not for the single metric that'd just wriggled into legibility from its original gorgon script.

Estimated Human Fatalities, Troglodan Inflicted: 78,387

Nate stared at the number, not comprehending. It was too big to even begin to wrap his head around.

Bear in mind, Ex said slowly, *that nearly twice that many humans die on this planet in a given day.*

Nate flexed his jaw, wanting to be furious that Ex would even think to draw a comparison between routine death and mass murder. He was too shocked to get there. In a way, Ex was probably just trying to give his grasping brain some iota of perspective.

Nearly eighty-thousand lives, gone. Just gone. Who knew how many hundreds of thousands more would be irrevocably ruined in the vacuum they'd left behind—how many millions had been injured today, scarred for life.

The second trog carrier began to lift up over Central Park, beating its slow, unapologetic retreat. Nate watched it go, suddenly wishing Iveera had torched them all from the sky. Quickly as it came, the thought disappeared down the bottomless pit in his gut, leaving him empty and tired, and more than a little bit lost.

Iveera closed her holos, and turned his way, her helmet peeling back to show her somber green face. He searched her alien eyes, looking for some explanation for it all. But there was none, he realized. None that he needed to hear anymore. Nothing but the guilt he'd known ever since the trogs had first arrived, and the slow, painful truth that'd been growing in his heart since he'd broken free from the waters of the Atlantic Ocean, twice-baptized by the twin furies of the drowning city and Iveera Katanaga.

Of all the reasons this catastrophe had unfolded, there was only one that had anything to do with him—just like there was only one thing left for him to do about it now.

"I'm coming with you," he said, not knowing where it was they'd be going, or how they were supposed to get there—only that he had to make this right. The trogs, the Beacon, the Merlin. All of it.

Ex practically purred at the sentiment.

"Yes," was all Iveera said. She didn't look particularly happy about it.

Nate released his helmet back to e-dim so he could see her with his own two eyes. "You're… okay with that?"

Her phosphorescent eyes returned from some distant thought. "I am not *okay* with any part of this, Nathaniel, but I can hardly allow you to stay here alone with a practically undefended Excalibur."

I believe she is calling you a weakling.

"I'm not—" Nate started, then he sighed and tried again. "I was offering my help," he told Iveera, "not signing up for daycare."

"Moreover," she said, as if he hadn't spoken at all, "I believe this arrangement is what the Merlin desired, should the impossible come to pass."

"I spoke with him briefly in the battle," she added, at Nate's confused look. "Released him from imprisonment aboard the Dread Knight's *Crimson Tide*. He had been captive for some weeks, though I cannot say what manner of sorcery held him there." She shot him a dark look, jin flattening. "Such a feat is well beyond the skill of any living Excalibur Knight."

"The Black Knight, then?" he guessed out loud, gross emasculation momentarily forgotten. "I think he was working with Groshna. I heard some of the trogs talking about it down there."

Iveera didn't disagree with the assessment.

"Did the Merlin… Do you know what that thing was? *Who* he was?"

She gave a soft hiss, her jin cutting the air. "The Merlin feared that a formidable foe had returned from the grave."

Nate considered the cryptic tidbit. "Well, I'm pretty sure the Black Knight knew the Merlin. I think this entire thing with the Beacon might've been a trap just to get his hands on him."

"Impossible," Iveera said, but the word was quiet, like she barely believed it herself. "One does not merely wake a dormant Beacon like the sparking of an ion engine. Even the Merlin does not command such power over the Lady's Light."

"Well… Maybe this Black Knight is beyond the Merlin too, then."

"No." Her jin swayed gently back and forth. "No, that's not possible either."

"But why not? I mean, if he was the one who imprisoned him… And hell, he did overpower him in a fight. How do you know what he could or couldn't do?"

"I know because I fought him, too," Iveera said, looking out to the horizon with a dark expression. "I know because the Merlin told me from where that blackened monster came."

She glanced back at him, jin flattening. "He used to be one of us."

Nate was pretty sure he felt Ex's surprise more sharply than his own. Maybe he was simply too ignorant to *be* properly surprised. A rogue Knight, returned from the grave bearing some kind of corrupted Ninth Excalibur? He didn't even know what to—

That was no Excalibur.

He flinched at the bite in Ex's voice. Ahead of them, Iveera looked even less happy about the revelation she'd just shared.

"So then… How did…?"

Iveera sliced the air with her jin. "All I truly know is that the Beacon and the Merlin must be recovered before they come to harm, or worse, fall into the hands of the Synth."

"The Synth?" Nate asked, wondering what Ex's so-called ancient evil— the one that had apparently been nothing but campfire legend for well over three-thousand years—had to do with a single mad Knight.

"Our oldest and most powerful foe," Iveera said, plainly mistaking his confusion. "Do not tell me… It is why the Excalibur Knights were created. Merciful goddess, surely the Merlin or the Lady must have—"

"No, yeah, I… I've heard of them," Nate said, raising his hands in peace and thinking back to the all-destroying swarm he'd witnessed sweeping through the asteroids on the final leg of his spacewalk with the Lady. "Ancient evil, right? Big swarm thing out in space? Eats asteroid belts?"

"Devours entire worlds," she corrected, looking only marginally appeased. "Entire systems. The entire plodding universe, perhaps, if we do not stand ready to stem the tide when it rushes forth from darkness again."

"Then, uh…" He frowned, still not sure what this had to do with the Black Knight, but strangely absorbed with her words.

Devour the entire universe? It sounded a bit dramatic. What did that even mean, really? He didn't know, but he couldn't seem to think of anything but the memory of that asteroid belt. The breathtaking ease and ferocity of that swarm ripping through gods knew how many millions of tons of asteroids, leaving nothing behind. The raw power, utterly silent in the dead vacuum of space. His heart beating faster. Cold terror slithering through his gut.

The Synth must be stopped.

The voice wasn't Ex's. His voice? He couldn't…

"Earth," he thought he heard himself mumble.

The word struck like a lightning bolt.

This thing was coming for Earth?

He couldn't seem to get the words out. Couldn't even remember where he was until an iron grip yanked him back to the quiet New York City rooftop, where Iveera had taken hold of his arm.

"If the Synth ever penetrates this far," Iveera said quietly, having apparently grasped something of his little episode, "all sentient life in the galaxy may already be as good as dead."

Nate tried to swallow against a parched throat, feeling clammy after whatever had just happened. "And the Black Knight? You think he's…?"

"The Merlin feared that Groshna's corrupted Excalibur might've had something to do with the Synth. That perhaps the Black Knight had been… repurposed by the enemy, so to speak. Resurrected out in the darkness, in the millennia following the Great War. Twisted into some manner of synthient servant, with the corrupted Excalibur to match—the dark seed of a plot to overthrow the Alliance's most powerful defenders before the new war begins."

Nate could barely think straight for the steady stream of Ex's oaths of *blackened hands* and *repugnant villains* and *vile sorcery.*

"But then Groshna…" His eyes widened. "But then *we're*…"

"I cannot say in either case," Iveera admitted. "I tell you this primarily to inform your Excalibur of the nature of the threat, should our brush with the corruption prove… persistent."

The blackened curs are welcome to try.

"Beyond that, the Merlin had not the time to tell me, just as we have too long tarried while that blackened demon escapes. We must return to the Atlantic for the ships, and depart for the Golnak relay posthaste." She lifted a few inches from the rooftop on silent gravitonics, fixing him with an expectant look. "Are you ready to fly?"

"I…" Nate dropped his gaze to the pavement, only then really registering what she was saying. Ships. Departure. Posthaste. As in right the hell now.

Suddenly, despite all the *I'm coming with you* bravado of a few minutes past, he couldn't help but wonder what the hell he was thinking, standing here in his neat little alien armor, talking with his alien pseudo-ally about their drastic non-plan to run off and… and what? Save the Merlin? Slam the lid on some unspoken darkness coming to gobble the universe up whole?

This wasn't how the world worked. This—

This is happening, Nathaniel.

"I… need to talk to my parents," he dully heard himself say. He wasn't even sure why he said it, only that the words rang with the empty echo of everything he was suddenly terrified at the thought of leaving behind. "I need to…"

What? Speak with your friends? Request a leave of absence from school? Look at what they have wrought on the world, Nathaniel. There is no going back.

His eyes traced down to the park—to the remnants of the troglodan invasion that had just changed the world forever, and to the seemingly endless list of reasons he couldn't go on with this madness, and the even longer list of reasons he couldn't *not*.

Ex was right. He knew Ex was right. But—

"I need to feed my dog, goddammit!" he cried out of nowhere, throwing his hands wide in helpless anger. He didn't know who he was trying to convince. Certainly not Iveera, who seemed less surprised at the outburst than he was. She just hung there in the air, watching him for a few long, degrading seconds before finally speaking again.

"Are you ready to fly?"

Somehow, those five words seemed to say it all.

Life as he knew it had ended, and something else was coming. Something none of them, not even the Excalibur Knights, were prepared to face. Not without their Merlin. Maybe not even then. But all he could do for sure was try. Or not.

"Okay," he whispered, beginning to nod.

Iveera was already drifting off on gravitonic wings. She turned eastward as he looked up, facing her back toward him and gently accelerating, silently expecting him to follow.

"Okay," he whispered to himself, reaching for his thrusters.

Nathaniel?

This is what you wanted, isn't it?

No, it's—

We're going, okay? I just—

Look down, Nathaniel.

Frowning, Nate followed Ex's instructions, honing in on the exact spot by nearly subconscious communication. He froze at the pair of tiny figures he spied below, looking up from the edge of the park. Froze until they clarified in his Excalibur-enhanced vision, not so much magnifying as resolving into unmistakable definition in every tiny detail.

It was Marty and Gwen.

He looked to Iveera, too stupefied to communicate that she needed to wait, that he couldn't leave after all. Back to Marty and Gwen, both squinting up his way like they were trying to figure out if it was really him. Back to Iveera, who had halted over the park now, watching him like she'd seen what was happening and was waiting to see what he'd do.

He could only stare down at his friends, barely daring to trust his eyes.

"I will return within three hours," came Iveera's voice in his head. "You should make whatever farewells you must."

It was only the word, farewells, that tugged him back to harsh reality.

"But your ship," he said, grasping at the mental image of the smoking wreck she'd ridden into Atlantis like a dying steed. "It can't just pull itself back together like that, can it?"

"Not quickly enough," she agreed, seemingly unconcerned by the detail, or by the additional fact that the ship was presumably still at the bottom of the ocean. "Which is why we are going to take yours."

"Mine?" Nate asked blankly.

"Three hours, Nathaniel," was all she said.

He looked up in time to see her copper form rocketing away between the buildings across the park, rapidly dwindling from sight.

Three hours.

Best make the most of your time, little hobbit.

He looked down to Marty and Gwen, who were turning back from the direction of Iveera's speeding departure. It was only then that he noticed Kyle and Kelsey in the park behind them, along with Todd and Emily and a few others—Tessa Kalders and her two SAS partners hovering nearby, keeping watch on the group and the proceedings in the park. Everyone was there.

Everyone but Zach.

The realization hit him with such sudden, awful clarity that he didn't even think about leaping off the building. He forgot to be afraid as he plummeted to the street, calling on his thrusters only toward the end in his desperate rush to correct his obvious misunderstanding—to reach street level and realize that he'd only missed Zach's face in the group.

He hit the ground harder than he meant to. Marty and Gwen gaped at the cracked asphalt beneath his feet. He gaped right back, searching the line of faces behind them. Searching it again. Zach's name caught in his throat.

Kyle couldn't meet his eyes.

Gwen couldn't look away, shock and devastation plainly written across her face.

He fixed his eyes on Marty, silently pleading with his friend to say it wasn't so, to tell him that they'd only been split up.

Marty just shook his head, red eyes brimming with tears.

"He saved us, Nate. He saved us."

CHAPTER 47
A QUARTER OF EVERYTHING

"It happened faster than…"

"Faster than any of us knew what to do," Gwen provided.

"Yeah," Marty whispered, closing his eyes and taking a deep breath, steeling himself to get back on track.

Nate sat there quietly, wanting to tell his friends that they didn't have to relive this now. That they could do it later, when they weren't surrounded by the watching eyes and muddling chaos of the lingering park evacuees. That he wasn't sure he could bear to hear it at all.

But he *needed* to hear it. And he could see it in Marty's face that his friend needed to say it. And later… Well, he couldn't think about later right now. Not beyond the next few hours.

So he sat there and quietly listened while his friends told him how the trogs had found them shortly after Iveera had taken him. How they'd been rattled and frantic, thinking he was dead. How Tessa and her two colleagues had whipped them into shape and gotten them moving, worried the abduction would draw attention to McClanahan's.

How they'd been too late anyway.

"We almost made it out before they got there," Marty said, shaking his head. "They hit the first car just after Tessa got it hotwired, thankfully before we could all load up."

Judging by her sooty face and clothes and the ugly gash over her eyebrow, he was guessing it must've been something of a close call for

Tessa, but she remained silent outside their huddle, not exactly pretending like she wasn't listening, but at least maintaining a respectful distance.

"Everyone ran for the one SUV after that," Marty continued. "The guys even brought one of the trogs down, I think, but..."

"It was my fault," Gwen said quietly. "If I hadn't been so..." She glanced over at Nate, then back to her feet, unable to finish.

"I'm the one who drew their attention," Marty said. "I'm the one who dropped the damn gun when..." He shook his head, lips trembling.

"It's bullshit," Kyle said, rousing for the first time since they'd sat down and looking from Gwen around the circle almost angrily, as if daring someone to argue. "You guys arguing whose fault it is, it's... If Zach hadn't..." He fought for control, lips and brow working, quivering back and forth between something like a snarl and a sob. "We never would've made it out of there," he finally managed. "They would've hit the SUV with that grenade, and... Fuck." He slouched back down, hanging his head. "Fuck."

Silence descended on the circle, thick and uneasy.

Nate found himself looking around, half-expecting Zach to step in and rib Kyle for his riveting command of the English language just to brighten the mood. The slip was like a phantom dagger nestled gently between the ribs. Almost worse was the way his friends, and even Todd and Emily, all avoided his eyes. Like they'd somehow let him down, and not the other way around.

I should've been there, he wanted to say, but the words hung in his throat. There was no end to the things he *should've* done since this had all started —since well before that too, truth be told. Sniveling about the fact had never gotten him anywhere. And much as he wanted to think Zach deserved his apologies, somehow, the thought of speaking them out loud only seemed like it would dilute the memory of his friend's sacrifice. So he sat there in silence, paying his respects and apologies to Zach and no one else.

You do your friend honor, little hobbit.

Nate swallowed against the sudden aching in his throat, gripped by unexpectedly powerful gratitude at the simple fact of being not alone.

Slowly, uncertainly, the creeping tendrils of life began to work their way back into the cold circle as the precious minutes ticked by. It started with a few comments about the ongoing trickle of evacuees, and about the group's rather abrupt journey, getting overtaken and abducted outside of Philadelphia—SUV and all—and summarily dished off here in New York, where many of the trog forces from State College had apparently congregated after Groshna had arrived, and where they'd just so happened to see the two Knights fly in to save the day.

At first, Nate tried to answer what questions he could about the trogs without saying too much, but soon enough, they'd slid into everything from Nate's encounter with Groshna all the way down to Atlantis and the Black Knight. Once he'd started, it was hard to stop. Hard to imagine snuffing out what feeble glints of curiosity and awe had returned to his friends' faces as he spoke.

Even with such surreal distractions, though, they never seemed to make it more than a few minutes at a time before the weight of Zach's absence settled back in on a heavy breath of silence, and they sat there absently listening to the fading din of the encampment, and the helicopters that'd begun swooping down, bringing troops and supplies in, and medevacking the badly wounded out.

Nate didn't tell his friends about the estimated fatality count he'd seen on Iveera's holos. It wouldn't bring them any more comfort than it'd brought him, knowing that their loss was only a tiny sliver of the total or that, all told, it hadn't been nearly as catastrophic a day as it could've been. The logic rang cold and hollow enough in his own head.

All he really knew was that, whatever pain he and his friends were collectively suffering right now, there was at least eighty-thousand times more of it striking across the globe right now. Probably more than that. A worldwide tsunami of loss and suffering, for reasons he still couldn't explain in any satisfying depth. He wasn't sure such reasons could even exist. Especially not when Kyle spoke up in the middle of one particularly lengthy silence.

"I just can't stop feeling like I'm missing... like *we're* missing... I don't know. A quarter." He shook his head, looking abjectly defeated. "A quarter of everything."

The words hung on the silence, immutably true.

"A quarter of everything is still everything," Marty finally said, his voice not much above a whisper.

The three of them shared a look then, and it was as if some part of Zach were stirring within them, amalgamating from the pieces and memories they each carried to surface as a near whole for some final farewell.

"Out-nerded," they whispered as one.

Nate wasn't sure whether he wanted to laugh or cry. He might've found out in short order, had that not been the moment he caught sight of Lieutenant Colonel Jaeger marching toward their huddle from the encampment with a few of his SAS crew in tow.

Just what he needed right now.

"Friends of yours?" Kyle asked.

Nate looked around to answer and realized the question had been directed not at him, but at Tessa, who'd risen to her feet and was ineffectively dusting off her grimy clothes. "Just the bestest," she said, rather lethargically, before straightening up and favoring the incoming officer at upright attention. Beside her, the other two SAS guys did the same.

"At ease, people," Jaeger said, as he drew up and looked his team over. "Glad to see you all pulled through."

Nate traded a look with his friends, and saw the same grim thought reflected in their eyes: they *hadn't* all pulled through. Somehow though, Nate didn't expect the Lt Col would be falling to his knees with the grief of their loss as he turned to regard Nate.

"Whatever you want from me," Nate found himself saying before he could think about it, "I don't have time."

"Why?" Jaeger asked, calmly looking around their circle before turning back to Nate, his dark eyes entirely too keen and discerning. "You got someplace to be, kid?"

Nate stiffened, all too aware of the round of suddenly attentive stares his friends shot him. He swore he could hear the realizations clicking into place —that he'd barely mentioned a word about Iveera, or what she'd gone flying off to do. Certainly, he hadn't mentioned *why*, or what his part was in all of this moving forward. He hadn't even realized himself, how thoroughly he'd kept the spotlight trained away from what happened next.

"This is our medic, Emily Carter," Jaeger broke into the uncomfortable silence, waving forward a twenty-something, five-foot-ten band of solid lady iron as if he were making a grand peace offering. "I thought she might have a look at your friends while we have a word."

Take it or leave it, his eyes said. Or maybe that was Nate's own inner voice, assuming that *emotional blackmail* was exactly the knife Jaeger had intended to twist. Either way, he kind of wanted to punch the clever bastard as he rose to his feet, waving down his friends' concerned looks, and turned to face his magnanimous extortionist.

"You've got five minutes."

～

"So what is it?" Jaeger asked as they drew around the decidedly non-private barrier offered by a few scraggly trees. "Rescue mission? Revenge?"

Nate frowned at the Lt Col, surprised by the acuity of the guess, and not really sure how to answer. He'd fully been expecting the man to open up with threats about how much trouble he was already in.

"I take it *something* critical slipped past you and your friend Katanaga out there in the Atlantic," Jaeger rolled on, unperturbed by his silence. "Imagine you two are looking to rectify."

Nate's frown deepened despite his best efforts. "How did you…?"

"We've still got satellites out there, kid. And believe it or not," he added, swinging a finger back and forth between them, "as far as I know, we're still on the same side here. So why don't you tell me what the gorgon's planning, and we can go from there?"

"Meaning you can decide whether or not to have your people try to drag me off to Area 51?"

Jaeger met him with an even stare. "Do you see me waving my dick around here, kid?"

"Kinda hard to tell, what with all the *kid* this, *kid* that."

"Okay," he said, raising his hands in a gesture of surrender that was still a few degrees too condescending for Nate's liking. "*Nate.* That better? Let's start with the thorn I'm guessin's still buried in your ass beneath that shiny armor, Nate."

"You mean that you're sorry you ignored everything I told you when it actually might've made a difference?"

He showed Nate a humorless grin. "That's the one."

Nate waited a few seconds, waiting for more. "Hell of an apology, there."

Jaeger's grin turned positively icy. "Who said anything about an apology?"

Nate bristled, but Jaeger pushed on before he could say a word.

"Look, we took what intel we had, and we passed it up the chain. Chain did the same. We did our jobs. Simple fact is the world wasn't ready for this."

"Seriously? You did your job, so it's not your fault? That's what you're going with?"

"We trusted generations of training and precedent, kid. It might not sound like much, but let me ask you somethin': how'd it go for you, playing hero all on your own out here, with no damn clue what you were doing?"

Nate opened his mouth to spit back that it'd gone a hell of a lot better than anything they'd tried—that he'd survived more than Jaeger could shake a condescending stick at. That he'd bonded with the Excalibur, dammit. Battled troglodans. Found the Beacon.

But what had any of it accomplished in the end?

He'd stumbled through it all, through failure after failure. He'd survived. But that was the sum total of it. He'd survived. He'd tapped into powers he never could've imagined. And he'd saved no one.

Most of the students he'd broken out of the brig had been promptly recaptured. Iveera, he had a strong feeling, might well have managed on her own if he hadn't happened along. And his friends? He didn't have to look any further than the somber gathering past the trees or the sick ache in his heart to remember how well he'd protected them.

When Jaeger finally spoke again, his voice was almost gentle.

"Aliens don't fall from the sky, Nate. It doesn't happen. Never has. Not until now." He looked out at the remnants of the park evacuee traffic, up to the small shape of the last retreating trog ship. "So no, I'm not sorry that we did our jobs the best we knew how, but I'm also not an ignorant tit."

He looked back to Nate. "It's a new world now. New rules. And for what it's worth, I'm pissed too. More pissed than you'd probably believe. Truth is, I don't think I would've done much differently, had I been in your place. But none of that matters anymore."

Nate just stared at him, wondering how he could stand there and dole it out like that. Eighty-thousand innocent lives lost in the shuffle for this brave new world, and none of that fucking mattered anymore? He wanted to shout. To *scream*. To demand answers. But part of him—maybe the part that was merely anticipating what Jaeger would say, or maybe another part entirely—already had the only answer that mattered.

They were dead. And there was no making it right.

"The only question now," Jaeger pressed slowly on, almost as if he'd been reading Nate's mind, "is do you wanna stand here bitching about how we fell flat the first time, or do you wanna help us make sure it never happens again?"

Nate scowled. "What is this, some kind of soldier pep talk?"

"This is me doing the job, kid. All my people want is—"

Not to be the bearer of ill-timed news, Ex broke in, as Jaeger continued on with something about a chance to talk, *but it appears Ser Katanaga has found our ship.*

Nate glanced inadvertently to the sky.

Not here, Nathaniel. Near Atlantis. The ship has been sequestered in e-dim aboard Ser Groshna's Crimson Tide these past weeks. That was why I couldn't find it. Captured, apparently, alongside the Merlin. The ship is quite distressed about the entire episode.

Nate was trying to process how a ship could even be distressed when Jaeger's voice cut into his thoughts.

"—didn't hear a word I just said, did you?"

"Sorry," Nate said, before he could remember he really *wasn't*. "I was thinking."

Thinking about how his precious time was almost up.

Jaeger gave a dubious grunt, clearly unconvinced, but deciding to move on anyway. "I'll ask again, then. Come debrief at UN HQ. No black bags. No dark holes off the edge of the map. Just a talk. Preferably with your gorgon friend, if she's available."

She will be presently. She is on the move. Quite quickly.

A trickle of panic burbled up in Nate's chest. He was vaguely aware Jaeger was saying something about potentially providing support, and the spirit of cooperation, but he really only caught the last words.

"So what do you say?"

Could be as little as ten minutes if she continues accelerating.

That, and the unfettered rush of panic it brought on, pretty much settled it.

"I say your five minutes are up, Colonel."

He needed to get back to his friends. Needed to tell them... Fuck. He didn't know what. Everything. Everything he'd somehow managed to hold back until now, trying to convince himself he'd have time later.

"Kid, now's not really the time for you to—"

He whirled back on Jaeger. "I might not be enough to scare off a trog armada, but I sure as fuck wouldn't push me right now."

The ferocity in his voice might've surprised him more than Jaeger. The Lt Col just went icily neutral, his weight subtly shifting to a ready position. Nate held his gaze a moment longer—the multi-voice in his head simultaneously shouting that Jaeger's request wasn't really all that unreasonable, and that it was also the height of all bullshit, and that he needed to get back to his friends, and that *maybe* they wouldn't have to leave the moment Iveera got back if this UN debriefing was actually pertinent, and that *why*, for that matter, did he even have to leave at all, save for the fact that his every strand of guilt and moral fiber was telling him it was the only way?

He turned wordlessly for the park—trying to blink away the buzzing hive of *crazy* in his head, Jaeger watching like a hawk—and nearly ran headlong into Gwen, who was edging hesitantly through the trees like she wasn't quite sure whether she was interrupting or coming to the rescue.

Jaeger looked between the two of them, assessing, then gave a *suit yourself* shrug. "I'll run your answer up the chain, kid. I'd say it's been a real pleasure, waving big ones with you, but I have a feeling we're not done yet."

They waited in uneasy silence as the Lt Col trekked back through the trees, no doubt bound straight for whatever comms they'd established.

"So..." Gwen said quietly once he was gone, looking uncertainly after Jaeger before turning back to him.

He showed her a sad smile, thinking of the moment they'd shared back in that quiet stockroom, before everything had fallen apart all over again. "So?" he asked, just as she had back then. "That's all you've got after all this?"

She bobbed her head, and for a second, he thought she'd smile or say something witty and perfectly Gwen, or that her eyes would fill with tears and she'd rush forward to throw her arms around him.

Instead, she just sobered, tilting her head after Jaeger. "Everything all right there?"

"Yeah," Nate said reflexively, feeling each second ticking by like a light smack to the heart. "No. I don't know. He was just... They want answers."

"You don't say." She tried to smile, then bit her lip instead, hanging on the edge of her next question. "So then that other thing about, you know..." She glanced in the direction of the group, almost like she wished she'd brought support, then turned back to him, seeming to remember she didn't need it. "Was he right? Are you going somewhere?"

Nate couldn't have said how many seconds he wasted floundering, mouth half open, trying to find the words. Even after everything she'd seen today, and everything he'd told her, it was all still too vague, too *arcane*, to explain to any satisfactory degree. He didn't even understand it himself: what was really at stake here, what dangerous and convoluted manner of Galactic Alliance politics he suddenly seemed to be caught up in, whether he liked it or not. Even what he owed to the Merlin, and to Earth.

So he gave up on words, and settled for a dumb nod.

She *did* surge into him then, gasping his name and wrapping him in a hug that might've been bone-crushing had he not been encased in powerful alien armor. Feeling her arms around him, though, he released that armor back to e-dim for the first time since Atlantis, and let her have a fair go at it.

Gods, did she feel good in his arms. Warm, and precious, and irrefutably *right* in a world that'd gone horribly wrong. He didn't know what to say other than that. Couldn't even seem to get those words out. For a long while, they simply held one another. He felt the seconds ticking by, felt the inevitable drawing closer, and he held her tighter. She didn't need to ask why.

"You have to?" was all she asked when they finally drew back enough to look at one another.

He swallowed, searching for his voice. It was only then that it really dawned on him just how terrified he was. "All I know is that I'm pretty sure the evil bastard behind this invasion got exactly what he wanted today. And if we don't make it right..." He gathered himself and met her eyes, tears pressing at his own. "I need to do this."

"Okay," she whispered, taking his face between her hands, fingers exploring along his jawline, through his hair, like she was trying to store it all up for later. "Okay," she repeated, nodding faintly to herself.

"I'm sorry."

She shook her head, tears welling. He prayed to god she wouldn't let go.

"I'm sorry I didn't—"

She kissed him, and he tasted tears. His or hers, he didn't know. He just pulled her close and kissed her back, closing his eyes, leaving the ticking time bomb of a world behind as best he could. For a while, he succeeded, and it was only the two of them, safe and warm in the darkness behind his eyelids. Only her eyes holding his when he finally found the courage to look again. Only those beautiful eyes, and the painfully deep ache of emotion they stirred within him.

He wanted to tell her that he loved her. Wanted nothing more than to close his eyes and disappear again. To wake up in bed twenty years down the road and look over to realize she was still there, right there with him, and that they were happy, and content, and at peace—her with her life-changing biotech breakthroughs, and him with... his art?

An odd wave of dissonance passed through him at the thought, like he'd queried his inner storage for the familiar fantasy only to find the file had been corrupted—all relevant data badly warped by the heat stress of a new reality. In a way, it almost felt like some part of him had died back there in Atlantis, replaced by the one that had bonded with Ex—the one that had kicked open an entire galaxy of unknowns, for better or worse.

Pandora's box.

Jaeger had been more right than he'd known.

"How soon?" Gwen whispered, her forehead resting lightly against his chest.

"Soon," he whispered back, flat and drained.

Too soon. Not soon enough. He didn't know. It just wasn't *fair*, some corner of his mind insisted, that he should finally make it to this moment only with the certainty that it couldn't last. The rest of him just watched in quiet acceptance as Gwen drew back and cupped his cheek in one hand, studying his face with a soft frown.

"You're different, you know," she said, stroking his cheek with a thumb, smiling a little at her own words. "I mean, of course you are, after everything, but... I don't know. There's just something in your eyes. Something that wasn't there before."

Nate took her hand in his, unnerved for some reason he couldn't explain, and resenting that he couldn't even seem to enjoy the feeling of her hand in his in that moment. "I guess the whole world's different."

She looked around the ruined park, then gave him a sad smile and leaned up to plant one last soft kiss on his lips. "I guess you're right."

Something fluttered back to life from the abyss, watching her descend back down from tip-toes. Something that, for one wild second, begged him to simply say *to hell with it*, scoop her up, and fly them off somewhere. Run for it and never look back. Have a chance to actually *be* together, to have anything more than this stolen moment at the tail end of a four year marathon of his self-pitying snivel-fest.

But he couldn't. And not only because he knew what was out there now, or because Iveera would probably hunt him down like a dog in a day flat. But because he just couldn't. Because he had a job to do, same as Lt Col Not-A-Tit Jaeger. And because, in some grim way, he actually kind of *wanted* to do it, he realized.

Merciful Sith, when had that happened? Three weeks in, one world crisis averted, and he'd officially lost his mind.

Just imagine where we'll be in three centuries.

The thought sent his head spinning. It was about the last thing he wanted to imagine right then. The faint patter of another approaching helicopter reminded him he didn't have the time to spare anyway.

"C'mon," he said, taking Gwen's hand and turning to head back to the others. "Better let the"—he flinched away from the word *squad*, thinking of Zach—"the guys into the loop."

As it turned out, though, there was little loop-letting to be done.

They'd barely made it out of the trees when Marty and Kyle both rose from the group, watching him with looks that said they already knew—had seen it coming since they'd first spied him atop that rooftop with Iveera. He couldn't even say if it was horror on their faces, or something more like shock and awe. Maybe all of the above. Whatever it was, it didn't make him feel any better about what came next.

Neither did the SAS team loitering nearby, or the odd looks they were all shooting him.

He didn't have time to parse it out, or even to speak a word to Marty and Kyle before he caught the first faint hint of a rushing *something* high above. He looked to the sky, not quite sure if he'd imagined it.

He hadn't.

It was only a speck in the sky when he caught first sight, but it grew with frightening velocity, moving straight for them so fast he could hardly make out the shape. By the time it decelerated enough to resolve into anything but a large blue blur, it was practically landing on top of them, kicking up a healthy gust of wind as whoever was at the helm—Iveera, he presumed— brought it to a crisp, calm hover.

The ship was long and aesthetically proportioned, all elegant curves and sleek matte panels of white and midnight blue. Based on his exactly zero knowledge of spaceship design, Nate thought it looked like it had been built more for speed and long voyages than for heavy warfare. It looked a little bit like Iveera's ship, he noticed. And there, etched across one of the port-side armor panels in faded, barely discernible letters was a one word explanation for the connection: *Camelot*.

"Dude," Kyle said beside him, gaping up at the vessel. "Fuck me."

Nate stared right along with him, not sure how to expound on the statement, stomach wriggling even as his heart leapt at the inexorable waves of change thrumming down from alien engines, permeating through every fiber of the life he'd thought he'd known.

He looked at his friends, and took each one by the shoulder as they pried their eyes away from the ship to look back at him. They fell into a group hug without a word. There didn't seem to be any words left.

It was only then, with his arms around two of the closest friends he had left, that he realized he wouldn't be there for Zach's funeral. That he hadn't even had a chance to contact his parents. He didn't even know if Copernicus was okay back in State College, for the love of Christ.

It was happening too fast.

He felt Gwen's hands on his back. Saw Todd and Emily holding each other nearby, prying their eyes from the arriving ship to give him a respectful nod. A somber farewell.

Breathe, Nathaniel. It is but one step on the journey.

Nate blew out the breath he hadn't noticed he was holding. Forced another. Saw Iveera appear from the belly of the *Camelot*, hovering down to collect him, and came to a decision. If he couldn't be here in person…

Yes, it would work, Ex said, almost before he was consciously aware of what he was thinking, *but are you sure, Nathaniel? It is still a risk, troglodans or not.*

He took Marty's hand, holding the thought in mind down to each tiny detail. *I'm sure.*

He felt it working, felt Marty stiffen as something took shape out of thin air between their palms.

"I think you know who that's for," Nate said, finding the hints of his first real smile as Marty turned his hand over and looked down at the chintzy looking gold medallion that had appeared there, embossed with two lines of all-caps text: *BEST DOGGO IN THE WORLD.*

"Just like the earpiece," Nate said, with a pointed look.

Marty's eyes widened. "This will… Even out there?"

"Keep it secret," Nate said. "And if at any point there's anything we need to let Earth know about, well…" He looked around at Kyle and Gwen, too. "Consider yourself my official liaisons." He frowned back at the quantcomm medallion, honestly not sure whether he was making a selfish mistake or a wise move. "Just…"

"Keep it secret," Marty finished.

"Keep it safe," Kyle added, still looking too flabbergasted to even appreciate his own reference.

"At least until we find the real wizard," Nate said, glancing around and wondering at the fact that Iveera hadn't already swooped in to yank him off. "I'll be back when…"

He trailed off as he spotted her talking with Jaeger, who'd reappeared among the SAS crowd beside the small pile of supply crates Nate hadn't noticed there before.

"… when it's safe."

What the hell was this all about?

It would seem Ser Katanaga has elected to take matters into her own hands on the question of the Camelot's crew.

Nate stared dumbly. *But that's not… I thought it was my…*

"Hey!" he called in their direction. "Just a second," he added more quietly to his friends, disengaging to stomp over to the SAS huddle.

Jaeger stepped out to meet him halfway, Iveera watching them calmly alongside the SAS bunch, who all looked some combination of grim, determined, and morbidly excited.

"Spoke with the brass," Jaeger said, before Nate could ask. "They reacted about like I figured they would." He shook his head, shooting a dark frown back toward Iveera. "Sure wish you two weren't in such a damn rush. Might've given us time to find more specialized volunteers. But at least one of you was willing to half-listen."

Nate looked from the Lt Col, to Iveera, to the SAS team, and back, following but not quite processing. Certainly not accepting. "You're saying..."

"501st Space Aggressor Squadron, reporting for duty," Jaeger said, looking one part glib and five parts grim steel serious as he glanced up to the ship, and back to Nate. "Let's go catch us a Black Knight, kid."

～

END BOOK ONE

AUTHOR'S NOTE
(UPDATED SEPTEMBER 5TH, 2020)

Let me ask you something, Book Fan...

Can you think of the last time a good story scene got you all stirred up?

Maybe it was a wham-bam fight scene, a-la Jason Bourne. Maybe it was something a bit more intimate and heated. (No judgies here!) Maybe just a poignant one-liner that carried the weight of a whole franchise on its shoulders. ("I am Iron Man.")

Me, I've always had this distinct memory of sitting there as a child, watching this action movie with my dad. (I think it was *Airforce One*. But that's almost beside the point.) What I REALLY remember (the part that stuck with me) is the way my dear old dad sat absorbed, subconsciously rocking with every on-screen punch. "I could do that," he'd say to himself, as Harrison Ford took down the next baddie. "Gun to my head, I could do that."

And honestly, maybe he could have. (He *was* a wiry, resourceful, brutally intelligent man.) But the part that stuck with me most wasn't the question of whether or not my dad truly was Action Hero material. It was that simple yet deeply ingrained feeling that he was *supposed* to be. That every person worth their metaphorical salt should aspire to be such a rugged, face-punching bastion of security in a hairy situation.

(Of course, I *say* "every *person*," even though back then, these noble life goals were *definitely* more targeted toward the male population. Nowadays, we have Certified Face-Punchers of all sexes, religions, shapes, and sizes. How's *that* for progress?!)

Mild sarcasm aside, the more I got into storytelling and began to probe and dissect the stories I loved, the more I started to notice there seemed to be something markedly different between the manly-man grit of the old school action movies and the wild sci-fi and fantasy tales I was becoming more and more enthralled with.

Sometimes this "something" looked like a radioactive spider bite, or a supersoldier serum. Sometimes it was a magic hammer or ring, or a mystical Force that permeated the galaxy, accessible only to a special few. Sometimes we just had a character who was simply born into godly power, be it from Asgard or Krypton.

Between all the amazing super strength, healing factors, and exciting magic powers, though, I couldn't help but notice one thing: In these worlds, it was no longer enough to simply be a gritty badass on the inside. If you wanted to Face-Punch in the Big Leagues, you *also* had to have a set of special powers dropped into your lap. Often by random chance.

In other words, these stories I loved (*and CONTINUE to love, despite what the tone of this note might suggest*) had begun to *externalize* a good chunk of the self-empowerment we often turn to stories to find or experience. And why not? Who *doesn't* want to imagine a world where the secret sauce to their ultimate potential could lay in a chance spider bite rather than on the far end of years of humble, disciplined pursuit?

Ultimate potential at the drop of a hat.

There's something *powerfully* alluring about that possibility. (Quadruply so in a world that's gotten pretty darn good at convincing us on a daily basis that we are NOT enough as we are today—that we need more money, less body fat, better stuff, newer stuff, *sexier* stuff. That being anything less than a flashy hero or celebrity is somehow unadmirable.)

And while it's definitely worth noting that most of my favorite characters DO still bring a ton to the table on their own two mortal feet... well, we also can't deny that Peter Parker becomes less fun to watch without his radioactive spider bite, right?

More than that, though, this externalization (and chance gifting) of power can also lead to some interesting... let's call them "shortcuts" in the developmental psychology of the "Hero Brain." Suddenly, we have more than a few stories about young—often untested—individuals taking up great power... and often having very little trouble wielding it with great responsibility and unwavering courage.

Sure, there might be a road bump or two. The loss of a loved one. One big, defining failure early on (which is often then negated once the hero learns their lesson and gets it "right" in the final showdown). But most of the time, these Average Joes go from zero to sixty on the Shiny Hero Scale in about one hiccup flat.

Why? Because it makes for a fun story! The kind of story that makes us feel like WE could do that too... if only that mystical power would fall into OUR lap. And as much as I love the narrative of the noble strength awaiting deep within each and every one of us, I've also never been able to stop myself from looking around at a lot of these stories and thinking, "Yeah, but what if they handled ANY of this shit like a genuine, everyday human?"

What if the Man of Steel *hadn't* grown up on a wholesome Kansas farm and learned all that humility and self-restraint? Moreover, what if NO amount of self-restraint could've ever truly tampered his ostensibly "human" ego once he'd realized he was *actually* strong enough to bring an entire planet to its knees and take whatever he wanted?

This is why I absolutely adore stories like Garth Ennis' "The Boys" *(recently adapted into an Amazon Prime TV show, which I also very much enjoyed)*, which dare to unflinchingly question what it might ACTUALLY look like if we warmongering human types were to ever develop superpowers. It's also why I wanted to ask my own question. Or several of them, actually.

Namely, I wanted to hop into the sandbox and explore what happens when that magic external power (and all the attached responsibility) is dropped like an anvil on a dude who's just NOT ready for it.

A dude whose parents hadn't been killed dramatically.

A dude whose greatest adversity throughout his uneventful white middle-class existence had been the simple struggle to get noticed by the girl he liked.

A dude who couldn't find that zero-to-sixty lever to acquire instantaneous Shiny Hero Brain largely *because* he'd spent most of his life idolizing the very same silver screen heroes discussed above.

Someone who'd already been benignly pushed into his little corner and told not to rock the boat, that this was just the way of the world. Someone who'd kind of made peace with his existence as a "sheep among wolves." Someone who, regardless of perceived scrotal fortitude, would probably crap their pants and fall into a shocked stupor, were a giant alien ogre to come falling from the sky, howling for their blood.

Someone kind of like the rest of us, in other words.

I had my character. Nate, I'd call him. Meanwhile, I'd also had this idea tumbling around for a while of this ancient, long-dormant evil (sort of like the Reapers from Mass Effect) returning from the depths to gobble up the galaxy whole, and a once-mighty but increasingly bureaucratic Galactic Alliance that would be hard-pressed to take up arms and stop them.

Their only hope? The equally ancient line of ultimate warriors known as the Excalibur Knights. Eight of the Alliance's strongest representatives, each chosen by the mystic Lady to wield a power unlike anything else in the galaxy—the only power strong enough to turn the tides against the coming darkness.

The two ideas seemed perfect for each other.

Just your average, nerdy middle-class college kid suddenly stumbling into a fight for galactic survival—and into exactly the kind of boundless power that could change everything, if only he can bring himself to accept it. The result was the birth of Nate Arturi and a sprawling Arthurian space opera series called the Excalibur Knights Saga.

And boy, did the first book rustle some jimmies...

∼

Hey there, Dear Reader!

Luke here again (for "real" this time), dropping in to provide a bit of context here — namely, that the above note was actually taken directly from one of my Sunday newsletters, in which I was basically seeking to explain to my readers what the hell I was thinking, opting to write an action hero who wasn't really much of an Action Hero at all.

That said—before I go any further—if you enjoyed that behind-the-scenes spiel, you should definitely come join us on the mailing list! You can signup right at: *lukermitchell.com/eighth-excalibur-signup*

In addition to occasional notes like these, you'll also get access to several free books and discounts you won't find anywhere else. First up on that list: two Excalibur Knights special features, both list-exclusives: *Flight of the Huntress*, and *The Last Good Boy*.

The former throws you into the weathered copper boots of Iveera Katanaga for the opening shots of the Terran Incursion. And the latter... well, you'll see.

Sign up at the above link to grab them both today (not to mention to grab the free Book Ones from each of my other series), and enjoy!

And now, with THAT out of the way (and with this note growing quite girthy already), I hope you'll allow me to just say a quick *thank you*.

Thank you, Dear Reader, for taking a chance on this book and coming along for the ride. I appreciate your time, and I sure hope you've enjoyed the time you've spent here. If you've read the reviews for this book, you'll already know that Nate Arturi really struck a nerve with a lot of readers. (Which—much as I never love reading angry 1-star reviews—was kinda the point of this series all along.) I *wanted* to write a "hero" who had a lot of growing up to do before he could reach that mythical *"Great power? Great responsibility? No problem!"* Hero Brain that is so commonplace in stories these days.

Needless to say, the phrase, "grow a pair," was bandied about more than once in response. But so too were ones like "depth of character" and "highly relatable." Or, as one reviewer put it:

"It's the perfect entry into the space opera genre that feels like it definitely could be you in his shoes."

An action-hero space opera for the rest of us, in other words.

One where our not-so-knightly Knight may take a little longer than an hour or two to come to grips with the weight of the galaxy being dropped on his shoulders, Atlas style.

One that might've even pushed all of *your* buttons, too.

But also one where you can bet your well-read keister you're gonna be able to watch our not-so-knightly Knight *grow*—grow into the big bad Hero Boots he's supposed to fill, and maybe even beyond. And that's the *real* beauty of the Excalibur Knights Saga. (Or so I'd like to think.)

So thank you, Dear Reader, for coming along for the journey. I sure hope you've enjoyed it, and if you've come this far, I suspect you're really gonna dig what comes next.

If you're ready for more, at the risk of sounding like a broken record, I highly recommend you join the mailing list at the above link for access to your two list-exclusive extras, *Flight of the Huntress* and *The Last Good Boy*— as well as for a nice discount on Nate's next adventure.

And if newsletters and email shenanigans aren't your bag, no worries. You can always visit *lukermitchell.com/books* to grab *The Black Knight* (Book 2) and continue the series today!

Me? I'll be tap-tap-tapping away over here, teasing the rest of the series out, one page at a time. Happy reading until next time!

Cheers,
Luke Mitchell

Acknowledgments

As always, I'd be remiss if I didn't start by thanking my ever-loving wife, Marina, for all of the wonderful things, big and small.

Thanks go as well to my obscenely supportive mom, to my family and friends, and to my steadfast publishing team, without any of whom I'd undoubtedly be lost at sea. (Except not sea, because I definitely wouldn't have left the house in this particular hypothetical. "Lost in chair," let's call it.)

Additionally, a very special thanks to the following Patrons, who directly support my work, rain or shine:

Mildred Ann Mitchell — James Mallison — Linda Lestha
Mark Frink — John Munson — Bartholomew Bacak
Bob Laughner — Simon Danner — Joan M. Combes
Janet Ober — Robert Stuart — Grant Wilson
Letcher Ross — Eldridge Newlin —Sharon Kenneson
Mary-Anne Mitchell — Andrea Johnson — Tony Tieuli
Toni Mcconnell — Steven Mathis — Howard Wolfgang
John Barnes — Lisa Hoffman — Ron Williams
Yaakov Bright — Aj Jain-Perkins — Debra Franklin
James M Blaine — Nicholas Ruppert — Daniel McNeese
Andrew Staples — Karl Hakimian — Faith Hakimian
Gordon Keller — Dan Andrews — Adam McIntosh
Sam Higby — Robert Poet — Dagmar Preusker

You gentlebeings are the blessed wind to my authorship's funny little sails. Love and peace to each and every one of you.

(Side Note: If you loved this book and would like to support more like it, hop on over to patreon.com/lukermitchell to learn more about the perks of becoming a Patron!)

Finally, my deepest thanks to you, Dear Reader, for coming along for the ride. I sure do enjoy you spending this time with my work. Thank you. And here's to many more stories to come!

Sincerely,
Luke Mitchell

ABOUT THE AUTHOR

Not a llama. Mostly human.

Luke is a storyteller whose dreams include learning the ways of the Force, becoming a sentient robot, and maybe even one day growing up. Also, lots of zombies… Don't ask.

Oh, and that "growing up" bit? That was a lie.

After studying engineering science at Penn State and neuroengineering at Drexel, Luke finally decided to throw in the towel on building a working Iron Man suit and opted instead to simply make things up and write them down. Boy, is he having more fun now.

When he's not holed up in his writing cave trying to string words together, he can often be found powerlifting, video-gaming, reading, and/or drinking the darkest, most roasty beers he can get his mitts on. Sometimes all at once.

But you know what? That's enough about Luke. He's really not that interesting. Still, if you'd like to say hi to him for whatever reason, he'd probably be glad to hear from you!

Go to **lukermitchell.com/eighth-excalibur-signup** to join up for fun emails, free books, and lots of other great deals and exclusive content you won't find anywhere else. (Content like the Excalibur Knights specials, *Flight of the Huntress* and *The Last Good Boy*, which you can read today by joining the list!)

Additionally (as you wish)…

Follow me on BookBub for new release alerts
bookbub.com/authors/luke-r-mitchell

Browse the rest of my published titles
lukermitchell.com/books

Join the Patreon team for digital copies of ALL of my work (past, present, and future) — and much more!
patreon.com/lukermitchell

Thank you for reading!